I0817768

DOMAINE DELAFAIRE

Vol. I

of

THE STEWARD

M.D. IRONZ

Published in the United States of America

Professorial Holdings

professorialholdings@gmail.com

Michael J. Moriarty

Necromancer

ISBN 978-1-7337594-2-7

Also by M.D. Ironz

THE STEWARD
Domaine Delafaire
Realms Of Possibility

Standalone
Dire Covenants

CH 1

MAUDE DELAFAIRE WAS dying. In this moment, she knew it.

She sensed that this lucid interlude would pass. Soon enough, she would once more slide down that well of vague awareness, floating among distorted memories. Even that thought, despite her determined focus, slipped away like a desperate minnow through a tattered net.

She shifted beneath the sheets in a sudden involuntary shiver. The sole window revealed only a dull overcast of thick clouds in the deepening dusk. It may well have been spring in Louisiana, but she knew darkness could surge from low places with the suddenness of flood, and the accompanying chill was not always merely the wind.

A set of patient monitors near the wall emitted pale light from small digital screens accompanied by soft rhythmic beeps.

She had been in this room, or one very much like it, for the past—*ah, three years, was it?* Her uncertainty frustrated and angered her; that seemed to bring her awareness into sharper focus. Yes, now she remembered.

This is an "assisted living, memory care facility". Hah! A nursing home and hospice! I've been here ever since that tentative diagnosis of Alzheimer's. Worse, it seems I've only grown weaker with the passing months.

No one had entered her room; the door remained closed. However, she sensed with an ominous certainty that she was not alone. Illuminated only by the diminishing light from the window and the pale glow of the monitors, the dim room held deep shadows. One shifted; a form was barely discernible.

She knew no fear, and felt no pain. The corners of her mouth twisted in a wry smile.

Him! I should have guessed he'd come.

His voice was low and controlled, with a shade of arrogance. "Greetings, my lady. I am pleased to find that you are so amused."

She willed herself to speak strongly, with resolve, but she only managed a dry rasp. "I see you, *Grimrald*. You are here without invitation. State your purpose."

"Lady, you wound me. You dare to name me—by my *true name*. I have done you no such discourtesy." His tone dripped condescension as he eased forth from the deepest shadows. Slender in build and pale of complexion, he wore his dark hair slicked back from his high forehead. A dark Van Dyke beard accentuated his narrow chin. His eyes were intense, the irises so dark as to be indistinguishable from the pupils.

"Very well . . . You go by *Salidar* these days, do you not? It will suffice?"

He stepped around a solitary chair and stood next to her bed.

"Indeed, m'lady. I accept your apology."

"I offered none. Nor am I convinced that you have done me no discourtesy. Now, state your purpose. Remember, you are here uninvited."

"Ah, m'lady, I am here because I promised that I would be present at your death. As you can see, I keep my word—your lack of invitation notwithstanding." He flipped a hand dismissively. "We have been in opposition on many occasions over the long years, have we not? Ah, but that is the past. You will forgive me for mentioning it, but you have no place in the future. Indeed, we both know you shall not see the morrow."

She had little strength for an argument, and none for any resistance should he offer violence. However, her mind was clear.

This pompous bastard is here to witness my death, as he promised ages ago. Since I didn't refute his impertinence then, there's nothing I can do about it now. I think I might know what he really wants.

I must stall for time.

She gathered her breath and whispered, "Salidar, your agenda is plain, and likely futile, as I may well see many more sunrises. My doctors are optimistic."

"Pah! They know nothing. This is your appointed time! And I am here!"

He strode to the foot of the bed and fixed her with a predatory stare. His confidence palpable, his smoldering visage seemed to will a hastening of her demise.

Her blood chilled with the realization that he would not be so certain, unless . . . *Had he a hand in my debilitation? But he could not have, could he? I always thought him a pretender, an inept nuisance bordering on annoyance, and certainly not capable of such strategy and tactics—but, now? Have I underestimated him all these years? Or does he not act alone? Damn the gods, I must know!*

"So, I have you to thank for my present circumstances, do I not? My, how *base* of you."

"But of course . . . well, not entirely, m'lady. I confess I can take some credit for your diminishing faculties. Of course, I am not the only one who would see you gone from the Council of Realms—and the Stewardship!"

He couldn't contain himself, gloating, strutting to and fro at the foot of her bed, smug beyond pretension. "And to be a bit crass, your old age was bound to catch up with you."

My age? She frowned. *How little this fool truly understands!*

However, she now knew for certain that Salidar was being used; someone else had manipulated this entire scenario. The cost would be her life; at this point, that was a foregone conclusion. She had always accepted that she would die; everybody did eventually. She had long ago taken certain precautions to secure the future.

She knew that her seat on the Council was a moot issue; one was elected thereto by the other members. However, the Stewardship—now, that was different. It was bestowed upon one by the last Steward. She frowned once more as comprehension dawned, her suspicions confirmed.

Salidar intends to seize the Stewardship for himself at the moment of my death!

She knew that wouldn't normally work—*but now?* If her mind were sufficiently addled, she might unintentionally convey the authority, or unknowingly agree to something that would have the same effect. While her faculties seemed sufficiently acute at present to deduce his intentions, she had no assurance that she could remain so lucid. Even further conversation with him could be dangerous.

She heard him softly chanting. *What? Casting a spell of some kind?* With mild alarm, she felt herself slipping into a subtle stupor.

She had no choice; the moment had come.

She allowed the spell to spiral her downward, in apparent surrender. With her remaining strength, she concentrated her very essence and accelerated the plunge. She felt a slight tug as she tore through the furtive strands that composed the web of the spell, where she would have been held in a highly suggestible state, and kept descending within herself.

She slipped past lingering whispers of corruption and malice, remnants of hidden sorceries that had contributed to her decline. These had been quite powerful at one time. And yet, it came as no surprise that there was no trace of their source. Her mind shuddered to think of the evil at work here; it had been very powerfully cloaked.

Alzheimer's—my ass! How did I miss this?

She continued plunging through the tapestry of her life. Threads of memories were now distinct and pure, diminished by neither time nor space; and there had been a lot of time. She felt the temptation to pause and savor a moment; but she knew that wasn't possible—all would be lost.

At last, she reached her point of origin, a bright warmth of quickening. She was free of everything—and yet, one with everything. She just *was.*

Have I shed this mortal coil? And yet, I am aware . . .

She remembered Salidar.

At that thought, she was once again in her room, but *not* in it. She saw it from all angles. Upon the bed lay her inert body, a cooling shell quite oblivious to Salidar's increasingly frantic pacing and chanting.

His voice rose as he approached the bed and fumbled beneath his shirt. As his chant reached its final crescendo, he pulled forth an amulet suspended from a thin chain, and pressed it to the forehead of the woman on the bed. He now spoke in a language not heard on Earth in thousands of years.

The amulet began to glow with a pale and strangely obscene light, pulsing in cadence to Salidar's rapid heartbeat. In its throbbing intensity, the profane light suddenly flared, fizzled, and went out.

An amused chuckle arose in Maude's mind, surprising her.

Salidar cursed vehemently in seven known and two forgotten languages. He kicked the bed and flipped the sole chair over. With an angry swipe of his arm across the wide windowsill, he sent a stack of old magazines fluttering like wounded birds to splay across the floor.

Maude wondered if his tirade would draw the attention of any of the attendants or nurses; their station was right down the hall. Then she knew; no one would come, because no one could hear.

A spell of silence? She didn't understand how she knew about the spell. She just *knew;* and she accepted that.

Salidar grew quiet, contemplating the dull amulet in his open palm. He seemed to focus inward, as if listening to something internal, and then sighed. He rearranged the room as if he'd never been there, righting the chair, collecting the spilled magazines and restoring them to the windowsill.

Then he surprised her—he spoke to her.

"Maude, I know you can hear me! You may think you have beaten us, but you are wrong! This has been coming for a long time! We have contingency plans! Now you cannot stop us! You are powerless—no longer an obstacle!"

Frustrated and angry, he took a deep breath, and began his rambling litany of curses once again. He stood near the center and addressed the entire room at first, as if he knew she was still nearby. But the habits of a long lifetime are hard to break; he kept glancing back to the body on the bed. He stalked closer, repeatedly jabbing a finger at the ashen face, overt virtual punctuation in accompaniment to his diatribe.

Even in her ethereal state, Maude was disturbed by his words. She wanted to convey her displeasure, but she didn't quite know how—*or did she?* She allowed herself a spectral smirk.

As Salidar sucked a breath through gritted teeth and leaned into the slack dead face, the eyes of the corpse flew open and stared into his own!

His jaw dropped; he choked on a strangled gurgle.

Crashing through the door, he bolted down the corridor for the exit.

Maude surprised herself once more—a spirit can laugh.

Oh yes, it seems I can. Well, that was interesting. Now what?

THE RINGING PHONE WAS an incessant annoyance, petulant and insistent. Ellen hunkered down at her cubicle, avoiding any eye contact, silently pleading for someone else in this vast office to take the call.

She didn't need or want any delays, distractions, or interruptions right now. She tried to concentrate once more on her laptop. Her resume needed to be completed today, but was still not polished to her satisfaction.

She pinched her eyes shut in frustration, and immediately scolded herself. *Oh, I've gotta stop doing that! I don't want crow's feet before I'm twenty-five! Come on, stay on task, girl! Finish this. No one else is gonna pay your bills, and Los Angeles is so-o-o expensive.*

She knew all too well that unemployment loomed on the horizon. Her temporary administrative position, mired in the bowels of a communications software company, would expire with the completion of the current municipal government contract.

Her job search, restricted to stolen moments on the phone and harried half-hour lunches, was not going well. She knew she was running out of time.

Fate granted her a small boon; the strident ringing was choked off mid-trill as some other employee relented and answered the phone. Near silence ensued, a moment of peace unencumbered by the usual rustle and bustle of an administrative office, just the sterile ambiance and low-grade static hum of the ubiquitous cube farm.

Ellen cocked her head, listening just to be certain. *Pleasantly quiet? Now, how rare is that? Oh man, how easily distracted I am! Focus! Now! You gotta find a new job! Or do you want to have to move in with your mother and Earl?*

The quiescent respite was not to last, shattered by the office intercom system's harsh initiation squelch. Ellen winced at the subsequent announcement.

"Ellen, call on line one! Ellen, call on line one! It's a GUY! Says he's your cousin—yeah, right!"

Ellen peeked over the partition and across the room at her friend, Stacy, who was grinning at her as she placed the caller on hold. Ellen could only smile and shrug.

Her friend was like a benign force of nature. In moments of whimsical conjecture, Ellen sometimes thought of Stacy as a dimensionally displaced nymph predisposed to romantic mischief. A pert and vivacious blonde in contrast to Ellen's brunette reserve, Stacy was ever the optimist. She was also determined to improve her friend's romantic life, which Stacy had often declared to be something less than optimal. In truth, Ellen quietly agreed, but to be honest, she was actually rather content with the status quo.

Ellen blew an errant lock of chestnut hair from her brow and eased her laptop closed. There was no doubt that Stacy would be perched at Ellen's elbow momentarily, the better to eagerly monitor her friend's conversation. In fact, Stacy was already navigating the maze of intervening desks and cubicles with an efficient hip-twisting glide that rendered most men in the room momentarily speechless.

Ellen paused for a moment to watch the show. Shaking her head in wry amusement, she reached for the phone. She actually did have a cousin, but they hadn't seen each other in years. He was now a lawyer, somewhere in New York, or was it New Jersey? Stacy had said it was a *guy*. Ellen was truly baffled; she had no idea who would be calling her at work.

Just as Stacy arrived, eyes twinkling above a mischievous grin, Ellen wondered if this was one of Stacy's little ploys to set her up with someone; but she dismissed the thought almost immediately. Were that the case, Stacy would not likely be so eager to eavesdrop.

"Good afternoon, this is Ellen Doyle, may I help you?"

"El', it's your cousin, Mark—Mark Paige. I—"

"Mark! Oh, it's good to hear from you! How are you?" She grinned at the memory; no one else had ever called her by that diminutive childhood nickname, *El'.*

She pointed to the phone and mouthed at Stacy, *"He really is my cousin!"*

Her lower lip thrust out in an exaggerated pout, Stacy shrugged and made her way back to her desk, oblivious to the wistful gazes of her male coworkers.

"I'm fine, El'. I'm sorry for calling you at work. I had no other way to get in touch. I don't have your home or cell number. I actually googled you and found you on your company's personnel roster."

"You did? I'm surprised I'm even listed; this is only a temp job. Oh well, no matter. So, what's going on with you, Mark?"

"Not much. Uh, listen, I'm afraid I have some bad news."

The rest of the conversation seemed to take place in a muted void, all sense of time and place suspended, as Ellen learned of the death of her Great Aunt Maude.

THAT EVENING, IN THE privacy of her apartment, she called Mark back. They had a lot of catching up to do. Ellen had not seen him for almost a decade. As they spoke, she felt those years dissolve. She rediscovered the cousin with whom she had shared childhood adventures and mischief in the beguiling woods and bayous of Chantilly Parish, Louisiana.

Eventually, the conversation returned to their Aunt Maude.

Ellen sighed. "So, Mark, how did you find out, about her passing, I mean?"

"I was contacted by a law firm in LaBorde, who formally advised me of Maude's death and the subsequent probate procedures. She had a will; and apparently had listed me as her primary next-of-kin contact."

"That makes sense; after all, you are a lawyer. What about a funeral? We're family; we should attend, right? So, are you gonna go?"

"Yeah, I'm going. As for the arrangements, there's to be a memorial service. I'm expected to be involved but I haven't gotten details yet.

"And another thing, both you and I are named as beneficiaries in the will. As such, we are expected—no, actually required per the will, to attend the reading. They inferred that the estate may be significant; but, they wouldn't give me details over the phone. We can suggest a mutually acceptable date for the reading, but it's gotta be within thirty days from Maude's passing. Are you okay with that?"

"Well, I'd go to her funeral, memorial service, or whatever anyway. So, yeah, I'm okay with it. Anytime is good for me. My job as a temp is winding down; so, I've got nothing holding me here. I'll call tomorrow to see if I can get flight reservations. What about you?"

"No problem. There is another thing though; I'm supposed to notify any other family members, and they told me I have to write an appropriate obituary."

"An obituary?"

"Yeah, it's actually a stipulation in the will. Jeez, El', I have no problem with the legal stuff, but I don't have a clue what to write for an obituary. I don't really know anything about her—you know, the personal stuff you'd expect to find in an obit. Can you help?"

"Mark, I really don't know if I can be of much help. I was only, um, thirteen or so when I last saw her. She never told me anything, you know, personal. I don't think she was ever married, or *involved*. Of course, that would be—or rather *was* her business."

"Yeah, okay, I understand. Maybe you could ask your mom? Aunt Millie would know more than us, wouldn't she? By the way, I haven't contacted her to tell her about Aunt Maude yet, since I didn't have *her* current number either. Do you want to tell her? I don't mind doing it, but I'll need her number."

Ellen's response was noticeably cool. "I could tell her; or you could, if you'd prefer. I'll have to look up her number for you."

"Well, let's figure out what we do know about Aunt Maude, and then go from there, okay?"

"Sure, but let's think about what is usually in an obituary. That's what you really need at the moment, right?"

"Right. Well, part of the problem is that no one seems to know how old Aunt Maude really was. The Louisiana attorney, Claude Fornier, told me that they could find no record of a birth certificate, social security number, or driver's license. Even the death certificate only articulated that she died at an indeterminate, albeit advanced, age. He said the cause of death was cited as *systematic organ failure.*"

"That sounds a little vague to me," Ellen offered. "Are there any more details?"

"Not really, and I asked," Mark assured her. "All the attorney could tell me was that when he checked with her doctors for more information, he was told that it's a fairly common scenario in the elderly wherein all systems seem to shut down at the same time."

"Okay, I guess, but *elderly* doesn't help narrow down her actual age, does it?"

"Not much," Mark agreed. "Claude Fornier also told me that there was some indication of dementia; Alzheimer's was suspected. Maude spent the past three years in a residential assisted living facility under the care of geriatricians. However, even they weren't certain of Maude's age. She would never discuss it, insisting that *a lady never discloses such matters.*"

"Ha!" Ellen exclaimed. "Now that sounds like her!"

"Yeah, doesn't it. You know, the earliest memories I have, per the family lore, are that Maude knew our great grandmother, and was a close friend of our grandmother. I guess I kinda thought Maude had somehow married into the family way back when. But, you know, that wasn't the sort of thing the *adults* ever discussed."

"Oh yeah, especially around us kids," Ellen confirmed. "I guess I just assumed things, like you did. I can remember my mother saying that Maude had actually babysat our moms when they were little. And of course, you know Maude occasionally took care of us when we were kids."

"Absolutely, I remember." There was a smile in his voice.

Ellen paused in thought.

"What? Did you think of something?" he asked.

"Well, yeah. You know, it's possible that Aunt Maude might not actually be related by blood *or* marriage."

"What th—oh, I get it! You mean it's possible that the honorific, *aunt*, was bestowed some time in the distant past, as was frequently customary when a well-regarded individual was in consistent proximity to a family and its affairs."

"Exactly, so children would show respect and acknowledge certain elders like family," she reasoned. "But would that change—"

"The will? No, we're specifically named as beneficiaries. So, legally—"

"No, not that," she interrupted. "I mean would that change how we should feel?"

"About Maude? No, of course not! You know better than that," he chided.

"I know, Mark. It really doesn't matter if the connection was by blood, marriage, or whatever; it was strong. You know, looking back on it, she was a loving aunt, all the same. She was just *always there, in the moment with us;* we loved that about her."

"Yeah, I do know," he agreed. "And now, it's like an essential part of our childhood reality is missing. It feels like a little hollow somewhere in the heart."

"Mark, that's sweet of you to say. I know just how you feel. But to be honest, I'm not sure I can be of more help; that's pretty much all I can remember that might help to determine her age. I don't know what else to tell you. Is it really that important?"

"You know, maybe not, but I gotta try, for the obit. I admit I'm stumped, too. I guess contacting Aunt Millie is my next step, maybe tomorrow; it's getting kinda late here."

Ellen winced. "Okay, I'll call you back with the phone number, as soon as I find it."

"No problem, I understand. We've got to coordinate our travel plans, too. I'm gonna get on that first thing tomorrow."

"Oh yeah, me too."

"Okay, good night, El."

"Good night, Mark."

Ellen reached across the arm of the couch and returned the cordless phone to its charger. As was her habit, she stood at the window to watch the subtle descent of night, that soft blurring of the city's harsher edges. She had always found dusk calming and comfortable. She snuggled back onto the couch, tucked her feet under her, and pulled a favorite cushion to her chest. With her chin tracing a small divot in the soft texture of the pillow, she stared unfocused at the smudge of dying twilight.

An image of her Aunt Maude, at least how Ellen remembered her, as an old woman with a kind yet knowing smile and an unabashed twinkle in her eye, hovered in her mind. A flush of guilt that she'd not made more of an effort to keep in touch evoked a wincing sigh and further saddened the moment. Aunt Maude had always been one of her favorite people. And yet, how had that bond diminished without her noticing? Were time and distance at fault, or at least contributing factors?

She realized that missing someone when you're just out of touch is one thing; but missing someone when you learn they are really gone is something else entirely. That utter finality can be a harsh moment of compelled acceptance.

In that sense, it was a kind of relief to hear from Mark after all these years. At one time he'd been her best friend and confidant; she had truly missed him. While she was happy to have her cousin back, she wasn't eager to get her mother, Mildred, involved.

However, she saw no way around it.

She wasn't even sure how her mother would react to the news; there had been some friction between Maude and Mildred many years ago. Ellen never knew the details, or cared. However, Ellen wasn't a teenager any longer; and this was a family matter. Mildred would just have to deal with it.

She smiled, realizing that whenever she was piqued at her mother she referred to her as Mildred, not *Millie* or *Mom*. Millie hated being called Mildred; she complained it made her feel *old*. So, of course, this was Ellen's little way of needling her, even if she only *thought* it.

Ellen could let Mark make the call, but that wouldn't be right. She would make the call, and do her best to be civil.

Her mental shields in place, she reached for the phone.

MARK SAT IN THE COMFORTABLE retreat of his New York apartment and began to organize his thoughts. A decade's worth of information had flowed between Ellen and him, upon which he felt he needed to impose some sort of order.

As was his habit developed in law school, he reached again for his ever-present yellow legal pad to take notes while the information was fresh in his mind. Much of what they had discussed about Maude was already duly noted on the first sheet, so he had nothing much more to add. He really needed to interview Aunt Millie; she *had* to know more about Maude.

Mark found himself nervously tapping his pencil on his legal pad, another ingrained habit from his law school days that seemed to manifest whenever he was faced with uncomfortable decisions or circumstances.

In retrospect, mentioning Millie to Ellen might not have been the best thing, since Millie and Ellen did not enjoy the traditional mother-daughter relationship; but, he'd had little choice. Nonetheless, he was not eager to get involved with whatever emotional tides were pulling at Ellen and her mother.

Mark viewed himself as a linear thinker, a problem solver, unburdened by the yoke of emotional distraction. He would much rather deal strictly with the facts, the solid legal issues. He tried to force himself to concentrate on the situation at hand. Besides, the turmoil between Ellen and Millie had been going on for as long as he could remember.

Wincing, he scribbled a *note to self:* STAY OUT OF IT!

He really disliked dealing with emotional issues. He wasn't good at it, and he knew it. He was always *in control;* and the antithesis of that state was, at least in his mind, *emotional chaos*. He shook himself free of such ruminations. He had other issues to address, like funeral and memorial arrangements, not to mention that confounded obituary.

Fortunately, in compliance with the will, there would not be a full funeral, just a memorial service. Evidently, Aunt Maude had long ago opted for cremation and a minimum of social fuss. Under the heading *Memorial Service* Mark listed attendees; Ellen, hopefully Aunt Millie, himself, and . . . He was stumped. Neither Ellen nor he had any idea who Maude's friends were, if any. Were they even still around, or alive? Who knew?

He really needed to speak with the attorney, Claude Fornier, again—and Aunt Millie. At least the LaBorde attorney should be available in the morning. Realizing he'd not get much more done on Maude's case, he shrugged, placed his notes in a file, and decided to get some sleep.

It's kind of odd that I'm thinking of this situation as a case. Perhaps it's just an unconscious mechanism to distance myself from the more uncomfortable emotional aspects. Oh man, how I hate the drama. I'm going to bed.

"STACY, ARE YOU SURE you don't mind taking me to the airport? I could just take a cab." Ellen dropped another overstuffed suitcase near the tiny apartment's front door.

"Forget it! I'm taking an extra long lunch today so I can do this; we can talk on the way. So, what's with your mom? She's not gonna go to the funeral or whatever?"

"No, when I called her she said she couldn't really get away. Something's going on with her work, you know, that diner she manages. She was kinda vague about it, hinting that the place might be changing hands, new owners and all. I don't really know that much about it. I haven't even been down in that part of town in ages."

Hefting a suitcase, Stacy agreed. "I don't blame you; that whole area's gotten kinda rough. I wouldn't venture down there without a real good reason. Wait! Doesn't your mom live near there with, uh, her boyfriend?"

"Yeah, with *Earl*," Ellen replied sullenly. "He's her latest, for almost two years or so. I guess I shouldn't complain; he treats her all right, I suppose. But I'd bet she still thinks she can *fix* him, like all the rest."

Stacy may be her friend, but Ellen was always uncomfortable discussing any details about her personal family issues, especially those involving her mother. "Sorry, but I don't really wanna talk about this, okay?"

"No problem. Come on; let's get these to the car." Stacy glanced at her watch. "We've got a little over three hours or so before your flight. Traffic is always a bitch; and, you know getting through security is gonna take some time."

Her car packed and her passenger aboard, Stacy drove toward the freeway.

"So, Ellen, tell me about your cousin. Is he cute? Who's older, you or him? What's he look like? Is he—"

"Enough already!" Ellen sputtered with laughter. "Jeez, Stacy! I haven't seen him in like ten years or so. I have no idea what he looks like now. He's older than me, by almost three years, and still single. He's a lawyer in New York now. We were the best of friends as kids."

"Wait a minute! He ended up in New York. You wound up in Los Angeles. And you're both from the same town in Louisiana, right? So, how did that happen?"

Ellen shrugged. "It's no mystery. His momma, my Aunt Margaret, died of cancer when he was nine. His dad, Luke, took it hard for quite a while; his auto repair business floundered. Eventually he took a job with a paper company as a traveling sales rep, and did pretty well. He was offered the Northeast Regional Manager's position, so he moved to New York. He took Mark with him, and they stayed."

"Okay, I get that," Stacy acknowledged. "But, what about you? You know, winding up in L.A.?"

Ellen frowned. She'd just turned thirteen when her mother decided on a whim to follow another man, her paramour of the moment, out to the West Coast. She took Ellen with her. Millie's capricious behavior and constant succession of boyfriends whom she thought she could fix were consistent sources of angst and embarrassment for teenaged Ellen. These were the thorns that would fester into the lingering shame and resentment that would taint their relationship for years to come.

"Let's just say it was my mother's idea," Ellen hedged. "She followed a guy she was fond of at the time to California. She must have thought he was *the one*—he wasn't. We wound up staying in Los Angeles; and the rest is history."

Enough said, jeez! How does Stacy do it? I didn't really want to talk about this.

CH 2

MARK GLANCED UP FROM his tablet as the flight attendant dangled a small package of pretzels just within his field of view.

"Snack? Beverage, sir?"

"Just orange juice, please." He waved off the proffered pretzels.

As she handed him the short plastic cup, he mumbled his thanks, and glanced out the starboard window at a bright carpet of endless cloud. He downed his three ounces of reconstituted orange juice and slid the cup of melting ice to the edge of his tray table.

He tried to focus on his tablet, but his thoughts wandered to Ellen. As promised, she had returned his call that morning. She surprised him; he had no need to contact Aunt Millie—Ellen had done it. Unfortunately, Millie had very little to add to the store of knowledge about Aunt Maude. Ellen also explained that it was very unlikely that Millie would attend the memorial service due to some sort of undefined issues with her job. Sensing something from Ellen akin to mild disapproval, and very leery of getting involved, Mark felt it wise to inquire no further.

Ellen was to travel to LaBorde today as well, but she would get in later that evening, several hours after his flight. She had insisted that he not wait for her, and urged him to keep an afternoon appointment with the attorney, Mr. Fornier. She would take a cab to the hotel. Later they could meet for dinner and catch up.

Mark tried to stretch his legs out and loosened his seat belt a bit. He peered out the window and thought about the LaBorde attorney.

In their last conversation, Mark apologized and explained that the requested obituary would be quite brief. Claude Fornier guardedly assured Mark that it would most likely not be an issue, and that he would see it appropriately published in the parish weekly newspaper, the Chantilly Clarion, as per the requirement stipulated in the will.

In retrospect, Mark was unsettled about the obituary. Why had *he* been so tasked? Something just didn't *feel* right. He would share his misgivings with Ellen at dinner later that evening.

He had not been back to Chantilly Parish in a decade. Had it changed much? It would be a simple matter to search on the internet and find out.

Chantilly Parish . . . It'd be a "county" everywhere else in the country; but, that's Louisiana for you.

He turned his attention to his tablet.

His patient probing proved fruitful. Chantilly Parish was still rural, boasting only a number of small towns and one small city, the centrally located LaBorde, which served as the seat of parish government. The population was barely over fifty thousand residents; just under half of whom lived in and around LaBorde. The rest were distributed among tiny townships, farms, and a few rustic hunting and fishing camps.

Aside from oil and gas concerns, the parish had little other industry, save for a long-established paper mill. However, there was the casino built four years ago on the Indian Reservation to the east. Consequently, tourism had seen modest gains. Of course, hunting and fishing were regional staples.

DeLorme University, a small but well-regarded institution, had its campus on the western edge of LaBorde. Its nursing school offered in-service training at the local hospital.

In an effort to revive the small downtown area, the city blocks around the central courthouse square had been successfully renovated as an *arts enclave* and now hosted a few galleries, cafes, and a coffeehouse. The square had become reasonably popular with college students and tourists.

The small airport south of town had extended its runway and added a heliport to accommodate the statewide oil and gas industry. The increased commercial flight traffic was a modest boon to the local economy.

As the flight attendant retrieved the empty cup, Mark leaned his seat back. He tried to relax. His mind wandered and he realized that he had subconsciously hoped to find no significant changes in his childhood home, at least not enough to further muddle his memories, already faded to soft sepia.

ELLEN SLEPT THROUGH most of her flight, at least the first leg, from LAX to Dallas-Fort Worth. Her connecting flight from DFW was delayed, so she had an extra hour on her hands. The novel she had begun to read on the plane was better than she'd anticipated, but was now in her purse. She would save it for her upcoming flight from DFW to LaBorde.

She decided to stretch her legs, so she wandered through the concourse, window shopping and people watching. She became aware of a subtle sensation, like a phantom itch between her shoulder blades, that she, too, was being closely watched.

Oh well, fair is fair; other travelers people watch, too.

ELLEN'S FINAL FLIGHT leg, from DFW to LaBorde, aboard a much smaller propeller-driven aircraft, was a bumpy ride; a rather rambunctious storm front dogged the flight's eastern progress. Her novel couldn't compete with the distractions of periodic turbulence. Touchdown at LaBorde Airport came as a welcome relief to all the passengers.

As she stood by the baggage carousel, enduring the inevitable wait, large windows afforded a view of angry clouds roiling forth in slow motion and swallowing the western end of the runway. The weak sun faded far too quickly; within moments, it became storm-dark.

Her luggage in tow, she stepped outside into a robust gust of wind that swirled about her. She had barely begun to look for a cab when a taxi whipped to the curb.

The wiry driver kept his head down and shoulders hunched as he stuffed her luggage into the trunk, and held the door open for her.

She mumbled her thanks, glanced at the ominous sky, and gave the name of the Ancelet Arms Hotel. She settled in the back seat, clutching her purse, and peered into the driver's rearview mirror.

Their eyes locked in the glass; he quickly looked away.

As the taxi left the airport, the storm broke with a furious shriek. Slashing sheets of rain and rumbling thunder rocked the cab as harsh lightning cracked reality. Tucking her chin and gripping her elbows, she erected her mental shields, shutting out the worst of the squall's fury, and sought her peaceful center.

Minutes later, still some distance from the hotel, and her mind pleasantly elsewhere, Ellen felt that something was amiss.

She tensed, sensing something looming to her right.

A sudden blinding light and jarring impact were followed by jumbled disorientation and a plunge into darkness.

CH 3

AWASH IN ANXIETY, SALIDAR stood tensely in the cone of light, his eyes downcast but ears alert for the slightest sound. He sensed that he was in a vast space; but, he was uncertain, for his eyes could not penetrate the deep gloom beyond the reach of his hands. He stood upon irregular, yet closely fit, smooth flagstones. When he looked for his feet, he was further unnerved to see they were swallowed by his own stygian shadow. He was not tempted to look at the light above; it would likely sear the orbs from his skull.

He endeavored to remain still and exert some semblance of control over his mounting fear. He was not brave by any stretch of the imagination, but he did have a very strong sense of self-preservation, which he had found to be eminently pragmatic, having served him well over his long loathsome life.

To venture beyond the cone of illumination would be the height of folly—anything could lurk beyond in the deep obsidian void. His subconscious screamed that all manner of salivating horrors stalked nearby, in the thick roiling shadows. Could he perceive things below the threshold of his senses? Were his ears playing tricks on him? Did he not hear a subtle snuffling off to his right? A guttural grunt of anticipation muffled to his left? Was that the scratch of claws on stone behind him? Was there just a whisper of carrion-laden breath across his neck?

The stench—ye gods! The stench was real; or, was it the stench of his fear? His terror was on the verge of total possession of his wits; he struggled to keep it in check.

His clammy sweat did not cool him despite the ambient chill. Waves of stifled nausea wracked his knotted stomach. Only his hidden anger and gritted teeth prevented him from vomiting.

He knew they would make him wait. They were patient. They would taste his fear and savor his terror. They would likely allow him to hover in soundless screams at the breaking point. Only then would he learn his fate. He was no fool. He knew more than his blood and flesh hung in the balance; his very essence, perhaps even his soul, was at risk.

Some time passed. He had no concept of its duration; years it seemed. He had long since collapsed to a huddled heap, and was about to slip from soft sobbing into witless gibbering, when a sibilant voice slithered through the shuddering tremors of his mind.

"Ssso, once again Sssalidar, you exceed the ssscope of your inssstructionsss."

"M'lords," he quaked, sensing other ominous presences in the murk. "It was too good an opportunity to miss. I thought it your intention, uh, implied at least."

"Fool!" roared another deeper, discordant voice. "You are not to *think*! You were to follow orders explicitly and not demonstrate initiative! This is the second time you have failed us!"

"Your sssoul isss now forfeit, you disssobedient pessstilence! I ssshall—"

"HOLD!" called yet another voice, firm yet light and musical—and cold, so very cold. "It seems our servant would benefit from a lesson; or, do we truly have no more need for such a one?"

No! Not her! This could not be worse!

"L-Lady Diere!" Salidar blubbered. His eyes darting unfocused throughout the darkness, he rasped, "M'lady, I am your loyal servant! Your interests are foremost in my mind! I am still most useful and . . . and, uh . . . have resources yet to call upon." He wheezed in another breath, as if to speak.

"Hear my judgment, Grimrald!"

That she *named* him stunned him into silence. This would not be good—no, not good at all.

"You were instructed to watch and observe the Steward's heir—*only* watch and observe. For that, you needed only your eyes. Instead, you exceed your instructions, *again!* Obviously, you do not need your eyes. So, I take your sight!"

Salidar's vision dwindled to a mere point of dim glow and winked out, leaving only dense blackness. He was blind—absolutely, totally blind. His breath caught in his throat as the shock filled his veins with ice. He was dimly aware that she had again begun to speak.

"You were instructed to converse with the dying Steward at the appointed time, that we might learn more of her plans, or something more of the intended heir. Instead, you attempted a suggestion spell using a dark amulet, its application well beyond your skill, which apparently led to her premature death. We learned *nothing!* I would wager you even foolishly used your right hand during the amulet ritual, hmm? So, I take the *use* of your right arm!"

His right arm convulsed and gave one final spasm. It was as dead, limp, an unfeeling weight dangling at his side. It wouldn't do anything. He couldn't even push off the stone floor. His sightless eyes flooded and he groaned.

The moment passed and he realized that she was not finished.

"I have yet to pronounce the full judgment; so, pay attention. You repeatedly failed to listen to your instructions. For that you only needed your ears. So they are obviously of no *use* to you. I take your hearing! Furthermore, I think you could also benefit from a period of contemplation in the void!"

Wrapped in sudden silence, Salidar was almost beyond caring. He could neither see nor hear as she gestured and spoke in a very old language, but he did register a sense of numb disassociation, the dead silence, and the endless dark of what she had called the void.

His body slowly rose from the smooth stones to rotate weightlessly, deaf and blind, suspended in midair at twice a man's height.

"IMPRESSSIVE, AND SSSEVERE. But, I ssstill want hisss sssoul!" whispered the watcher.

The deeper voice resonated, with a subtle mixture of fear and awe. "He can't hear or see us, right? I agree that was very well done. Now what? Kill him?"

"No, I think not." She sighed. "The truth is, we still need him. George, only you can go about your business unnoticed in the Realm of Man without certain aids or assistance. And you cannot be in two places at once."

"Not yet," he quipped.

She smiled in the dark, laid her unseen manicured hand on his arm, leaned into him and breathed, "Patience."

She steered him, arm in arm, toward the light, and indicated the floating Salidar. "I'll bring him back, perhaps not whole, lest he forget this lesson. We have reports that the Steward's heir still lives, near comatose and critical. So, it appears that we still need this pawn."

Lady Diere now stood fully in the light, tall and slender, graceful and poised. Raven hair clasped back from her high forehead fell in an ebony cascade over her slight shoulders and dropped to her narrow waist. Slanted deep violet eyes almost overwhelmed her small face and dainty chin. She ran her long fingertips past her temples capturing a few stray strands of hair and tucked them behind her elegant, pointed ears. She was proportioned well, and quite obviously female, but just a bit too ethereal to be human.

Reflected light danced upon tiny onyx beads suspended in the matrix of delicate black lace that trimmed her sheer crimson gown. Close fitting, such attire was considered simple and understated for a Fey of high status, appropriate for casual court functions or *other business*. It would be otherwise scandalous anywhere but a Parisian fashion runway in the Realm of Man.

"Enough of thisss! What of the men he usssed?" rasped forth from the deeper recesses of the dark.

"George, they were yours, were they not?" She leveled her gaze at the graying man in the blue pin-striped business suit.

"Yes, three thugs from New Orleans, displaced by the hurricanes; they won't be missed." He scoffed and tossed a hand nonchalantly. "In fact, I recently learned that one was an unreliable junkie. I would have had to dispose of him eventually anyway."

"He wasss the taxi driver who wasss killed in the *accident?*"

She glanced toward the unseen questioner still shrouded in the dark. With the slightest tilt of her head, she indicated that he should join them in the light.

George, oblivious to her gesture, nodded his assent to the question. "Burned to a crisp in the fire, they probably will never even identify him."

Lady Diere's violet gaze fixed him, penetrating his carefully maintained façade of aloof detachment like a lepidopterist's steel pin through a hapless butterfly's thorax. She stared until she was certain he could feel the icy shaft of her disdain twisting in his own guts. In a voice of crystalline frost, she chastised him.

"Never underestimate the curiosity and creativity of your own species. If they have his body, they will eventually identify him. There can be no link to you—to us! Am I clear? See to it!"

Clearly chilled to his very core, George could only nod in affirmation.

She held him transfixed for a moment more. "Are we certain that the heir traveled alone? There are no other *loose ends*?"

George paled, but responded with growing confidence. "She traveled alone. I even had some *associates* observe her when she changed planes in Dallas. They said she spoke to no one, and kept to herself."

She looked down her nose at him. "So, the long range plan is still in play, notwithstanding Salidar's curious initiative?"

George gulped, but found his voice. "It is, despite that fool."

"And what of the othersss, thossse who aided Sssalidar?"

The unseen speaker eased into the edge of the light. Of medium height, he appeared to be a hairless male of modest, yet compact, stature, a ruddy yellow tinge to his rough dermis. As he turned slightly, his sallow complexion seemed to blush with hints of rust as the light refracted off his exposed skin. A loose hooded robe hid all but his hands, head, and an open laced V across his chest. Beneath a heavy brow, his amber eyes held saurian pupils that squeezed to mere slits as he entered the full light.

He spoke, his forked tongue slipping between his lips, as if to punctuate his point. "Pleassse, we mussst ssspeak of thisss."

"Why, Lord Addecus, I saved them for you," George answered smugly, despite his obvious discomfiture at the proximity of the Were Lord. He then executed a slight bow and made a gesture in a direction to their left. Another cone of light illuminated two figures, sprawled unconscious. "You see, I have managed a small degree of competence with the limited powers at my disposal."

"Sssplendid, sssimply sssplendid! We may make a mage of you yet, young one. What think you, Lady Diere?" Lord Addecus inclined his head courteously to her, but his unblinking eyes never left George's own. He smiled, his forked tongue flicking between barely glimpsed fangs.

"We shall see, my lord, we shall see," Lady Diere said evenly. The thinly veiled sarcasm of the shape shifter's remark was not lost on her, but she was not so certain about George. *Is he too clever for his own good?*

She shrugged and tossed a beckoning command over her shoulder as she turned, disappearing into the dark. "Come George, it would be best that we leave Lord Addecus to his distractions, such that you have so thoughtfully provided. We have preparations to make. Lord Addecus can join us at his leisure. Can you not, m'lord?"

"Asssuredly, m'lady. I ssshan't be long, to be sssure. Tisss quick work that awaitsss me," he hissed in amusement as George hurried away.

MOMENTS LATER, ADDECUS made a gesture and the cone of light widened considerably. Confident that he was alone, but for the helpless Salidar and the two unconscious men, he set up a rumbling vibration in his throat that summoned a pair of large shaggy hulks that seemed to materialize at a distance within the gloom. They gained definition as they approached the light, loping upright on two legs. Huge furred shoulders cast the bodies in shadow, but the long muscular arms swung in and out of view as the massive clawed hands, almost paws with opposable thumbs, scraped knuckles upon the flagstones in their easy haste.

It was their heads that commanded attention; the elongated snouts, the long teeth, and the panting. The heads resembled those of massive wolves—dire wolves, the likes of which had not been seen on Earth in an age. Elements of man were evident in their carriage, but the aura of the predator and the features of the wolf were overwhelming. Most frightening of all was the evident intelligence in their yellow eyes, a malevolent glint in their gaze.

Stopping a pace from their summoner, whom they dwarfed by twice his size, each werewolf sniffed the air and cocked tall pointed ears as Addecus spoke in a guttural language. He indicated the supine figures unconscious on the stone, and conveyed that they were to be taken to a place he named, unharmed, for he had plans.

The beasts caught Salidar's scent, and one started salivating, taking a few steps toward the floating body.

"Ssstop! Not that one. He ssservesss Lady Diere'sss purpossse!"

The werewolf froze in mid-step, flinching at her name, and scurried back before Lord Addecus.

The Were Lord hissed to himself. *But sssoon enough he'll ssserve mine! The fool! He fearsss thisss punissshment, thisss sssensssory deprivation, this void, beyond all reassson. Little doesss he know how vulnerable he really isss! I ssshall have hisss sssoul yet!*

SALIDAR, A LONER AT heart, still felt isolated with only shattered portions of his wits for company. A more lucid segment of his subconscious noted that his tattered mind was host to several conversations amongst various aspects of his personality—*or should that be personalities?*

He struggled to make some sense of the chaos of images, recriminations, hatred, and fear. He found a thin strand of raw cunning and grasped its harsh edge, instinctively focusing on the one reliable trait that offered any potential for recovering his wits. Forcing himself to a fragile state of reasonable calm, he tried to assess his situation. For the moment, he lived; his soul, however dark, was intact—a good place to start.

More facts surfaced in his muddled brain; he had been banished to the void. That was not too surprising; he'd been punished thusly before, and it didn't really bother him that much because he knew he'd be retrieved. The void held few immediate horrors that he was aware of, nor was the forced solitude much of an imposition for a self-absorbed loner. He thought of the void as his brier patch; of course, he was always careful to react with abject fear whenever it was threatened as punishment. Had the *Mad Elf* sought his death, neither he nor his soul would now likely exist. She must still need him. She hadn't killed him, or given him to that were-hybrid monstrosity, Addecus.

At that thought, his ravaged mind shuddered anew.

He remembered more. She had blinded and deafened him; and, she'd done something to his right arm. The terror he had felt then now floated just below the surface of his dubious control; he gripped ever tighter to his anger and cunning. He reasoned that he would be retrieved, and his faculties restored. He was still of use. He was needed; he instinctively knew it. She would come to regret her misuse of his many talents.

He gave no thought as to why she had treated him so severely; he didn't actually care. His only regret was that his plans had gone awry; and he'd been caught. He would plan more carefully in the future; and, he would have his revenge. The only variable that lay beyond any semblance of his control was time. But time held no meaning in the void. He had learned to be patient. Of course, that didn't mean he liked it; but, he could wait. After all, he was far older, even for a halfling, than most would believe, an unintended but selfishly gratifying result of his long service to those of darker intentions.

Yes, he would wait and plan.

ELLEN WAS BECOMING aware, much like waking from a deep sleep, but finding herself in a strange place, one that she didn't remember going to, or how she got there, or when—or anything. Everything was grey, or shades of grey. She sensed that she was standing—well, maybe standing, as she had no real sense of gravity either—on a grey floor, in a grey place, yet not in a room, but not outside. There were no walls, but there was a vague grey limit or horizon. Something seemed to define this greyness; it didn't *feel* infinite. She stared at her hands, both of which appeared leeched of all color as well.

She was trying so hard to comprehend where she was that she almost didn't hear, or rather sense, the voice calling her name—or was it just in her mind? *Telepathy?*

At that very thought, she seemed to hear someone speak—but with her ears? She hoped so.

. . . Oh very well, I suppose that would be better under the circumstances . . .

Slightly startled but somehow unafraid, Ellen asked, "Who? Where are you? Where am I? What's going on? Where are you?"

. . . *Oh, sorry . . . Give me a moment, please . . .*

The voice was vaguely familiar, which Ellen found even more unnerving as she twisted around in search of the speaker. Several paces away, the grey matter began to eddy and swirl in place as the form of a petite woman took shape. Ellen stared in fascination as memories flooded forth, and familiarity warmed to full recognition.

"Aunt Maude? B-but you're—" she stammered.

. . . *Yes, don't remind me. And hello to you too, Ellen . . .*

Maude seemed to be grey as well, but somehow that fit, as she waved a hand in the grey air as if to dismiss the obvious.

"Does that mean that I'm . . . " Ellen's voice hitched a bit and she tried to swallow.

. . . *No, you're not dead—not that somebody didn't try!* Maude's visage took on a cross look as she pursed her lips and shook her head in obvious frustration.

"What? Somebody tried to kill me?" Ellen blurted. "What's going on here?"

. . . *Quiet! And listen! It's important! This telepathy stuff takes practice; it'll get easier for you. But right now it's too slow, so I'm going to try to speak aloud. At least it'll seem that way to you, but you have to be receptive . . .*

"Uh, okay, I guess . . . " Ellen was still bewildered.

Maude struggled to speak urgently, but could not utter a word. She paused, calmed herself, and quietly found her voice.

To Ellen, it still felt like much of the message formed within her conscious mind.

"We don't have much time, and you can't stay here. The only reason you're here is because you came close to dying; but it's not your time. You have to go back,

soon." Maude began to pace. *"In fact, I doubt this opportunity for us to communicate was anticipated. Someone has made a big mistake; and we can take the advantage.*

"This place, it's not in your, uh, reality. It'll help if you think of this as a dreamscape, at least for now. There are rules of a sort here. Think of them as the laws of physics in your world. I can't tell you all I'd like. I'd try, but it just won't come out. So I'll tell you what I can, while I can. You just listen, okay?"

Ellen just nodded.

"You may be able to find your way back here, without benefit of a near-death experience, but you'll have to discover the technique on your own. I've left you some help, a journal and some things—the spectacles are important. There are some people, friends, whom you can trust; you'll know when the time comes. I'll likely still be here, but that's a story for another time.

"You're in danger, and I'm afraid it's my fault. I've named you as my successor to the Stewardship, but you have to agree and formally accept the responsibility, and . . . ooh, damn it! You'll have to learn a lot as you go; but remember this, true names are very important and powerful. It's very important that you accept and do this."

Maude stopped pacing and tilted her head, as if listening. *"You have to go back now. No argument. Go! Just will yourself back into your body. Do it! This place is not safe for you, or me either for that matter. Please, Ellen, do as I ask."*

Ellen was overwhelmed. A part of her wanted to believe she was dreaming, but somehow she knew the truth of Maude's words was undeniable—someone had caused her deliberate harm. A sudden insight rocked her; had someone also deliberately harmed her Aunt Maude? Killed her? Should she ask?

Maude shook her head. *Just go, now!*

Maude's image began to fade, her features softening into the grey mist. Her sad smile seemed to be the last to go; a Cheshire moment, thought Ellen.

That was the point at which her resolve solidified; she would find out just what the truth was, for herself and Maude.

She became aware of another nearing presence, ominous and foreboding. Just sensing it was not a pleasant experience. Could this approaching entity have sensed her? It was now focused on her—she was certain of it.

She closed her eyes and willed herself back into her body, wherever that was, and felt herself falling, disoriented and breathless into a maelstrom. Her senses faded; even the subtle concept of time's passage eluded her.

SHE BECAME AWARE OF gravity. She was pressed down on her back—no, not really *pressed*, it was merely her own weight she felt. Then the pain registered, a dull pulsing ache that mimicked her heartbeat. She tried to take a deep breath, and froze as more pain flared on her right side. Taking little hitching breaths, she managed to fill her lungs and slowly exhale.

That hurt! Broken ribs? Oh man, I hope not! What else?

She managed to open her left eye to a squint; but her right didn't cooperate. She realized that side of her face, and her head, were bandaged. Her neck was stiff, or rather held immobile; she sensed some sort of collar.

I'm flat on my back in a bed? My ribs hurt badly and bandages are on my head and face. I'm sore all over. Okay, I must be in a hospital. What happened? The plane? No, we landed just fine. The taxi? Omigod! The taxi—an accident! The grey place—Maude? This hurt was deliberate?

She noticed the room was small. Something was visible to her left; an IV pole, and softly beeping monitors—a hospital for certain. It was very quiet, the lights dim. She could barely hear soft voices to her right, as if through a closed door, fading with the receding patter of purposeful footsteps.

Okay, now I have a good idea of where I am. But, am I all here?

With much conscious effort she went through a ritual of wiggling her toes and fingers. Satisfied with the inventory, she found she could move both her legs, although her right knee complained. Her arms were stiff; but she could move them.

I can see an IV in the back of my left hand. I can't see my right hand, but it feels like it's taped up—maybe another IV?

Satisfied, at least for the moment, Ellen realized she was extremely tired.

Maybe I should just nap for a bit and I'll feel better. Maybe then I can get some answers.

Within the span of a few breaths, she had burrowed into a realm of dreamless sleep.

SEVERAL FEET AWAY AT the nurses' station, a small patient-alert light had been flashing for several moments. The senior duty nurse was down the hall checking on another patient. Her volunteer assistant for the evening, a young nursing student, reached over and toggled off the flashing light.

She glanced down the hall, saw that the duty nurse was sufficiently preoccupied, picked up a clipboard, and walked into Ellen's room. Standing at the IV pole, she adjusted the sedative drip to dramatically increase the flow.

With a penlight, she quickly observed Ellen's undamaged eye and whispered, "We can't have you waking up now, can we?"

CH 4

DR. MARIE LATRICE-JOHNSON, Chief Neurologist, shifted uncomfortably at her desk as she studied the patient file. She sifted through chart notes, and checked her monitor screen for corresponding images of imaging scans, and the electroencephalograph readings for the past forty-eight hours.

The scans gave no indication of any head or neck trauma beyond the initially diagnosed concussion sustained to the right anterior of the skull, just above, and slightly forward of the ear. The file clearly articulated that there was still no indication of intracranial bleeding or increased pressure, a very good sign.

There were no fractures, but there was considerable evidence of strained muscle tissues throughout the patient's body. The blow to her head must have been reasonably significant, not that unusual in the case of traffic accidents. The soft tissues of the upper cheek and around the orbit of the right eye were bruised and swollen. Fortunately, the patient's overall condition, while still serious, was showing signs of improvement, but Ellen Doyle was still lightly sedated—or was she?

The source of the doctor's puzzlement was displayed on her computer screen, the digitized EEG chart as recorded at about midnight last night.

Prior to that time, the EEG record was consistent with an unconscious patient under light sedation. In fact, had circumstances warranted, a deeper sedation regimen that mimicked a coma-like condition could be chemically induced when deemed appropriate in certain treatment strategies, but was not applicable in this case.

However, about eight hours ago the digital EEG record reflected a significant increase in brain wave activity that would be consistent with an awake and alert patient. But within two hours of that time, the brain wave patterns dropped significantly below the previously established threshold and into a much deeper, near-comatose state.

Upon discovery of the EEG anomaly, Dr. Latrice-Johnson had immediately reexamined the patient. What she found raised her professional ire; the patient's IV sedative flow had been set significantly higher than the prescribed rate as specified on the patient's chart.

The EEG unit in the room was apparently functioning normally; however, the printout from the previous night was not in the patient file. Fortunately, the monitoring systems, to include the EEG, were digitally networked to a server for remote access and backup, so doctors could monitor patients remotely with a few key strokes on networked devices.

So, Dr. Latrice-Johnson caught the apparent mistake in time, and took immediate corrective action. As she treated Ellen Doyle, a cloud of doubt hovered. All her instincts were practically shouting that something was dreadfully wrong with this scenario.

Nurses are not prone to make mistakes like this!

At the nurses' station, the doctor questioned the day shift duty nurse, Roberta Beckett, who indicated that all had been well according to Eloise Smithers, the night shift duty nurse, when they had met at shift-change this morning.

Unsatisfied, the doctor pressed. "Did she mention anything at all unusual about last night's shift?"

"Not that I recall," Roberta insisted, "except for, well, it's probably nothing. She said she had a student-nurse volunteer for the shift last night. And I thought that was unusual because those college kids usually don't want to pull a night shift, especially over a weekend."

ALONE WITH HER THOUGHTS, the doctor wrestled with the ethical dilemma of notifying the hospital administrator immediately, or waiting until she had spoken to the night duty nurse. The Administrator, Dr. Gerald Hollis, was not fond of being presented with problems without proposed solutions. Nevertheless, she found herself walking through the administration wing in the direction of his office.

So be it; I may as well tell him now. Something just doesn't feel right.

She entered his outer office and smiled at Dr. Hollis' secretary. "Good morning, Nancy, is our fearless leader in?"

"Good morning, Dr. Latrice-Johnson, I'm sorry but Dr. Hollis is unavailable."

Nancy was not usually so formal, as she and Marie were old friends; so, such courteous formality alerted the doctor that they were not alone. An Emergency Department intern and a morgue attendant were seated in the reception area. Marie acknowledged them with a nod, and noticed that they were positively fidgeting like a pair of misbehaving schoolboys sent to the principal's office.

Stifling a chuckle at that image, she turned to Nancy, a question perched upon her lips—but Nancy preempted the inquiry with one of her own.

"Doctor, could I have a word with you, please?" Nancy led Marie into the Administrator's office and closed the door.

Marie stuffed her hands into the deep front pockets of her lab coat, absently fingering the cool disc of her stethoscope with one hand and her pager with the other. She was growing concerned, as she cocked her head attentively. "Okay, Nancy, what's going on? Where's Gerald?"

Nancy took a deep breath and sputtered. "Oh, M-Marie, I'm so glad to see you! You have no idea!" Nancy tended to accelerate her speech when stressed; right now she was passing *impulse* and working up to *warp speed*. "Gerald's at this funeral, his wife's sister's ex-husband, kind of like an ex-brother-in-law once removed or something. Anyway, he's *who-knows-where*, somewhere out of cell coverage range, and we need him! We have a problem! But now you're here; and you're the senior staff person here today, so you can handle it! Oh, I feel so much better already!"

"Huh? I mean, what's the problem?" Marie was confused, thinking it couldn't possibly be the same burden she hefted. She hadn't discussed it with anyone but the duty nurse, who was still busy on the ward. Then she remembered the two anxious young men in the outer office.

"Well . . . um . . . uh," the secretary stammered. Her eyes wide, Nancy now couldn't manage to speak with any alacrity; words seemed reluctant to leave her lips.

Marie would have likely found the dichotomy amusing under normal circumstances, but she sensed that Nancy thought the issue indeed dire, if not an absolute crisis. So, she probed soothingly.

"What is it, Nancy? I'm sure we can handle it."

"We've lost a body!" She sputtered, slipping into acceleration mode again. "The burnt one! It's missing from the morgue!"

Marie sought to calm her, and had her repeat what few facts she knew.

"So that's why the intern and morgue attendant are waiting in your office?"

Nancy nodded affirmatively.

"Okay, send them in and let me hear it all. Please don't let anyone interrupt us, okay?"

"No problem, Marie," assured a relieved Nancy. "I'll be right at my desk if you need me."

Nancy scurried from the room, waved the men into the office, and closed the door.

Marie took the liberty of sitting in Gerald's chair while she listened to the men explain how, this very morning, they realized that the body was missing. When the intern and attendant were finished, she asked them to wait again in the outer office.

"Well, this is sufficiently bizarre!" Marie mumbled and pinched the bridge of her nose. She looked up to find that Nancy had entered and now stood before the desk, as if awaiting orders, pen and notepad in hand.

Marie shrugged. "Okay, please keep trying to reach Gerald. I told our two *boys* to sit tight in your office until told otherwise. They are not to talk to anyone, just yet, except Gerald—and the authorities, of course. I'll make that call. Okay?"

"I'm on it," Nancy acknowledged, her confidence restored. "Contact Gerald; and the 'boys' talk to no one." She slipped from the room, easing the door closed.

Dr. Marie Latrice-Johnson, Chief Neurologist, sighed deeply, reached for the phone, and dialed the Sheriff's Office.

What a day this is turning out to be.

DETECTIVE CONNOR REDHAWK returned to his squad room desk with his second cup of office coffee. Morning sunlight streamed through the east windows, splashing about the room, tugging dust motes in its wake. He settled in his chair, and blew across his steaming mug. A sunbeam warmed his face causing him to squint as he noticed Sheriff Frank Tatum enter Captain Lou Miller's glass-walled office.

Two more of the day shift detectives, partners Billy Swift and Gordon Cormier, shuffled into the squad room and headed for the coffee. Billy mumbled, "Morning, Hawk." Gordon merely grunted, nodding in the younger detective's direction.

Connor, more often than not, was referred to by the other cops simply as "Hawk". He was resigned to it, having learned that somehow, nicknames were inevitable in law enforcement circles. He grinned, grunted an appropriately unintelligible acknowledgment, and sipped his own hot coffee.

Gordon Cormier hefted his cup toward a vacant desk. "Where's your partner, Hawk?"

"Trey's in court, a preliminary hearing. It shouldn't take all morning. You guys are in suits; so, you've got court today, too?"

"Yeah, this afternoon," Billy Swift confirmed. "It might get continued; the D.A.'s office has a problem with a witness—"

"Yeah," interrupted Gordon, "she got locked up last night for DUI. She's one of our good sergeant's old informants."

"Whoa! Are you kidding?" Hawk chuckled. "Does Trey know?"

His partner, Trey, the senior man on the squad, Sergeant William Robert Bassett, or *Billy Bob Bassett*, *Trey-B*, yet most often just "Trey", had an impressive assortment of confidential informants. It wasn't unusual in the least for any one of them to periodically get into trouble, and expect the sergeant to help them out. He never did, of course, unless the District Attorney saw an advantage and approved.

Billy Swift smirked and nodded. "Oh yeah. He got the call last night before we did; she called him from the jail. He called us so we wouldn't be surprised in court today. The Assistant D.A. still hasn't told us." Billy shrugged. "Go figure."

Hawk just smiled and shook his head; surprises in court were no fun for anyone.

He was thankful that he had no court appearances scheduled this week, so his usual casual garb of slacks and knit polo shirt, bearing the Sheriff's Office logo, would suffice. He donned a suit only when required by circumstances. He favored a loose multi-pocket utility vest, similar to a photographer's vest but designed for law enforcement, to discreetly carry the rest of his gear; and, of course to conceal the Glock 23, .40 caliber, semi-auto pistol, that rode canted forward, high on his right hip, just aft of his badge, the six-pointed star on his belt.

Hawk made no claim to being a *morning person;* he definitely needed his ritual infusion of caffeine. Stiffening his back with arms laterally extended, he stretched at his desk, noting distinct muscle stiffness at the base of his neck and in his lower back—no doubt residual reminders to maybe take it a bit slower in the gym. Rolling his broad shoulders to work out the kinks, he took several deep breaths and relaxed with a deep sigh.

"You okay, man?" Gordon asked.

"Yeah, just stiff."

"None of us are getting any younger, kid." Billy sipped from his mug. "Just wait `til you hit thirty; it's all downhill from there."

Hawk grinned and shook his head. He wanted to stay active and healthy. Still single, there was no spouse to scold him for not taking care of himself. He sipped his coffee and wondered if he ought to consider switching to decaf once he'd had his morning ritual, a couple of cups of *real* java. Like most cops, he drank a lot of coffee throughout the day, maybe too much? If he didn't start looking out for himself, who would?

"Hey, Hawk," Gordon asked, "is that the sheriff in with the captain?"

"Yeah, he came into the squad room a few minutes ago."

"Do you know what's up?"

Hawk shook his head.

"I bet it's that robbery we closed from two nights ago," Billy suggested.

"No way, Billy," Gordon countered. "That's a real ground ball. The sheriff wouldn't be digging into that. I finished the prosecutorial report and submitted it late yesterday. I've got our approved file copy right here." He tapped a finger on a case file folder on his desk.

Hawk reached for the file. "Can I see that? Trey said there's been an increase in armed robberies lately. He even mentioned your case, but he didn't tell me any details."

"Sure, here y' go. I can wrap it up in a nutshell for you; a late night robbery of a convenience store. Lone armed robber fired one pistol shot into the ceiling to compel the clerk's compliance; fortunately, no injuries. It was all captured on video tape. A glimpse of the license plate on his getaway car sealed it. Patrol stopped the car after a brief chase and made the arrest. They recovered the firearm, still in the perp's possession. Ballistics from the spent round matched. The eyewitness, the store clerk, ID'd the suspect at a lineup yesterday morning. Like I said, a real ground ball. Case probably won't even go to trial; a plea deal is likely."

Hawk nodded. "How about the perp? Got a record?"

"Oh yeah, ex-con, couldn't even make bail. No connections to the local community, just another lowlife flushed from New Orleans by *the storms*."

Hawk sighed; now he more fully understood. Quite a few criminal types had surfaced throughout the Gulf States after the infamous twin hurricanes had wreaked their havoc. Most folks had come to refer to the brutal pair of successive storms that had roared up through the Gulf of Mexico only days apart simply as *the storms*. Hawk knew bad weather was just a part of life.

It had happened before; and, it'll happen again.

It was a shame actually, he mused. Hundreds of people had perished; bodies were still being found months later. Thousands of residents had been forced from New Orleans and a host of devastated communities along the Gulf Coast. In a matter of days, the destructive hurricanes and subsequent levee-busting flooding had rendered untold numbers virtually homeless. Some had made arrangements with relatives or friends for interim shelter and subsistence, but many would not return to the crippled Crescent City.

FEMA struggled to help, but the situation was far worse than could have possibly been anticipated. Recovery would take years.

In the meantime, a good portion of the criminal element, those who preyed upon the decent folk, faced a diminished pool of potential victims. So like most opportunistic predators, they simply moved on and extended their range. Before the storms, there had not been a great deal of crime in Chantilly Parish, but enough to keep the Sheriff's Office moderately busy. Now things were rapidly changing; the workload for the Sheriff's Office had significantly increased, especially that of the Criminal Investigations Division and its eight detectives.

The captain stood at his open office door, surveying the squad room. His eyes came to rest on Hawk. He crooked an index finger, summoning the young detective into his office.

Hawk debated only a moment before deciding to take his coffee as well as his notebook. Gently closing the door behind him, he nodded to his seated superiors.

"Morning, Captain, Sheriff . . . What's up?"

"Morning, Hawk," acknowledged the sheriff. "Sit. You doin' okay?"

Hawk nodded over his coffee mug as he settled into a chair.

Captain Miller sipped from his own cup and winced. "Whoa! Someone made this pot too strong again. Hawk, you and Bassett caught that fatal traffic accident last week, the one where the Doyle woman survived, right?"

"Yes sir, in fact, we were the second unit on the scene." He flipped through his notebook. "A two-vehicle accident, taxi cab and a pickup truck, and a subsequent fire. One fatality, the cab driver, whose ID is still pending, and one survivor, who was probably the fare passenger. We found her, uh, Ellen Doyle, white female, twenty-three years, in the brush about sixty-five feet from the actual impact point. She had apparently been thrown from vehicle number one, the cab; no indication she was wearing a seat belt. In fact, the CSI guys are not convinced the taxi, an older model, even had working seat belts for rear seat passengers. No sign of the truck driver, and no other witnesses."

"Any status updates from the CSI Unit, Lou?" inquired the sheriff.

Captain Miller glanced at a case file on his desk and indicated the CSI tech's preliminary report. "A couple things; the taxi post-impact fire was so intense, an accelerant is suspected, based on some recovered evidence; they're looking into that. They're still processing the pickup; it's not as severely damaged or burned. As for the fatality, the ID is gonna be an issue. We have little to work with, just some tissue samples taken at the scene and the badly burned remains in the morgue, pending a complete forensic post-mortem. As Hawk mentioned, the survivor, Ellen Doyle, is assumed to have been the sole rear seat passenger. She's in the LaBorde hospital, and as far as we know is still sedated. So, she hasn't been interviewed yet."

"Okay, stay on top of this." The chair creaked as the sheriff leaned back and tucked his thumbs into his belt. "Now give me an oral synopsis that I can share with the D.A. His office has already called this morning. I think he smells some ink. "

The captain shook his head. "We haven't gotten any media inquiries, at least not yet."

"We probably will. The D.A. is rarely wrong about publicity." The sheriff shrugged. "So, let's hear it."

At the captain's nod, Hawk paged through his notebook. He understood the sheriff's request; some of it would cover what they had just discussed, but it would be delivered the way the prosecutor would want it.

"As of this morning, we can prove that on Thursday of last week, at approximately 18:20 hours, vehicle number one, the taxi, northbound on Parish Road 9, was struck *right-side-center* by vehicle number two, the truck, traveling westbound on Parish Road 16. A fire ensued.

"Weather was bad, a severe thunderstorm had hit, and visibility was only about one hundred feet. It appears the storm let up just after the collision. Speeds have not yet been conclusively determined, but are estimated at fifty-five and seventy miles per hour respectively.

"The operator of the taxi was the sole fatality on the scene. The operator of the truck was not found; and, is presumed to have fled the scene. It was during a cursory search of the area that we found the unconscious victim, Ms. Doyle. Fire Department EMTs transported her to the LaBorde Hospital ED.

"We learned that vehicle number two, the late model Ford F-150 pickup, was stolen from a used car lot near Alexandria, but not reported until two days ago. There are no security cameras on the lot. So, we don't know for certain when it was stolen, but Alexandria PD can roughly pin it down to within a week prior to the wreck. It did not suffer as extensive damage as the taxi, from either the impact or the subsequent fire. The fire department had the fire under control within minutes of arrival, so CSI hopes to have more luck with the truck. It's unclear if the impact actually started the fire, but they found traces of an accelerant, an ethanol and petroleum gel mix of some type, kind of like napalm. They also found some blood and partial latents. The prints are pretty poor, not really sufficient for an AFIS search, so an examiner/analyst is following up. Hopefully we'll know more this afternoon.

"The injured victim, Ellen Doyle, is actually from here, but has lived in Los Angeles for the past ten years or so. She returned for a funeral and a subsequent probate matter; she's named as a beneficiary in the will of the recently deceased Maude Delafaire.

"Trey and I got all this the night of the accident when we interviewed her cousin, Mark Paige, at the hospital. He's from here, too, but he's been gone about eleven years or so. He's now an attorney in New York; and he's also in town for the same reasons. He's staying at the Ancelet Arms, and we have his contact information. I contacted the local attorney handling the probate matter, Claude Fornier, and he has corroborated this information."

Hawk closed his notebook. "Funny thing, I don't remember Ellen Doyle or Mark Paige. As kids they would have been a coupla years or so younger than me; but then again, only a few years can be a huge gulf from a school kid's perspective. However, Trey said he remembered their mothers, sisters, Margaret and Millie. Margaret Paige died fifteen or so years ago. Millie Doyle moved to California, uh, a while back, ten years or so."

"That's it so far?" asked the sheriff.

Both Hawk and the captain nodded.

"Okay, not to throw a wrench in the works, but . . ." The sheriff stood. "I got a call just before I came here from Dr. Latrice-Johnson at the hospital. She wants to talk to us about her patient, our Ms. Doyle. She wouldn't go into it on the phone. And, there's another problem; your cab driver's corpse seems to be missing from the hospital morgue. When was the *post* scheduled?"

Captain Miller shook his head. "It hasn't been. The forensic pathologist isn't available until early next week. He's under subpoena as a witness in a trial up in Shreveport."

"Okay, Lou," Sheriff Tatum acknowledged. "Where's Trey, in court?"

"Yes sir, but he should be free by mid-morning," assured the captain.

The sheriff nodded. "Good. He and Hawk can follow up with the doctor, and look into the missing corpse. I don't like the way this situation is shaping up. I think we all know we may have something other than just a traffic accident here. This arson aspect strikes me as significant—*napalm?* It's clear there's something else going on. Let's find out what."

DETECTIVE SERGEANT Trey Bassett eased himself out of the courtroom, letting the double doors close softly behind him. Smiling broadly, he would have likely been laughing aloud had such an outburst not offended his sense of proper court decorum. He couldn't wait to share this tale with the other guys in the squad room.

He strode down the solemn hall, eschewed the elevator and opted for the stairs. Trey always chose stairs over elevators these days, if time and circumstances allowed. He had few illusions about the effort it took to maintain his waistline now that he was solidly in his mid-fifties. He was carrying more than twenty extra pounds, and he felt it. He was finding it increasingly difficult just to stay in shape. This aging process was tough—until one considered the alternative.

He was on the fourth floor of the five-storied courthouse. The Sheriff's Office occupied the basement and first two floors of the structure; the CID offices were on the second floor.

Just as he swung into the stairwell, his cell phone silently vibrated. Without breaking stride, he retrieved the phone and switched it from *vibrate* to *ring*. It was a good habit to maintain whenever one ventured to the upper three floors of the building, that august domain of the courts, judges' chambers, and court support offices; one should always silence a cell phone's audible ring. Having a cell phone suddenly ring in a courtroom, disrupting a proceeding, was considered disrespectful of the court. One could find oneself cooling one's heels in the cellblock, mulling over the contempt citation—not to mention the ribbing one would take for the rest of one's career, a real rookie mistake.

Trey didn't bother to answer the call until he reached the window on the third floor landing. The building was quite stout, built in the 1930s; an art deco-style granite and marble WPA project that had earned a place on the National Historic Register. Tons of steel and quarried granite comprised its structure, which unfortunately was not conducive to cell phone reception. He knew windows were therefore pragmatic locations for cell phone calls.

"Hello?" Trey held his hand over his other ear when he heard the slight echo in the stairwell.

"Trey, it's Hawk. You out of court?"

"Yeah, just now. Man, you won't believe what happened! Brewster was going to make bond—"

"Save it! Meet me at the car, you can tell me on the way."

"Okay, where?" Trey didn't even need to finish the question; partners often developed such rapport.

"Hospital; talk to the doctor about Ellen Doyle, and a missing body."

Trey was already moving down the stairs, losing the signal as he descended.

HE FOUND HAWK AT THE wheel of the unmarked cruiser idling near the rear door marked *Staff Only*. Trey shed his suit coat and draped it neatly across the rear seat. As he settled into the front passenger seat, Hawk handed him a large capped to-go cup of squad room coffee.

"Thanks man, I'm going to be really hungry by lunchtime." Trey winced as he sipped from the cup. "Oh man, that's strong."

Hawk chuckled as he drove from the lot. "Yeah, I think it's been brewing for a while this morning."

"No kidding, I think I could peel paint with this." Trey took another sip and reached for the radio mike. Pausing for *clear air* so as not to override any other unit's transmission, he depressed the mike key. "Control, 304 and 318, 10-8."

The dispatcher responded. "Copy your 10-8 at 10:39 hours. 304, landline 610 at CSI, at your convenience."

"10-4, Control. We'll be en route to the hospital for interviews." Trey reached for his phone and speed dialed the CSI office.

Hawk glanced over and asked, "610? Sgt. Melancon?"

Trey nodded as his call was answered. "Hey Mel! It's Trey, what've you got? Uh-huh . . . good job . . . nothing? No, that's at least something. Hold one, I gotta write this down: C-A-N-T-U. Okay, got it . . . Take it easy." Trey slipped the phone back into his pocket and turned to Hawk. "CSI managed to get the VIN off the cab. That was a piece of work; that VIN plate was a melted blob!"

"Yeah," Hawk agreed. "Those plates are usually aluminum or thin steel, melt or warp real easy."

"You know it!" Trey grinned in admiration; the CSI crew never ceased to amaze him. "They ran it NCIC and got nothing, no stolen, *zip*. NLETS query got registration info; the owner is one *Carlos Cantu,* address in the ninth ward, New Orleans. He's only got a traffic record, no criminal history. They sent a *locate lead* to NOPD. We'll know in a day or so, and then we may have a name for our toasted vehicle fire victim."

Trey sat back, a half-smug smile sliding up his cheeks, until he noticed Hawk's wry smirk. "What? No! Don't tell me that's our missing body!"

"I understand that's the case, Sgt. Bassett, sir."

Hawk's deadpan delivery had Trey groaning and chuckling simultaneously. "Great! Yeah, that's just great. Nothing is simple any more."

Hawk changed the subject. "So, what were you going to tell me? What happened in court today? You know, that I wasn't going to believe?"

"Oh yeah! This is rich! Today was the preliminary hearing on the Fenton Brewster fraud case. It's partially based on an old case I had before you transferred into the squad; but I'm getting ahead of myself. Anyway, this slick old con artist had been ripping off people for years, mostly elderly folks, with bogus stocks, loan schemes, pigeon-drops, roofing scams, the works. Lately he's gotten into computer hacking, data mining and identity theft.

"Well, today I had to testify as to the probable cause we developed in support of a search warrant for some of his records and documents. Now this was a warrant we executed about five years ago; that case *still* hasn't gone to trial. Brewster's had three attorneys over the intervening time; they all get that case continued for various reasons. But that wasn't the same case before the court this morning.

"The D.A.'s Office has filed a new *bill of information* alleging an even broader scope of fraud activities, and my old case supports the premise of an *on-*

going criminal enterprise. The D.A. is obviously coordinating with the U.S. Attorney in laying the groundwork for a later federal racketeering indictment.

"So today, just after I finish being cross-examined by this latest defense counsel, the assistant district attorney announces that the state feels it's proved sufficient probable cause and moves to hold Brewster for the Grand Jury.

"Now Brewster has been in jail since Friday of last week, when the warrant on this new case was issued and he surrendered with his attorney. He thought he'd get out on *personal recognizance* but he didn't know then that Judge Pearson had placed a $250,000 cash bond on the warrant. He couldn't make that bond; he had to wait for the hearing.

"Well, of course, today the defense argues the probable cause issue, which they lose, but not by much. Sensing weakness in the D.A.'s case, the defense makes an impassioned argument for a reduction in bond, if not outright personal recognizance.

"Now get this; Brewster takes the stand, against his counsel's advice, I'll bet! Anyway, under oath, he testifies as to his ties to the community, his desperate financial status as a small rancher, and even articulates further details about his ranch operation under cross-examination by the ADA. I noticed that the defense attorney was starting to look uncomfortable, so I decided to hang around."

Trey was grinning now.

"Brewster gave answers to every question, without hesitation. He even ignored an objection from his own lawyer. Finally he was finished and stepped down. The ADA said that the state still opposed any bond reduction, and of course the defense argued for it.

"Well, Judge Pearson ruled that a reduction was reasonable, so he lowered the bond to $100,000 and allowed real property collateral—you know, put up your house or other real estate in lieu of cash, but you gotta have sufficient equity or own it lien free. Now remember that Brewster's just testified that he owns and runs this ranch, with the oil leases and gas wells, and such; so of course, that's the offered collateral."

Trey took a deep breath, smiled broadly, and continued.

"Then the ADA surprises everyone and indicates that the state has no objection. The judge is prepared to accept the property as bond collateral, and asks if there's anything further. The ADA stands up and says that he's just learned that another warrant has been issued for Brewster's arrest by the federal court, and the real property in question may be subject to seizure and forfeiture. And right then, through the courtroom doors come Deputy U.S. Marshals Todd Simmons and Willis Hebert from their Alexandria office, Eva Quantrell from DEA, Jim Franklin from the FBI, and another man, an IRS criminal investigator I hadn't met yet.

"The ADA introduces them to the court as representatives of OCDETF—you know, the Organized Crime Drug Enforcement Task Force. He explains that they have a federal warrant for Brewster for wire fraud, money laundering, and the kicker, manufacture of narcotics, methamphetamine, and a whole list of bootlegged pharmaceuticals. They've had long-term surveillance on a major drug lab on the very ranch that he just admitted, under oath, he owns and runs. They've identified his suppliers, cooks, mules, distributors, customers, and money trails. The Feds are sweeping them all up starting today, and asset seizures and forfeiture actions will follow.

"And now, the con artist has conned himself into a major federal beef, or perjury!" Trey sucked in a huge breath. "Fenton Brewster is toast! Just like our missing body!"

They both laughed, long and heartily. Irony could be so poignant.

Trying to catch his breath, Trey wheezed, "I had to leave while they were arguing over custody and speedy trial issues, or I would have lost it in the courtroom!"

At which point he did lose it, slapping his thighs in a spate of incongruous hilarity.

Hawk chuckled as he pulled into the hospital parking lot. "Okay, get it together Big Guy, we're here. Let's go visit with the doctor. And please, no more toast jokes; or, *I'm* liable to lose it."

Catching his breath, and some semblance of control, Trey snorted, "I'm okay. It's cool. Just listen." He reached for the mike, and in the stoic monotone of the seasoned and unflappable street cop, he flatly intoned, "Control, 304 and 318, 10-6 for interviews at the hospital. Please advise 301 our status."

The radio squelched. "Copy your 10-6 at 10:57 hours. 301 advised."

Trey and Hawk settled into their *official mode* mindset, checked their gear, and exited the car. Trey took a portable radio with him.

As they approached the doors, Hawk asked, "How do we handle this? I haven't met Dr. Latrice-Johnson."

"I know her; she's good people." Trey stopped and faced Hawk. "She's from New Orleans; she's stunning, about forty, and one of the smartest people I've ever met. She's a first-rate neurologist, with some forensic pathology background. She treated my wife a few years ago for migraines, and found a small brain tumor. Fortunately, it was benign. She's aces in my book. She'll cut to the chase, no drama. You'll like her, but it'll seem like she can see right through you. Don't let it get to you. She can be a little intense."

Trey pulled one of the doors open, and in his best *training officer* voice recited, "So, how do we handle this? We inquire, listen, learn; we repeat as necessary. We corroborate or refute all data via proof. Does that sound familiar, young rookie?"

Hawk grinned as he passed into the lobby. "Familiar indeed it is, *O Wise One*. Embarrass you not, I shall."

With a pained smile and a shake of his head, Trey followed.

CH 5

IN THE PRIVACY OF THE absent hospital administrator's office, Dr. Marie Latrice-Johnson recounted the facts as she knew them for Detective Sgt. Bassett and Detective Redhawk. They listened patiently, without interruption, to the circumstances surrounding the missing body, and to the doctor's suspicions regarding possible tampering with patient Ellen Doyle's sedative.

Upon finishing her account, Sgt. Bassett guided her through a repetition of the facts, asking a number of questions in the process. This did not surprise her; in fact, she acknowledged the effectiveness of this interview technique, as she had frequently employed it in patient interviews. Besides, she found Sgt. Bassett, or "Trey", as he was known, always quite professional and easy to talk to. She remembered treating his wife some years ago for a benign tumor, and the successful subsequent treatment. She remembered Trey's affectionate and patient dedication to his wife's recovery. She had liked them both.

She realized her mind was on two tracks, a situation not the least unusual for her; multitasking was second nature. So, she relaxed, continuing to answer his questions in precise detail as she subtly turned her attention to Detective Redhawk.

She estimated him to be considerably younger than the Sergeant, mid to late twenties. His dark hair, somewhat angular features, and slightly bronze skin tone hinted at Native American heritage. *Hmmph, as if his surname were an insufficient clue.*

She thought him a handsome young man, in a rugged, wiry way. She was particularly taken with the light brown color of his eyes, somewhat unusual in her estimation of his presumed genetic heritage.

Her analytical inclination to probe, or at least speculate further, was interrupted by the buzz of the intercom.

"Doctor," the receptionist, Nancy, announced, "Eloise Smithers, the night shift nurse is here."

As the detectives rose at the middle-aged woman's entrance, the doctor greeted her warmly, effectively putting her at ease. The doctor introduced the detectives and asked Miss Eloise to describe what had happened during her previous shift. It wasn't long before the topic of the *student-nurse volunteer* became the focus of the inquiry.

Trey eased into the interview and elicited as much descriptive information as Miss Eloise could provide. This student, a female of very pale complexion and intensely green eyes, wore her auburn hair pinned up. She seemed to be in her late teens or early twenties, of medium height and build. She had introduced herself only as "Leigh Ann". Miss Eloise did not recall her offering a last name.

The doctor made several calls to the nursing college in an effort to ascertain more information about this student, but to no avail. "I am sorry, detectives, but there is no assignment or credit record of any student volunteering for ward duty over the weekend."

Apparently frustrated in their collective efforts, they sat in contemplative silence, pondering potential options.

"Well, if it's of any help," offered Miss Eloise, "I think she said she might be volunteering again tonight. That would be around seven o'clock this evening."

"Well," Trey drawled, "I do believe we can be on hand then." He glanced to his partner in an unspoken question.

Hawk nodded in silent agreement, and resumed taking notes.

"Thank you, Miss Eloise. We'll see you later this evening. Please don't discuss this with anyone," cautioned Trey as he escorted her to the door and bid her a good day.

Standing with his back to the closed door, Trey knit his brow.

"Doctor, I'm concerned that there's more going on here with your patient than meets the eye. We'd appreciate your notifying us of any change in Ms. Doyle's condition. We'll need to interview her; I suspect the sooner the better."

"I understand, Sergeant. I agree that something just doesn't feel right about all of this."

"Now, regarding this missing body, I'll have our CSI team meet us at the morgue. We'll interview the morgue attendant and the intern. Ready, Hawk?"

"Ready. Thanks, Doctor. We'll be in touch."

ELLEN'S MIND SLOWLY ascended from the murky depths of chemically induced stasis. She was increasingly capable of cohesive thought as faint recollections and vague scenes sifted through the shadows still clouding her mind. Her confusion began to dissipate as she consolidated her memories and ordered her thoughts.

Her memory of meeting and conversing with Maude was firm and clear. She somehow accepted that without question.

She assessed her situation. *Still hospitalized, for sure. Am I experiencing some sort of relapse? I think—no, I'm sure I remember being conscious. It hurt then, too; but, I was alert, wasn't I? And now, do I feel a sense of setback? Yeah, that can't be good. I was either injured more seriously than I thought, or did someone try to harm me, again?*

Her mind bristled at the thought.

Finding her will thus galvanized and focused, she concentrated on ascending to full consciousness. She sensed the last tendril of the drug slipping its hold as she strove to make slow but steady progress back to the surface of her own life's reality.

Ellen could feel the pain once more. That somehow familiar, dull, yet steady, pulsing ache demanded her attention. She was easing into full consciousness as before, but this was different. For one thing, it was even more uncomfortable.

Oh man! It hurts! I'm sore all over!

She fought a moment of panic, and forced herself to calm down. Opening her left eye a crack, she recognized that she was in the same dimly lit room as before. She went through the finger and toe wriggling ritual she'd found so reassuring the last time.

She could discern voices and the patter of footsteps growing louder.

Suddenly, the room brightened. A gentle hand held her cheek as the small harsh glare of a penlight flared briefly into the pupil of her undamaged eye.

In another moment, she could focus on the soft features of a concerned face the hue of warm caramel hovering above her own. Ellen felt immediately at ease with this woman, whose competence she sensed as she submitted to the scrutiny of those dark eyes. The face smiled and spoke softly, in a firm voice laced with reassurance and compassionate support.

"I'm Dr. Latrice-Johnson. Can you tell me your name?"

Ellen tried to speak, but her mouth was so dry she could barely croak. "Ellen."

"Very good. Do you know where you are?"

Ellen tried to lick her lips; it didn't help much. "Hos-hospi-tal?"

"Yes, very good. I'm sure your mouth feels very dry." The doctor held a tiny paper cup of cool water to Ellen's lips and cautioned, "Sip very slowly, just hold some water in your mouth and swallow a little bit at a time. Then we'll give you some ice chips to work on. There, that's good."

The doctor handed the drained cup to a nurse who filled it with ice.

Ellen thought the water wonderful, but found the ice exquisite. The melting chips were easy to focus on as the doctor completed a more thorough examination.

Ellen took a hitching deep breath and winced, her ribs protesting.

The doctor noticed. "Easy there, try slow shallow breaths; it'll get easier. I'm certain you have a great many questions, but I don't advise trying to speak too much, or too soon. So, if you'll just listen, I'll tell you what I know. But first, I have one question; do you remember being in an accident?"

Ellen nodded.

"Okay, that's good, that you remember. We'll come back to that, I'm sure."

The doctor made some notes on a chart, leaned over the edge of the bed, and placed a soothing hand on Ellen's shoulder.

That light touch, a warm affirmation of the solidity of another human being, served as both beacon and anchor for Ellen's focus and grip on this reality. She appreciated the compassion and implied rapport of the gesture, as she listened carefully to the doctor's words.

"You were apparently involved in a severe traffic accident. You sustained a concussion, a bad bump on the right side of your head, and have been unconscious and sedated. The orbit of your right eye, the bony part of your skull, was impacted; so, the soft tissues in that area are bruised and swollen. You should have no problems with the sight in that eye when the swelling subsides. You have no internal injuries or broken bones, although you sustained some fairly severe bruising on your right side from blunt force trauma, impact during the accident, no doubt."

"Wha-what happened?" Ellen croaked.

"I don't know the details about the accident, just that it happened last Thursday, four days ago. Today is Monday, early Monday evening, actually."

Ellen winced. "I-I'm so sore."

The doctor offered a sad sympathetic smile. "Yes, I'm certain you feel sore in almost every muscle in your body. Ironically, that's a good sign; it means there's likely no neurological, nerve damage."

The doctor mused in thought for a moment, and made a few more notes on the chart.

"I think you'll be with us for a few more days. We have some more testing to do. I'll be monitoring your recovery closely. We are weaning you off the sedative for the pain, but I think we'll keep you on a saline IV for a little while longer. In a day or so, we'll get you started on some physical therapy; that'll help with the soreness you're feeling."

The doctor leaned toward Ellen and asked softly, "Do you have any more questions?"

Ellen nodded and whispered, "I woke up . . . a bit . . . not now, earlier."

"You did? Hmm, I thought you might have. We'll talk about that later."

Ellen nodded and sucked on the ice slivers.

The doctor seemed lost in thought for a moment. "Ellen, I'm going to have you moved to another room. Oh yes, you've had some visitors; and the authorities want to speak to you about the accident, when you're up to it."

Ellen sank into the pillow. *Visitors? Of course, Mark was already here! And the police would certainly look into an accident.*

The doctor tucked the medical chart under her arm and smiled. "We'll get you moved first. You'll be going upstairs to the ward on the floor above us. Then we'll see about any visitors you might have this evening. That is if you feel up to it, of course."

Ellen mumbled a weak response. "Thank you."

AT THE NURSES' STATION, the doctor reviewed her written instructions. Fingering Trey's business card, she considered her patient's current condition. That, in conjunction with the related circumstances and events of the last several days, culminated in a twisted sense of the sinister. Something was very wrong here; she could feel it.

She came to a decision, grasped the phone and dialed.

Surprisingly, it was Detective Redhawk who answered.

After exchanging the usual pleasantries, she advised him that her patient had regained consciousness. "Yes, she is lucid and coherent. We will be moving her to another ward. I see no reason why you can't proceed with your interview."

"That's excellent news, Doctor! In fact, it couldn't be better! We will be heading your way shortly to discuss some developments in the case. I can't go into it over the phone. The sergeant and I are about to go into a meeting, but right after that, we'll be on our way."

"Very well, I'll be available in my office if you need me."

"Thank you, Doctor. Could you keep Ms. Doyle's movement and new location as confidential as possible? Keep it to only those staff who have a need to know. Could you not reuse her old room for the time being? We'll explain when we arrive."

She thought that was a bit strange, but no stranger than anything else that's been going on around here lately. "Well, assuming no immediate need for the room, I believe we can comply with your request."

"Thanks, Doctor, we appreciate it. We'll see you shortly."

Ending the call, she huddled with the head nurse and made the necessary arrangements.

Her pager went off. A digital message from Nancy read, "DR HOLLIS CALLED LEFT NUMBER".

As she strode toward her office, a smirk briefly slid across the doctor's countenance.

Now maybe I'll get some answers around here!

DUSK HAD COME AND GONE; full night reigned.

The *student nurse*, she of no last name that anyone could seem to recall, stood in the dim hospital stairwell listening carefully and sniffing the stale antiseptic air. Neither her acute hearing nor sense of smell found any reason for concern as she adjusted her nursing attire.

Satisfied with her appearance, she unwrapped a small cloth bundle. Within was a syringe, one previously pilfered from this very hospital. It now contained a very unsavory liquid. She held it up to her gaze and watched as tiny subtle currents within the mixture flowed and folded in on themselves; minuscule bursts of sickly colors shimmered and faded. With a feral smile, she delicately wrapped the syringe, placed it in her pocket, and began to climb the stairs.

She had not been told what was in the syringe. However, she was not stupid; she had a fair idea of its intent. Her instructions had been simple; inject the Doyle woman, preferably via an existing IV. *Hmm, that's smart, no extra needle marks that way.* Then simply observe her, inconspicuously of course, for the rest of the night.

She anticipated no real problems. She had spent the previous night performing a similar mission. She'd even had the foresight to *lose* the EEG printout once she had noticed the very active lines on the rolling paper tape. But for the unexpected and hasty instructions to assist in the removal of a body from the morgue, all had gone as planned.

Concentrating her focus on the moment, she spent a few minutes at the door of the landing, just listening and sampling the air. The heavy scent of disinfectant masked, but could not completely obscure, the fetid miasma of human illness and suffering.

Easing the door open, she saw no one in the hall. She sensed people in the rooms; mostly patients, an occasional visitor, and the few staff going about their business. It seemed safe to proceed.

Gliding soundlessly down the empty hallway, she paused at the door she sought. After a quick glance in either direction, she slipped inside. The light in the room was very dim. No matter, her vision was quite sharp in the dark. The woman on the bed, still swaddled in bandages, was breathing shallowly. IVs stood on both sides of the bed.

This should be easy . . . now, which IV?

Dipping into a deep pocket, she removed the cloth bundle and retrieved the syringe. Approaching the bed, she grasped the nearer IV line at the tube juncture and aimed the needle at the orifice. Gently piercing the membrane, she began to apply slow pressure to the plunger.

The room suddenly flared with intense light!

Momentarily blinded, she spun, slashing out at empty air with her left hand! Something seized her right wrist—something on the bed!

Relinquishing the syringe jammed in the IV junction tube, she easily jerked her arm free, but was shocked to see a handcuff firmly locked on her right wrist, its open-clawed twin dangling on its short chain.

A voice boomed behind her; two men now blocked the doorway.

"Don't move! Show us your hands! Do it NOW!"

Shrieking with rage, she spun and faced them. Bunching her muscles, she prepared to spring, but was suddenly slammed face down on the floor, the weight of another body on her back.

The body on the bed! Not the Doyle woman! It's a trap! I must flee! Now!

With a strength that belied her modest form, she shoved off the floor with one hand. With the other, she tossed the person on her back across the room, slamming the body into the wall. She saw it was the *patient*, an unfamiliar woman who now lay senseless, crumpled at the base of the wall.

No bandages, they're in a heap on the bed! It's all a ruse!

With a loud hiss, she charged the two stunned men at the door. The bigger one made as if to grab and tackle her, but she dove over his grasp with such speed that he missed her entirely. The other man was faster, delivering a side kick that barely connected as a glancing blow to her hip as she flew past him. But it was enough to upset her balance; she tumbled headlong across the hall and into the wall.

Before she could rise, he was astride her back, grabbing the open handcuff, and reaching for her left wrist.

She went limp for just a second, and felt him lean a bit off balance. With explosive force, she rolled under him, ripping the open cuff from his hand, slashing his palm. Planting both feet in his chest, she shoved upward driving him airborne and away. Scrambling to her feet, she ran down the hall.

Too late, she realized it was the wrong direction.

Hearing pounding footsteps behind her, she glanced back to see her pursuer back on his feet and closing fast; but, he was alone, and bleeding.

Enough of this! She ran into the next open door she saw, a darkened vacant room—mops, buckets, rolls of paper products—a storeroom. She grinned ominously when she saw the window.

HAWK SLOWED AS HE REACHED the room he was certain the student nurse had entered and looked behind him to see Trey running in his direction. Pausing at the door, his bleeding hand throbbing, Hawk was not willing to again underestimate his quarry. She displayed such strength and speed. Had he not seen it firsthand, he would not have believed it.

In the flash of an instant, an arm reached out from the shadowed room; its clawed hand snatched him off balance and into the darkness. With incredible strength, the lone hand held him by the scruff of his neck and pinned his chest against a wall, his feet dangling inches off the floor. His face pressed to the side, he tried to grab at the hand and arm that held him, but his bleeding right hand was torn away and held in another vise-like grip.

Hawk could see nothing. He fumbled for his pistol with his free hand only to realize his holster was too light; it was empty. He hadn't dropped his sidearm; he hadn't even drawn it. That could only mean he had been disarmed when he was grabbed.

His mind raced! *Who or what is holding me? No mere student, surely! Where is Trey? What is going on? What the—?*

His mind suddenly blanked! A shudder of revulsion, and curiously *pleasure,* surged from his damaged hand to his spine. Pulsing outward throughout his body, the sensation intensified until it was almost unbearable, bordering on the shamefully erotic.

A muscle spasm caused both his hands to clench; but his right closed on her face. In that moment of shock, he realized that she was *licking the blood from the wound in his hand!*

It was the last thing he would remember.

HAWK WOKE, GROGGY AND confused. He saw that he lay on a gurney in a curtained alcove. His right hand throbbed; it was bandaged. An IV trickled a clear fluid into a vein in his left arm.

He started to get up and realized he was only wearing an open back hospital gown.

Oh no, this won't do . . . Where's Trey?

As if in answer to his question, he heard Trey's gruff voice.

"I'm here—you all right?"

"Yeah," Hawk mumbled. "What happened?"

"Hold on." Trey pulled the curtain open. "Hey Doc, he's awake."

Dr. Latrice-Johnson entered with a nurse and another doctor. "How are you feeling, Detective?"

"I'm okay."

"Good. This is Dr. Bates, a resident physician assigned to the Emergency Department. She'll be checking you over. Please cooperate with her."

Dr. Latrice-Johnson gave Hawk a smile while the ED resident gave him a quick examination. Dr. Bates shushed him when he tried to speak and stuck a plastic thermometer under his tongue.

Trey smirked. "Okay, Hawk, give me a second to be sure no one else is within earshot, and I'll bring you up to speed."

Hawk rolled his eyes in impatience as Trey stepped beyond the curtain for a quick look around.

Upon his return, Trey kept his voice low. "You're the only patient in this part of the ED, so you can't complain about not getting full care and attention." He nodded toward the nurse and two doctors, chuckling at his own joke.

Dr. Bates removed the thermometer, allowing Hawk to speak.

"So? A sit-rep, please?"

Trey relented, but still spoke softly. "First of all, she, our perp, got away through the window. Yeah, I know, three floors to the ground—go figure. All I found was you, bleeding, and Anita's empty handcuffs. We have a BO-

LO out on the subject with still photos from the surveillance camera hidden in the room. We have no further ID, except that we know for sure she isn't a university student."

"Excuse me, BOLO?" asked a new voice.

"Dr. Hollis, you're back!" exclaimed a relieved Dr. Latrice-Johnson. "Allow me to introduce Detectives Bassett and Redhawk; they're investigating the matters we discussed on the phone this afternoon."

Greetings out of the way, Trey provided a few more details for the hospital administrator's benefit.

"BOLO is an acronym for *Be On the Look Out*. Now, we are authorized to share certain aspects of our investigation with you, since the hospital is involved. But you must understand that what we discuss is to be considered confidential and kept on a *need to know* basis."

"I understand. My staff has kept me informed as best they can." Dr. Hollis glanced gratefully at Dr. Latrice-Johnson.

"There are essentially two issues," Trey explained, "the body missing from the hospital's morgue, and the attempts on the life of a patient, Ellen Doyle.

"The missing body has not yet been found; positive identification is moot at the moment. Whoever took it left no trace. Our CSI techs did not find anything in their examination of your morgue facility, not a single latent print, not even the morgue attendant's; that's highly unusual. We interviewed him again, to be sure. He indicated that he only used his key to unlock the door, and his shoulder to push it open when he arrived at work yesterday. So, that would explain his prints not appearing on the outer door. But he was certain that he was not gloved when he opened the cooler doors; so, there should have been prints. There were none whatsoever; it's just too clean, wiped most likely.

"Now regarding the patient, Ellen Doyle; Dr. Latrice-Johnson had informed us of her suspicions regarding someone tampering with her patient, specifically increasing her sedative intake via IV to near life threatening levels. Our subsequent investigation developed a suspect and with the cooperation of your staff, we set a trap. Unfortunately, our trap didn't work so well. Two of our law enforcement personnel were injured, and the perpetrator got away.

"In view of what has transpired this evening, which our report will characterize as an alleged *third* attempt on Ms. Doyle's life, we believe the doctor's suspicions are validated.

"We deeply appreciate the hospital's cooperation. We will do our best to bring this to a satisfactory conclusion."

Dr. Hollis was about to ask a question when his pager went off. He read the message and opened his palms. "I apologize, but I'm afraid I'll have to leave you. Thank you, Detectives, for all you've done. Please keep me informed, and of course if there's anything I or the hospital can do to assist, please let me know."

Trey shook the administrator's hand. "Of course, Doctor Hollis, thank you. We'll be in touch."

Dr. Hollis smiled. "Marie, could you please join me in my office. The dean of the nursing college awaits me there. I think I'll need your assistance in this matter."

"Dr. Hollis," cautioned Trey, "I trust you'll be discreet in dealing with the dean?"

The hospital administrator nodded. "Don't worry, Sergeant, I understand the concept of *need to know*. We can handle the dean. Your investigation will not be further compromised."

"Thank you, Doctor," Trey responded as the administrator and Dr. Latrice-Johnson departed. "We really appreciate it."

Dr. Bates turned to Hawk. "Detective, you have no other injuries, but you lost consciousness, most likely because you lost blood. We found no evidence of a concussion. Replacing your fluids is a priority, thus the saline, which we can dispense with now, but I want you to drink lots of water. The injury to your hand is fairly superficial. However, there was a problem with the bleeding; we found traces of an unidentified anticoagulant. You've received a tetanus shot and a couple of stitches; you're going to have to take some oral antibiotics for the next ten days just as a precaution. Keep the hand dry, and change the bandage daily. The stitches can be removed in a few days."

"Okay," Hawk acknowledged. "What about Anita? I saw her hit that wall."

"Ah," said Dr. Bates, "Deputy Marshal Jackson sustained a dislocated shoulder, and a number of bruises, but otherwise she'll be fine. She's been treated and released."

Trey cleared his throat. "Uh, Hawk, you won't get all your clothes back today." He held up a clear plastic evidence bag containing his partner's bloodstained vest.

Hawk groaned, knowing his vest was now treated as evidence, but brightened as he remembered that he had another one at home, albeit older and faded across the shoulders.

The color drained from his face as he remembered his missing pistol.

As if he had read Hawk's mind, Trey held up his other hand and displayed Hawk's holstered pistol, belt, and belt badge. "I found your gun on the floor of that little storeroom, unfired. CSI checked, no prints; but you know a Glock has poor surfaces for latents. So, it's not evidence." He grinned. "But, you can't have it back until you wear some pants. And you're lucky they didn't cut your clothes off you with scissors; you can thank me later."

"Oh yeah, my clothes. Uh, Dr. Bates, can I have my clothes back, and get out of here?"

She smiled. "Of course. Remember what I told you."

The nurse held up a plastic bag containing his clothes.

With everyone standing around there was no convenient place for him to dress.

Dr. Bates noticed his discomfort. With a small smile she and the nurse stepped away and pulled the curtain closed.

As he dressed, Hawk queried Trey. "CSI won't come asking for any more of my clothes, will they?"

"No, not if you promise to launder them at your earliest convenience," retorted his partner.

Hawk mumbled something unintelligible and Trey just chuckled.

THE NEXT MORNING, TREY activated the CID conference room phone's speaker mode.

"Okay, folks, I think we're ready to commence this after-action briefing and status report. On telecom we have Lieutenant Sansone, New Orleans Homicide. Are you there, Lieutenant?"

"Yes, I'm here. Go ahead, Sergeant."

"Yes sir. Present are Detective Terri McPherson, NOPD, Deputy U.S. Marshals Anita Jackson and Brian Soudelier from the Fugitive Apprehension Strike Team, Captain Lou Miller, Detectives Connor Redhawk and Trey Bassett, Chantilly Parish Sheriff's Department.

"We learned this morning that the registered owner of the involved taxi, Carlos Cantu, never left New Orleans. The vehicle was not reported stolen. He's been dead for some time, a homicide victim, possibly as long ago as when the hurricanes hit. He was found in his locked home, hands and feet bound with duct tape. The medical examiner hasn't advised of a cause of death yet, but drowning is suspected.

"New Orleans PD CSI got some partial latents and some blood traces from the duct tape and a good set of prints off a damaged television that someone dropped trying to remove it from Cantu's home. So, NOPD came up with a suspect, *Wilson 'Bubba' Cutler*, an ex-con who does home invasions and robberies with his half-brother, *Ignatius 'Iggy' Simpson*.

"Now, Iggy is wanted by the U.S. Marshals as an escapee from a federal halfway house. They had thirty of them just walk away when the hurricanes flooded them out. Well, they found twenty-five without too much trouble. Three more were dead, drowned, presumed storm victims. That left just Iggy and an old cellmate, *Orlando 'Ratso' Ratalondo*, a small time druggie and car thief. So, the U.S. Marshals are hunting for Iggy and Ratso. They've been keeping periodic track of Bubba in the hope he'll contact Iggy, or vice versa. But several weeks ago, Bubba just dropped out of sight, and there's been no word on the street about him, Iggy, or Ratso.

"That is until the accident involving Cantu's taxi last Thursday, here in Chantilly Parish. Our CSI guys found traces of blood and some partial latents in the stolen truck that hit the cab. The latents and blood types appear to be close matches for what was found at the Cantu crime scene. The AFIS searches were good, but not sufficiently conclusive, so the U.S. Marshals are following up with DNA testing. We're not one hundred percent certain yet, but it definitely looks like our New Orleans trio of Bubba, Iggy, and Ratso are the involved parties in the events of last week.

"From this point, we're speculating that this was no accident, more likely an ill conceived *hit* on the taxi passenger, Ellen Doyle. The *why* we don't know, not yet.

"It appears that something went wrong. The cab driver may, or may not, have survived the accident, but he certainly didn't survive the subsequent fire. By the way, the fire is definitely arson; the accelerant was a mix the U.S. Marshals have seen before in another case."

"Not to interrupt, Sergeant," Detective McPherson interjected, "but the accelerant, how was it deployed? I mean as a spray, liquid, or gel? Do we know?"

"Good question, Terri," Trey acknowledged. "Most likely liquid. Two five gallon jerry cans, the wide-mouthed military type, were found in the burned debris. The arson investigators are pretty sure that was the means. Their lab will probably confirm it in a couple of days."

"And the taxi driver?" the captain prompted.

"That's a problem," Trey admitted. "The driver's remains, badly burnt, went to the LaBorde General morgue, from where they went missing, and are still missing.

"Initially, we thought that body might be Carlos Cantu, but since his remains have been located at his house in New Orleans, we now suspect it's one of our trio of hoodlums.

"As it so happens, when the body was removed from the vehicle, CSI took tissue samples when collecting accelerant evidence. So, we may not have the body, but we do have some tissue samples, and DNA testing is underway.

"As you know, Detective Terri McPherson from New Orleans PD, Homicide, is the primary on the Cantu case. She was working it with Anita and Brian from the U.S. Marshals FAST unit in New Orleans because of the suspect associations. Our DMV inquiry on the taxi got their attention. They got in touch and we confirmed the links.

"We exchanged our information and determined that finding this student nurse was possibly a key to all these related cases. So, when we learned that Ellen Doyle had regained consciousness and would be moved to another ward, we formulated our plan to protect the patient and catch our student nurse if and when she returned to the hospital. Unfortunately, when she did we could not contain her; and two of our people were hurt. But Ellen Doyle is safe; we have a security detail outside her room.

"We recovered the syringe that was used to introduce whatever concoction it contained into that IV. We'll probably know the contents of the syringe by tomorrow. CSI will conduct a thorough analysis."

Looking around the table, Trey asked, "Does anyone have anything to add?"

Everyone shook their heads; Trey's report was complete and succinct.

"Very well. That concludes our report. Captain, any questions for us, sir?"

"No, not at this time, Sergeant. Lieutenant Sansone, you have the floor."

"Thank you, Captain." The NOPD Lieutenant's voice was accompanied by mild static on the phone line. "Regarding the Cantu case, y'all may be right about *Ratso*. I'm sure Terri has advised you, that as of yesterday, our techs located a red-light camera photo of what appears to be him operating Cantu's taxi. The time stamp is within the period we anticipated, but the resolution isn't that great, so the ID isn't that conclusive. Our lab is trying to enhance it, but they're not real optimistic. I'll send Terri an enhanced copy as soon as they're done. But overall, it does tend to support your theory that your three suspects are the involved perpetrators."

"Thanks, Lieutenant," acknowledged Trey. "That does help. Maybe the DNA tests will nail it down; we'll see."

"All right, Trey, what's next?" asked the captain.

"Well, sir, we'll keep a security detail on Ellen Doyle for now; we still have to interview her. I know that Anita and Brian have their own report to file with their office, and Terri does as well. That's it, unless you have anything further, sir."

"No, I'm good. How about you, Lieutenant?"

"I have nothing further. Let's let them get back to work."

"Okay . . . Carry on, people; keep us informed."

CH 6

ONCE AGAIN SALIDAR found himself in a crumpled heap on a smooth stone floor. He dared to slowly unravel from his painfully cramped position, and was surprised to hear the small scrapes and scuffing of his efforts. *So, I can hear once more; but only, it seems, on my left.* He forced his eyes open. *Ah, I can see again as well, but only with my right eye.*

He recognized that he was illuminated in a familiar cone of light, holding at bay the twisting shadows and deeper gloom beyond. *I know where I am.* Trying to right himself into a sitting position, he found that his right arm was still useless.

He knew that Lady Diere had brought him back for a reason, just as he had expected. He was still needed; therefore, he was of value. That meant he would have the opportunity to improve upon his present circumstances. Oh, but he would have to be very, very careful. He could not afford to run afoul of the *Mad Elf* again, or at least not too soon.

Salidar expected her to make him wait, as was her habit, to stew in his own juices until his fears ran amok. So, it came as a surprise that she did not. The cone of light widened and she was suddenly before him, imperious in a shimmering gown of iridescent purples and greens.

"Well, Salidar, I wonder if you can now follow instructions; or is your usefulness truly spent?" She slowly walked around his abject form, regarding him much like a cat would assess a wounded mouse.

He managed to stand, thus salvaging a shred of his presumed dignity, and murmured, "M'lady, I live but to serve thee."

"Indeed you do," she cooed. "And I would further test your loyalty. I have a task for you. As I deem that you will need certain faculties to perform successfully, I have returned half your sight and hearing. I am sure you have noticed."

Salidar bowed his head, mumbling, "I am in your debt, m'lady. I shall not fail you."

"See that you do not! In fact, perform well and you may earn the further return of part of what you have lost."

"I am your servant, m'lady. Please, name this task; you may consider it done," he effused, his curiosity nonetheless aroused.

Lady Diere beckoned to the darkness, and the grey haired *businessman* stepped forth.

"Tell him!" she snapped at the newcomer, folding her arms and scowling.

Hmm . . . So, it appears that all is not well amongst the powers that be. Salidar looked on attentively, *and appropriately submissively,* as he bowed toward the man known as "George".

George glanced at Lady Diere, nodded, and turned fully toward Salidar.

"There's this guy, a human, named Fenton Brewster, who's kind of a threat to, uh, security, and our plans. He's gotta be eliminated; it's gotta look like an accident or maybe suicide. His body, it's gotta be found; you got that?"

"Of course, m'lord, and where can this man be found?" Salidar had posed the question poker-faced, but his mind was racing. *A threat to "security, and our plans"? Oh, what can this really be about? I sense opportunity here!*

"You can find him in the Chantilly Parish Jail." George looked uncomfortably at Lady Diere after he had spoken those words.

"Ah, that is a complication," remarked Salidar, "but one I can assuredly manage."

"Hold that thought, Salidar," said Lady Diere sweetly.

Her comment immediately alarmed him; but he nodded attentively as she continued.

"Your role will be to merely arrange access for another, and assist with escape and evasion if necessary." Her wry smile did not assure him in the least.

Lady Diere again beckoned into the darkness.

Another form began to take shape, gaining substance with its approach, a woman. Her very pale face, framed in flaming auburn tresses, held green eyes that gleamed with a cold radiance. Wearing a gown of pale olive, long sleeved and snug of fit, she seemed to glide rather than walk. She stopped at the edge of light, as if reluctant to depart the shadows.

At another gesture from Lady Diere, the figure stepped forward.

Salidar felt his blood run cold; his breath froze in his lungs. He didn't know *who* she was, but he was relatively certain as to *what* she was. That was the cause of his distress.

George, on the other hand, appeared utterly confused. In the presence of this beautiful redhead with startling green eyes, his face betrayed his more primordial instincts, a yearning lust warring with a subliminal and barely perceptible dread.

Lady Diere paused savoring the moment, obviously well pleased with the reaction her little surprise had caused.

"Gentlemen, allow me to introduce the Lady Leanan of the Sidhe, an esteemed member of the Unseelie Court. She has graciously consented to assist us in this present situation."

Salidar was dumbstruck. This was one of the most dangerous minions of the Unseelie Court, an elder vampire, and a female at that! He was so shocked that he almost missed the vampire's subtle flare of anger in response to the slight tone of condescension deftly laced within Lady Diere's comment—*almost*, but he did notice.

Lady Diere demanded his attention, and got it.

"Salidar, heed my words! You will arrange for Lady Leanan to have the required access to Fenton Brewster. And, you will assist her, if necessary, in her return to me. You are to stay by her side unless she instructs otherwise. Fail her, and you shall answer to both of us."

Salidar swallowed. "There will be no failure, m'lady. You may rely upon it."

"Very well, I suppose you may both now go."

The Dark Elf casually flicked her wrist in a dismissive gesture, and murmured a small incantation.

Salidar and Lady Leanan stepped back, faded, and disappeared.

FOR SEVERAL LONG MOMENTS Diere considered George; he just stood there, clearly befuddled. She had intended to make an impression upon him by introducing Leanan at this juncture, but had she overplayed her hand? He had gaped like a besotted fool. *Did he not appreciate how deadly she is? Did he miss my thinly veiled threat entirely?*

As if in unintended confirmation, he blurted, "Wow! Just who was she, really? She's a real looker, quite beautiful!"

"Fool! You try my patience!" She spat in disgust. "I should let her have you! You have certainly bungled enough. You do not even know that she is the reason those two dolts you sent to recover the body were able to succeed. I had to interrupt what she was doing and have her assist their feeble efforts. No, do not even ask; you do not want to know what she did with them afterward. Let us just say that they are in no condition to betray you, unlike your other associate, this Fenton Brewster!"

She whirled on him, her rising ire apparent. "Have you any more surprises for me? Any more criminal associates of yours who could possibly compromise us?"

"No, no, of course not," George hastily responded. "Brewster was only a financial arrangement; I just backed some of his, uh, more lucrative enterprises. None of his people ever saw me. I dealt only with Fenton, alone."

"Pray that is the case, lest I begin to wonder if you are not *that* essential to our plans."

She strode to the edge of the light and faced him. For a long moment she just assessed him. She could see that he clearly feared her; that pleased her.

"George, it is time for you to return, and await word of this endeavor. If successful, I shall send Salidar. If not, I shall summon you, as he will no longer be among the breathing; and we will plan accordingly. Go now."

At a gesture and word, George was gone.

SHE PACED FOR A MOMENT, then stood still and composed herself. She concentrated on a summons, an incantation, and then relaxed. She knew she would not have long to wait.

Moments later, a figure materialized in the shadows. Lord Addecus silently stepped into the light, his forked tongue tasting the air. Without preamble, he hissed in distaste. "The Sssidhe wasss here!"

"Aye, she was; it could not be helped. She failed in her task to inject the heir with the prepared spell. She walked into a trap, and caused quite a stir in her escape. Somehow we were anticipated. I suspect George has not been as discreet as we require. You know of the arrest of his criminal associate, this Brewster?"

Addecus nodded. "Yesss, I have been ssso informed."

She picked at the sleeve of her gown, brushing imaginary lint. "Well, I have recovered Salidar, not whole of course, and sent him with Leanan to address that loose end."

"I sssee, and may we asssume George hasss no other isssuesss that dessserve sssuch attention?" Addecus cocked his head attentively.

She sighed and drew her lips into a pout. "Hmmph, he assures me that he does not, but I think he would bear watching."

Addecus considered that for a moment. "I have jussst the one for sssuch a tasssk. I would be honored to asssissst in thisss matter."

Her lips pursed sweetly and a delicate eyebrow rose in guarded response to his offer.

Apparently sensing an advantage, the Were Lord pressed his case. "You need not call upon the Sssidhe. I am quite capable, and have many resssourcesss at my dissspossssal."

She turned fully to him, a stormy look upon her fair face. "Addecus, I am well aware of the mutual dislike between the Were and the Sidhe. But that is irrelevant in the greater scheme of things. We cannot afford to work at cross-purposes; there is too much at stake!"

Addecus gripped his elbows as his head bobbed up and down; soon his shoulders mimicked the motion. His breathing was suddenly a series of hissing gasps.

With mild surprise, she realized he was laughing!

Addecus gained a semblance of control. "You sssaid *crosss* and *ssstake!*" He was off on a laughing jag again.

Lady Diere stood stiff-armed, fingers balled into fists of frustration, her face pinched in a grimace. *Never, ever "pun" with a Were, intentionally or otherwise! Arrgh! They find it so maddeningly funny!* She had no choice but to endure his spate of laughter.

Eventually, his episode subsided and he wheezed his apology. "Pleassse, forgive me, m'lady, but that wasss ssso appropriate."

She sighed, and tried to refocus. "We have much to gain, all of us. Do not forget that."

"I ssshant, m'lady, but . . . " All humor had fled his demeanor; his amber eyes smoldered. "Do not expect me to forget that vampire'sss frequent asssertionsss of her preference for the blood of Weresss!"

In a low voice colder than death she decreed, "I have asked only for cooperation. Keep wary, if you must; but, cooperate you will, both of you."

ELLEN'S NEW ROOM WAS slightly larger, boasting three visitors' chairs and a generous westerly window, but otherwise it was very similar to her former hospital accommodations. Her heavy bandages were gone, all but for a smaller square on her right temple. The IV in her right hand was also gone, but the one in her left was still there.

She had napped off and on for several hours at a time, but was now awake and bored. Periodically she could hear soft conversation just beyond her door, and for some reason she found that comforting. She estimated it was mid-evening, and she was hungry.

A light knock on the door drew her attention. As Dr. Latrice-Johnson and a nurse entered the room, Ellen noticed a group of three men and a woman clustered in quiet conversation at her door. One of the men glanced in her direction, his eyes locking on hers. He held her gaze until the door slowly closed, severing the contact. Her breath had caught, and she felt herself blush as her right hand drifted unconsciously to her hair. *Oh man, I must look awful. I'd love a shower, or a long soak in a warm bath.*

"Well, your color certainly looks good," said the smiling doctor, snapping Ellen's attention back into the moment, "and I'll bet you're a bit hungry?"

"Uh, yeah . . . I am very hungry, but still sore." Ellen's voice had regained its strength. "And I'd like to get up and move around."

"That's good, because that's exactly what I have in mind for you." Gesturing to the remaining IV infused into Ellen's left hand, she continued, "I think we'll dispense with the saline first thing in the morning, but you will have to keep up your fluid intake. Drink lots of water."

Ellen nodded. "Of course, anything you say, doctor."

"That's just what I want to hear. We need to get you on some solid food."

Ellen brightened. "Oh good! I've been so looking forward to a big bowl of gumbo."

"Gumbo?" The doctor chuckled. "That may be a bit too spicy to start. Your digestive tract has been somewhat suppressed from the sedation and may be a little sluggish in getting back to normal; so, too spicy too soon is not a good idea. Our staff nutritionist will prepare something appropriate. Don't expect too much; it *is* hospital food. It'll be bland, but it's what you need right now. Tomorrow, you'll start physical therapy. I promise you'll be moving around."

"Oh, I'm more than ready. By the way, who's outside my door?"

The doctor's smile faltered, but remained. "There are some detectives here to speak with you about the accident, if you feel up to it."

"I may as well do it now, if that's okay?"

Ellen sat up a bit, allowing the nurse to plump another pillow behind her head. Her hand was again fluffing her hair, sadly with little effect.

Ushering two men into the room, the doctor introduced them as Detective Sgt. Bassett and Detective Redhawk. The younger detective was the man in whose brief gaze she had seemed pleasantly lost. Her cheeks felt warm and she tried to find distraction in the weave of the bedsheet.

"Well, I have rounds to make," the doctor announced. "So, we'll briefly leave you gentlemen with my patient. She needs her rest, so please don't overtax her."

"No problem, Doctor," Trey assured her. "We only need a few minutes of her time."

As the door closed behind the nurse, Ellen asked, "I have to know; was anyone else hurt, um, in the accident?"

"I'm afraid so," the older detective admitted. "The driver of your taxi did not survive, but I can't get into the details. Now, we do have some questions. Did you speak to the driver?"

"Uh, I probably did. I mean, I must have told him where to go, but I don't really remember. I'm sorry, but I can't even remember what he looks like."

"I see. It's okay, that's not a problem," the detective acknowledged sympathetically.

As the interview progressed, Sgt. Bassett had initially asked most of the questions, but Ellen found herself seeming to give most of her answers to Detective Redhawk. Soon she was responding solely to the detective with the haunting eyes.

As the interview wound down, a nurse knocked and entered. "Excuse me, but it's time to take your vitals. How is our patient feeling?"

"I'm fine, really, still hungry, though."

"Good. Your supper has been ordered; it'll be here shortly," she responded and commenced to notate the patient's chart.

A uniformed deputy sheriff poked his head in. "Sarge, she has some more visitors out here."

The detectives shrugged at one another.

"No problem, we're done for now," Trey answered. "Thank you, Miss Doyle. We'll be in touch."

"Yeah, thanks, uh, sorry if I—*we* overstayed our welcome," Detective Redhawk added a tad sheepishly as he followed his partner from the room.

"Are you willing to see more visitors?" asked the nurse.

"Yes, of course," Ellen answered.

The nurse smiled and stepped into the hall.

She heard a muffled conversation at her door.

It opened; in came *her mother! Then her friend, Stacy!* A taller, older, somewhat harried version of her cousin, Mark, at least as she remembered him, followed.

Ellen was surprised to see Stacy, but shocked to see her mother. A flush of gratitude flooded her heart as she realized what Millie had potentially sacrificed to be here for her.

As for her cousin, Mark, she still saw the teenager in him to whom she'd bid good-bye when he'd left for New York with his father over a decade ago. Now, he appeared careworn and in need of sleep.

"Ellen, are you okay? You had us so worried!" Her mother pulled a chair to her bedside, and reached for her hand.

"I'm bruised, Mom, but I'm going to be fine. Sorry for all the fuss, but this really wasn't my idea."

Her visitors smiled sympathetically, and they began to just talk.

"I'm a little confused," Ellen conceded, and gestured to her mother and Stacy. "How did y'all find out about my, uh, *predicament?*"

Both of them grinned and pointed to Mark.

"Uh, yeah, that was me, I'm afraid," Mark admitted and went on to explain that he was notified about the accident by the local sheriff's department. Since he never did get Millie's phone number from Ellen, he contacted Ellen's office, thinking they might have it listed as an emergency contact. Was it just luck that Stacy took the call, or capricious fate?

Stacy took up the narrative. "I called your mom at the diner. We decided to come to LaBorde as soon as possible. I called Mark back and told him our plans."

"He was kind enough to pick us up at the airport early Sunday afternoon," Millie added. "Since then, we've been splitting our time between the hotel and the hospital waiting room. They let us see you briefly, but you were still sedated. You looked so . . . I was so worried—"

"But they told us yesterday," Stacy interrupted, laying a hand gently on Millie's arm, "that you were doing much better, and we could visit you today. So, here we are!"

The recent worrisome days had clearly taken a toll on her visitors. But now, relief was palpable.

Even Ellen, despite her aches and bruises, felt uplifted and buoyant. "I'm really glad to see you—all of you. So, tell me what else you've been doing; I want details."

In a torrent of words, spiced with dramatic gestures and pauses, Millie and Stacy fussed over her and recounted their tales that led to them both being there for her.

Mark just leaned against the wall smiling sheepishly, obviously having already heard the details, but he was good-natured enough to listen to it all again.

It did not escape Ellen's notice how frequently Mark stole long glances at Stacy. She smiled to herself. *Now isn't that interesting.*

A soft knock on the door announced the arrival of an orderly with her supper.

"Oh, we'll let you eat," Millie insisted.

"Oh, yum! Hospital food!" Stacy teased. "That'll make you want to get better!"

"We should get going," Mark suggested. "We can come back tomorrow during regular visiting hours, okay?"

Ellen nodded. "That's fine. I'd like that."

"Maybe we'll smuggle you in a cheeseburger." Stacy stage-whispered, behind a raised hand, "Even the vending machines in the visitors' lounge suck."

Ellen glanced at her hospital food and winced. "Make that *two* cheeseburgers and a chocolate shake, okay?"

Everyone said their good-byes, departing amidst promises to return in the morning.

ELLEN FINISHED HER meal and pushed the tray table to the side. Within a minute there was a soft knock on her door and a smiling face surrounded by gray curls appeared.

"Hello Ellen, I'm Madeline Dupree, the hospital librarian; you can call me Madeline. Dr. Marie sent me. I suspect she doesn't want you to grow bored during the recovery process, so she asked that I help you select some reading material." Her smile was infectious and her eyes twinkled as she added, "Of course, in my opinion reading is always therapeutic." Her tone grew more somber. "However, even if you do select some books now, you might want to wait to actually read, you know, until you feel up to it; don't push yourself. Once you do start reading, if you should experience any difficulty, double vision, headaches, any discomfort at all, please notify a nurse immediately."

Now this was a prescription Ellen could enjoy. "I understand. Don't worry; I love to read!"

They chatted briefly about the types of books Ellen enjoyed, which was of a fairly broad spectrum and variety. This seemed to delight Miss Madeline, and she began shuffling amongst the books in her cart, selecting that which might interest Ellen. At length, she deposited some paperbacks and a well-worn hardback on the bedside table.

"Now, if you don't find these hold your interest, just let me know; I have thousands more at my shop." Madeline cocked her head and smiled, almost as if waiting for the question.

"Shop?" Ellen asked.

"Oh, yes!" Madeline nodded. "The hospital doesn't have its own library, so I loan books to patients from my secondhand bookstore. The title 'hospital librarian' is somewhat honorary, kind of a little joke. It's okay; I like it."

Ellen could not help but warm to this woman with a consistent smile and a sparkle in her eye. She returned the librarian's smile and picked up the books one at a time, examining the covers.

Miss Madeline handed her a business card, *Tomes & Scrolls*, bearing an address and telephone number. "You can use that for a bookmark, or in case you need to reach me."

Ellen picked up the last book, the hardback. Its faded cover barely held traces of the title. She tilted it to and fro in the light trying to read the lettering; finally, she gave up and looked inside for the title page.

OLD BLOOD

A Speculative Treatise

On Myth and Folklore

Dr. Armand Dupree, PhD

Dept. of Cultural Anthropology

Delorme University

Ellen noted the author's name, and looked up at Miss Madeline.

Before she could ask, Madeline said, "Yes, my husband wrote that book. He was always of mixed emotions about it."

Ellen didn't know what to say, but she had to admit she was intrigued. "Your husband, he's—"

Madeline laughed. "Oh he's just fine! He's retired now from teaching, just dabbles in what he calls 'cultural parallels and anomalies' research. He sometimes helps out with the bookstore. However, he tends to lecture the customers; although the regulars take it pretty well, sort of tongue-in-cheek."

Madeline's laugh was infectious, and Ellen was soon chuckling along.

Then Madeline surprised her. "You may not know it, but we were friends of your Aunt Maude, yes, for many years. She asked us to keep her dogs when she went into, uh, that place, the rest home. I imagine they're yours now."

Ellen was stunned. "Dogs? I didn't know she had any pets. I can't imagine—"

Madeline held up her hand. "Now don't fret, they're fine and healthy. When you get out of the hospital, you come see me and we'll have a long talk, maybe over some nice tea. You like tea, don't you?"

Ellen was at a momentary loss for words. *Here was someone who knew—no, more than that, she was a friend to Maude! Of course I want to talk with you!* She nodded wide-eyed, sputtering, "Tea? Oh yes, of course, definitely!"

"Good! Then it's settled. Read your books and get well. Then come see me. You have my card with my number, just in case you need me. Now you get your rest, young lady. Good night!"

With that, Madeline trundled her cart into the hall and was gone.

FENTON BREWSTER WAS not usually subject to claustrophobia, but spending twenty-three hours a day in the five by eight solitary confinement cell was beginning to get to him.

His lawyer had been of no help with this complication at all; so, he had decided to fire his current attorney. That high-priced shyster had gladly taken Brewster's initial retainer deposit, but now he wanted more money, a lot more, to deal with the federal warrant now hanging over his head. The feds had filed a detainer with the parish jail, which meant that if he made bond on the state fraud case, he still wouldn't be freed. The U.S. Marshals would immediately sweep him up, assume custody and execute the outstanding warrant. He'd find himself before a federal judge by the next day, on a much more serious set of charges. He was in deep trouble; and his own damned lawyer was squeezing him for more cash.

Well, he had a surprise coming for that greedy mouthpiece. When he was allocated telephone privileges, he'd made some calls, and left word for *Papa George*. He wanted new counsel, from a top-drawer firm with the heavy legal firepower to make the warrant, or even better, any indictment, go away. Fenton knew George Papadolis not only had the resources to engage such a firm, but he had a vested interest in seeing that Fenton Brewster did not go into federal custody. Papa George would want to keep his silent-partner status in many of Fenton's enterprises from the light of exposure. Brewster knew that pressuring Papa George could be dangerous, but he was running out of options.

George Papadolis, Greek on his father's side and Sicilian on his mother's, had successfully straddled the factions among organized crime in New Orleans for a generation. He was the money man, the *bank*, a whiz with finances and money laundering. While he didn't maintain a large contingent of *muscle*, he could easily contract with any of his customer factions to meet any specific needs. He was known to savor his insulated anonymity, and enjoyed the perception of being behind the scenes, all powerful yet mysterious. So, Brewster had left the subtle hint that such anonymity might be compromised should he be abandoned, or worse, left to fall into federal custody.

His message must have struck a chord.

A guard appeared at his cell door. "On your feet, Brewster. Your new attorney is here."

Brewster gathered a few documents, a copy of the detainer letter and notes on his fraud case, and accompanied the guard to the attorney/client interview room.

The small room, austere in its pale yellow walls and antiseptic in its brushed stainless steel fixtures, was divided by a hip-high steel bulkhead topped with thick wire mesh all the way to the ceiling. A long steel bench on the prisoners' side was bolted to the floor beneath a narrow steel tabletop that ran the length of the bulkhead. A more generous twin surface was mirrored on the attorneys' side, accompanied by a handful of dull grey folding chairs.

Brewster sat opposite the lone occupant on the attorneys' side, a slight man in an expensive suit, with dark slicked-back hair, a thin Van Dyke beard, and very dark eyes behind horn-rimmed glasses.

This new attorney rummaged one-handed in a briefcase, as Brewster watched deep in thought. *This guy looks like even more of a snake than my last lawyer. Oh well, so long as he's good.*

In a lowered voice, with just the barest hint of condescension, the man spoke in a deliberate yet cultured tone. "Good afternoon, Mr. Brewster. I am Mr. Salidar. I am here at the request of our mutual benefactor. Do you understand?"

Fenton nodded, but kept quiet. The attorney/client room was not supposed to be electronically monitored pursuant to *attorney/client privilege*, but Fenton didn't trust the authorities.

Apparently neither did this new attorney. "We won't be discussing your case right now. I have a few questions and some instructions for you. Do you understand?"

Fenton nodded once more.

"Good. Are you separated from the general population?"

Fenton kept his voice low, his eyes shifting from one side of the room to the other. "Yes, in a solitary cell; I think because of the federal detainer."

"You are entitled to one hour of exercise, even when in *lockdown*. Are you getting it?"

"Well, yeah. They let me out alone on the roof from ten to eleven every night, with two guards." Fenton parsed his words carefully, his curiosity growing. "There's a basketball court up there. It's not that well lit, but it's got two cameras and an eight foot fence with razor wire. I get to smoke."

"Hmmph, really? Smoking will kill you. You know that don't you?"

"So what? What else am I gonna do in here?"

"This fenced rooftop, is it open at the top? No overhead mesh?" Salidar asked, leaning closer with every word.

"No mesh, just the razor wire along the top of the fence. The center is wide open." Fenton's imagination was in high gear.

"Excellent!" Salidar whispered. "Please do nothing to cause the jail staff to alter that schedule. Keep to your established routine. That will be of the utmost importance."

Fenton could hardly contain himself; visions of helicopters danced in his head. *This is even better! I'm getting out of here! Maybe tonight!*

Forcing his voice to some semblance of normalcy, he whispered, "I understand. I'll be ready."

Salidar stood, collected a few papers, and in a normal conversational tone said, "Thank you, Mr. Brewster. I'll get to work on this matter right away. Please have a good day."

"Thank you, Mr. Salidar. I believe we will work together just fine."

Fenton watched as Salidar left the room. Making an effort to compose his face in a neutral expression, he turned to await the guard.

The next several hours in his solitary cell would seem the longest in his current incarceration.

AT TEN O'CLOCK, TWO guards opened Brewster's cell. "On your feet, Brewster. Exercise time. Let's go."

Brewster forced himself to maintain a calm outward appearance despite his racing heart and raging sense of anticipation.

They ascended the staircase that took them to the exercise area on the roof. Two gates locked down a ten foot long hallway; only one gate could be opened at a time, thus creating the *mantrap*. One guard held Brewster at the mantrap gate. The other guard proceeded onto the roof to conduct a routine security search and check the fencing and wire.

Brewster was familiar with this routine. Although the roof was sixty-five feet from the parking lot below, people had been known to throw things like drugs, weapons, and other contraband onto the roof for retrieval by inmates. The roof was routinely searched before any use.

His search concluded, the first guard waved Brewster onto the roof. The other guard followed, securing the gate behind him.

Brewster looked around, trying to be casual, and lit a cigarette. He wandered about, deliberately not looking up, yet listening for any hint of a helicopter's signature *whop-whop-whop-whop*.

His imagination was in overdrive, but his straining ears heard nothing.

He kept pacing . . . and smoking . . . and pacing.

"OUR BOY LOOKS A LITTLE antsy," remarked the duty sergeant who was overseeing the shift observing the closed-circuit television monitors.

One of the control room deputies noted, "Yeah, that's his third butt; he usually smokes two. He's nervous about something."

The sergeant grunted. "No doubt that federal indictment. I heard they've got him good; he's *done*."

BREWSTER FIRED UP ANOTHER cigarette as he paced. His hour was seeping away.

He hadn't noticed that the two guards on the roof with him had casually drifted toward one another to pass the time in quiet conversation. He was too distracted to care.

Maybe it wasn't supposed to be tonight? Yeah, that must be it. I get it; they're watching. Yeah, they're watching the pattern so they can bring in the chopper at just the right moment. That's smart. Of course, it'll be tomorrow night. Damn it!

He thought he heard a muffled *thonk* and he turned toward the guards; but he couldn't see them in the shadows. A few steps closer and he realized they were sprawled flat, not moving.

He spun around! *This must be it! Where's the helicopter?*

A figure stood before him, seeming to take substance from the darkness, a pale woman with red hair.

Shrouded in some sort of dark cloak, she smiled.

"Who are you? Where's the bird?" he demanded, stepping back. "Answer me!"

She opened her cloak; she was nude. Her feral smile widened; her luminous eyes flared in cold green radiance.

He paled, dropping his final cigarette.

SEVERAL FLOORS BELOW, the deputy seated at the monitors called out, "Hey Sarge, something's wrong with the roof cameras! I'm looking at stars and night sky here!"

The sergeant pressed an alert button on the console. "React Team to the roof! Expedite!"

BREWSTER GASPED. HE had never known such pain, or such ecstasy. Even now, a small part of his unscrupulous mind was thinking that he should try to somehow get his hands on this drug, or whatever it was, and deal it on the streets. He'd make a fortune! However, a more rational inner voice started to scream and rant in panic, but faded in pale echoes. He flailed weakly, sighed, and stopped moving.

THE SIDHE RELEASED his throat, licking a trace of blood. Despite the rampant hunger surging throughout her being, her instructions were clear; she could not drain him. This was to look like an accident or suicide.

She easily picked up Brewster, confirmed that he still had a heartbeat, and carried him to the perimeter fence. Placing his throat along a strand of razor wire, she vigorously slashed his neck back and forth, obliterating her teeth marks. Then she did the same with both of his wrists.

Assured that he still lived, however weakly, she tossed him to the top of the razor wire and jerked him right and left, gashing his chest and abdomen. Satisfied with her handiwork, she tipped him over the uppermost wire.

He plummeted to the street level below. A small mercy, his spirit departed on the way down.

THE REACT TEAM BURST through the gate and onto the roof.

"The guards, found `em! They're out cold!" declared the man on point.

"Call the paramedics!" ordered the team leader. "Where's the prisoner?"

No one answered. There was no sign of Brewster.

"The cameras' mounts are loose, aimed at the sky," observed a team member.

"Hey, I've got blood here," announced another man, "on the razor wire."

That was just about the same time a responding patrol unit found Brewster's corpse in the parking lot directly below.

A BLOCK AWAY, STANDING in deep shadow, Salidar watched as more deputies flooded from the building into the parking lot to set up a perimeter. Some began stringing yellow crime scene tape in the harsh alternating blue and red strobe lights of marked units just arriving on the scene.

Salidar removed his horn-rimmed glasses, casually wiped the optically clear lenses with a handkerchief, and mumbled to himself.

"Fool! I told him smoking would kill him."

CH 7

THE MORNING AFTER FENTON Brewster's death, Sheriff Frank Tatum called a meeting of his detectives in the CID squad room. He was not in the best of moods, and the reports in his hand did not help.

"All right, settle down. Detectives Jones and Barrows have the Brewster case. It's currently classified as a suspicious death. It has not yet been determined whether or not it's a suicide. That'll depend upon the forensic results and a decision from the medical examiner's office. Jones, give us a synopsis."

"Sure thing, Sheriff." The lanky detective stood and cleared his throat. "There was little evidence on the scene. The two guards, Montgomery and Yashida, who were found unconscious, are gonna be okay. They have sufficiently recovered to offer statements, but have little to add. They did not see their attacker. Both vaguely remember Brewster smoking and pacing, and then nothing.

"Both men sustained concussions from their heads being slammed together with just enough force to render them unconscious. They have no other injuries; they were bruised, but neither bled. We don't know if Brewster was responsible; but we haven't ruled it out. The blood found on the roof and the wire, not to mention the parking lot below, was Brewster's. That's it so far."

Sheriff Tatum nodded. "Thanks. Okay, anyone got any ideas?"

For the next ten minutes the squad room buzzed as details of the case were discussed in depth and investigative options analyzed.

"All right, if that's everything," the sheriff said in conclusion, "I want everyone to examine all their cases for any related links, and to assist Detectives Jones and Barrows should they request help. Remember, no one is to speak to the media. Send any such inquiries to my office; I'm headed there now."

He knew he was in for a trying day.

SHERIFF TATUM WAS NOT to be disappointed; by noon his office was getting crowded.

FBI Special Agent Jim Franklin and his boss, Assistant Special Agent-in-Charge Manuel Scherer, stood before the sheriff's desk. Behind the two FBI agents stood Eva Quantrell from DEA, and Deputy U.S. Marshals Todd Simmons and Willis Hebert.

A windmilling Manny Scherer was furious. "How in the hell could you let this happen? Brewster was the key to this OCDETF case! He was *the* link to 'Papa George' Papadolis! We would've had him!"

The FBI ASAC went on like this for several moments. Frank just elected to ignore him, and calmly studied the faces of the others in the room.

Jim Franklin looked crestfallen and embarrassed, no doubt at Scherer's tirade. Eva Quantrell had found something of deep interest in the vicinity of the ceiling and gave it her full attention. The two Deputy U.S. Marshals just stood relaxed, leaning against the wall, arms folded, alternatively grinning at each other or the back of Scherer's bobbing head.

Frank tuned back into Manny's rant to hear " . . . and I want all files and documents, and that includes all personnel records for everyone on duty that night, especially those two *allegedly injured* guards!"

The sheriff stood, and being a head taller, looked down on ASAC Manuel Scherer, who, for the moment, went quiet.

"ASAC Scherer, are y'all formally opening a homicide investigation?" Frank asked softly.

Manny blinked and sputtered, "Ah, that decision will be made at Washington, based on my recommendation, after I, uh, review everything."

"I see," intoned Frank. "Well, until such time as a federal investigation is officially opened, the Chantilly Parish Sheriff's Department will conduct *its* investigation and turn over all reports and evidence to our district attorney for potential prosecution. At that time, and in the interest of inter-agency cooperation, this office will happily share with you everything so vetted by the district attorney. Anything you'd like prior to that, you'll have to seek pursuant to a subpoena. Now, do we understand one another?"

ASAC Scherer was grinding his teeth, audibly. He spun to face the others in the room and seethed, "With me, people! We are *out* of here!"

Jim Franklin shrugged his shoulders, and rolling his eyes turned to follow his boss from the room.

"That means you, too!" ASAC Scherer spat as he came abreast of the Deputy U.S. Marshals.

"Now Manny," Todd Simmons drawled, "we don't work for you."

"That's ASAC Scherer to you!" Scherer was livid, the veins in his temples pulsing.

Willis quipped, "Yeah sure, Manny, whatever. Listen, we'll see you later. We have some other business with the sheriff."

ASAC Scherer spun on Eva, who quickly jabbed a thumb toward the marshals. "I rode with them."

ASAC Scherer clamped his jaws and stormed out of the office with a hapless Jim Franklin in his wake, whose wince and pursed lips spoke volumes.

After a long moment Frank asked, "So, y'all didn't ride here with him?"

"Nope," replied Eva as she meandered over to the window overlooking the parking lot. "Manny made Jim drive him, just him alone. Y'all might wanna come on over here and watch."

They crowded around the window and observed as ASAC Scherer approached the polished black cruiser, stopping at the right rear passenger door. Then he just stood there, hands on his hips.

Jim was walking around the front of the car when he noticed that Scherer was just an akimbo statue at the right rear door. He stopped, retraced his steps to Scherer's position, and opened the rear door for his boss. Scherer seated himself, and with an exaggerated flourish put a cell phone to his ear.

Jim's lips thinned as he stared through the open door for just a moment longer than was probably wise, but it appeared that Manny had already dismissed him as irrelevant and ignored him. Jim closed the door and trudged around to the driver's door. He glanced skyward, and with a sad smile, closed his eyes and shook his head.

As he drove away, the witnesses in the window chuckled and guffawed.

Todd chuckled and pointed. "Y'all see that? Manny got into that cruiser like it was a limo, and he was a VIP!"

Willis added, "Yeah, he doesn't realize sittin' in the back like that makes him look like a *perp* on the way to jail!"

Laughter burbled forth once more. They commiserated on behalf of Jim Franklin, a very well liked and excellent investigator, who now had to waste time acting as chauffeur to a bureaucratic *prima donna.*

"Don't worry, Sheriff," Todd remarked, "Manny's got no jurisdiction in a local homicide or suicide. Brewster never made bond in the state case so we never assumed custody and executed our warrant, ergo, no federal jurisdiction. Of course, he may try to play the 'civil rights of the defendant have been violated' card, but there's no sound basis or any evidence whatsoever to that effect. Besides, a civil rights case requires DOJ approval, something he knows he'd never get under these circumstances."

"I know and I'm not concerned," Frank acknowledged. "Now, did you really have other business with me, or were y'all just avoiding being drafted into the ASAC's departing motorcade?"

Eva squealed with bright laughter; the rest all smiled in amusement.

Willis regained his composure. "It's about that taxi-pickup truck accident and arson your detectives are working, the one in which the Doyle woman was injured. We now know that the Cantu homicide case out of New Orleans is linked; and that the taxi was stolen from Cantu's home in New Orleans, although it was never reported as such. We've been told that the DNA from the recovered tissue of the fatality, whoever was driving the stolen taxi, appears to be a match for Ratso, so he's probably your missing corpse. Still missing, right?"

"Yeah, afraid so," Frank admitted, "but if y'all are right, we'll at least have a firm ID to work with."

Willis nodded, and his partner, Todd, continued the narrative. "As you know, there were latent prints recovered from the stolen truck. We've received confirmation that they include those of Iggy and Bubba. So, at some time, each was in it. There were two types of blood found in the cab of the truck. We think the subsequent DNA blood work will put both Iggy and Bubba in it at the time of the wreck."

"So, we had *two* perps in the stolen truck, not just the operator?" Frank asked. "If not seriously injured, they could've set the fire, and then fled the scene?"

"Yes, we think so, too," Todd confirmed. "There was some speculation that Ratso might have been the intended target. He was documented as a small time CI with the NOPD, but the detectives who handled him said he hadn't been credible for some time, and they'd lost track of him. Street intel indicates that other criminal elements knew he was loose-lipped, and probably a *snitch*, but there was no indication that he was to be taken out, or any money offered for a hit. The word on the street was that he was just to be avoided. If Iggy and Bubba were going to kill him, they'd have had plenty of other opportunities in New Orleans."

Willis nodded in agreement and spoke guardedly. "On the other hand, we think it's entirely possible they may have planned on killing him in the accident; we don't know. We do agree it looks more like an attempted hit on the cab's passenger, but we have no clue as to *why*. Ratso may have just been acceptable collateral damage. We'll be tentatively closing our escape file on Ratso upon receipt of the final DNA report, assuming that'll pretty much confirm he's now a corpse, albeit still missing. Unfortunately, there's nothing else, no further leads, on Iggy and Bubba in your parish."

Todd nodded, and continued. "Our escape warrant for Iggy is still outstanding. NOPD will have a warrant for Bubba, and maybe Iggy, too, in the Cantu homicide case in short order.

"Our people were happy to lend assistance when Trey and Hawk wanted to trap the mystery 'student nurse', because it sure looked related. But that gambit, and the rest of our leads, didn't pan out.

"The point is, our borrowed assets are needed on some of their own cases. Detective Terri McPherson is still the lead NOPD investigator on the Cantu homicide, but her captain needs her back in New Orleans because she's got court on Friday."

"So," Willis explained, "the Fugitive Task Force personnel from New Orleans have to pull out; and, we've got a threat case in Alexandria that just came up. That shouldn't take us more than a couple of days. After that, we don't have anything hot pending for a week or so. If you need us, just call."

Frank sighed. He knew their assistance, however valuable, would be limited by time factors and circumstances beyond his control. "Well, you know I'm grateful for all you were able to do. Do you know when the final DNA reports will be ready?"

"A week, maybe ten days," Willis acknowledged. "We'll either hand deliver or overnight hard copies as soon as we get them. We'll e-mail Trey and Hawk, too."

Frank turned to Eva and offered an apology. "I'm sorry if this Brewster matter has screwed up your OCDETF case, or caused you any other grief."

She shrugged. "It hasn't, really. Don't worry; Manny's histrionics don't get to me, Sheriff. Besides, he doesn't think long term. If we don't get a shot at Papa George with this case, we will with another. He's just too connected to everything foul in this state. Hell, the whole Gulf Coast! Either we'll get him or his *customers* will. He'll get his eventually."

Frank nodded in agreement, knowing she was very likely right. "Well, thank you all once again. I assure you we'll call if something breaks on Iggy and Bubba."

As he bid them good-bye, Frank thought that at least some of this news might be helpful for Trey and Hawk. Reaching for his phone, he was beginning to think his day wasn't so terribly bad after all.

SALIDAR LIKED CASINOS; and he liked New Orleans. He savored the ambiance of chance, thinly veiled promise, and greed. It reeked of opportunity and risk, especially for one who knew how to take the advantage.

He was here at the behest of Lady Diere to communicate further instructions to George. Salidar scoffed. *I am no fool. My presence is intended to impress George with the successful resolution of the Brewster problem, something George could not seem to accomplish on his own. She's practically rubbing his nose in his failure.*

He knew he had performed well, despite having to work with the Sidhe. His reward had been the return of the use of his right arm; but, he still had to *earn* the full recovery of his sight and hearing. He straightened the lapels of his lawyer's suit as he entered the reception area of the casino's executive office suites and approached the exceptionally attractive blond receptionist.

"I am Mr. Salidar. I am here to see Mr. Papadolis."

"Of course, one moment, sir." She then seemed to speak into thin air, conferring with someone he couldn't see.

He noticed the small wireless device hooked over her ear and the opaque glass ceiling dome that surely hid a camera. He stifled the urge to smile and wave. *Ah, yes, technology, mankind's soulless magic.*

Despite his diminished hearing, he was startled by a metallic hiss and spun to see a pair of carved wooden panels slide open, an elevator.

A tall woman with striking Oriental features and long raven hair stepped delicately into the room.

Salidar was momentarily bemused at the juxtaposition of the two women, the darkly exotic oriental in counterpoint to the western idealized blonde.

The inscrutable *femme fatale* nodded to the receptionist, and bowed slightly to Salidar. "Mr. Salidar, please come this way."

Her voice held a slight husky tone, but betrayed no discernible accent. Her Mandarin silk dress shimmered in shades of grey as she turned toward the elevator; hints of crimson flared from long side slits from ankle to mid-thigh. She had an easy, yet powerful, grace about her movements, and a distinct sense of confident competence.

Salidar did not move. No fool, he took a moment to assess the situation. This woman was dangerous; he sensed it in every cell. He could ill afford to be other than cautious; after all, he was here on Lady Diere's business.

"Why, thank you, dear lady. Might I be permitted to know your name?"

"If it pleases you, know me as Ling." She smiled coyly as she invited him into the elevator with a small sweeping gesture of an exquisitely manicured hand.

He entered, graciously nodding, and noting that her smile never reached her eyes. *Ling, eh? Not your true name, I'll wager.*

The car ascended several floors; the doors opened into a large office suite. Two men, wearing the uniforms of the casino security staff, were busy packing a number of cardboard boxes. They stopped at the sight of Ling and just stared.

She ignored them, slipping sinuously around stacks of boxes with Salidar following in her wake. She knocked at a closed door.

Salidar recognized the voice bidding them to enter.

George, a cell phone to his ear and his back to the room, stood behind a large desk. A number of files and ledgers were arrayed upon its surface. Sealed moving boxes were stacked along one wall.

George mumbled into the phone, ended the call, and turned to his guest. "Welcome Salidar, forgive the mess. You've come when I'm in the middle of a move."

"So I see, m'lord. My apologies for such inopportune timing; but I have come at her ladyship's request. May we speak in private?"

"Ah, yes, of course." Turning to Ling, he said, "Please see that the workmen are busy in another area of the suite, and then return to us."

She bowed and passed silently from the room.

"I see you've met Ling." George eased into his chair and watched Salidar carefully. "What do you think?"

"A beautiful woman," Salidar offered cautiously, "one whom I should think it would be unwise to offend."

"You'd better believe it! She comes highly recommended. You just can't be too careful these days, or too obvious. No one's gonna figure a woman as a bodyguard, especially dressed like that!" Smiling broadly, George leaned back. He appeared quite pleased with himself.

"Indeed so, m'lord, indeed so," Salidar acknowledged agreeably. *Bodyguard? What a fool! This woman is more than a mere bodyguard, more likely an assassin, at the very least. I wonder from whence her "highly recommended" status came.*

"So, I take it, since you're here, that means the *Brewster matter* is no longer a problem?"

"Quite so, m'lord," said Salidar, as he bowed and gestured with exaggerated flourish, using *both* hands. *Good! Let him think I've recovered all my faculties, not just the use of my right arm.*

"Ah, that's very good. Well, I have a lot to do, so if there's nothing else?" George reached for his cell phone.

"Actually, there is, a message from her ladyship, for your ears alone, m'lord."

That stopped George cold. He slowly lowered the phone.

Salidar almost grinned, but he remained stoic. "You are to make yourself available to summons any time within the next ten days. The council is planning to meet to contemplate the, uh, recent vacancy. M'lady will certainly summon you, but you are to be prepared to answer a summons from the council as well."

George appeared stunned, but he managed to respond. "Of course, uh, whatever." He seemed to gather his wits, and stood. "You can inform your boss-lady—"

"Ah, you mean *her ladyship,* of course?" Salidar smiled smugly as he delivered the correction.

George balked, but quickly recovered. "Uh, yeah, right. Tell her *ladyship* that I am moving my base of operations to the casino on the Indian reservation outside of LaBorde. One of my subsidiary holding companies has acquired an outstanding mortgage of sorts on some related property. My location will otherwise be kept confidential. Is that clear?"

"Of course, m'lord, will there be anything else?"

"No, that's all."

George sat, glancing over Salidar's shoulder. "Ling, please escort Mr. Salidar back to the casino's main floor. I'm certain he's eager to return to his bos—er, *her ladyship.*"

To his credit, Salidar did not flinch when he realized Ling was behind him and just to his left. *My blind side! Did she know? I can hear on that side; but I heard nothing! How long has she been there?*

Salidar bowed. "Then I shall take my leave, m'lord, and bid you good-day."

He turned and followed Ling to the elevator. They rode down in silence.

As the doors opened, Ling leaned toward Salidar and purred, "So nice to meet you, Mr. Salidar. Perhaps we shall encounter one another again. Tread carefully."

He nodded amiably, but the hairs on the back of his neck were on end as he exited the elevator.

Distance, my sweet, I want some distance between us. Oh George, thou poor fool! Methinks thou hast taken an adder to thy breast.

ELLEN WAS MORE THAN ready to get out of the hospital. Thank goodness her mother, Mark, and Stacy visited daily; otherwise the boredom would have been too much.

In between the tests, physical therapy sessions, and visits, Ellen started reading Dr. Dupree's anthropology text. While indeed scholarly, she did not find it so esoteric that her interest lagged; in fact, she had begun to find it intriguing and imaginative.

Speculative evolution and alternative realities? Oh, that just spurs my imagination on; this is fun!

DETECTIVES BASSETT and Redhawk visited once more as well, ostensibly to see if she had remembered anything else about the accident since their first interview.

"I'm really sorry, Detectives, but I don't remember any more than I've already told you. And please, call me Ellen."

"As you wish, Miss Ellen," Trey agreed genially. "If there's anything else that occurs to you, please don't hesitate to contact us."

"Uh, yeah," added Detective Redhawk. "Um, my first name is Connor. I'll—uh, *we'll* be in touch, to check on you."

Trey looked askance at his partner and smirked, just as a nurse poked her head in and motioned for Trey to follow her into the hall.

Ellen noticed the young detective's bandaged hand. "Are you okay? How did you hurt your hand?"

"This is nothing, just a cut. I had some stitches, but they were removed a few days ago. It's pretty much already healed, but the doctor insisted I keep it covered for a couple more days. Really, it's no big deal." He slipped his injured hand behind his back, and glanced away, a slight reddening to his cheeks.

She noticed. *Oh, he's uncomfortable talking about himself, how cute!*

"Well, I'm glad you're all right."

To her utter amusement, his cheeks flared once more. *Oh, that is so endearing. I like him.*

His partner returned to retrieve him and pulled him toward the door. "If you'll forgive us, Miss Ellen, we really have to go. I understand your family has arrived for their visit. We're glad to see you're doing better. Call us if you remember anything."

"I will. Thank you!" she called out as the young detective was pulled from her room, looking equally surprised and chagrined.

She hoped she hadn't offended him. She'd rather enjoyed the visit and wouldn't mind spending more time with him.

Well, at least this time I'd had a shower and didn't look so, uh, unkempt?

ON THURSDAY AFTERNOON, Dr. Latrice-Johnson pronounced Ellen sufficiently fit for discharge sometime early Friday morning, absent any problems arising in the interim.

Ellen was subsequently delighted, relieved, and a bit anxious.

Of course, Mark took the news to mean he could make arrangements as necessary. Within hours, he returned to the hospital and found Ellen in her room.

"Hey, El', I've made sure your hotel room will be ready as soon as you're discharged."

"Thanks, Mark, I appreciate it."

"Oh yeah, I should mention that your mom and Stacy got you some clothes. When the police told us everything in the cab was a complete loss, including your luggage, I figured I'd get some stuff for you, but Stacy wouldn't hear of it. She and Aunt Millie insisted on shopping for you."

Ellen smiled. "It's okay, Mark. I admit that had been in the back of my mind, that I'd need some new clothes and stuff, I mean. Stacy does know what I like; so, it's fine that she and my mom went shopping, But thanks for thinking of me."

"No problem. If there's anything else I can do," he assured her, "just ask."

"I will; don't worry. Now, what about Maude's service?"

"All taken care of; don't worry. The memorial service is scheduled for eleven on Friday morning at the local funeral home's chapel. The funeral director told me it'll be brief. You know, your attendance isn't really necessary; after all, you'll have been out of the hospital only a few hours."

"No, I'm going! There's no way I'm not going to Maude's memorial service, hear me?"

"I hear you!" Mark smiled, obviously encouraged by her resolve. "Well then, would you also feel up to attending the reading of the will later that afternoon at two o'clock? The time's not fixed in stone; the attorney, Mr. Fornier, will accommodate your wishes."

The simple truth was that her curiosity could not be restrained much longer. She felt strongly that the sooner she learned more, the better off she'd be. So firm was her conviction that she was now determined to attend the reading of the will, notwithstanding how tired she might feel by then.

"Two o'clock is fine, Mark. Don't worry about me; I'm gonna be all right. I am definitely attending the memorial service *and* the reading."

FRIDAY MORNING ARRIVED soaking in a steady spring rain. The dismal leaden sky promised no respite from the inevitable drenching. Lake levels would rise and swollen bayous would abandon their lazy sluggish pace. The gutters of LaBorde were almost awash. Carefully tended lawns and gardens softened with saturation. All life in the region calmly took it in stride, as another manifestation of Mother Nature's timely bounty.

To Ellen's mind, it was nonetheless a fine day to leave the hospital, despite the weather and the pending memorial service. Her discharge procedures included the totally unnecessary, yet required, ceremonial departure via wheelchair. She refused to allow that minor indignity to dampen her mood as she bid Dr. Latrice-Johnson good-bye at the lobby doors. She let Mark bundle her into his rental car for the short drive to the hotel, where she had insisted she be permitted to freshen up before attending the memorial service.

NEITHER ELLEN NOR MARK saw the dark unmarked cruiser that discreetly followed them as they left the parking lot. But the doctor noticed; and she nodded in approval when she recognized the young Detective Redhawk at the wheel.

CH 8

THE RAIN HAD SETTLED into a gentle cadence that promised to lull the day into a drowsy languor.

Ellen thought it appropriate ambiance for a memorial service.

As Mark parked the car, Ellen pointed at the unexpected number of people milling about the entrance to the small chapel.

"My goodness, that's a lot of people! Are they all here for Maude's service?"

"Gotta be," Mark concluded, "that's the only service scheduled today."

She smiled at her cousin. "And here you were worried about the obituary and who might attend. That's quite a crowd."

Millie patted his shoulder. "You did good, Mark."

Mark shrugged sheepishly. "I'll admit I'm a bit relieved. Shall we go?"

As they approached the chapel, her mother hovered at Ellen's elbow, pointing out and acknowledging a few people she had known years ago.

Mark guided Ellen and Millie into the vestibule, where they were greeted by the funeral director, Mr. Sheldon, who organized a sort of receiving line.

There were so many attendees that Ellen suspected that she would likely forget some names and some personal details. Thankfully, Madeline Dupree stationed herself within the range of a soft whisper, and kept Ellen apprised of *who was who, kin to whom, when and how.*

Millie remained rather stoic, acknowledging expressions of sympathy with mumbled thanks and patient nods.

Ellen found that sometimes Madeline's breathless commentary betrayed her dry wit. Amused yet restrained, Ellen was successful in keeping her responses limited to polite acknowledgements and small pained smiles. Nonetheless, she was grateful for her mother's presence and Madeline's subtle quips; they gave her a sense of being grounded in unfamiliar circumstances.

The attendees were very solicitous of Ellen and her family. Many offered very gracious personal comments, sharing experiences they'd enjoyed in Maude's company. More than one person remarked about her strong support for the local ecology and her staunch defense of the natural forest habitat.

In a quiet moment, Ellen whispered, "Madeline, are these people university faculty members?"

"Oh yes, most are; does that surprise you? Maude may have been a very private person, but she was popular, well respected, and humorous. Her laugh was infectious—somewhere she's probably laughing at what I'm saying! The point is her wisdom, wit, and insight were deeply appreciated by these folks."

Ellen could easily accept that, for there were a lot of people here.

It was also clear to her that Mark had been very busy helping to arrange the service.

STACY TUGGED MARK ASIDE and whispered, "You look tired; I think you might need a break. Let Ellen and her mother handle the rest of the arrivals. Come on, let's look at the floral displays. They're important, you know."

"Uh, okay, this way, through here."

Standing before the displays, Stacy spent considerable time evaluating each with a critical eye. Flora was obviously her passion. Mark was a bit apprehensive upon realizing that fact; after all, he had made some of the selections on the family's behalf.

However, as minutes slipped by, her generous smile and nods of appreciation eventually alleviated his concerns. It surprised him that he so much desired her approval.

"Hmm, not too shabby, Mark. You did good," she confirmed. "Come on, we'd better take our seats."

IT WAS A RATHER GENERIC memorial service, more secular than religious, as Maude was not a member of any church. Her ashes resided in a funereal urn, which to Ellen's eye was more of a fancy rose-colored marble box, displayed on a small, yet elegantly carved table draped with a wide black velvet runner.

Once the service concluded, people milled about socializing briefly. After a few minutes, most began to depart in small groups.

Mark sought out the funeral director.

"Thank you, Mr. Sheldon. It was a lovely memorial service. If you don't mind, I'll be in touch to make arrangements regarding the urn."

"Of course, that's no problem whatsoever, and again, my deepest condolences. If you need me, I'll be in my office; and of course, you have my card." Mr. Sheldon excused himself.

Ellen gripped Mark's arm. "I know you put this all together for us. I just want to thank you. I don't think I could have done it, you know?"

Mark patted her hand. "Don't underestimate yourself, El'; you could've done it. As for me, I needed to *do* something; and this needed doing. I'm just glad to help, okay?"

She gave him a tired smile. "It's okay, I understand. But listen, what was that about the urn?"

"Oh yeah, Maude's ashes. I haven't had the chance to talk to you and your mom about that. I think that's a decision that needs to be made together, don't you?"

"Oh, I see. Yes, you're right. We'll need to think about that, right Mom?"

Millie nodded. "Yes, I suppose so."

"Right," Mark confirmed. "Are we ready to go?"

"One moment, please, Ellen." Madeline stepped forward.

"We, Armand and I, are hosting a little get together this evening for some of Maude's closest friends, a sort of wake, and we'd like you all to come. Eight o'clock, at our bookstore, *Tomes & Scrolls*, it'll be very informal. Oh yes, there will be spirits, beer and wine, too! Please come."

Madeline winked at them and went off in search of her husband, whom she found with practiced ease, deep in an amiable philosophical debate among several lingering faculty members.

On the way back to the hotel, Ellen decided that this was one group she was determined to meet.

CLAUDE FORNIER HAD instructed his secretary, Miss Mavis, that the firm's conference room was to be reserved for his use that afternoon, and prepared for a will reading session.

Miss Mavis knew without asking that it would be the Delafaire probate case. She was uncomfortable as she made the preparations. However, she was a professional; she would do as Claude had instructed.

Standing before the ornate grandfather clock in the corner of the conference room, she checked the time displayed upon its faded painted face against that of her watch. As always, it was accurate, despite its great age. The wonderful old clock would not need winding for days. Placing her hand on the side of the dark walnut cabinet, she could feel as much as hear the seconds ticking away in that measured cadence she had always found soothing and reassuring. In some ways she identified with this masterful timepiece, silent witness to the passage of events and lives, and yet unable to change a thing.

She would be relieved when this afternoon's business was finished. She reached for the phone to make the final notification; for this probate case, the sheriff would attend the reading of the will.

BY TWO O'CLOCK, ALL parties were present, including Sheriff Tatum, and Detectives Bassett and Redhawk. Claude began by making introductions all around, and added, "I will explain the sheriff's presence in detail after the will is read; suffice to say there are taxes due. Shall we begin?"

The last will and testament of Maude Delafaire was relatively simple; nonetheless, Claude patiently explained every detail. There were several firm provisions: the real property, the land, could not be further subdivided; nor could it, or any portion thereof, or interest therein, be used as collateral, leased, or sublet. The main house and other buildings, and the immediate five acres of the tended grounds, were to go to Ellen and Mark equally. All personal property, to include any and all bank accounts and their contents, and the remaining thickly forested land, approximately 2,195 acres, to include all water and mineral rights, were to go to Ellen, provided she accepted the stewardship. There was no further explanation as to the term *stewardship*.

All eyes turned to Ellen. Puzzled faces and murmured questions around the table contributed to her momentary confusion.

In dim memory, she heard Maude's voice: *"I've named you steward, but you must accept . . . very important that you do this . . . for both of us."* Ellen must have paused for longer than she realized.

Her mother took her hand and asked, "Ellen, are you all right?"

"I'm fine. I'm not certain that I understand this stewardship. Is there any further information about it?"

"Not in this document," answered Claude. "I wouldn't be surprised if she meant it in an ecological sense, as in the preservation of the old-growth forest. However, absent any explanation or articulated requirements beyond your acceptance of the *title* or *position*, in this official document and court record, it may well be open to your personal interpretation."

Ellen sensed that her next words would be significant, perhaps more than she could appreciate at the moment. She acknowledged to herself that she wanted and needed to proceed. *Well, why not? This was Maude's intention, and it may be the only path I have to the truth.*

"Very well, I hereby accept the stewardship."

Miss Mavis eased out of her chair, walked around the table to Ellen's side, and placed a document before her. "Please sign here, my dear. Then Mr. Paige can sign. I'll sign as a witness. Sheriff, would you be so kind as to witness their signatures as well?"

"Certainly, be happy to." Frank grunted as he rose from his chair.

Claude announced, "Your signed and witnessed acceptance of the terms of the will become part of the permanent court record. That will conclude the reading of the will. We do, however, have a related matter to discuss, the taxes due."

The room was very quiet. Claude sighed and plowed ahead. "There is a tax lien on the property, approximately $60,000. That's several years of property taxes and penalties in arrears. That's one reason why the sheriff is here. You may not know that in Louisiana, the Parish Sheriff is also the Tax Collector. I know you have questions, but please let me explain. Then, we'll deal with any questions.

"First of all, my law firm is handling this probate case at the request of the court, because the attorney of record, Mr. Perry Wilkerson, is not available.

We're doing so *pro bono,* at no cost. So, you need not expect a bill for our services.

"My dear friend, Perry Wilkerson, was one of the founding partners in this firm. Many years ago, Maude Delafaire engaged Perry as her attorney of record, and he handled many things on her behalf. About four years ago, Perry left the firm and began a solo practice, taking a number of clients, including Maude, with him. He spent a considerable amount of time in New Orleans, where he had previously practiced law."

Miss Mavis was looking decidedly uncomfortable.

"Miss Mavis," asked Claude, "could I please trouble you to arrange for coffee or tea for everyone?"

"Of course, please excuse me." She gratefully accepted that duty, and slipped from the room.

Claude did not resume until she had departed. "Three years ago, Maude Delafaire had an incident with a minor fire in the kitchen at her home, and subsequently went into an assisted living facility. She gave Perry her *power of attorney* and limited access to her financial assets. He was to maintain her property and investment interests."

The look on Mark's face was growing darker as Claude continued.

"What no one knew at the time was that Perry had developed a gambling problem and was exhausting his own personal resources—"

"So, he ripped off his clients?" Mark interrupted, a scowl harshening his tone. "And that included our Aunt Maude?"

Claude's pain was obvious. "Sadly, yes, he took advantage of his clients, to include Maude Delafaire, apparently to pay off gambling debts. In Maude's case, he used funds that were intended to pay the annual property taxes. She was never the wiser, no doubt assuming that all was well. He never told her, or anyone else, otherwise."

Mark was obviously steaming. "How could something like this go unnoticed? Surely unpaid annual property taxes are a *flag*?"

Sheriff Tatum stood. "I'll answer Mr. Paige, if you don't mind, Claude."

The attorney shrugged and deferred to the sheriff.

"It takes months to manually collate the annual incoming property tax payments. We are not computerized; we have to do it by hand, and that's just with two part-time tax clerks in my office. So, figure six to eight months to confirm a nonpayment or an overdue payment, and then 120 days after the late notice is served for the taxpayer to request consideration for an extension. Pretty soon you're close to a year past due.

"If an attorney gets involved and requests an extension citing extenuating circumstances, a delay of up to twelve months can be granted. That delay can be extended or renewed by the court. Now you can easily be in the neighborhood of thirty months past the original due date.

"This is not unusual in an agrarian region; farmers can lose their primary crop and find themselves in tax arrears for years. In this case, Perry kept filing for extensions citing 'medical expenses' as the extenuating circumstances."

Mark was not deterred. "As I understand the law, he is still liable. The state bar would surely take action; it's clearly an ethical violation, if not a criminal act! I would think disbarment and restitution would be required immediately! He's clearly open to civil liability! This is just outrageous!"

The room grew painfully quiet.

Ellen asked, "What aren't you telling us? Where is Perry Wilkerson now? As Mark points out, isn't he ultimately accountable for this?"

Sheriff Tatum and Claude exchanged pained grimaces and glanced at Miss Mavis's vacant seat. Claude nodded, and the sheriff spoke softly. "We believe Perry Wilkerson is dead. His car was found in Lake Pontchartrain near Mandeville about six months ago. His body has never been recovered."

The mood in the room was now more somber.

Not quite knowing why, but sensing the appropriateness of the sentiment, Ellen said, "I'm sorry for your loss."

Claude and Frank shared a knowing glance, mutely acknowledging Ellen's perceptiveness.

"We both grew up with him," Claude admitted. "It was a terrible blow. And as you can imagine, we have no wish to exacerbate the situation in which you, as heirs, find yourselves. Neither the parish nor the state has the option to waive the back taxes; they still must be paid or the property faces seizure, forfeiture, and subsequent auction on the courthouse steps to recover the unpaid taxes. Of course, there is always the option of selling the property; it is worth considerably more than the outstanding tax debt, and there would be a substantial residual."

"Not happening," Ellen announced firmly, surprised at the strength of her heartfelt conviction.

"I see." Claude glanced at a document, cleared his throat, and continued. "The rest of Maude Delafaire's liquid resources were placed in an interest bearing account designed to meet her financial requirements as a resident of the assisted living facility. Perry did not have access to that account, but the facility did. That account has been severely depleted by Maude's extended residency, but it is not exhausted. A bit over $12,000 remains, which is to be held in Miss Ellen Doyle's name. You'll need to meet with Mr. Foster at the bank. Of course, I'll be happy to arrange and facilitate the meeting."

Sheriff Tatum, still standing, added, "As new owners through inheritance, you're entitled by parish law to a one hundred twenty day period of adjustment, to arrange new title, insurance, any other related details, and of course, to address the tax issue. If you can pay the full amount before that time, the tax lien will be lifted. If not, the legal process that culminates in an auction proceeds. I do not have the authority to stop it; only the court can grant any delay."

An uncomfortable silence descended upon the room. Only the steady ticking of the stately grandfather clock marked the passage of dispirited melancholy seeping through the minds of those present.

A soft knocking at the door heralded the return of Miss Mavis with a tray of drinks. Everyone took a few moments to compose themselves as they sipped.

The secretary turned to Claude and gestured to the stack of documents that comprised the Delafaire file.

He nodded. "Yes, please, we're done with these. You can prepare the originals for the court, and appropriate copies for the clients and our files."

She scooped up the paperwork and disappeared from the room.

Claude stood. "If I could have your attention once again, please. We have another matter before us. But first, I would like to volunteer my legal services, and the resources of my firm, for any matter you deem appropriate, at no fee, of course. While neither I, nor my firm, bears any legal liability or direct responsibility, I do feel a certain moral responsibility. I'd like to help if I can."

He turned to Mark. "Mr. Paige, I can sense your frustration. You're an attorney, admitted to the bar in New York, but you're not a member of the Louisiana bar, so to a large degree your hands will be tied. So, let me help you, if you'll allow.

"The practice of law in Louisiana is a unique blend of English common law and the Napoleonic codes, further spiced by centuries of multicultural influences like old Spanish land grants, French allocations, and displaced Acadian heritage. Spend some time in our offices and we'll get you prepared for admission to the bar here in Louisiana. If you sincerely want to be an asset to your family, be a fully capable asset."

To the others in the room, he said, "If you would retain my services, please advise me so, now. Otherwise, in the interest of privacy, and in compliance with the rules of ongoing investigations, I must step out of the room while Sheriff Tatum speaks to you further."

Ellen looked to Mark and Millie; both nodded affirmatively.

She stood and addressed Claude, "Mr. Fornier, we accept your offer. You are now engaged as our family's legal counsel. Please stay."

"Excellent, thank you. Please, Miss Doyle, resume your seat." Claude nodded to Frank. "Sheriff, you have the floor."

"Thank you, Claude." Frank paused. "I'll have to ask that whatever you hear today, you keep confidential, because it pertains to an ongoing investigation. We do not usually share such information, but there are certain requirements when someone may be in danger. We have such indications in regard to Miss Doyle. I'll give you a brief synopsis, and Detectives Bassett and Redhawk can answer specific questions. There may be some questions we can't answer; we'll tell you so, should you ask one.

"We believe the traffic accident that injured Miss Doyle was no accident. We believe someone meant to harm, or possibly kill her. The driver of the taxi was killed. The truck involved was stolen; and, it turns out the taxi was stolen as well. We have identified three male suspects, one of whom is deceased, the driver of the stolen taxi. The other two, we believe, were in the truck and were injured. We don't know the extent of their injuries, nor do we know where they are now. We believe the fire at the scene was not caused by the collision, but was deliberately set using an accelerant. We think the perpetrators were unaware that Miss Doyle had been ejected from the vehicle. Detectives Redhawk and Bassett found her some distance away.

"While she was recovering in the hospital, there was an incident involving an IV sedative flow increase that may or may not have been deliberate. Beyond that, we believe there was clearly another attempt to harm her. A female suspect attempted to inject her with a syringe, via an IV. The suspect was not successful thanks to Detectives Redhawk and Bassett, and some other law enforcement officers. However, that suspect got away."

Millie gasped, one hand covering her open mouth and the other grasping Ellen's wrist. Eyes narrowed, Ellen stared straight ahead, her lips drawn in a grim line. Stacy leaned forward and knit her brows in determination. Mark forestalled her from making any comment by squeezing her elbow, as the sheriff continued.

"We've had constant security around Miss Doyle while she was hospitalized. There have been no more attempts to harm her, so our security coverage has loosened somewhat. We will likely curtail any further active coverage, unless something else happens. We will be around, and of course, you can call us anytime. Okay, now, any questions?"

Of course, there were many questions. Most were to clarify details already disclosed. Frank could answer those; but some he had to toss to his detectives.

Mark asked, "What was in the syringe in the hospital attempt?"

Sgt. Bassett read from the CSI lab report. "A concoction consisting of 'digitalis, amanita muscaria, mertensia virginica'—that's foxglove, fly agaric, and bluebell. All of which are organic; one is a strong hallucinogenic, and all are poisonous in sufficient quantities. There were some other unidentified elements that stumped the lab. Just to be sure, and to add to their database, a sample was sent to the CDC. They'll attempt further analysis."

Stacy spoke up. "You could find all three in a garden. They're old herbal folk remedies; although I've never heard of them combined. That's certainly strange."

"Well," said Claude after a moment of silence, "if there are no more questions for the moment, allow me to offer my first advice as counsel."

Once he had everyone's attention, he dangled a set of keys. "These are the keys to the Delafaire house and the outer buildings. I suggest that you take Detectives Bassett and Redhawk with you when you inspect the property. It has been secured for three years, although Madeline and Armand Dupree have kept an eye on the place, at Maude Delafaire's specific request."

Claude handed Ellen the keys and remarked, "Oh, by the way, Miss Doyle, you should know that Madeline has Maude's two dogs, Chow Chows, a male and female. Uh, Max and Sophie, as I recall. Anyway, they're yours now as well."

"Oh yes, Madeline told me. What am I supposed to do with two dogs?"

"Oh, don't worry, sweetie!" Millie chuckled. "You've always been good with animals. Are they cute little dogs, you know, like lap dogs?"

"Ha! Not hardly!" Stacy scoffed, her excitement obvious. "They're an ancient Chinese breed; they were used to guard palaces and temples! They're real cool; they look like little bears! Well, they're not that little, actually."

Claude was smiling as well. "Okay, folks, that's all I have. Sheriff, do you have anything else?"

Frank nodded. "Yes, a couple of things. Let's all exchange cell phone numbers. Remember, please call us if anyone feels the least bit threatened. When do you all plan on inspecting the property?"

Ellen shrugged and glanced around the table. "Tomorrow? If that's convenient for everyone, of course."

Sgt. Bassett said, "No problem for me; but it is Detective Redhawk's day off—"

Hawk interrupted his partner, "Actually, it's not a problem, I'll meet y'all there."

"You know how to get there?" Trey probed.

"Sure, I know where it is. Uh, what time?"

Millie spoke up. "Let's say ten-thirty. That'll give me time to inspect the kitchen, especially since there was a fire there once. We can bring some food, have lunch."

"Okay," Ellen quipped, "ten-thirty it is. Sergeant Bassett, will you be meeting us at the hotel? We're not real sure of the directions."

"Sure thing," Trey acknowledged.

Ellen gestured to Claude and asked, "Would you care to join us on our inspection tour, Mr. Fornier?"

"Please, Miss Doyle, call me Claude; I'm your lawyer now! And I wouldn't miss the opportunity to see the estate again. Thank you."

Ellen nodded. "Very well, Claude, but please, call me Ellen."

Claude beamed. "As you wish, Miss Ellen."

Miss Ellen? She had to chuckle, having forgotten that such polite courtesy was as ingrained in the fabric of southern culture as the persistent heat and humidity.

"Okay, Claude. We'll see you in the morning. Sheriff, thank you, I'm sure we'll see you again."

As the family and the detectives filed out of Claude's office, they thanked Miss Mavis for her assistance as well, and bid their good-byes.

THE SHERIFF AND ATTORNEY remained behind. For several moments the only sound in the comfortable silence was the subtle ticking of the stately old clock.

Frank ventured an observation. "You know, Claude, I think our Miss Ellen Doyle may be a quite formidable young lady. I've got a good gut feeling about her."

Claude sighed. "You know *my* gut feelings usually mean I'm hungry. But for some reason, I agree. And I hope we're right, because I have this uneasy sense that something is on the horizon. I hope they can hold on to the farm."

"What do you mean *something?* For her, for somebody else, or just in general?"

"I don't know . . . Nah, it's probably nothing; just forget it. You know, I think I *am* hungry."

THE SECONDHAND BOOKSTORE, *Tomes & Scrolls*, was only a few blocks from the hotel.

The light rain had diminished to a steady drizzle. Had she been fully recovered, Ellen would have considered walking. However, Mark insisted upon driving, so the four of them had gathered in her room.

"I'd forgotten what this climate does to my hair," Millie groaned, standing before the mirror.

Behind her, a brush in hand, Stacy contemplated Millie's unruly curls. "Yeah, it's the humidity, but we can deal with this."

Millie watched her reflection as Stacy pulled her hair back. "Do y'all think we should tell one of the detectives where we're going, just to be safe?"

"I'll do it!" Ellen offered, and speed-dialed Detective Redhawk's number.

In the mirror Millie and Stacy shared a look, nodded to one another, and smiled.

"I think it was sweet that that cute detective gave up his day off," Stacy teased and nudged Millie. "I think he *likes* Ellen, don't you?"

"Oh my, I wouldn't know," Millie retorted. "I suppose we could ask him."

"*Mother!* Stacy, enough! " Ellen spat. *Jeez, what are we, back in high school?*

Hawk answered his phone. "Hello, Ellen."

"Uh, hi . . . How did—?"

"Caller ID. Is everything all right? Are you okay?"

"Oh, yes, of course, everyone's just fine." She suddenly felt guilty for calling him, and a bit embarrassed. "I just called to let you, and Sgt. Bassett, too, uh, both know that we, that is, all four of us, are going to attend a wake for Aunt Maude at the Tomes & Scrolls bookstore this evening. Um, we thought it would be a good idea to let someone know where we were, just in case, you know?" *Omigod, now I'm babbling like a high school girl! Just stop talking!*

"Oh, I see. Well, we certainly do appreciate that."

"Well, um, okay then. So, I guess I'll see you tomorrow?" Ellen winced and gnawed her lower lip. *Oh great! Now how did that sound? Too hopeful? Desperate, or what?*

"Absolutely, ten-thirty at the Delafaire house, or as I probably should say, *your* house."

"Oh, I'm not too sure how I feel about all this just yet. It just doesn't seem right to call it *my house,* well, at least not yet anyway. Besides, it's half Mark's, too."

"Yeah, I think I understand. Tomorrow things may fall a little more into place for you; at least I hope so."

"Thank you, that's sweet . . ." *Sweet? OMG! What's wrong with me?*

Ellen finally noticed that she was the center of attention in the hotel room. Millie, Stacy, and Mark were all grinning broadly at her. She blushed uncontrollably.

"Um, well, I see I'm holding everyone up here, so I've got to go. Thanks again, Detective. Have a nice evening."

"You too, Ellen. 'Bye now."

As she ended the call, Stacy smirked and said, "Aw, wasn't that swee—"

“No! Don’t even!” Ellen cried out with a scowl, waving a warning finger at her friend.

It didn’t work; they both erupted in laughter.

CH 9

TOMES & SCROLLS huddled in the midst of the block; a weatherworn stone and brick edifice that had spent a patient century observing LaBorde gradually evolve. Over the years the old post and beam construction had sheltered a warehouse, a general store, and a succession of small businesses before its latest incarnation as a bookshop. To either side of the tall and ornately carved wooden doors, large multipaned windows softly glowed with welcoming saffron light. The other buildings on the street were lifeless and dark; the business day done, the proprietors were long gone, snug in their homes.

More than a few cars were parked close to the bookstore, metallic moths drawn to the beckoning glow. The drizzle had paled to a mere mist as dusk deepened and shadows pooled. Mark found a parking place close by; so, the foursome shared two umbrellas for the short walk to the shop.

Before they could ascend the steps, Madeline swung open a smaller door set within one of the massive double doors. "Ah, welcome one and all! These large doors are not generally used, although they do open. We use this modest portal as the main entrance. Please, come in and get out of the weather."

The shop was much deeper than it appeared from the street, its width somewhat narrow by comparison; although that too was deceptive. A large oval counter on the left held a small cash register and computer workstation. Facing the large front windows, two long library tables supported carefully stacked books and periodicals artfully displayed for sale.

Rows of bookcases stood in ranks between the towering bookshelves lining the sidewalls. Rolling ladders accessed the uppermost shelves.

A series of wrought iron chandeliers hung suspended from soaring rafters. The glow of their incandescent bulbs was softened and diffused by small tapered shades the hue of old parchment. In the rear, a large loft could be accessed by a broad staircase that twisted upon itself at a wide landing.

Madeline kept up a steady narrative as they walked toward the quiet voices and snatches of muffled laughter that beckoned from the rear of the quaint bookshop.

"Armand, my husband, delights in indulging me," she confided, her eyes sparkling. "This little store is my hobby, passion, and vocation. I just really love books. So, years ago we acquired this old building, and then bought the bookcase stacks from the school board when the old local high school was demolished in order to build the new school. We even got the oval librarian's desk and use it as the checkout counter."

"Oh my gosh!" Millie exclaimed. "I went to that high school, the one they tore down."

Ellen sighed wistfully as she strolled past laden shelves imagining how many student hands had tugged books free, and innocently returned them too frequently to the wrong shelves. *I know I did that often enough.* Smiling to herself, she savored the musty ambiance and the comfortable sense of familiarity.

A large stone fireplace dominated the rear wall, where a small cheery fire flickering in a large grate sent dancing shadows across a generous hearth.

Two tables, heavy with food and drink, were illuminated by sets of pharmacy lamps of bright brass. Each table stood to either side of the hearth area, surrounded by an eclectic collection of side chairs.

A fair number of people milled about, conversing easily while sipping cocktails, wine, or beer. The comfortable buzz of light conversation was punctuated by the occasional hearty laugh and guffaw. A pause floated across the gathering as those assembled noticed, and began welcoming the newest arrivals.

"Ah, here he is now." Madeline pointed as her husband strode down an aisle to greet them.

"Armand Dupree at your service, my friends." The slight man with bushy gray eyebrows displayed a broad and welcoming smile. "Please, make yourselves comfortable. What can I get you to drink?"

The evening was indeed pleasant. Armand and Madeline played the gracious hosts, assuring that everyone was well met and comfortable. Guests could snack from clever displays of *finger food*; small sandwiches, cheeses, and sweets.

Madeline and Millie discovered a shared penchant for cooking, and were soon deep into shelves of old cookbooks.

Stacy and Mark found a collection of Audubon prints that drew the attention of a local naturalist, who was only too happy to discuss the local flora and fauna.

Ellen found that everyone had something nice to say about Maude. Most in attendance seemed to be faculty members from the university, Ellen was quite comfortable with these friends of her aunt. She found their conversations stimulating. However, she felt like she still didn't know that much more about her great aunt.

Leaving Millie temporarily engrossed in a nineteenth century Cajun cookbook, Madeline sidled up to Ellen who was standing near the hearth. "Have you given any thought to your dogs?"

"Oh my gosh! I completely forgot! Are they here?" Ellen cast about anxiously.

"Goodness, no!" Madeline laughed. "They're at our home, outside of town, and they're just fine. But I think they're a bit anxious to go home. We take them with us when we go to check on the property. To be honest, I think they're reluctant to leave. When do you take possession of the property?"

"Tomorrow morning at ten-thirty, we're supposed to inspect the place. Is there anything we should know?"

"Well, let's see . . . The electricity is on. You'll have to contact the power company to have the account put in your name. As far as I know, the well is fine. The house and buildings are kept locked." Madeline pursed her lips. "That should be about it. I'm sure everything will be just fine."

"Um, Madeline, would you and your husband like to come out to the house tomorrow with us? Perhaps you could bring the dogs?"

Madeline grinned. "Why that's just a wonderful idea! Thank you so much! We'd be delighted to bring your puppy dogs home."

Ellen just rolled her eyes and smiled.

Madeline leaned toward her. "Don't worry, my dear, I think Max and Sophie will surprise you."

Turning Ellen toward the tables of food, Madeline declared, "There are some homemade chocolate treats on the dessert tray. I will be simply crushed if you do not sample my wares, young lady. Off you go!"

Just as Ellen sampled something chocolate from the sweets tray, *actually the third something* she shamefully admitted to herself, Armand approached her.

"Are you finding this affair to your liking?"

"Oh yes! Thank you, Dr. Dupree; this is all very kind of you." Ellen's sweeping gesture included the entire assembly. She noticed a trace of chocolate on the tip of her finger, and discreetly licked it off. *Never let excellent chocolate go to waste.*

"Not at all, my dear Ellen. Please, call me Armand. Your aunt was a very dear friend to us. This is the least we could do." The diminutive professor smiled, his eyes twinkling as he leaned in to whisper, "In fact, it wouldn't surprise me one iota if she was among us right now, wondering where I put the sipping bourbon; she liked the good stuff, you know."

For just an instant, Ellen's eyes widened and she almost looked about, but Armand's humor was practically contagious. She found herself laughing along with him.

"Ah, now here's someone you simply must meet. Ellen Doyle, may I present my esteemed colleague and dear friend, Dr. Isaac Johnson, head of the De-Lorme University Astrophysics Department?"

Ellen shook hands with one of the biggest men she'd ever seen. Dr. Johnson was massive, easily six and one-half feet tall with an enormous set of shoulders; and, when he spoke it was in the softest of bass tones highlighted with the lilt of New Orleans.

"Delighted to make your acquaintance, Miss Doyle. If you'll forgive my impertinence, I believe you know my wife; she's your doctor." Dr. Isaac Johnson positively beamed when he mentioned his wife. He nudged Armand playfully. "You didn't spoil my surprise, Armand, did you?"

"Nope, Zack, I didn't tell her. I wouldn't spoil your surprise." Armand's bushy eyebrows rose as if in indignation; but, he couldn't pull it off. Soon they were both laughing.

"Of course," countered Ellen, "Dr. Latrice-Johnson! Oh, I think she's wonderful. Is she here this evening, Dr. Johnson?"

"Please, call me Zack. And I agree that she's wonderful! But sadly she's not here tonight. She's *on-call;* she's already back at the hospital. It's possible she may join us later."

"Well, I'm sorry that she was called away. And please, call me Ellen."

She was completely at ease with Armand and Zack, who were quite obviously the best of friends. She remembered the easy rapport and familiarity between Dr. Latrice-Johnson and Madeline Dupree at the hospital, when Madeline was distributing books.

Oh, the book . . .

"Oh, Dr. Dupree," she began, and received an instant scowl from him. "Forgive me, *Armand*." She winced cutely, earning his smile. "I've been reading your book, *Old Blood,* and I've been finding it quite interesting."

Both men went quiet, glanced at one another, and stared into their drinks.

Ellen sensed the obvious change in atmosphere but decided to press on a bit. "It's a fascinating theory that evolution is responsible for a number of curious branches on the human tree, but in this day and age of DNA analysis and testing, I'd think you could actually prove or disprove at least some aspects of such a theory."

She had hit a mark; Armand stared at her with renewed interest. That encouraged her to continue.

"And as for alternative realities, every science fiction fan understands the concept. Multiple dimensions, warping space, even time travel gets serious attention these days. Science-based television shows offer plausible theories for these sorts of things all the time. I guess my point is, well, have you considered publishing a revised or updated second edition perhaps, taking full advantage of current technology and general popular knowledge? Who knows? Maybe you could have a *best seller* on your hands."

Armand and Zack just stood there, stunned.

Armand recovered first. "Ellen, did Madeline show you our loft? It's quite nice and has its own fireplace; and of course, some very comfortable armchairs and sofas. Why, even our erstwhile and ever erudite book club, *The Middle Earth Society*, meets up there occasionally. I suspect that many of our guests will be leaving in the next half hour or so; if you could stay, we could reconvene upstairs and continue this conversation in more relaxed surroundings. I'll mention it to Madeline, whom I'm sure would be delighted if the rest of your family were to attend as well."

He turned to his hulking friend. "Zack, you'll join us?"

"Of course, if you think it wise?"

"I do," Armand said firmly. "After all, she's asked; she deserves to know."

"Very well," Zack nodded. "You play host for a while and I'll slip upstairs and make preparations. Miss Ellen, until then?"

Zack gathered a few bottles and glasses, and with a grace that belied his size, slipped silently up the broad stairs.

Armand chuckled and directed Ellen's attention to the front of the shop. Madeline and Millie were laughing as they walked back toward the gathering, their arms loaded with more cookbooks. And behind them came Dr. Latrice-Johnson, laughing as well.

Ellen was delighted, and called out, "Doctor!"

To her chagrin, a dozen heads turned in her direction. The room burst into spontaneous laughter.

Dr. Latrice-Johnson reached her blushing patient in time for both to hear Armand's stage whisper.

"Ah, that's the problem with such an august assemblage; everybody's a doctor!"

Of course, that comment brought more laughter, as Armand shuffled away theatrically shrugging his shoulders.

Smiling broadly, Dr. Latrice-Johnson took Ellen's hands and said, "Armand never gets tired of that old joke; but it's true, and suitably confusing. So, when we're among friends, please call me Marie."

Ellen smiled. "Thank you, Doctor—oops, Marie."

Marie gave her a careful look that Ellen realized was a quick professional assessment of the state of her health.

"How are you feeling? Any tiredness, headaches, dizziness or loss of appetite?" inquired Marie.

"I was a little tired earlier today, but I took a nap this afternoon and feel good." Ellen grinned. "And as for appetite, the chocolate desserts Madeline made are, well, just *amazing!*"

Marie laughed. "Aha! Chocolate? Where?"

Arm in arm, they were off to the snacks.

ON THE OTHER SIDE OF the gathering, Mark successfully disentangled Stacy from the eager and earnest naturalist, whose knowledge of the works of Audubon seemed annoyingly endless, and guided her deeper into the stacks, on a thin pretext regarding a search for some obscure book.

Stacy playfully tugged his sleeve, pulled him toward some shelves marked *Erotica* and coyly asked, "Is this the section you're looking for?"

Mark's face went crimson, and he sputtered, unable to form a complete sentence.

Stacy erupted in laughter, mercifully pulling him away as he found his voice.

"Uh, no, not exactly, um, now I've completely forgotten!" He was laughing as well.

She cocked her head, blowing blonde bangs from her eyes. "Do you really like New York? I mean compared to here? I just love this place; it's so green and earthy! The people are so nice and friendly. I like the pace. No one's in a rush. I think it's so much better than Los Angeles, at least for me. There's no traffic, no smog, and no *plastic people*. Do you know what I mean?"

Mark paused and seriously considered that perception for a moment. "Yeah, I think I do. This place will always be special to me. I grew up here; I didn't move to New York until I was in my teens. Don't get me wrong; I like New York. I mean, I work there, in the city, but I spent a lot of time upstate, too. I like the seasons. However, it can get really cold in the winter.

"But to be honest, it can get really hot here in the summer; and the humidity can be brutal. There are seasons here, too. They just tend to be variations of summer. In fact, my dad used to joke that *there's the cool, then warming up to summer, then high summer, then mild summer, and finally some cool comes around again.* That's not too far off the mark."

Stacy shrugged. "In Los Angeles lately it's been more like rain, warm, then hot, drought, brush fires, then too much rain, mudslides; it can be a real mess. Then the cycle, more erratic than not, begins again. I don't think Mother Nature intended that as seasons. We get the Santa Ana winds, the effects of *El Nino* and *La Nina*; these are not kind to gardeners. You know fruit and vegetable production is a major deal in California; water is always an issue. Sorry, I'm rambling."

"No, you're not. You're just passionate about nature; you appreciate it."

That clearly surprised her. "I guess I am, uh, and I do. Thank you."

"You're welcome. Well, it appears that I'm now a property owner in this lovely garden spot, so I'll no doubt be spending more time here. Perhaps you'd like to visit, of course in the interest of seasonal comparisons and cultural exchange?" He smiled, feigning a mock leer.

Tilting her head, hand to her throat, she purred in the dulcet tones of the antebellum south, "Why suh, ah'd be so 'onored to comply and accept y'all's kind and considerate invitation." She leaned into him and breathed huskily, "But y'all bes' be careful what y'all wish for now, y' heah?"

With a wink and an impish grin, she twisted away; her bright laugh left spinning in the air, as she disappeared up the aisle.

"Hmm, are you sure you're not from around here?" he called softly after her, his smug grin overwhelming his face.

IN DUE TIME, MOST OF the guests departed, having paid their respects to Maude's family.

Armand banked the coals in the lower level fireplace as Madeline ushered Ellen, Mark, Stacy, and Millie upstairs to the quaint loft. Marie was already there with Zack, who had a modest fire crackling in the loft's small fireplace. A pair of sofas and a number of overstuffed easy chairs were pulled up in a cozy semicircle. Fresh drinks were poured all around, and everyone settled in quite comfortably.

Madeline swept her hand about the loft, careful not to spill any of her wine. "Cozy, isn't it? We frequently hold the meetings of The Middle Earth Society, our book discussion club, up here. Maude often joined us; she sometimes referred to us as the 'think tank'. We would discuss anything actually, not just books. As it happens, Ellen has asked some interesting questions regarding a particular book. So, with that as an appropriate segue, Armand, my dear, you have the floor."

Armand noted the knowing look his wife bestowed upon him, cleared his throat, and slipped unconsciously into his stylized lecture mode.

"Very well then, let us begin with the book, *Old Blood*, published over thirty years ago. When I wrote it, it was purely an exercise in speculative theory; of course, it could be argued that all theories are speculative at some point. Nevertheless, as a cultural anthropologist, I had observed certain cross-cultural consistencies within myth and folklore. That is to say that there seemed to be common beliefs among diverse human cultures of coexistence with other humanoid species.

"Permit me to explain what may appear to be a tangential point, but I assure you is quite relevant.

"Coexistence with other humanoid species is indeed possible. Science has provided ample forensic evidence to prove it. For example, we know that our direct ancestor, *Homo sapiens*, shared the planet contemporaneously with *Homo neanderthalensis*. Both species can, no doubt, trace their lineage to a common ancestor in the genus *Homo;* but, over time, each took a different evolutionary path. Consequently, we have two humanoid species existing at the same time, in roughly the same environment. Each developed a culture and assuredly had contact with each other. However, only one survived.

"Why *H. neanderthalensis,* Neanderthal Man, apparently did not survive and *H. sapiens,* early Modern Man, did, had been traditionally attributed to certain adaptations, or beneficial evolutionary mutations, that led to things like enhanced adaptation skills in response to environmental changes, more comprehensive group dynamics, and perhaps the development of more articulate language. Presumably early Modern Man was thus better able to flourish, whereas Neanderthal Man simply failed to adapt and subsequently became extinct.

"Today, of course, the prevailing theory, amply supported by considerable mitochondrial DNA evidence, which I personally find eminently more pragmatic and persuasive, suggests that *H. neanderthal* was simply genetically resorbed over a number of generations by *H. sapiens.* In time this led to the species to which we belong, *H. sapiens sapiens,* Modern Man . . . Oh, forgive me, I digress.

"Now, as to cross-cultural consistencies within myth and folklore," Armand paused for a long sip of wine, "we must examine the cultures.

"All cultures at some point try to explain that which is, for them, the unexplainable. *H. sapiens* consistently demonstrated two characteristic traits, which could arguably be deemed behavioral because they prompted man to take overt action in order to understand and comprehend the unexplainable, *curiosity and creativity*.

"In the simplest terms, when man would experience curiosity, he would try to learn, to understand. If his efforts fell short of full comprehension, he would consider what he did know and extrapolate creatively—he would craft an explanation that fit with his current *world view* or environment. Thus, we have the genesis of myth, folklore, and even magic in a cultural sense."

Armand sipped a bit more wine. "Allow me a tangential diversion for the moment, as it will be pertinent later. *Magic,* what is it?

"Human cultures tend to agree on the following definition: magic is the manipulation of energy and/or matter by a means not yet understood. If this were a class, I'd say *take note, you may see this material again*.

"There is an old adage, frequently cited in various forms by some very wise people, that holds that any sufficiently advanced technology may appear to be some sort of magic to the uninformed or uncomprehending. In other words, anything observed for the first time, but not understood in a given culture, was perhaps considered *magic*, or the appropriate equivalent terminology of that culture. Firearms were considered magic by cultures upon their first exposures, so were cameras, telephones, aircraft, television, and so on. It's simply magic until fully explained and understood.

"Everything in our reality follows a set group of proven physical laws, the Laws of Physics. Physicists generally hold to a generic belief that essentially everything that *can* be understood, eventually *will* be understood, no longer unexplainable, no longer considered magic. Now bear in mind that both the level of education of the observer and his reference point, or perspective, do tend to dictate his actual perception and subsequent level of comprehension.

"Now, let's consider evolution, and genetic mutations. In simple terms, mutation is the natural method of evolution. Some mutations are successful and flourish, thereby altering the standard definition of a species. If the mutation is significant enough, it might qualify as a new classification within the genus altogether. On the other hand, some mutations fail and face imminent or eventual extinction. We know that mankind has evolved, that is to say, experienced a number of mutations in the evolutionary process. In fact, we are still, and will always be, in that process.

"Decades ago, I and some colleagues began collecting and collating data on common and similar characterizations in cultural folklore and myth from over a thousand known cultures. Now, I know that may not sound like a very large sampling considering that we have ample evidence of many more diverse cultures, especially since the last Ice Age, some ten thousand to twelve thousand years ago. But documented cultures, those with some sort of self-initiated record or history tend to come much later. So, we selected samples from the last six thousand years that offered a recorded history or a rich oral tradition; although in some cases, it was both.

"We found much that was to be expected; a series of gods to whom celestial and/or terrestrial phenomena were attributed. By that I mean weather, the seasons, and any local geological aberrations, volcanoes, and so forth, and, of course, the spirits or ghosts of the dead.

"However, what really surprised us, in terms of similarities of folklore and mythology, was the frequency and scope of humanoid beings that were believed to coexist, yet were *once removed* from the cultures in question. Even taken in context, that struck us as significant.

"The only differences in the general descriptions were the names of these different classes of humanoids. We realized, of course, this was the result of the inherent language diversity among the cultures under study. This was a consistent problem; the literal translations and subsequent correlations could be at issue. Consequently, we found ourselves using the familiar European terminologies or the equivalent English translations; elves, dwarves, fairies, nymphs, and such. By no means was the use of these terms ethnocentric, but rather merely convenient.

"While many are somewhat familiar with Western folklore and myths, Far Eastern folklore and mythology is just as rich; Japanese Yokai, Chinese Yaoguai, Asian demons, etc. African myth and folklore was equally varied, and often more likely to be an aspect of firm contemporary belief.

"And lest we forget, there were those humanoids of more ominous natures; vampires, skin-walkers, shape-shifters, werewolves, ghouls, goblins, and the like. Almost every culture sampled made some mention of variations of these types of beings, as well. It was no great task to find something similar or reasonably equivalent in their respective folklore, myths, or legends."

Ellen nodded. "I can remember taking a philosophy class where we examined common traits of old world religions, and it was surprising how similar some things were. I mean other, um, sorts of beings, not necessarily spirits exactly, or the gods and demigods of Greek and Roman mythology. There are some even among those religions still widely practiced today. I don't just mean the more common angels and devils or demons. For example, Jews and Christians had references to the nephilim and elohim, and Islam had its jinn. I realize that references to these and other lesser known beings have been diminished or trivialized by most organized religions today."

"But Armand," interjected Stacy, "you and your group weren't looking at religions exactly. You were looking at folklore, myths, and legends. And as I recall, most religions tend to ignore, co-opt, or demonize these things. So, what did you do?"

Armand drained his glass; Zack refilled it.

Armand nodded to Stacy. "Good question. We did what scientists always do; we speculated and wrestled with the interpretation of the data. We had to eliminate any preconceived notions, expectations, or bias, and just examine the evidence, ignoring any outside influences, and that included any current religious dogma. We could always look at that later, and make comparisons with earlier versions wherever warranted."

"That makes sense," Stacy agreed.

Armand paused, swirled the wine in his glass, and sighed heavily. "When looking at the evidence through the clarity of pure objectivity and rational logic, we came to realize it was staring us in the face. *What if* . . . "

The loft was deathly quiet, but for the soft crackling of the fire.

"What if these beings existed, as evolutionary mutations that achieved something short of what we would consider exceptional evolutionary success, but nonetheless did not face extinction? Or at least had not become extinct at the time of the folklore's origin?

"Of course, that precipitated debate upon the concept of *exceptional evolutionary success*. If a viable mutation of a species exists, is that not *prima facie* evidence of successful evolution? Or need it be measured in successive generational terms? Well, as you might imagine, we spun our metaphorical wheels for quite a while.

"Some of our colleagues invited a few guests, a biologist, a psychologist, and a medical researcher, to one of our *skull sessions;* and our perspectives were broadened considerably.

"It was fairly well determined that biologically, the premise was possible, perhaps even likely, that these beings, as interesting offshoots from the genetic tree of *H. sapiens*, were essentially human with specific mutations that would tend to culturally separate them from the rest of mankind. The point we hadn't yet explored to any great depth was that these beings could be cross-compatible genetically; after all, they were essentially human and capable of reproduction. Would not the mutation transfer to offspring? Most likely yes, albeit to varying degrees. So, what about potential hybrids or new species?

"That left us with more questions. If they did exist at one time, where were they? Or even more intriguing, if they still exist, where are they? Why has there been no discovery of such a culture, or conclusive forensic evidence of a past culture? Well, we don't really know. Perhaps we have stumbled across something without realizing it.

"It finally dawned upon us that they would have likely been among us for generations, intermingling genetic material and diluting the original mutations, in a very real sense, adding to the rich stew of humanity. Remember what I said about the Neanderthals? Was extinction truly their fate, or rather protracted genetic assimilation?

"Now, keep in mind that we are talking about an evolutionary epoch that may have commenced over ten thousand to twelve thousand years ago, or approximately five hundred to six hundred generations, assuming a twenty year generational standard.

"Our biologist and medical researcher generally agreed that in slightly less than half that time, five thousand years or around three hundred generations, it would be possible for specific genetic strains characterized by specific mutations to have firmly established distinct subsets within the human species, or conversely, be subsumed as recessive traits in the genome.

"Our psychologist proffered that in the case of distinct subsets, it would be typical for such people to associate, to band together in a tribal-like group structure, having limited interaction with those outside the group, ergo, the micro-genesis of a new culture.

"For want of a name, we decided—I'm not sure I remember exactly *how*, although I vaguely recall Maude offering the suggestion—to refer to these groups, these ancestral subsets, as 'Old Blood'.

"Of course, the uniqueness of these groups would slowly change with the parallel evolution of trade or commerce. Over the next five thousand years, or approximately three hundred generations, trade-initiated interaction would lead to integration and intermingling of both cultural aspects and genetics. This tends to support the contention that these mutations would become recessive genetic traits.

"Therefore, many people today could bear traces of 'Old Blood' in their genetic makeup, encoded in their DNA. Now bear in mind that this study was undertaken almost four decades ago, well before the advent of widespread DNA analysis, so we had no way to test our theories. And, in all candor, I'm not entirely certain, given the current technology in use with DNA analysis, that any testing would be conclusive. Marie, could you elucidate?"

Marie put her glass down, and cleared her throat. "Deoxyribonucleic acid, or DNA, has been studied for over sixty years, but only recently has the human genome finally been read. Three billion base pairs are arranged in a double helix held together by hydrogen bonds between pyrimidine and purine bases. These are the instruction packets for protein creation; but we don't fully understand the codes and the nuances of their intended applications. We can identify certain base pairs and associated functions, but we are a long way from full comprehensive analysis and understanding specificity of function and subsequent interrelationships of all three billion.

"DNA analysis at this stage is commonly used for identification and comparison purposes, and as such is approximately ninety-nine percent accurate. The point is that we could not yet identify the specific markers of 'Old Blood' genetic characteristics without unadulterated samples for comparison. In other words, find living examples of beings of the 'Old Blood' and subsequent DNA analysis would establish a baseline, at least for identification purposes, of other persons having similar characteristics."

"Thank you, Marie." Armand paused, raising his index finger. "We ran into another problem. One of our book club members, a medical doctor who also served as a medical ethicist, conferred with our psychologist, and they subsequently pointed out that, in view of human nature, persons with certain mutations may well elect to hide such differences; while others may not. In fact, some might endeavor to maintain the genetic uniqueness, or 'purity', of that mutation.

"This led to discussions related to anticipated patterns of subsequent behavior. For example, some, knowing they are different, might view themselves as *inferior* and expect social rejection. Whereas others may just as well consider themselves to be *superior,* suggesting an entirely different attitude and potential behavior.

"In any case, it is entirely possible that they would prefer isolation from the rest of mankind, and be fearful of exposure. In fact, they could well be quite defensive, perhaps even hostile, in their resistance to integration of any kind, a sort of *lost tribe* deliberately staying hidden from the rest of the world. We found this fascinating premise to actually be a statistically likely scenario. Unfortunately, that brought us back to the original question. If they exist, where are they?"

Millie quipped, "I just saw a special on television about a 'lost tribe' recently discovered in the Amazon. They were even supposed to have been cannibals! So, this sort of thing still happens, doesn't it?"

Mark scoffed. "Ha! Yeah, right. I wouldn't be surprised to learn they decided to let themselves be 'discovered'. Small groups can remain unnoticed and undetected for considerable time, if they work at it, only to come forth when it meets their agenda—or that of someone who stands to profit, like television producers."

"Oh, for crying out loud, Mark!" Stacy scolded, and playfully swatted his arm. "I seriously doubt they were out to hustle some airtime! Don't be so cynical, you—*lawyer,* you!"

To his credit, Mark grinned sheepishly and apologized to Millie. That earned him a quick kiss on the cheek from Stacy. Laughter commenced.

Shaking his head and grinning, Armand refilled his glass and settled into the sofa next to Madeline.

She glanced at his refilled glass and gave him a look of mild disapproval.

He winked at her and turned to his hulking friend.

"Zack, why don't you pick it up from there?"

"Certainly, Armand." Zack stood. "Now, as to *where can we find them?* Well, we currently have two theories. They are among us, having integrated and diluted the 'Old Blood' line, perhaps even hiding in plain sight, or . . . "

Zack and Armand locked eyes for a moment. Armand sighed, closed his eyes, and nodded affirmatively. Zack acknowledged with a trace of a smile and continued.

"Or, they have found a way into another reality, or perhaps, and more likely, a little of all of the above."

"Is another reality possible?" Millie asked.

Zack and Armand exchanged another guarded glance. Armand smiled and nodded once; Zack shrugged and continued.

"Theoretical physics says *yes,* but I'll need to give you a little background. One of my mentors, Dr. Felix Garibaldi, was involved in reviewing an early draft of the 'Old Blood' research. As an astrophysicist he had always held a notion, however whimsical, that some 'vanished civilizations' may have simply departed our universe. Debatable phenomena like the Bermuda Triangle and the Dragon's Triangle had never ceased to fascinate him.

"At the time, a physicist named John Wheeler coined the term 'black hole' to describe a singularity so dense that even light could not escape. Of course, Stephen Hawking would later prove that certain radiation did escape . . . Oops, now *I* digress.

"Anyway, Dr. G, uh, please forgive me, but that's what I called him, and quite a few physicists were intrigued by the possibility that black holes were gateways of a sort to another universe. Later study tended to disabuse them of that notion as surviving the trip was quite problematic. The point is that multiple universe theories are quite common in physics. If we were to further assume that travel between them might be theoretically possible, then how to get there, and back, now that's the problem.

"Without going into a complete physics lesson, just let me say that Dr. G, like most physicists, was fascinated with Einstein's unfinished *theory of everything,* the Holy Grail of physics, the explanation for everything. Sadly, we're not there yet, but we like to think we're close. Of course, the eight hundred pound gorilla in the room is the *moment of origin* of our universe, the *singularity*, the *big bang*. Any *theory of everything* must be able to explain that . . . Oh, sorry, I'm getting off point again.

"There is another theory that references probability within path-integral formalism of quantum field theory, or the *sum-over-histories* concept, formulated by Dr. Richard Feynman, which has been subsequently interpreted to suggest that our universe has more than one single possible history. Multiple histories suggest multiple realities, and it would follow multiple timelines and futures. I know that this sounds confusing, but to a physicist, it makes sense, trust me. By the way, Dr. Feynman won the Nobel, albeit shared, in 1965 for his work in quantum electrodynamics, which led to a new way of thinking about quantum mechanics."

Noting that his audience was beginning to take on that glassy-eyed *thousand yard stare*, Zack said, "Oh, quantum theory—I'm getting too deep, aren't I?"

Four heads nodded as one, while Marie, Madeline and Armand snickered.

"Okay, I'll cut to the chase. Dr. G was an early proponent of what would become known as *string theory* and later *super-string theory* which holds that matter, the basic objects of our universe, are one-dimensional strings that can vibrate at specific frequencies. He sensed a great potential and struggled with this concept for years. Unfortunately he did not live to see the inherent issues resolved. As one of his students, I endeavored to finish his work. Please bear with me for a moment, as I explain. I promise it will be relatively painless.

"Most physicists now accept that there are multiple dimensions, perhaps eleven, of space, of time, even more of mathematical certainty, some of which are infinitesimally small, and, of course, gravity. They further agree that there are essentially five string theories. In the mid-nineties, an eminent physicist, Edward Witten, realized the five string theories were but different limits of a single theory. In fact, when the five string theories are mapped by certain rules called *dualities* and combined in a web of equitable relationships in regard to the eleven dimensions, to include gravity, the results suggest an overall united framework of a single theory called 'Membrane Theory'. It is sometimes referred to as 'Brane theory', or simply 'M-theory'. M-theory strongly suggests that multiple universes are possible, perhaps even probable, thus the *Multiverse.*

"Of course, the challenge is in finding what will be accepted as tangible proof. And in that regard, there have been some promising developments at research facilities like LIGO—"

"Huh? What?" interrupted Mark.

"Oh, sorry." Zack winced, and followed with a smile. "I guess you were *listening* after all. I meant the Laser Interferometer Gravitational-Wave Observatory in Livingston, down in South Louisiana; there's another such facility in Hanford, Washington. They have done some amazing work; in fact, three scientists, Drs. Weiss, Thorne, and Barish were recently awarded a Nobel for their pioneering work in the detection of gravitational waves.

"Furthermore, if certain findings related to theoretical particles like *gravitons* can be corroborated, for example, by the scientists at CERN who have found the *Higgs Boson,* using the Large Hadron Collider on the border of Switzerland and France, we may be much closer to some amazing revelations. Uh, sorry, but I'm not really at liberty to get into any details; much of the relevant data is considered classified for the present. I'm afraid I could jeopardize my clearance."

"That's okay, Zack. I, for one, wouldn't understand the details anyway," Ellen assured the chagrined astrophysicist. "Let's get back to the good part. Now, assuming other universes exist, how would one go there, and hopefully, return?"

"Now that's the real question," mused Zack, as he swirled the untouched wine in his glass, "isn't it?

"We are in an area of speculation, but it has been suggested that the membrane that is our universe touches other membranes, other universes, at various locations and times. Try to think of the membrane as a cylindrical curve, in fact, think of it as a torus, a doughnut shape, perhaps somewhat lumpy. Imagine it in a bag with other doughnuts, making contact here and there as this cosmic bag is jostled about by the inherent expansion of these universes. If the collision is sufficiently violent, a great deal of energy might be released, perhaps a viable explanation for the *singularity,* the *big bang,* and the birth of a new universe. On the other hand, membrane contact might be quite gentle or sticky; they might softly bounce or adhere, perhaps even be drawn to each other under the right circumstances. At each point of contact, it may be possible that matter and energy could be passed from one to another. This suggests that travel from one membrane to another, from one universe to another, is possible.

"So how does this relate to the 'Old Blood' subsets, or tribes, if you prefer? Consider that many people hold that modern man commonly uses about ten to thirty percent of his estimated *brainpower*, or focused *problem solving* energy, in a given circumstance. I readily admit this is a gross oversimplification, but bear with me. The truth is that we understand very little, comparatively speaking, about the human brain in relation to the process of thought. Right, Marie?"

Marie gave a resigned nod from the sofa and explained. "All right, I've heard that 'ten to thirty percent' range a lot, and it's often misinterpreted. Let me be clear; we use one hundred percent of our brains to function as living creatures. But how we use our brainpower in problem solving is conceptually vague by comparison. We know a great deal about which areas of the brain control certain functions, but our current knowledge base is minuscule compared to what we have yet to learn.

"For example, if a part of the brain is somehow damaged, let's say some neural pathways are interrupted or blocked, there have been cases where new pathways are grown, think of a detour around the damage, and certain compromised functions are restored. We can only speculate and theorize at the dynamics involved here. At one time it was believed that nerve tissue once damaged could not heal, not regenerate. Now we know that sometimes it can, but we really don't yet fully understand how or why.

"We strive to understand the process of thought and surmise that it is an electrochemical and biological miracle that we have yet to fully comprehend."

"I have to ask," interrupted Stacy, "what does this have to do with finding these multiple universes?"

"Excellent question, young lady," Zack declared. "And very well timed, I might add. Now let us suppose an evolutionary mutation occurred within the physiology of the brain that allowed certain individuals, or related groups, to use more or different parts of the brain to somehow sense these M-theory contact points, perhaps even pass through from one universe to another. That would offer potential explanations for a host of heretofore unexplained disappearances, would it not?"

Zach grinned at the four open, yet speechless, mouths before him. Armand and Madeline sat there smirking. Marie sipped her wine and stared into her glass.

Madeline gently patted Ellen on her knee. "Didn't I tell you we have very interesting discussions up here?"

Ellen was a bit stunned. Millie looked a little confused. Mark was scowling under a furrowed brow, but Stacy wouldn't let him brood.

Grabbing his arm, she squealed, "That is so cool! Now that's an adventure worth having! I'd want to go just to see the difference between the universes."

Zack smiled. "There might not be too much difference. It's just as likely you would find yourself on another Earth. Well, at least the geography and topography might be the same; but as for anything else, like its history, or even the laws of physics in that universe, who knows?"

"Now hold on a minute." Mark stood. "I want to be sure I understand what I'm hearing. These other humanoid beings that are common in folklore, myth, and legend may essentially be mutated human beings, who just evolved differently, and either blended back into the human race as we know it today, or manage to somehow hide in plain sight, or left our universe through some sort of membrane and went into another universe, or maybe a combination of these scenarios? Have I got the gist of it?"

Armand and Zack exchanged glances, looked to Mark, and nodded affirmatively.

"And you have no evidence to support this claim?" Mark was definitely sounding like a lawyer.

"On the contrary," rumbled Zack, "*evidence*, as you put it, may be forthcoming at any time. I'd be happy to show you the math that supports the physics—"

"Please, don't bother," Mark interrupted. "I wouldn't understand it." His hands to his chest, he added, "I mean no disrespect, but I'm just skeptical by nature, and a lawyer by training." Jabbing his index finger into his open palm, he rationalized, "Now, give me something concrete, something I could put before a judge and jury and perhaps you'll persuade me. But, convince me? I don't think so. However, I must admit the concept is at least entertaining."

Armand shrugged and smiled. "Oh, we take no offense, Mark. We're *academics*. We argue theories and defend positions all the time. We savor healthy debate and controversy, which always seems to follow whenever we publish our work."

Zack nodded in agreement. "Remember that theories are by their very nature dynamic rather than static, morphing with any changes that new information or interpretations thereof might suggest. For example, lately I've been studying some recently published papers dealing with *dark energy* and *dark matter.* I don't yet know whether or not these concepts will have any bearing on some of the theories we've been discussing this evening, but it's entirely possible that they could."

"Zack, might I suggest that we not go down the *dark energy/dark matter* path tonight?" Armand cautioned. "I suspect we've already given our guests quite a bit to digest."

The astrophysicist grinned and nodded. "Yes, of course. I guess it is a bit of a *rabbit-hole.*"

Marie chuckled and tugged her husband back down on the couch next to her.

Mark shook his head, sighing in mock surrender, and resumed his seat next to Stacy.

"Speaking of digestion," Madeline began.

"Doughnuts?" Stacy interjected, grabbing Mark's hand. "Somehow, now I want a doughnut, or two!"

Madeline laughed. "Well, I have a pound cake with lemon sauce. Will that do? Now, who'd like a piece?"

A number of hands went up; and Millie rose to help Madeline serve the cake.

"Wait a minute, Armand, I get it," declared Ellen, her mind still on the speculative discussion. "I mean I understand what you and Zack are saying, in general. But this brings me back to my original question; why not publish a revised and updated second edition of your book and take advantage of the state of current technologies, you know, like DNA, to prove or disprove your theories? Even if it were offered as pure speculation, Mark is right, it would certainly be entertaining!"

Everyone paused, awaiting Armand's answer. He looked at Zack and Marie, and then to Madeline.

His discomfort evident, his wife gave him a sad smile and the briefest of nods.

Finally, staring into his empty glass, Armand sighed.

"Because you see, Maude asked us not to."

CH 10

TWO FIGURES MATERIALIZED from the darkness, on opposite sides of the solitary cone of light. Salidar stepped forth still wearing his suit and bowed with practiced flourish before a frowning Lady Diere.

Her dour countenance considered him for a long moment as he held his low posture with an effortless grace. She could sense his growing confidence; she resented that he should feel such ease in her presence. Begrudgingly, she accepted that she still needed him, however distasteful she might find that fact. She masked her pique with a façade of cultured indifference, and deigned to notice him.

"You may speak."

"Your servant, m'lady," he oozed as he rose from the bow. "As you have commanded, so it was done. M'lord George has been informed to hold himself in readiness for your summons, and perhaps that of the Council, as you instructed."

She gently tugged at the long sleeve of her black and silver gown, smoothing an imperceptible wrinkle in the ebony fabric at her wrist. Cocking her head, she examined his face. "You learned more. Continue."

"Indeed, m'lady," Salidar agreed, daring to risk a small smile. "M'lord George has moved his 'base of operations' to the casino on the Indian Reservation near LaBorde. One of his minion companies has gained control of an outstanding debt, a *mortgage.* He intends to secure offices there, and keep his efforts secret, but of course, not from you, m'lady."

This news was a surprise to her; but she was loath to let him see that.

"Additionally, m'lady, he has taken on a *companion*, whom he characterizes as a *bodyguard,* a tall female called *Ling*. I sensed that there is a great deal more to this woman than meets the eye. I believe her to be quite dangerous."

That he offered his unsolicited opinion would normally anger her, but she held her ire in check. She knew there was more to learn from him. She let her gaze grow glaringly intense, willing him to divulge whatever he knew.

"M'lady, if I may?" He gestured with empty hands and a slight bow.

"You have been quite observant. I am pleased." She slowly walked around him, in quiet thought. She faced him once more, and nodded her assent. "Proceed."

"May it please you, m'lady. While he said nothing, I got the impression that m'lord George harbored some resentment at being summoned, as if he were sufficiently competent to effectively transit here under his own power, perhaps thinking that an *invitation* was more to his liking than a summons. So, I wondered, is his blood so strong, or his craft skills sufficient, that he could do so? Does m'lady need to be so warned?"

She leaned forward, her face mere inches from his. Her voice chilled the air between them. "Salidar, understand this; when you act on my instructions, all of your skills are mine, and I expect you to make full use of them. I will know all you learn *and* all you suspect. I will tell you *what* you need to concern yourself about, and *when*.

"As for Ling, I expected something like this. You are to give her a wide berth, unless I tell you otherwise. You need not worry about George on my behalf. He bears only a trace of strength in blood, although he has been led to believe otherwise. Furthermore, he is quite weak in craft; he cannot transit to any of our realms, or *special places*, unassisted. He shall remain so untutored until it otherwise suits my purpose."

"As you wish, m'lady," Salidar bowed once again. "I only hope to serve you better."

"And so you shall," she confirmed icily. Looking down her nose, she considered him for a moment. She nonchalantly gestured an arcane sign while murmuring under her breath.

With the suddenness of a rushing wind, his hearing was fully restored. Salidar fell to his knees in supplication and gratitude, emotionally mumbling his thanks.

She allowed his self-abasement to continue for another few moments, but soon grew impatient. "Indeed, now stop your blubbering. I have another task for you. Perform well, and you may enjoy the full return of your eyesight as well.

"You are to seek out Padraic the Rogue. You are only to locate him and return to me. He is not to know that I seek him, at least not yet. I know not in what realm he may abide, so you may discreetly call upon any vassals of the Unseelie Court for assistance in my name. However, any who so participate are to be sworn to secrecy; any who dare to violate this troth shall feel my wrath. Do you understand?"

"Yes, m'lady. How soon shall I begin the search?"

"On the morrow, after the Council has met. I may then have further instructions for you. For now, go and make your preparations."

Salidar bowed and stepped backwards from the light. In an instant, he was gone.

LADY DIERE WAITED ONLY a moment before speaking. "Come. You heard?"

Lady Leanan of the Sidhe glided quietly into the light, her expression betraying nothing, and spoke evenly. "I did. While I don't trust Salidar, I don't disagree with him in that your human pawn, this *George*, shows disturbing initiative. And for what it is worth, I know of this *Ling*, as, I suspect, do you."

Lady Diere stifled an angry retort, composed herself, and fixed the Sidhe with a frigid stare. "It would be best if you did not concern yourself with what I know. Ling was sent by Lord Addecus, ostensibly to watch George."

Lady Leanan stared unblinking into the surrounding gloom. "Ling is, as Salidar so aptly put it, 'quite dangerous'. And now, I suspect you have a problem; and you would like that I arrange a *watch on the watcher,* do you not?"

Lady Diere remained stoic, but she was slightly unnerved that the Sidhe had so readily deduced her purpose. "You are very perceptive, my dear. Can you arrange such a thing, with the utmost discretion?"

"It depends. If George stays in the casino, we shall have no problem. But if he goes anywhere else on the Indian lands, we may not be able to follow. These are a very old and wise people; some among them may be strong in blood and craft. We could easily be discovered; they could be a danger to us."

Diere knew it had cost Lady Leanan to admit that last bit of information. However, she would have been remiss were she to fail to disclose it; notwithstanding that she probably suspected that Lady Diere very likely already knew it.

Diere smiled in silent gloat; but her tone was even and betrayed nothing. "Rest assured, George will not wander about the reservation; he will stay within the casino. He rarely goes anywhere in daylight, and is quite paranoid about surveillance by law enforcement authorities. He is far more concerned with manipulating his criminal enterprises from behind the scenes. He will, no doubt, stay within his *ivory tower* unless summoned." Her mood darkened at that last thought.

Lady Leanan nodded. "Very well, I shall make the arrangements. Remember our limitations. If we risk exposure, we must desist. I am sure you understand. Now, I must return; my House prepares for the Council meeting. So, if there is nothing else?"

Lady Diere slowly shook her head. "No, that should suffice, for now. Thank you for your assistance."

The Sidhe remained expressionless as she stepped back, simply faded and was gone.

LADY DIERE SPENT SEVERAL minutes in quiet reflection. Her plans, no matter how carefully crafted, seemed to demand constant attention and adjustment. Too many unpredictable factors were in play; but she found it invigorating and challenging. It was far more stimulating than the petty intrigues of the Unseelie Court, and far more dangerous.

She sensed a change in the ether, and smiled. "Welcome Lord Addecus, how have you fared?"

"Well enough, Lady Diere." Addecus stepped into the light, his forked tongue tasting the air. "I sssenssse the Sssidhe. Gone now?"

"True enough, Addecus. Be warned; I will not have you, nor she, bickering at, or about, one another. So, do *not* start! She performed a task I set for her, admirably well I might add, and now has departed to prepare for the Council meeting, as should I. Do not waste my time."

Addecus raised a rough hand from beneath the folds of his dark robe to forestall further scolding. "Pleassse, I merely noted her recent presssence. May I continue?"

Lady Diere relented. "Very well, we have much to discuss. George must be properly prepared for his role. Which raises the question, his status?"

"Ah, he isss moving to another location, and I have sssomeone very clossse to him, conssstantly." The Were Lord smiled smugly, obviously quite pleased with his arrangements.

Diere could almost feel his subtle impertinence; so, of course, she could not resist. "Ah, that would be the Indian casino? And you refer to his new bodyguard, Ling?"

Addecus betrayed no reaction but for his eyes; his pupils narrowed to mere slits. "Ah, I sssee you are very well informed. Of coursse, I ssshould expect that you would have your own ressourcesss in play."

Lady Diere could see Addecus was not pleased with her obvious lack of trust. *But then, he does not entirely trust me either.*

"I mussst point out," he insisted, "that I have only done that which we previousssly dissscusssed asss a prudent precautionary meassure."

She waved a hand dismissively. "So you have, but let us move on. We have much to do and time grows short. I am about to summon George. Ling will not accompany him, I trust?"

"Ssshe will not. He isss unaware of her true nature. Ssshe hasss been insstructed to maintain hisss ignorance, unlesss we decide otherwissse." Addecus tilted his head, and bowed slightly, a token of deference that was neither sincere nor convincing.

"And may I know her true nature, Addecus, as it may influence or impact our planning?"

Addecus spread his open hands. "Alasss, m'lady, asss you likely know, among the Were it would be quite rude of me to divulge the ssspecificsss of her true nature, akin to divulging one'sss true name, without her consssent. But I do sssee the problem. Perhapsss it would be appropriate to think of her asss a rather dark natured *feline.* Will that sssuffice?"

Raising one elegant eyebrow, Lady Diere shrugged, but her mind savored this minor triumph. *Ah, that I could wrest that tidbit from you with so little effort only serves to prove the superiority of Elfin lineage and breeding.*

Addecus clasped his hands in apparent supplication.

She relented. "Let us hope so. Now as for George, I propose to tell him only enough to facilitate his performance, as we direct it. One more thing is clear; there is no point in making another attempt upon the heir at this time. I am certain it would only prove counterproductive; we need only let the plan in play proceed. However, we require George for the final stages, and his impatience concerns me. I do not want him demonstrating initiative. I trust that Ling can contain his impetuous inclinations, as we may deem necessary?"

"Ling hasss my complete confidence." Addecus licked at a loose scale of dried skin on the back of a scarred knuckle. "Ssshe will follow inssstructionsss precisssely."

"Excellent."

"M'lady, that bringsss to mind another quesssstion. What of Sssalidar? He hasss befouled our plansss with hisss own initiative and failed to follow insssstructionsss."

Lady Diere stared icily into Addecus. "You need not concern yourself with Salidar. He was suitably chastised for his infractions, and he has since performed well a difficult task under certain arduous conditions. He still bears a mark of his *lesson,* and will so until I deem otherwise. I have given him another task to perform, which will in part effectively remove him, for some considerable time and distance, from the vicinity of our more immediate endeavors."

And you, Addecus, need not know the nature of his task, nor its role in my plans.

"I sssee," responded Addecus guardedly, "I wasss only curiousss. I had no doubt that you would adequately deal with thisss annoying minor isssue."

Her gaze narrowed. *Was this condescension? Does he dare mock me?*

Apparently oblivious to her semantic suspicions, he blithely changed the subject. "I ssshare your concernsss with regard to our friend, George, and sssuggessst we proceed asss you have proposssed relative to the depth of hisss knowledge."

"Very well." She settled herself and nodded. "I shall summon him now."

Folding her arms to her chest, she began a soft incantation. She continued slowly dropping her arms to her side. At her final word, she clapped her hands together once. An amorphous shape began to materialize just beyond the light at the edge of the deeper dark.

George blinked his squinting eyes, anxiously looking all around. As he focused on the cone of light, he hastened forward out of the dim gloom, and stopped before the two figures he recognized.

"Lady Diere, uh, Lord Addecus, how y'all doin'?"

Lady Diere, a trace of annoyance skirting across her countenance, sighed and acknowledged him. "Welcome, George. It is time to instruct you in the role you are to play at this stage in our plans. You have been granted a small amount of *power* in return for your cooperation thus far. If you are successful, you will be granted a great deal more. Are you prepared to proceed?"

"Absolutely, Lady Diere, you bet!" George leered, the gleam of greed bright in the depth of his eyes.

"Excellent! As you were told, the death of Maude Delafaire created a vacancy on the Council, and we intend to propose you for that vacant seat. You are eligible as you are native born to that realm and you are sufficiently strong of blood."

His look of confusion caused her to pause.

Addecus interceded. "Think of it like thisss; you were born on that world, and you are, uh, genetically sssuperior. That isss why you can ussse thisss bit of *power* in certain circumssstancesss."

His ego so obviously stroked, George nodded enthusiastically. "Okay, now I understand! What sort of authority, you know, *power* will I have on this council? What can—"

"A fair amount," Lady Diere interrupted, "but we shall get to that momentarily. There are important things you must understand first, especially about the make-up of the Council.

"There are eight seats, one for each realm, or *world.* Three are of the Unseelie Court; the realms of the Dark Elves, the Were, and Shadow. Three are of the Seelie Court; the realms of the Light Elves, Dwarves, and Mer. The two remaining seats are the realms of Man, and of Dragons. We intend to seat you in the Chair of Man."

Addecus raised a scaly finger to make a point. "You ssshould alssso know that the Dragon Chair hasss not been occupied in over five hundred yearsss. Ssso, the sssix realmsss of the two Courtsss of Faerie tend to vote as blocksss, frequently in opposssition to one another. Asss you can sssee, the Chair of Man often cassstsss the deciding vote."

"Oh, I understand politics; how to manage votes, lobbying, and such. I've even *arranged* a few elections in my day." George chortled, rubbing his hands together. "But what authority does this council have, and over *who* exactly?"

This was not going to be easy, Lady Diere realized; he was far too focused on power. But on the other hand, that made him more susceptible to some subtle and deft manipulation. She smiled; she was easily up to such a challenge.

"The Council has complete authority and power over the affairs of its members in those realms as might impact the other Council realms, with the exception of the Realm of Dragons; that world is closed to all. Members of each race, Elves, Dwarves, Weres, the Mer, and so on, to include some humans, may be found residing in almost all of the realms. However, only one race is tasked with the administration of a particular realm. Transit among the realms of the Council is open to all strong enough in blood or craft. As a council member, you could visit all realms as you please, with the one exception, of course."

George surprised them. "How many other realms or worlds are there, besides those overseen by the Council?"

Addecus and Diere looked at one another in silence. Finally, she responded.

"There are many, but they are wild, uncivilized places. Few who venture there ever return. It is even said that the Dragon Lords set forth, and have not been seen for over half a millennium. Their council seat remains empty to this day; but none would dare suggest its elimination."

George considered this for but a moment. "What power will *I* have in my own world? What will I be able to do that I can't do now?"

Addecus stepped closer to George and hissed. "I think you fail to appreciate the circumssstancesss. You would represssent your world on the Council, and you would enjoy whatever additional power the Council would grant you, in order to further Council busssinesss. Once we control the voting block and the deciding vote from the Chair of Man, there may potentially be no limit to the level of power available to you. Now do you understand?"

Diere saw that George was very uncomfortable with Addecus almost in his face as he listened to the Were Lord's explanation. *Was that a flash of resentment in my pawn's eyes? Or is it as it appears to be, simple fear? Nonetheless, he will bear watching.*

Stepping back a pace, George sputtered, "Yeah-yeah, all right, I get it, okay? So, what do y'all want me to do now?"

"For the moment," Lady Dire said as she began pacing in a small circle around him, "nothing more than *pay attention.*

"The Council meets tonight, on the full moon, at which time the *avatar*, or representative, of the Dark Elves will submit the recommendation for your nomination. Presently on your world there are insufficient numbers of humans of strong blood, or who are even adequately aware, to elect their own representative, so another Council realm may make the recommendation. The members will consider it for another moon and meet again. They will no doubt summon and question you. Do not worry; we will spend some time tutoring you as to what they might ask. As early as two moons hence, they could hold a vote."

"Excuse me," interjected George, "but aren't you two members of the Council?"

Lady Diere laughed coldly. "No. As I just explained, the members are nominated by their peers in their respective realms and then voted to membership by the existing Council. Lord Addecus and I serve our respective realms and the Unseelie Court in, ah, *other* capacities."

George nodded and opened his palms. "So, I just go back to running my businesses until I hear from you, and we begin my tutoring sessions?"

Growing impatient, the Mad Elf bit back a retort; but Addecus interceded once more and nodded affirmatively. "Yesss, that would be bessst."

George held up a hand. "I have another question. What about this 'stewardship'? You were very interested in that, it seems to me, especially when Salidar first came to me a few years ago. I manipulated that lawyer, Wilkerson, into debt as instructed, and now that land is gonna come up for auction in a tax sale, maybe later this year. So, I can still get my hands on it, despite Salidar's most recent stunt. So, what about this stewardship? Does that come with any power? Just what is it anyway?"

"That isss ssseveral questionsss," hissed Addecus dangerously as he stepped closer.

Lady Diere balled her fists and froze George with a gaze of icy anger.

"*You . . .*" She took a deep breath. "George, you are not to concern yourself with the Stewardship. It is merely a caretaker's position for some forestland, and bestows no power. As for Salidar, that ever presumptuous knave, he was mistaken as to our intentions. Worse, he was twice impudent and impatient in his unsanctioned initiative to secure that position. The original plan was more than adequate. As I recall, he even involved some of *your* people in his second ill-advised attempt. All have paid dearly."

"Sssome paid more dearly than othersss," added Addecus, flicking his forked tongue inches from George's flinching face.

"Hear me," demanded Lady Diere ominously. "There will be no further attempts on the life of the heir. You are to inform me should you hear of such. We have a solid plan in place to deal with this matter, all in good time. George, be assured that you are involved in all pertinent aspects of our plans. So, be patient; keep your focus on our Council strategy and your pivotal role. Remember, great rewards and great powers await those who would so strive!"

"Yeah-yeah, I hear you," George acquiesced. "I'll need to make some arrangements with my, uh, ongoing enterprises, since I may not be there to run things."

Lady Diere pinned him with a frigid stare. "That is not my concern! Do as you must, but speak of this to no one. Be patient until I summon you. You may go now."

George balked at her rebuke, but backed away as she began a soft chant. In another instant he was gone.

Addecus sighed and shook his head. "We will have problemsss with that one. He isss either too ssshallow and greedy, or too deep and Machiavellian to trussst. I do not know which."

Extending her arms before her, she considered her elegantly manicured nails. "Well, I for one am leaning toward 'shallow and greedy', as long as he is malleable, and, of course, expendable."

CH 11

CLAUDE FORNIER RATHER enjoyed the short leisurely walk from his office to the hotel. The previous day's rain left the air cleansed and crisp on this cool bright morning.

Downtown LaBorde seemed reluctant to wake from a peaceful sleep. Few small shops would open this early on a Saturday; so the streets were momentarily devoid of life save for a few songbirds and bold squirrels. A brisk easterly breeze wafted through the town square park carrying the wet musky scent of fresh mulch.

As he approached the hotel, Claude saw Trey Bassett leaning against the fender of his unmarked cruiser.

"Good morning, Sergeant! Not too early, are we?"

"Morning, counselor, and no, we're right on time. Mark drove Miss Millie to the grocery store to get food for lunch. I expect them back any time now." Trey nodded toward the hotel's entrance. "Miss Ellen and her friend, Miss Stacy, are in the lobby having coffee. I reckon you've got time to join them and have a cup, if you'd like."

"Well, I'd better go in and say hello, but I'll pass on the coffee. I've had two cups already. That's my limit these days, too much caffeine and a nervous bladder. Say, Trey, how long will you be staying out at the estate today?"

Trey shrugged. "I'll have to come back to the office after lunch; I'm working day shift today."

"In that case, might I ride with you? I really need to be back this afternoon as well."

"Sure thing. Just let me call my office and advise the lieutenant that you'll be riding along." As Trey reached for his phone, he noticed Mark's rental car coming down the block. "Look, Claude, here comes Mark now."

Mark parked behind Trey's cruiser. He and Millie climbed out.

As if on cue, Ellen and Stacy stepped from the building.

"Good morning!" Ellen exclaimed. "Armand and Madeline are supposed to meet us at the estate. So, I guess we should get going."

"Okay," acknowledged Trey. "Claude's gonna ride with me. Mark, y'all can follow me."

THE UNMARKED CRUISER in the lead, the mini-motorcade departed the hotel. A few minutes into the drive, the quaint cityscape gave way to a neighborhood enclave of stately older homes, edifices boasting strong hints of an architectural heritage that paid homage to designs popular sometime deep in the last century. A cathedral of magnificent oaks shaded quiet streets of Victorian and Georgian styled homes, and seemed to hold the bustle of the outer world at bay.

As the road rambled on, the huge trees became fewer and the shaded canopy diminished. Generous suburban lawns surrounding modest homes were revealed. A few ambitious souls were already mowing grass and tending gardens.

From gardens to carefully cultivated farmland, the miles rolled by. Rows of early corn stood over low acres of soybeans and peas. Hay fields, nearly ready for cutting, waved with the breeze. Only the recently turned cotton fields were without some bright spring growth; that would require the relentless heat of summer.

The road climbed among rolling hills thick with tall pines whose deep shadows would hold the morning chill hostage in the low hollows until banished by the persistent warmth of high noon.

Where slash pines surrendered to a wall of hardwoods, two huge white oaks flanked a gated drive. Both cars pulled off the parish road and idled while Trey opened the gate. Returning to his car, he slowly led the way, tires softly crunching on the gravel of the private road.

The track gently twisted and rolled for almost two miles through a stunning old growth forest, crossing a succession of bridges that spanned lazy bayous and trickling streams. The bridges were of such stout oaken timbers and large blocks of quarried stone that they barely registered the passage of the vehicles.

Weeping willows and cottonwoods crowded many of the streambeds; flowering dogwoods and redbuds favored the dappled shade of towering oaks and hickory. Sweetgums, magnolias, and silver bells shone in angled sunlight near tall yellow poplars. A stand of ash harbored a small clearing where a doe nibbled in the short grass. The deer calmly noted the cars passing by, and resumed her breakfast.

Millie rolled her window down. Lilting birdsong and fresh pine scent teased the senses. "Oh, this is just wonderful! Oh my goodness, look there!" She nudged Stacy. "That's longleaf pine! I didn't even know any had survived. I thought it was all gone."

Stacy stared in awe. "These trees, this whole place is special. It's like *holy* or something."

Ellen and Mark shared a concerned glance. The broad scope of their situation, the enormity of the responsibility for this land, was finally sinking in.

Trey's car slowed as he came to another gate. As before, he opened it and left it so. They continued on. Within moments, they were in an open area, driving between long rows of evenly spaced trees.

Millie recognized the layout immediately. "We're in a pecan orchard! These trees must be over a hundred years old, maybe older! They're huge!"

Stacy strained to look far ahead. "Those look like mimosas up there beyond the pecan trees. Those splashes of white, pink, and red must be the blooms!"

As they neared the line of mimosas, their sweet fragrance became discernible. Dozens of brightly iridescent hummingbirds chittered and buzzed about the delicate feathery flowers.

Beyond the sweetly scented trees stood a long row of tall crepe myrtles not yet in bloom, their green leaves a counterpoint to the riot of color unfolding in a patchwork quilt to either side of the drive. Flower gardens basked in the sunlight, unkempt and undisciplined, flaunting their blooms audaciously, shouting color at the sky. White gardenias bordered upon a sea of yellow, blue, and purple irises. Soft purple wisteria and fading yellow jasmine vied for dominance over a leaning grape arbor. The cloyingly sweet scent of wild honeysuckle hovered at the edge of everyone's senses.

The vehicles moved on.

In the distance, the main house came into view. Situated atop a slight rise and facing south, the building stood sheltered and shaded by two large oaks in the front, and several tall hickories in the rear. Its stately walls were the faded white of old chalk, its windows framed in dull black shutters, and its peaked metal roof the soft green of streaked verdigris. A broad and welcoming front porch was further shaded by a balcony of equal length. To the right, a spiral staircase wound counterclockwise from the porch to the balcony in a graceful arc. Four tall chimneys ascended past the roofline, two each on the east and west walls of the house. Each chimney thrust an ornately filigreed lightning rod defiantly into a cloudless sky.

As they drove closer, more architectural details became evident. The four columns supporting the porch and balcony were topped with elaborately carved capitals. Arched transom windows rode the lintels above the front door and the three sets of French doors on the balcony. The waist-high front porch splayed forth a wide set of stone steps. The foundation was entirely composed of large blocks of quarried stone, closely fitted and mortared.

Where the driveway curved in front of the house, Trey stopped and parked.

Mark followed suit, and everyone disembarked.

For a long moment they just stood there in quiet awe.

"This is really something," Ellen murmured, "much more than I expected."

"Maude lived here alone?" Mark asked. "This place is huge! And so much land!"

Narrow driveways to either side of the main house led to more buildings sheltered beyond the massive oak trees standing sentinel in the front yard.

"Is that a barn?" Mark asked, pointing to the left, and slightly to the rear of the house.

"Indeed, it is," replied Claude, indicating the large white building that had caught Mark's attention. "I believe it hasn't been used much for animals, but rather for storage and potting for the gardens, which, as you can see, are extensive. Also, there's a carriage house and stable that was converted to a garage to the right of the house. And as I recall, there's a pump and generator shed just off the kitchen in the rear, near an old cistern."

"Generator?" echoed Ellen. "I can see power lines running to the house, and from the house to the other buildings, and what? Phone lines, too?"

"Yeah, probably," Trey said. "This place is served by the local power grid. But if a farmer can afford it, a generator backup is always a good idea. You likely have a well and septic system because this is way outside the city water district. It's pretty self-sufficient, actually."

Claude pointed to the overhead lines running to the house. "Your speculation is correct, Miss Ellen. The upper line is electric power and the lower is the phone line. The power is on, but you'll have to make arrangements with the local phone company for landline service."

Stacy elbowed Ellen and shoved her phone toward Ellen's nose. "Or you could just use cell phones. I've got a good signal, four bars. See?"

Ellen just laughed, pushing Stacy's arm away.

"I hear something," said Millie. "Like a motor?"

The sound grew in the direction from which they had come. A lone headlight came into view; a motorcycle was revealed.

Trey chuckled. "Y'all can relax. I think that's Hawk, uh, my partner, Detective Redhawk. Only I'm not sure which one of his bikes he's riding." Peering into the distance, he shrugged. "Yeah, that's him; he's on his old BMW."

The motorcycle's lone rider pulled up near the steps and coasted to a stop. With the flip of a keyed switch the muted rumble died. Hawk climbed off, undoing the D-rings that secured his helmet. Freed, his hair went all awry. He made a few futile efforts to regain some tonsorial control before giving up, mumbling *sotto voce* about *damned helmet-hair*.

He waved to the group as he removed his leather jacket and spent a few moments securing his riding gear on the seat of the bike.

Stacy whispered to Ellen, "I see your knight in shining armor rides a motorcycle, too!"

"He's not my knight!" Ellen hissed, trying not to smile.

"Ha—as if! Riding that bike, he looks so cool. Bet you'd go for a ride if he asked," Stacy teased. "Look, his hair's all tousled, kinda sexy. You ought to get him some mousse."

Ellen elbowed her friend and smirked. "What? A *moose?*"

Stacy elbowed her back. "Hair product, silly!"

Ellen stifled a laugh. "I knew what you meant! Hush!"

Mousse? How does Stacy do that? I was thinking the same thing. And, yeah, I would go for a ride.

"Good morning," said Hawk. "I hope I'm not late. It was such a nice morning, and I was so into the ride. I was starting to worry that I might be holding y'all up."

He shuffled toward the group, trying not to look only at Ellen, and failed miserably. He deliberately cast his gaze down the long driveway, paused and pointed.

"Look, somebody's coming."

A light blue minivan slowly made its way toward the house.

As it drew closer, they could all see a cautious Armand Dupree at the wheel. His frowning passenger, Madeline, was gesturing and talking nonstop.

"Hmm," mused Hawk aloud, "I think I passed them on the road a little while ago; but I didn't recognize the vehicle."

Armand finally arrived at the house. An exasperated Madeline was out of the van and fussing before her husband had even shut off the ignition.

"I'm so sorry we're so late! I just can't get *Mario Andretti* here to drive any faster than five miles an hour under the posted speed limit!"

"Now, now, my dear," cautioned Armand as he approached. "Speed limits are maximums; and velocity at approximately seventy-five to eighty percent of the recommended maximum is statistically quite safe—"

"And boring," she interrupted, "and irritating to following traffic! We even had an old motorcycle pass us in a cloud of smoke." Madeline pointed as her voice spun down, "It looked a lot like that one, there . . ."

Hawk raised a hand. "Guilty, as charged, Miss Madeline. It was me. I guess you couldn't recognize me with my helmet on. But, I didn't know about the smoke—sorry about that. I put new rings and valve seals in last winter. I guess they haven't seated and sealed all that well just yet."

Undeterred, Madeline rebounded. "Well, weren't we going so slowly, that—"

Claude could hardly keep a straight face as he interrupted, "As an officer of the court, Detective, I advise you not to answer that. In fact, I advise all present to resist the temptation. Miss Madeline has been giving Armand grief over his driving habits for decades. I think they both like it. I submit for your consideration, the big grins both of them are displaying right now."

At that, everyone smiled.

Madeline just shrugged her slight shoulders and gave Armand a quick kiss on his cheek. His brief effort at maintaining a dignified façade collapsed in a snorting chuckle, and he hugged his wife.

Once more composed, Madeline pulled Ellen aside. "We've brought the dogs, Maximilian and Sophia. Are you ready to meet them?"

"Yes, actually this is their home, isn't it?"

"It is. But first I need to speak to everyone about them."

Madeline gestured for their attention. "Okay, I'm going to need everyone to stand over here, on the lawn, away from the house. We will let the dogs out of the van in a moment. I assume no one has a fear of dogs, no? Good!

"Chow Chows are special; they're rather unique as a breed. I should add that they're somewhat territorial; and they know this is their home. Everyone will be perceived as strangers, except for Armand and me, of course. We always brought them with us when we came to check on the place.

"They won't have a problem with anybody, though. We'll sort of *introduce* you. Let them smell you. Like all dogs, they recognize others primarily by scent, not necessarily appearance.

"Don't expect them to act like other dogs; they actually act more like cats, somewhat independent. I *told* you they were unique. Well, I'm getting ahead of myself. They generally don't expect to be petted, although they'll permit it if they know you. If you want to pet them, calmly extend your hand under the chin and scratch there first. If they like it, they'll stay for more. If they're not in the mood, they'll just walk away from you."

"Wow," Stacy interjected, "that sounds *exactly* like a cat!"

"Yes, very much so," agreed Madeline. "It's good to keep that in mind if you want or expect them to do something; they have to want to do it, too."

Ellen asked, "How old are they?"

Madeline shrugged. "We don't really know. We've had them to a vet annually, and he estimates they're four to six years old. He doesn't think they're from the same litter, but he isn't sure. Are there any other questions?"

There were none, so Madeline nodded to Armand who slid open the side door of the van and said, "Okay, Max."

A large russet mass of fur bounded from the van and stood to one side scenting the air, his short muzzle swinging in a large arc. His focus centered upon the people as he continued scenting. He did indeed look like a cinnamon bear with thick shoulders and a lion's mane; his black tongue added to the exotic impression. His dark eyes and steady gaze hinted at a deeper intelligence.

Armand said, "Okay, Sophie."

A smaller version, about two-thirds the size of Max, leapt from the van to take a position beside and slightly ahead of Max. She mimicked his actions, scenting the air and focusing on the group of people.

Madeline gestured with both hands, rolling them towards her. "Max, Sophie come. Meet your guests."

Both dogs trotted to her side and followed as she approached the line of spectators, stopping at Claude, who happened to be standing at one end.

As if following a formal ritual, she made an introduction. Placing a hand on Claude's arm, she looked at the dogs and said, "This is Claude. He's a friend."

Both dogs took their time sniffing his shoes, trouser legs, and finally his hand when he carefully scratched beneath their chins as Madeline had instructed.

This greeting ritual was repeated for everyone. The only difference was that Sophie felt compelled to twine catlike through Hawk's legs, depositing a streak of shed fur on his jeans, and then looking over her shoulder as if to say . . . *You're welcome.*

That left only Ellen.

When Madeline said, "This is Ellen," both dogs circled in opposite directions around the surprised young woman, and came to a stop on either side of her. Each licked her nearest hand, and promptly sat down, staring up at her.

Ellen felt a terrific urge to hug them both; so, she squatted down and enveloped them in her arms. A tremendous sense of peace, warmth, and protection flooded her heart. Her eyes almost welled with tears and her breath slightly caught as she sensed Maude smiling over the three of them. Sophie placed a paw on Ellen's knee, and Max just sort of leaned on her and gave a soft *huff.*

Ellen sniffled and smiled. *You even sound like a bear, big boy.*

She wasn't sure, but she could have sworn that Max smiled at her.

Madeline said softly, "Well, I've never seen them do that. Ellen, they certainly have taken to you."

Mark remarked, "That was interesting how you 'introduced' us, almost as if they could understand what you were saying."

"Well, now that we've all been introduced," Claude chuckled, "shall we go in? Ellen, do you have the keys?"

"Of course, right here." She stood, dangled the key ring at arm's length, and turned toward the house—only to stop short. "Hey, what the—? Look!"

There, on the front porch, a large gray cat sat complacently grooming its fur.

"Oh my, I don't believe it," breathed Madeline. "Smokey! It has to be Smokey, Maude's cat. We haven't seen him in what? Three years?"

"Quite so," Armand agreed. "When we took the dogs in, we could not find the cat. After a month or so, we assumed him gone. Are you sure that's Smokey?"

Ellen looked at the dogs; neither had budged from her side despite seeing the cat. "Wouldn't the dogs know for certain?" she asked.

As if she understood, Sophie trotted directly to the house and right up the steps. The cat barely acknowledged the approaching dog until she was on the porch, then he stood and faced her, nose to nose.

Everyone held their breath, expecting to witness an explosion of snarls and fur. But to their surprise, the two animals merely brushed alongside, rubbing their coats against one another. Sophie sat down to one side and faced the people; the cat just sat and resumed grooming.

Ellen scratched Max behind his ears. "Well Max, it seems that Sophie has made a confirmation. Do you agree that's Smokey?"

Max just *huffed* and licked her hand.

"That's good enough for me. That's gotta be Smokey; and he's come home." Ellen smiled and ascended the steps with Max at her heels.

Once on the porch, Max and Smokey sniffed each other, then ignored one another.

Ellen reached down and scratched behind Smokey's ears. The big cat purred loudly and promptly collapsed on his back, begging for a tummy scratch, much to Ellen's surprised delight. As she rubbed his belly, he batted at the keys dangling from her other hand.

Stacy cocked her head at the tableau on the porch and murmured, "Actually, it looks more like Ellen's the one who's come home."

Ellen pulled the screen door open, and faced a white wooden door of generous width that boasted an arc of wavy glass panes in its uppermost panel. She remembered these were called *lights*. She was impressed with the stout appearance and the meticulous trim work.

A large wrought iron ring, the size of her hand, and obviously very old, hung at eye level and served as a robust knocker. The metal was well worn, but she could see remnants of stylized scales beneath its dark patina, and the slight bulge of a snake head consuming its own tail at its lowermost circumference serving as the actual contact point for the elaborately engraved striker plate, a testament, no doubt, to the standards of dedicated craftsmanship of long ago. In a flight of wistful imagination, she decided to assume this knocker was original to the house.

She had always loved antiques and their secret untold stories; so, she found this small discovery and her fanciful speculation both comforting and pleasing.

Ellen snapped out of her reverie and allowed herself a private smile. She fumbled with the key ring for a moment, found the right combination of keys and opened the front door.

Before she could step across the threshold, Sophie blocked the entrance as Max and Smokey slipped inside. No matter which way Ellen stepped, Sophie moved to block her.

The rest of the group arrived on the porch and bunched at the door, behind Ellen.

"Is something wrong?" asked Claude.

Puzzled, Ellen responded, "I think Sophie doesn't seem to want to let me past her."

Armand inquired, "Did Max go in first?"

Ellen nodded. "Yes, and Smokey, too. Does that mean something?"

Madeline answered, "I don't know for certain, but the dogs would do this when we came here with them to check on the house. Just wait a moment for Max to come back."

Max and Smokey returned in less than a minute, each sitting in the front hall to either side of the front door.

Sophie stepped across the threshold and to one side, allowing Ellen to enter—but no one else.

Both Max and Sophie resumed blocking the doorway. Smokey sat behind them.

Ellen stared at them, still puzzled.

Madeline chuckled and raised a finger. "I think they've acknowledged you as the mistress of the house. You'll have to invite us in, before they'll allow our passage."

Ellen was taken aback. "Are you serious?"

"Ellen, just do it," Stacy urged. "I think the animals are very smart about this stuff. Just humor us, please?"

Ellen shrugged and smiled. "Okay, whatever . . . Max, Sophie, and Smokey, these are my friends and I now invite them into the house."

To the surprise of all, the dogs and cat promptly abandoned the door and wandered off down the hall.

Hawk pulled his partner aside. "Trey, did you just see what I saw?"

"You mean the pets *clearing* the house before they'd let her in, and then blocking the entrance until she *invited* us in?"

"Yeah, they're pretty well trained, or something," Hawk mumbled, as they entered.

Mark and Stacy stepped into a parlor on their left. Mark grumbled, "I shouldn't have to be invited in. I own half of this house, after all."

"Aw, poor baby," teased Stacy, as she tugged at him to follow her deeper into the house. "Now all you have to do is convince the animals!"

Her bright laughter echoed in the empty front hall as the heavy front door swung gently closed of its own accord.

CH 12

ILLUMINATED IN THE familiar cone of light, Salidar stood before Lady Diere in his usual obsequious pose, carefully hiding his distrust and growing suspicions of her motives. He was about to set out on her latest assigned task, but she had insisted upon a final meeting prior to his departure. He hoped it would prove to be to his advantage to have complied.

"As you no doubt know," she began, "the Council briefly met; and among other things, there was ample opportunity for the various support staffs to mingle and exchange the latest court gossip. I was able to acquire certain information that may be of assistance in your imminent quest." She deliberately paused, smoothed the pleated layers of her dark blue diaphanous gown and regarded him with a small smile.

Ah, she intends to make me ask . . . Ye gods! How I tire of her petty mind games. Careful! Keep smiling like the idiot—her idiot, as hopefully she believes me to be. Very well, let us play the game.

"I am most grateful, m'lady." He groveled. "I am ready to attend and serve."

"Excellent." She sauntered around him as she spoke. "It would seem that Padraic the Rogue has once again lived up to his reputation. He has apparently sullied the honor of a certain noble lady elf of the Seelie Court—a duchess, no less! Duke Briar is furious! He has put a price on the head of the Rogue."

"M'lady, if I may, will not others now seek him, for the bounty?"

"True enough, but that works to our advantage as well. Now any inquiries you make will be thought to be in pursuit of the bounty. Of course, the disadvantage is that someone else may find him first." She stared coldly into him. "But you will not allow that to happen, will you?"

"Of c-course not, m'lady," he said with just a touch of deliberate tremor in his voice. That seemed to please her, so he dared venture a question. "If you please, m'lady? As I understand it, Padraic was declared *Rogue* because he refused fealty to either the Seelie or Unseelie Courts, despite being of Faerie himself, and travels freely in those realms. Although I know him to be human in appearance, I have not personally seen him in almost a century. Can you advise me if his countenance has greatly changed? I ask only that I might more readily recognize my quarry, and determine from what quarter he might more readily seek aid and assistance."

She regarded him stoically. "You are thinking, Salidar; and in this case, that pleases me. Padraic *is* of Faerie, and as such is very long-lived; thus, his appearance will not have changed much in a mere century. It is true that he was declared *Rogue,* in part, for his refusal to swear fealty to either court, but also because of his randy behavior. He has admitted on occasion to thinking of himself as an *incubus,* as if that might excuse his lustful pursuits, a predilection that heralds his present circumstances.

"As you might imagine, he will not likely find succor within the realms administered by races loyal to the Seelie Court since Duke Briar's influence is considerable. Within the realms of the Unseelie Court, there are those who will hunt him just as eagerly for the sport as for the bounty, not that such would truly deter him.

"I would not be surprised to learn that there are also those who secretly admire, and even approve of, his exploits. But as for any who would actually help him, I would look to the darker realms. In fact, the latest news is that he was seen recently, within a fortnight, in the Realm of Shadow. You are to begin your search there."

Salidar couldn't quite manage to suppress a shudder. The Realm of Shadow was, at best, terribly depressing during daylight, and at night always dangerous, often deadly. He had managed to avoid spending any length of time there for several decades, but now he silently cursed his luck. All things that shunned the light and relished the dark, intelligent or otherwise, gravitated there.

Snapping him out of his reverie, Lady Diere handed Salidar a small sealed scroll.

"Present this scroll to the innkeeper, Boltar, at the *Crying Cup Inn* in the Shadow Realm. Are you familiar with this establishment?"

"Ah, I believe so, m'lady," he acknowledged, bowing slightly. *A dim and rustic place I'd not care to frequent, but with occasionally interesting clientèle. How is it she chose that primitive den of iniquity?*

"Excellent!" she declared. "He will expect your arrival within two days. He may have further information regarding Padraic."

She paused in apparent thought; and he became instantly wary.

"Salidar, you understand that you are merely to locate the Rogue and report back to me, do you not? However, since we know others will be searching as well, it may be necessary for you to assist him in keeping hidden until I summon him. If you must be in contact with him, it might be better if he does not yet know of my involvement, if that is at all possible. Do you understand?"

"Absolutely, m'lady." He bowed again, his caution unabated.

"Salidar, have you ever ventured outside the Realms of the Council?" she asked, in a mild tone of seeming innocence.

He was further alarmed, but struggled to betray no outward sign. *She could not possibly know! No one here does—no one alive, that is. But she at least suspects something. Perhaps a shaded truth would serve well?*

"Ah, on occasion, by accident, m'lady, when a transit spell went somewhat awry."

"I see. Where did you find yourself?"

"M'lady, in truth I had no idea. It was a hot barren place of sand and rough rocks. I had kept the thread of the spell in my mind and carefully repeated the incantation to summon the globe. It worked, and I transited to the intended destination."

"You were lucky, Salidar. That trick does not always work. It occurs to me that Padraic may have gone to one of these wild places. I would have you follow. Do you understand?"

"I do, m'lady, but I have limited abilities. I can transit among the Council Realms easily enough, but beyond that, I fear I am out of my depth."

Lady Diere smiled; he felt himself chill.

"You are wise to acknowledge your limitations, Salidar. However, you would better serve me if you had more adept transit skills. So, I will temporarily enhance those skills for the purposes of this task."

She gestured briefly and whispered softly in an old language that he did not recognize.

Salidar felt nothing; he bowed deeply nevertheless. "Your servant, m'lady."

"You now have enhanced transit ability; you can retrace your passage in order to return. In fact, in some cases it may be that returning the way you came is absolutely required. It will last for one moon; you must return to me by then." She focused intently upon him, as if his most secretive thoughts might be laid bare. "Am I clear?"

"Indeed, m'lady, I must return within one moon," he responded as guilelessly as he dared. *And by then, I may have learned how to keep this enhanced ability.* "When shall I depart?"

"Depart at the dawn. I know you maintain hidden accommodations in my realm. No, do not bother to deny it. As it happens, it suits my purpose. Wait there until daybreak and speak to no one. I would rather that you are not impeded; so, you should travel through Shadow in the daylight. You are resourceful; so, do what is expedient. Find Padraic!"

"By your leave, m'lady," Salidar intoned, silently cursing that she clearly knew of his private rooms taken under an alias. He would have to make other arrangements soon. One was wise to have alternative options, secret places of respite with some degree of safety, available in any realm.

Bearing a bland and subservient expression, he backed away from her presence and was swallowed by the darkness.

IN THE DEEP HOUR BEFORE the dawn, Salidar awoke and made his own preparations beyond those needed for the task. Unbeknownst to all, save a select few, Salidar was a member of the *Thieves Guild*, and had been for most of his long life.

In olden times, the guild was formed as a mutual protection pact among thieves and smugglers who plied their trades in the Council realms and beyond. Mutual agreements regarding territorial rights kept strife and internal bickering to a minimum.

More importantly, certain fiscal obligations, annual *dues* and a *tax* assessed on smuggled goods, financed and maintained a hidden realm, *Storm Haven*, somewhere in the wild, outside of Council influence. Informally known in ages past as *Thieves Hold*, it served as a hub for smuggling activities, and of course, the bartering of stolen goods.

There had always been a healthy black market for magical artifacts, despite their dubious effectiveness and random results when employed in different realms. There were many habitable realms other than those overseen by the Council, but most were harsh and dangerous places where *wild magic* was potentially encountered. Consequently, items of *power,* especially those presumed to be of a defensive nature, were always in demand.

In recent years, other commodities had become quite popular items of this illicit commerce, information and knowledge, especially that thought to be secret and of restricted access. This is what piqued Salidar's interest.

I lack pertinent knowledge and information. Something big is going on, but I can see only a small part, that in which I am personally involved. I must go to Storm Haven and make further inquiries; and, of course, inquire there about Padraic the Rogue as well. After all, one never knows.

Salidar prepared a coded message on a small scroll, and assumed a position of meditation on the cool stone floor. After a few moments of composing himself, he softly recited a simple incantation.

In the air before him, a small wavering sphere appeared, dim and unsubstantial. Slowly it expanded to the size of an apple. It grew more solid until it hung suspended like a dark ball with a small amber light deep in its core. The light flickered, taking on the definition of a small hearth fire, setting shadows dancing within the floating globe.

Steeling himself, Salidar leaned forward, whispered his true name, and delicately passed the small scroll into the surface of the sphere. At first, it met some resistance, like pushing at a child's balloon; but then passed through the surface and moved completely within, as if another's hand had accepted the burden.

Salidar waited patiently, staring at the flickering orb. He was nonetheless apprehensive. He had never been comfortable using his true name in this ritual. However, it was an absolute requirement, one that he dared not get wrong.

One could not enter Storm Haven unexpected. Any such attempt would be instantly diverted to a deadly realm from which no one returned, a hellish place of molten lava and searing heat.

The sorcery that protected Storm Haven was very strong, and constantly monitored. An unsanctioned school of magic had arisen in Storm Haven, a result of the vast accumulation of purloined secret knowledge. The matriculated mages were on a par with, if not superior to, those found within any of the Council Realms; only the foremost senior mages among the elves *might* be more adept.

After a few moments, a voice. "You will be expected."

Salidar was never quite sure if he heard the response with his ears or just in his head. He acknowledged the message, and watched as the light within the globe died, and the orb faded and shrank. There was a barely perceptible *pop* as it winked out of existence.

He had taken the first step; his impending visit had been approved. All he need do now was to stay alive in Shadow. *Ye gods be damned! It would have to be Shadow, a realm I've successfully avoided for years. Maybe I can escape notice by the Vampire Administration, however unlikely I know that to be.*

Salidar knew he would have no choice while under Lady Diere's scrutiny but to transit directly to the fixed entry point of the Shadow realm upon the break of dawn, and make his way toward the Crying Cup. It was two days travel if he walked the entire distance, an effort he had no intention of making.

Certain that his arrival would be observed and reported, he planned to disappoint no one, and would act as expected. However, he also had no intention of spending the night on the road; he would never do so in Shadow, given his druthers. As soon as he safely could, he would transit to Storm Haven in furtherance of his own agenda and transit back into Shadow late the following day, hopefully somewhere in the vicinity of the Inn of the Crying Cup.

If he could find this Boltar immediately, he would deliver the scroll right away, and be done with this hazardous realm, assuming Padraic was not there. Otherwise, he saw no alternative but to take lodging at that disreputable inn for the night. No doubt, that was expected of him as well.

AS THE FIRST RAYS OF the rising sun broke over the eastern horizon, Salidar donned a hooded cloak, gathered his pack and walking staff, and stood quietly in the center of the room. After a moment of stilled silence, he began a soft incantation.

Another sphere began to form before him. However, this one grew considerably larger as it gained mass and solidity. Stabilizing at his height, he could see a blurred hall within, and weak morning light beginning to illuminate a distant doorway. He waited a moment more than really necessary, until the daylight strengthened and the large hall came into sharp contrast.

He pushed into the orb—and stepped into chaos.

HIS ENTRANCE WAS NOW a dim and disjointed memory flailing in a stygian morass. The cloying darkness began to fade, but his head ached horribly. He became aware of the dull rhythmic rasp of something being dragged across bare stone. The wrenching pain in his shoulders and sickening pitch of motion focused his wits.

Arrgh! I am being dragged across a rough stone floor! I cannot see well, not enough light.

He thought it best to feign unconsciousness, in hope of learning more. This was certainly the Shadow Realm; he was already in deep trouble.

With a sudden jerk, he was briefly airborne, thrown through a doorway, only to slam to the ground outside. His breath driven out of him, any pretense of unconsciousness was beyond his ability as he fought to breathe.

"Stand back! Let him have full sun!" rumbled a deep voice. "Stay alert, lads!"

Sucking wind, Salidar rolled to his side. He held one hand across his brow to shade the bright sun. He found himself surrounded by half a dozen mailed and armored men-at-arms who held spears and drawn swords at the ready. He didn't move. He just tried to breathe; his ribs hurt with the effort.

"Well, he's not burnin' up," observed a gruff voice from behind him.

"So he's not a revenant; might be a Were!" warned another.

"Not for us to decide," grumbled someone else. "Clap him in irons—no, use the silver restraints, just to be sure. Take him to the baron!"

"Aye, Sergeant, what of his pack and its contents?"

"You've searched it?"

"Aye, some clothes, food, and a sealed scroll." A rotund man with a livid sword scar across one cheek hefted the pack for the sergeant's inspection.

"Sealed scroll? Keep everything together and bring it." Turning away, the sergeant bellowed, "Ferris, bring the packhorse! Samuel, secure our prisoner on the pack mount and keep him in your custody. Corporal, recall the rest of the patrol and make for the castle!"

So, suffering the indignity of capture by some low noble's men-at-arms, Salidar kept silent as the patrol formed a column and set out.

These men are obviously well trained. They move silently as a group through this dark forest. None have tried to question me. Unusual that, most humans are very curious. They are certainly disciplined and competent. What irony! Were these the hours of darkness, I would welcome such an escort. Nonetheless, I must be cautious.

By mid-morning they approached a small castle, more of a fortified manor house in Salidar's estimation, but surrounded by a surprisingly deep moat. A nearby river was tapped by a canal that fed the moat with running water. Another series of smaller canals drained some of the flow into irrigation ditches watering adjacent fields of crops.

Salidar noted the efficiency of the arrangement. *Defense and irrigation, that is indeed creative. Are things so different here now? Have I been away too long?*

The patrol came to a halt a short distance from the moat.

The sergeant rode forth a few paces and stopped. The steed tossed its head snorting nervously and stamped a forefoot. The sergeant settled his mount and took a deep breath. Holding his arms out to either side, he softly chanted, too softly for Salidar to hear. Then he waved an arm and the patrol started forward.

To Salidar's shock, the sergeant's horse seemed to step into thin air over the moat and calmly walk toward the rising portcullis. The mounted men-at-arms followed.

Salidar's breath caught in his throat as the horse he was astride followed. He felt a mild shock, as if passing through a barrier, and found his mount clomping upon a very solid drawbridge which was only visible once he was upon it. He also realized that he hadn't heard any hooves upon the wood until he passed whatever barrier he had sensed. Looking over his shoulder, he saw that the drawbridge appeared normal in all respects.

This is a complicated spell, indeed.

In the courtyard, he was taken from the horse by two soldiers and led down a winding staircase to an iron-strapped oaken door that opened silently on well-oiled hinges. His guards urged him forward. The door shut behind them and a lock clicked into place. The other end of the short hallway held an identical locked door, toward which his guards prodded him. Salidar recognized this space.

A mantrap! No doubt I am being scrutinized by hidden watchers even now. What spells are in use here? I must remain calm.

At their approach, the other door opened and they proceeded through.

After several twists and turns through a number of passages and up a long staircase, he was led into a room furnished with a cot, small table, and a simple wooden chair.

One of the men-at-arms said, "You may wait here. Make yourself comfortable."

Salidar presented his shackled wrists and offered a wry expression. The guard smirked, but did not remove his restraints.

Ah, well, it was worth a try. In truth, I could be free of these whenever I please, but I suspect it may be more prudent to play along. Who knows? These are silver; so, I might take them as a souvenir, perhaps to fetch a good price in certain markets?

Another guard brought in a flagon of water and a short pewter mug.

Salidar was then left alone. The door locked with an audible *click*.

He walked around the perimeter of the room, noting several things. The dark hole in the floor in one corner held the sound of flowing water, a primitive but effective toilet. A small iron-barred window set high in the outer wall admitted a surprising amount of daylight. No torch or candle was in evidence, nor did any soot marks appear on the ceiling. *Aside from the sole window, well out of reach, what do they use for light after sunset? Surely, no one in Shadow would forgo illumination in darkness, would they?*

His gaze fell upon the flagon of water, and he shrugged. If they'd intended to seriously harm or kill him, they could have easily done so on the road. He quenched his thirst with only a passing thought to poison.

These were not the typical men-at-arms he had previously seen in his none too frequent forays into the Realm of Shadow. They were quite disciplined and truly professional. They had managed to take him completely unaware; and, to be honest, that rankled him.

I must be on my guard; much has changed here. What else do I know for certain? What has not changed? No doubt the elite among the vampire lords still rule, and enforce their will through a system of trusted familiars elevated to positions of pseudo-nobility, such as this baron I am to be brought before. When I was last here, this was still a world of sword and spear, rife with superstition and fear. The human population was considered little more than amusing cattle by the realm's administration, to be periodically culled and managed, much like a violent and rapacious game preserve. Even members of the two Faerie Courts were not assured of their safety in this realm, notwithstanding any skill with magic. But now, is it somewhat tamed, or even more dangerous?

He pondered the details. Had he noticed anything in the transit globe, anything unusual? It was often a good idea to walk around such a summoned sphere, one could then see what might lie in wait in all directions; but, he did not remember doing so. No, they were waiting for him, or more likely *someone* or *something,* when he happened to emerge.

Even more surprising, these common soldiers, mere *humans,* had used some relatively sophisticated magic. This baffled him. Apparently, a great deal has changed since he last trod this realm.

He sat on the cot and contemplated his silver restraints. *Well, it seems not everything has changed; they still hate and fear the Were. Now there's another realm that I would very much like to avoid, far too similar to this one, but for being controlled by the elite among the shape-shifter clans.*

So, these silver restraints . . . Do they fear that I might serve the Were? I must convince this baron that I am no such threat. And I must be about the Lady Diere's business. Aye, the Lady Diere, now there be a thought. I wonder if the enhanced transit ability she bestowed might allow me to get out of here? Tis no harm in trying, eh?

Despite the constraint of the manacles, Salidar awkwardly eased himself to the flagstone floor and assumed the position of meditation. With a final glance at the door, he cleared his mind and focused on summoning a transit sphere.

The silver restraints began to glow with a dull blue light. Since he was not of the Were, he ignored it; the silver could not harm him. He closed his eyes and concentrated, channeling the ambient energies to form the transit sphere.

He thought he noticed a dull red glow through his right eyelid. Suddenly, he was on his back, shrieking in agony! There *was* a red glow, from the walls!

He felt he was afire! Burning skin crackling to a crisp, his very breath a silent scream of superheated steam, and the humors of his eyes boiling in his head! Overcome with agony, he passed out.

MUCH LATER, HE HAD no idea how much time had passed, Salidar returned to consciousness. His clothing was drenched in sweat and plastered to his shivering body. The stench of his panicked fear hung about him like a fog of rot. Bringing his trembling hands before his face, he saw that his skin was not burned. Pressing hesitant fingers to his cheeks and eyelids, he found his face and orbs intact. He spent long minutes on the floor, regaining self-control and taking stock of his situation.

Trapped! I am truly trapped!

He realized his attempt to transit had triggered a counterspell that had almost killed him. Losing consciousness stopped his attempted spell-crafting; the counterspell abated. Irony indeed, that his low threshold for pain very likely saved his life.

When he could move without too much discomfort, he crawled to the lone chair, struggled to rise, and collapsed into its seat. He spied the pewter flagon and drained its remaining water in one long draught.

Spent, he stared listlessly at the looming walls as his headache diminished and he slowly recovered his wits. The large smooth stones, without evidence of mortar, yet so closely fitted, resembled old Dwarven work.

He had a sudden inspiration. *Of course!*

Exhausted yet determined, he rose and clumsily tugged the chair to the center of his cell. He sat heavily and took a moment to slow his breathing. He would have to be careful; he didn't want to trigger any more counterspells. *Once was quite enough.*

He relaxed his exhausted body and worked on calming his thoughts. What he had in mind was essentially a childhood trick thought to have originated in Dwarven households to *see without looking.* By simply using an unfocused gaze one could learn to sense, and sometimes *see,* traces of a hidden or lingering spell without activating it or otherwise tripping its trigger.

Children in realms of magic learned the knack of it early if they wanted to raid the family sweets larder without their parents' knowledge. It was a totally passive process. One did not gather any ambient energy; that alone was very often a hidden trigger. One merely opened both mind and senses, and relied on one's impressions. If it was a strong enough spell, a trace might be perceived, even by one's normal senses.

Salidar slumped in the chair. He let his mind go blank, and his right eye no longer focused. He was close to a state of daydreaming, and could easily slip off into true sleep. Very slowly he became aware of a slight red glow at the corners of the room that seemed to flow along the junctions of floor, walls, and ceiling. The longer he stared unfocused, the more distinct the glow grew. At some point, he realized that letters, a script flowed within the glow, e*lfin runes!*

He snapped his eyes closed with that thought, and braced himself for the onslaught of the counterspell.

Nothing happened.

He slowly relaxed again. He found it hard to believe his mishap with the counterspell had gone unnoticed; and yet, no one had come to check on him. *Did that mean that no one knew? Or is someone already aware of what had transpired? Caution! Perhaps someone watches, even now?*

As if he was being watched at that moment, Salidar crawled onto the cot and closed his eyes. Sleep was not his intention, just his ruse. He had to think.

Why has a very potent elfin spell been cast upon this place, this room, this cell? More importantly, for whom is it intended? What is going on here? Hmmph, no doubt someone will want answers from me as well; how could they not?

HE DID NOT HAVE TOO long to wait. The ambient light in his cell diminished as the sun set; a sharp-edged evening shadow crept up the inner wall. With the *click* of the lock, the door swung open and two soldiers in livery stepped into the chamber; two more waited in the dim hall.

Salidar recognized none of them.

The first man glanced at the stones of the ceiling, made a deft yet elaborate hand gesture, and murmured a small word of power. A soft glow emanated from overhead, slowly brightening the spare room.

Salidar was stunned! *Wizards' light! These men, mere humans, use wizards' light! Well, that explains the lack of soot marks. But how can this be?* Nonetheless, he managed to maintain his composure and offered the newcomers a disinterested yet mildly curious expression.

"Yes, gentlemen?"

One man gestured toward the open door and spoke with practiced courtesy. "Sir, if you would be kind enough to accompany us, the baron will see you now."

Salidar found the deferential courtesy slightly unnerving, since they both knew he had no choice in the matter. Mustering what dignity he could, he rose, tugged at the hem of his rumpled tunic, and walked to the door.

"Very well, gentlemen, shall we go?"

They walked through a succession of hallways, each somewhat wider than its predecessor. Elaborate sconces held multiple candles, neither lit nor needed, as a soft yet uncanny glow seemed to hover overhead and illuminate their progress past faded tapestries and portraits of ancestral nobility stiffly portrayed in poses of stoic indifference. Displays of ancient armor, to include swords and shields bracketed by racks of spears and halberds, lined the broadest of halls. Elaborately woven carpets covered the smooth stone floors.

Stopping before a tall set of ornately carved wooden doors, the lead soldier knocked politely and waited.

From within they heard the muffled command.

"Enter."

The great doors opened to reveal a large room that Salidar took for a library. Here the eerie overhead glow was augmented by a host of candles casting golden light upon heavily burdened bookcases that covered almost all available wall space. On the left, a huge hearth held a modest fire. Two large mullioned windows were set shoulder-high in the far wall. The glimmer of starlight shone through the uppermost panes of wavy glass, confirming the slippage of dusk into the full fall of night.

At a broad and well lit table of polished wood sat the room's sole occupant, an unremarkable young man of thinning hair and sloping shoulders. Clothed in a comfortable house robe of deep crimson, he gave his full attention to a tattered scroll which he carefully scrutinized with a large magnifying glass. He glanced up briefly.

"One moment, if you please."

He carefully rolled the ancient scroll in a piece of soft vellum and placed it to one side. He studied Salidar in a protracted silence.

Two more liveried soldiers entered from a passage on the right that Salidar had not noticed, its entrance hidden amongst the bookcases. One soldier carried Salidar's walking staff and cloak, the other carried his pack.

The seated man rose and motioned for the items to be placed before him on the table. His gaze considered the pack for only a moment, then locked on Salidar.

"I am Baron Frederick Von Kestel, and this is my home. Who are you?"

"I am called Salidar, your lordship. I am an innocent traveler who was accosted by your men-at-arms as I entered this realm." Salidar huffed, doing his best to sound indignant and affronted. "I have done no wrong. Why am I treated so?"

"I shall ask the questions at this point, if you do not mind," replied the baron evenly, but Salidar heard the steel in the man's voice.

"Well, then let us proceed to clear up this, um, misunderstanding," acquiesced Salidar, with a calculated bit of bluster.

"Excellent. Whom do you serve, and why are you here?"

The baron rummaged through Salidar's pack, slowly removing each item and carefully placing it on the table. When he found the small sealed scroll, he reacted with raised eyebrows and pursed lips. He set the scroll to one side, separate from the other, more mundane items.

The baron looked to Salidar, "I'm waiting."

"Your lordship, I serve the Unseelie Court. I am in this realm to deliver a message."

Salidar watched the baron closely for a reaction to his answer, but there was none.

Instead, the baron gestured to a chair indicating that Salidar should seat himself.

Salidar did not miss the subtle extra flourish in the baron's gesture. So, the slight disorientation he felt as he sat came as no surprise. *Ah, a truth spell of some kind, no doubt associated with this chair. But that he, a low noble and human, makes such easy use of uncommon magic, there is more to him than meets the eye. I must be careful.*

"You were saying?" queried the baron.

And what do you know of truth spells, my dear baron? Are you as familiar as I? Do you know that in essence, a truth spell of minor potency cannot compel anyone to speak the truth, or at least what they believed to be the truth; it can only alert the spell caster to a deliberate lie? Whereas, a very potent truth spell is another matter entirely, and can compel one to speak only the truth. Yet it too shares the same shortcoming; under its influence one would speak what they believed to be truth. It is certainly not conclusive, and can be quite frustrating for the interrogator. I sense that this one is a truth spell of only modest potency. But my recent experience with the elfin counterspell suggests the utmost caution. Fortunately, I have not lied, at least not technically.

"As I said, your lordship, I serve the Unseelie Court."

A lone eyebrow rose as the baron inquired further, "Specifically, whom at the Unseelie Court do you serve, may I ask?"

Salidar's expression betrayed nothing; but, he knew this was dangerous ground. The rules of the Seelie and Unseelie Courts generally protected the disclosure of the identities of its members in relation to certain court activities from all who were not members of the respective courts. Courtiers did not lightly abandon anonymity, nor would their staff or minions breach this protocol of discretion unless the individuals involved granted specific permission for their identities to be known. This was, no doubt, an extrapolation of the fierce protection of one's true name. As a noble, the baron should know this. Salidar surmised this was a test of sorts.

"You may well ask, your lordship, but I am constrained by the rules of court from responding." Salidar cocked his head and executed a small, but nonetheless graceful bow, even constrained by his seated position.

This seemed to satisfy the baron. He made a motion to one of the soldiers, who unshackled and removed Salidar's silver restraints.

Determined to maintain what he thought would be the dignity and decorum of one who serves the courts, Salidar ignored the urge to rub his wrists.

"I take it then, that *this*," the baron hefted the sealed scroll, "is the message you are to deliver?"

Salidar saw no harm in agreeing to the obvious. "It is, your lordship."

The baron watched him closely as he asked, "Are you aware that there is an enchantment upon this scroll, a particularly dark spell?"

It came as no shock, nor was it hardly a surprise to Salidar that Lady Diere might protect her message with something unsavory and not tell him; but then, *that* was Lady Diere. *Appearing to be somewhat surprised would be the appropriate response, I should think; and, as a happy coincidence, it is true, as well.*

"Indeed? No, your lordship, I had no idea. Is it dangerous for me to be carrying?" *And just how is it that you have discerned this, my dear baron?*

The baron scrutinized him, then took up the magnifying glass to further examine the scroll. Several moments of complete silence passed before he spoke. "I think not, provided only the intended recipient breaks the seal. Carrying it appears to present no immediate danger."

The baron carefully replaced the scroll on the table.

"Thank you, your lordship. I am relieved." Salidar sensed the pendulum of suspicion swinging away from him. "May I now inquire as to why I was set upon at my arrival?"

The baron resumed his seat and gestured to a servant. A liveried man appeared with a wine tray, and proceeded to serve them both. Salidar took a moment to sample the vintage, and found it surprisingly good.

Apparently the baron was now prepared to play the congenial host.

"Please, you must forgive us. We were expecting someone, or perhaps *something* else. There has been some trouble. I have only recently assumed the title of baron, upon my father's death, less than a fortnight ago." The nobleman stared unfocused into his goblet, as if he could divine an augury from the dregs.

"My condolences, your lordship, I was unaware of your loss. It was untimely?"

"Quite, if you consider murder *untimely!*"

"My apologies, your lordship, I meant no disrespect, intended no offense," Salidar soothed.

"Ah, none was taken," replied the baron in a tired voice. "He, my father, was apparently the victim of a cursed Were, or a revenant. We are not certain, as he was attacked at night. We believe the culprit may still hide in the forest close to where you were, um, *found*." His voice was firm, yet tainted with a morose bitterness thinly veiled, its edge as raw as fresh steel. "My men search constantly and thoroughly, but with little success thus far."

"I am sure you will prevail, your lordship." Salidar assured his host. "Upon reflection, that explains why I was thrown into the sunlight and forced to wear silver restraints. But, I must say, *revenants?* I travel a great deal, and I've not heard of any revenant problems in cen—uh, a very long time. Is this something new?"

"I do not know." The baron sighed. "The last talk or rumors of revenants were in my great-grandfather's time. Stories told of persons selected by the vampire lords who did not successfully complete the metamorphosis to attain the elevated status of lord or lady, and reportedly lost their minds in the process, running amok, until stopped." His hand to his eyes, the baron paused. Then pulling his hand down his face, as if wiping away the memory of a horrid scene, he sighed heavily. "Of course, that was generations ago."

Salidar remained silent. He was still seated in the chair associated with the truth spell, so he dared not comment, for he knew better.

Those unlucky persons culled by the vampires were slowly bled over a period of time until drained and killed. There had been incidents; when a victim had been partially bled, but managed to escape before being fully drained and slain. Those who survived typically fell into one of two categories; ghouls or revenants.

Some were reduced to ghouls, near mindless eaters of the dead. Individually timid and typically satisfied with carrion, they shunned the living. But, formed into a pack, they would hunt any living thing if an opportunity arose within the hours of darkness.

On the other hand, should a partially-bled victim have sufficient contact with vampire blood, not an unusual circumstance in the process of vampire feedings, and subsequently escape, that victim is destined to become a revenant. These were not true vampires, but rather dull-witted halflings of a sort, yet still compelled to seek the blood of living creatures. Revenants were savage, not particularly cunning, but very dangerous nonetheless.

All of these unfortunates were, in truth, never intended to become vampires. The vampires killed all those they culled as a general policy, having no interest in creating more of their kind. They viewed themselves as the top of the food chain. They typically wanted *no* competition.

The vampire elite tended to ignore the ghouls and revenants, unless their predations seriously threatened the balance of their food source, the humans and any other prey.

Over time, the resident humans had proven to be quite capable of dealing with the vampires' mistakes, these revenants and ghouls. The vampire lords found this amusing, and to some degree, entertaining. Salidar had often wondered if such *mistakes* were not loosed upon the population periodically, for the sheer entertainment value.

Ghouls and revenants shared many of the same vulnerabilities as *most* vampires; sufficient direct sunlight was usually fatal, as was decapitation, incineration, or the traditional wooden stake through the heart.

As the baron seemed mired in a moment of personal reflection, Salidar sipped sparingly from his goblet and studied the man. *This new baron appears to bear his burden rather well. May fortune favor him. And may he trust me, and let me go.*

"M'lord Baron, again you have my deepest condolences. I am most sorry for your loss."

"Hmm? Oh, yes, of course," the baron mumbled, waving away his sense of displaced distraction.

"I presume I shall be permitted to fulfill my assigned task, your lordship?"

"Of course, Salidar, of course," acknowledged the baron. "Please forgive my woolgathering. Tomorrow's light will see you on your way. I offer the use of a horse and a cavalry escort to the limits of my lands."

Salidar smiled and nodded as the baron spoke, but his mind was ever calculating.

This will not work well with the schedule I had originally planned. Alas, I must adapt. How can I turn this complication into an opportunity to my advantage? Perhaps with more wine, the baron might care to engage in a philosophical discussion of magic? I could learn more about such magic as I have seen here, like the spell at the moat, the wizards' light, the truth spell, mayhap even that damned elfin spell? Perhaps this is not so bad a turn of events after all?

But before he could vocalize an appropriate acceptance to the baron's gracious offer, a new voice, soft and clear, yet somehow ethereal, interrupted.

"That is all very considerate of you, Baron Von Kestel, but Salidar will be leaving with me, tonight."

The baron and Salidar stood and faced a shadow of gently swirling mist slowly gaining substance and definition as it drifted closer.

Salidar was stunned. His stomach dropped and his blood ran cold.

The baron bowed deeply in recognition, and held his deferential pose.

"Lady Leanan, good evening. As always, your ladyship is welcome in my home; your presence is an esteemed honor. I see that you are acquainted with my guest, Salidar."

"I am indeed, my dear Baron. I am about to get to know him so much better."

The Sidhe smiled.

CH 13

DELAFAIRE FARM EXCEEDED Ellen's expectations. She stared wide-eyed at the opulence of the front hall.

Madeline nudged her husband and winked. "Armand, why don't you give Ellen and her guests a narrative tour?"

"I'd be happy to, my dear. Ladies and gentlemen, we are now in the entrance hall, or the foyer, if you please. I draw your attention to the architectural details of the house; ten foot ceilings are typical, delineated by ornate crown moldings, and in most rooms chair rails line the walls."

"Oh man, I really like these floors," Mark commented. "Is that heart pine?"

"Quite so. Polished wooden floors, of very rare heart pine wood, are found throughout the house, except in the kitchen and baths which are tiled."

"How many rooms altogether?" Ellen asked.

Armand paused. "Well, let's see . . . On this floor, there are three large rooms; a parlor and library to the left of this central hall, and a ballroom that extends the length of the main house to the right. Oh yes, there's a half bath between the parlor and the library. At the rear of the house is the dining room, with the kitchen just beyond. So that's five rooms and a bathroom on the first floor."

"This is some staircase," Stacy remarked, as she ran her hand along the cherrywood banister and let it come to rest on the polished newel-post knob the size of a grapefruit. "So all the bedrooms are on the second floor?"

"That's correct." Armand smiled and swept a hand toward the top of the stairs. "There's a wide hall on the second floor, with four large bedrooms, two to either side. Each pair shares a full bath. French doors at either end of the upstairs hall and the respective bedrooms open to either the front or rear balconies. The rear balcony has been converted to a screened sleeping porch with four overhead fans."

"So," Ellen surmised, "that's nine rooms and three baths, or twelve rooms in all, not counting porches or balconies, right?"

"That's correct," Armand agreed. "I should mention that aside from a wood-burning cookstove on a large brick hearth in the kitchen, there are eight wood-burning fireplaces as well. Years ago that was the only method of heating a home."

"Do they all work?" Mark asked.

"Oh yes," Armand assured him. "Some may appear decorative, but they all function. Most of the fireplaces are brick with wooden mantles, but for the two in the ballroom that are fronted in panels of white marble with identical marble mantles."

"These walls look to be real plaster," remarked Trey.

"Oh, they are indeed. However, the library is an exception. Let me show you."

Following their guide, they entered the library; no plaster walls here, but rather paneled woodwork and shelves of polished cypress darkened with age. Books of many sizes lined all available shelf space, even to the high ceiling. A small set of rolling steps promised access to the otherwise unreachable. A narrow table and matching writing desk of burnished mahogany centered the room. The modest brick fireplace supported a polished oak mantle above which hung a gilded convex mirror. To either side of the hearth, two overstuffed club chairs sat upon a thick Oriental carpet and promised many a cozy evening for readers lost within favorite books.

Mark stood entranced. By the hush that fell over the group, it was clear he was not alone in his appreciation.

Stacy broke the spell. "Cool! Can we explore now?"

"I don't see why not," Armand responded and shrugged with open palms.

Madeline tugged at Millie's sleeve. "Would you care to see the kitchen?"

"You bet!" Millie exclaimed. "I can tour the rest of the house later. Please lead on!"

THE PETS FOLLOWING at their heels, Madeline explained the layout as she guided Millie toward the rear of the house.

"The kitchen is in the rear, behind the dining room. Traditionally, the kitchen would be housed in a separate building to preclude the introduction of cookstove heat into the main house during the warmth of summer. To protect the serving staff and hot food from inclement weather, the kitchen was often connected to the main house by a covered porch called a *dogtrot*. At some point, the dogtrot was widened and enclosed with a succession of tall glass windows and French doors in the east and west walls, and now serves as the formal dining room."

Millie stood stunned at the rear of the long main hallway, staring through the ornate beveled glass of a set of fluted cypress doors.

Madeline pulled them open, revealing a broad slate landing, and said, "This is the dining room. Be careful on the steps, please; they're polished stone."

"Oh!" exclaimed Millie, as the pets slipped past her through the open doors. "I didn't even hear them."

"Yes, they can be very quiet. Don't mind them; they're off to the kitchen, I'm sure. I suppose we should keep these doors open now." Madeline propped the doors open and then gestured to either side of the landing where shade loving potted plants, ferns, pothos, and ivy, overgrew their pots and stands. "We've kept the plants watered. I know they need attention; some need repotting. Now that it's spring, they could all go outside. Sadly, Armand and I just haven't found the time to do it all. Hold on a second; let me turn the dining room lights on."

Millie offered a distracted nod, for the dining room commanded her full attention.

Twin crystal chandeliers hung from the high ceiling glowed in delicate grace, casting multihued dots of refracted light across a long table covered in a white linen sheet. In awed silence, Millie picked up one end of the sheet, revealing a highly polished walnut table inlaid with designs in cypress. Pulling off some of the dozen smaller white sheets disclosed hand-carved chairs of cypress with woven cane seats. The entire ensemble rested upon a large oriental carpet that covered most of the room, the heart of pine flooring visible beyond its perimeter along the walls.

"Oh my," Millie whispered breathlessly. "Such dinner parties she could've had. Oh, the holidays would've been so special." She sighed heavily and gently shook her head.

This personal moment of wistful melancholy did not escape Madeline's notice. She smiled kindly and sought to offer a gentle distraction by opening the French doors in the west wall.

"And here, Millie, we have a flagstone patio, shaded by this magnificent magnolia. Another shaded patio lies through those French doors in the east wall."

It worked; Millie brightened.

"Ah, I see. This is lovely, with great light! You'll see sunrise at breakfast and sunset at supper!"

Proceeding through the dining room, they came to two leather covered swinging doors, centered on the rear wall. Millie immediately recognized the design of commercial kitchen serving doors, complete with round windows at eye level.

"Now these look familiar; counterbalanced and swing both ways, right?"

"Oh, yes," Madeline confirmed. "Even the pets have no problem using these doors."

With the grace of one long practiced, Millie easily pressed through the one on the right and found herself in quite a large modern kitchen with white tiled walls and stainless steel appliances. Two sets of large windows in the east and west walls streamed daylight into every nook and cranny. A large butcher-block table was centered in the space, surrounded by half a dozen mismatched kitchen chairs and overhung by a rack of suspended copper pots and pans. A huge recessed brick hearth dominated the rear wall, upon which squatted a large, and obviously very old, cast-iron cookstove replete with silvered nickel trim.

Madeline just stood back and smiled as Millie whirled around the kitchen, inspecting cookware, opening cabinets and pantries, tugging drawers open, and assessing appliances.

When she found an apron hanging in a pantry, Millie donned it and began humming, lost in the moment. Finally she sat on a chair and looked around the room in awe. "The lawyer, Mr. Claude, told us at the reading of the will that there had been a fire in here, but it's hard to believe. I don't see any damage."

"Well, it was more smoke than flames, or so I was told." Madeline sighed. "It was on the old cookstove, something Maude was supposed to have been cooking in a stewpot. I was never told the details, but I did see the blackened ceiling before everything was cleaned up. Some of the ceiling plaster had to be replaced, and everything was repainted, of course."

Millie nodded. "Well, they certainly did a good job. As for the rest of the kitchen, it's great! There's good counter space and ample storage. The appliances aren't that old; they're good quality. The gas is on; the stove and grill are working. They're very similar to professional models in common use today. You could run a modest sized restaurant with these tools."

"Maybe so, but I'd bet everyone will settle for a little lunch." Madeline chuckled. "How can I help?"

Millie grinned. "We've got bags of food in the trunk of Mark's rental car. Let's get those, and we'll get started."

ARMAND AND HIS TOUR group were exploring the second floor. Each bedroom boasted a fireplace and overhead fan, a mirrored dresser and night tables, and a queen-sized bed. A pair of stuffed chairs, usually of different styles, sat before each fireplace, with floor lamps at their shoulders. As Armand had described, each pair of bedrooms shared an adjacent full bath.

Stacy and Ellen just had to open every closet. Each one held a modest assortment of womens' clothing, much of it very dated. Surprisingly, a small amount of dated man's clothing was in one closet.

Ellen sensed that the right rear bedroom had been Maude's. A quick look through the dresser's contents confirmed her hunch. Maude had evidently also used this bedroom as her sitting room, as a pile of well-handled books stacked beside a slightly sagging overstuffed club chair suggested.

Armand called for their attention. "If you've seen everything on the second floor, I suggest we go back downstairs. You may have noticed that most of the furnishings in those first floor rooms were covered with dust sheets. The library was an exception, of course, because that's where Madeline and I would spend some time when we came to check on the place. Anyway, shall we further explore the covered furnishings? I assure you, things are not always as they seem. I invite you to guess before each item is revealed. Shall we?"

THAT WAS FUN. THEY took their time, going through each room, pulling off the individual white sheets that covered almost everything. Each unveiling was becoming an event; everyone was caught up in the childlike anticipation, trying to guess at what article lay hidden beneath each shroud. Armand, who knew of course, kept silent counsel, refusing to give hints, encouraging them to guess.

Much of the furniture was easily identified by shape, but some items were quite obscure. Stacy was particularly delighted when one misshapen lump was revealed to be an early Victrola phonograph. Mark surprised himself by correctly guessing that a harpsichord was hidden in the ballroom, next to a readily obvious baby grand piano.

The furnishings might best be described as eclectic, to include quite a few antiques, some early Americana, art deco, and assorted pieces from the '50s, or more properly described, Stacy insisted, as *mid-century modern*.

Of course, Mark found the library particularly inviting. He would have lost himself therein, had not Stacy found him so enthralled and tugged him away.

"Mark, come on! Can't you smell that? It's making me hungry. We've gotta follow the others down through the dining room."

"Oh, right. To the kitchen, I guess."

BY THE TIME THEY REACHED the kitchen, Mark's appetite had fully succumbed to the tantalizing aroma of blackening spices and charring hamburgers.

Even the dogs had taken positions by the old stove where two large bowls sat empty on the tile floor. The cat, Smokey, peered out from under the cast-iron behemoth, completely unfazed.

Ellen poured a bowl full of water and placed it on the floor before the animals, and whispered, "Don't worry, you guys, I haven't forgotten you."

Millie had found a well-seasoned cast-iron skillet which she had employed with consummate skill to prepare a lunch of Cajun-style blackened hamburgers. A pot of bacon flavored red beans and *andouille* sausage simmered on the stove, and a steaming rice-cooker burbled merrily on the counter.

Madeline and Ellen distributed napkins, silverware, and glasses of iced tea around the butcher-block table, which was large enough to accommodate everyone comfortably.

Ellen set aside three cooked, but unseasoned, meat patties to cool for the animals. She glanced in their direction. *Hmm, I don't think sharing the beans with you guys might be such a good idea, but a little rice would be nice.*

The room grew quiet as everyone happily stuffed their faces.

Once his first hamburger disappeared and his grin couldn't get any bigger, Claude broke the spell. "I declare! That was the best burger I believe I've ever had the honor to consume! My compliments to the chef!"

"Hear, hear!" added Trey, as Hawk started clapping and all joined in the applause.

Ellen reached over and hugged Millie. "That was great, Mom! You're the best!"

Surprised, Millie's eyes filled, but she quickly dabbed at them with a corner of her apron, and smiled at Ellen. Turning back to the table, she said, "Why thank y'all kindly. Now, we've got more burgers and red beans and rice, but don't fill up because I've got some peach cobbler and vanilla ice cream for dessert. I know it's store-bought, but it looked pretty good."

The prospect of dessert suited everyone just fine.

The peach cobbler had been warming in the oven, so scoops of cold ice cream were soon losing spherical integrity; melting vanilla glaciers oozed across flaky crust, forming sweet puddles that lapped at the edge of each plate. It was unanimously declared delicious.

"Does anyone know just how old the house really is?" asked a satiated Mark, scanning the faces at the table.

"Not really," replied Claude. "When we did the title search for the court, the earliest record we found confirmed that the entire property was originally articulated in a French land grant, about 1720, as I recall. Later, when the Spanish controlled the area, the Spanish Crown honored most of the original French land grants, provided new taxes were paid. Control subsequently returned to the French, who in turn sold the entire colonial claim to the United States in 1803, the Louisiana Purchase. The United States chose to honor both French and Spanish land grants, dependent upon *new* taxes being paid of course, to encourage growth and commerce. That was a very wise move actually, as it capitalized on the existing infrastructure and established trade."

He paused in overt contemplation of his now empty dessert plate, and glanced sheepishly in Millie's direction.

With a twinkle in her eye and an overly dramatic tone in her voice, Millie said, "Oh dear, your plate is empty, Mr. Claude! Would you care for another bit of the cobbler? I fear it just won't keep, and it'd be such a shame to waste what's left now, wouldn't it?"

Everyone laughed, and one by one began holding up their own empty plates.

Grinning as Millie took his plate, Claude continued. "But as for this house, it appears that a dwelling of some type has always been located here; at least, it is so indicated in some of the earliest documentation that dates to shortly after the original grant. By the way, the original name of the property was 'Domaine Delafaire'; but now it's referred to as Delafaire Farm."

"Domaine Delafaire," Ellen repeated. "I like the sound of that; kinda romantic, isn't it?"

"Quite so," agreed the lawyer, "from the original French. Of course, it stands to reason that whatever structure was here has been added onto or perhaps rebuilt several times. I think it's safe to say that we now sit in its latest incarnation."

"Well, it's pretty obvious," observed Trey, "that Miss Maude kept updating the building. I've noticed that the electrical work seems to be up to code, and the vents throughout the house suggest she installed central heat and air conditioning."

"Oh yes," confirmed Armand. "She had natural gas heat and central air added decades ago. In fact, she upgraded the HVAC system to a high efficiency unit about four years ago and had additional insulation installed. The furnace and cooling unit is in the cellar, you know, the basement."

"Basement?" asked Claude. "I didn't even know the house had a cellar. Of course, it's on a good size knoll, so it should be okay."

"Why would it be strange to have a basement or cellar?" asked Stacy.

"The water table," replied Mark. "It's usually pretty high in Louisiana. You don't have to dig too far before getting wet, so cellars, or basements, are rare. But this house is on fairly high ground, so it should be dry."

"Where is the entrance to the cellar?" asked Claude. "This is only the second time I've been here. I came out here with Perry, uh, my law partner, at Maude's invitation years ago. However, I never really had a good look at the place."

"There's a set of storm cellar doors at the rear of the house, and a narrow interior stairwell behind a panel door between the parlor and the library," replied Madeline. "It's not exactly hidden, but not easy to find unless you know where to look, opposite the bathroom. I can show you. Maude had to show Armand and me when she asked us to look after the place. There's an attic, too."

"Well, I'd love to continue the tour," said Trey, "but I'll have to take a rain check. I have to go back to the office; I have the duty this afternoon." He winked at his partner. "Although, it *is* Hawk's day off."

"Regretfully, I, too, must return. I have a case to prepare," intoned Claude, "but, before I go, may I inquire as to your collective plans? Can you spare a few minutes, Sergeant?"

"Sure," said Trey.

"Well, I've got to go back to Los Angeles, probably next week," Stacy offered as she stole a look at Mark. "But I've got some vacation time coming, so I just might come back for a little while."

Millie nodded in agreement. "Yeah, I've got to go back to work, too, but I think I might be persuaded to visit." She smiled at Ellen, who smiled and nodded in return.

However, Mark had a pensive look about him. "Well, there's still the issue of $60,000 in back taxes that we have to address. So, I'm inclined to return to New York long enough to work out a leave of absence from the firm, and come back to resolve this tax issue."

Finally Ellen said, "Well, I don't have to go back to Los Angeles. My apartment is a sublet and my lease is almost up. So, I guess I'll stay here, at least for the time being." She thought for a moment. "Look, why don't all of you check out of the hotel and we can all stay here until you have to leave? We certainly have the room!"

"Oh, I'd love to!" squealed Stacy. "We've got so much more to explore!"

"Well, we'll need some more food," cautioned Millie. "Except for what we brought with us, the cupboard is bare."

"That's no problem, Aunt Millie. I can drive us back to the grocery store, once we check out of the hotel," Mark offered. "I need gas, anyway."

"Okay then," Ellen declared, "that's decided! Madeline, Armand, you'll stay for supper? Good! How about you, Hawk—um, can I call you Hawk?"

"Sure, I mean, yeah, call me Hawk. Supper sounds great, especially if Miss Millie is cooking," he answered, grinning.

"One last question, before the good sergeant and I depart," said Claude, raising a lone finger. "Actually, it's an observation that surprised me. I gather from your reactions to seeing the house today that the family members, specifically Millie, Mark, and Ellen, have never been in this house before?"

The three shook their heads.

"No, I'm certain that we, Ellen and I, haven't," Millie insisted. "As I recall, Maude was always at our homes, I mean Margaret, my sister, and me. She spent the night with us, our families, lots of times. Although, I remember Maude invited me to visit her here, back when I was seeing Ellen's father, way before she was born. But I knew, well, *sensed* that she somehow didn't approve of him or my seeing him. So, I never came here, despite a few more invitations. Once we were married, the invitations stopped. I never brought Ellen here. But, like I said, Maude was most often at our homes."

An uncomfortable silence descended. Mouth slightly agape, Ellen simply stared at her mother.

Mark fidgeted. "Uh, I haven't been here, either. I never gave it much thought; but, I didn't even know where she lived, Aunt Maude, I mean, much less was ever invited here. I don't know if my dad was ever here. I do know that after my mother died, Aunt Maude would stay at our house when my father was traveling on business trips. If she wasn't at our house, she was usually over at Aunt Millie's."

"Ah, forgive me. I didn't mean to pry," commented Claude, as he nodded to Trey and they prepared to depart. "I'll bid y'all a good afternoon, and thank you for a wonderful lunch."

Trey echoed Claude's sentiments as he headed for the front door. "Yeah, thanks again. Great lunch! But we gotta go."

Everyone followed to the front porch.

As Trey's car dwindled down the drive, Ellen shoved her hands in her pockets, leaned against a column, and gazed out at the grounds. *I can't believe we never came out here; I never thought about why. I'd have loved this; it's just awesome. However, there's a tremendous amount of work here, just to maintain these extensive gardens. I can't imagine doing it alone. Just how had Aunt Maude managed?*

No apparent answers were forthcoming, so she shrugged and turned to her mother. "Mom, can I help you clean up the dishes?"

Millie smiled and nodded.

Stacy started to follow, but Madeline called to her. "Stacy, dear, could you help me with something?"

"Sure!" Stacy joined her. "How can I help you?"

"Two ways, actually," Madeline whispered. "Firstly, let's give Ellen and her mother some private time. And secondly, help me identify some of the small plants in the herb garden. I don't see things as well as I used to."

Stacy smiled knowingly; together they made their way down the steps into the garden.

ARMAND TROOPED DOWN the steps and motioned for Mark and Hawk to follow him.

Holding up Ellen's set of keys, he asked, "You boys feel up to walking off that wonderful lunch? Maybe do a little exploring with me?"

Mark grinned. "You bet! There are at least three more buildings to see."

Hawk agreed. "Sure, where to first?"

"The barn, I think. Can I perhaps ask you something, Detective? Or might I call you Hawk, too?" Armand winked, and started down the steps.

Hawk chuckled and followed. "Of course, what's on your mind?"

"I hope you don't find this too personal. As I understand it, your people were here long before the earliest European explorers arrived. So, my question is, does this place, this land, this *Domaine Delafaire*, have any particular significance in your tribal folklore?"

Without breaking stride, Hawk shook his head. "That's something you really ought to ask my grandfather, Wendell Small Owl. He's the last of our tribal shamans. All *I* can remember is that the forest, this old growth forest, was considered a place of power and spirits, and best avoided. At least that's what we were told as kids."

Armand stopped at the barn doors and examined the keys, looking for the right one for the large padlock which secured the double doors. He tilted his head toward Hawk. "So, Wendell Small Owl is your grandfather?"

Hawk nodded. "Sure is. Do you know him?"

"You could say that," Armand admitted with a smile. "We used to play chess at the University Club, and he was an occasional guest lecturer in my department. But I haven't seen much of him since the casino opened." Armand found the correct key and popped the lock open.

"Well, he serves on the board of directors," Hawk explained as he tugged one door open, while Mark swung the other wide. "So, he spends considerable time in Baton Rouge dealing with the legislature and the gaming commission."

Light streamed in, illuminating a dusty tractor with assorted attachments and a long potting table. Bales of hay were stacked along one wall. The other wall was lined with broad shelves holding dozens of different sized pots. Above their heads, a loft held more bales of hay.

The floor and foundation were of large smooth stones similar to those of the house. Post and beam construction, and walls of stout white oak planks suggested that this was a robust barn of considerable age.

They moved on to the pump house which was located behind the main house, off the rear porch and next to a large cistern. The cistern resembled a large barrel, approximately six feet in height and ten feet in diameter.

"Wow," Mark exclaimed, "this thing is huge!"

"And very efficient," countered Armand. "Rain drains from the roof into gutters, and is then funneled into a screened hole in the cistern's top. See there, at the base, a series of three common garden spigots are plumbed off a single drain. Hoses can be used to send the stored water wherever it might be needed. If treated to be potable, this could also be used to augment the deep well that primarily serves the main house and outbuildings."

Inside the pump house, a number of hoses were rolled and hung on one wall. Armand pointed out the deep well access, and the auxiliary generator. "You see, it's plumbed for natural gas or propane, so the generator is capable of supplying adequate power for the house and other buildings in the event of an electrical grid outage."

Both Mark and Hawk were suitably impressed with Maude's foresight and contingency planning.

Armand had saved the best for last.

The converted carriage house and stable was a two-storied building of similar post and beam construction as the house and barn. Of more generous width than length, it was originally designed to shelter a dozen horses. Two sets of wide double doors in the north and south walls would allow a rig to be driven straight through. Now, serving as a garage, it could hold six full-sized vehicles, three to either side, and an open center.

Armand had Mark and Hawk open both sets of doors. Daylight poured in and Armand flipped a switch. Rows of overhead fluorescent lights brightly flooded the interior, banishing all but a few lingering shadows.

To the left of the front doors, a narrow staircase was now visible, the access to the second floor.

"I'll check it out," Hawk announced and ascended.

A moment later he returned. "It's basically an unfinished storage space with a big trap door in the center. There are some old trunks, broken furniture, desiccated harnesses and tack. All the leather looks cracked."

"No surprise," Mark observed, "this building isn't insulated; it must get pretty hot up there."

On the ground level, two unidentifiable vehicles, each shrouded in a tarp, were parked in two of the stalls.

Mark approached one and turned to Armand, "May I?"

"Of course," responded Armand, with a twinkle in his eye.

Mark grasped a corner of the tarp and lifted. Hawk stepped up to help. Together they folded the cover back to reveal a faded white pickup truck, its front and rear axles suspended on stout jack stands.

"Hey!" exclaimed Mark, "It's an old Ford truck!"

"More specifically," intoned Armand, "it's a 1984 Ford F-250 with only 40,000 miles on the odometer. It's been in storage for at least ten years, maybe longer. I don't know for certain."

Mark opened the hood and pointed. "Check it out! This is a 5.8L HO. They were stock with a Holley four-barrel. Isn't this a *Cleveland* engine?"

Hawk leaned in under the hood. "I don't think so, not in '84. This would be a *Windsor* High-Output motor, 351 cubic inches with, what—a C-6 auto transmission? Now that's a healthy combination. It might even have a limited slip differential."

"I know how to check!" Mark grinned and opened the driver's door. "I learned a lot about cars from my dad. You need the parking brake *off* and gear selector in *neutral*. Whoops, good thing the key's in the ignition, locking steering column."

Walking to the left rear tire, he said, "Okay, it's in *neutral*, brake *off*, and up on jacks. So, I'm going to manually rotate the left rear axle forward. Hawk, watch the right rear wheel. If it rotates forward, too, it's a limited slip differential, but if it rotates to the rear, it's not. That means it's an *open rear end,* no *posi-traction* equivalent."

At first nothing happened, the wheel refused to budge, and Mark mumbled, "Damn, the brake shoes must be sticking. Hawk, give me a hand. Let's just rock the wheel forward and back to break the shoes loose."

They did, and with a sudden *ka-sha-aack* sound, the wheel rotated freely. In fact, both rear wheels rotated freely in the same direction.

Mark shouted, "Yes! Limited slip differential!"

He and Hawk bumped fists.

Armand just smiled. "Well, you boys seem to know a bit about motor vehicles. Aren't you going to look under the other cover?"

Both laughed and started removing the other tarp.

"I don't believe it," Mark breathed. "Isn't this a '62 Chevy?"

Hawk agreed as he continued removing the tarp. "Yeah, maybe a Bel Air? No, it's a Biscayne, a two-door sedan."

The car, now completely exposed and held off the floor by another set of robust jack stands, offered no reflection or shine, almost as if its dull surface swallowed ambient light.

Hawk walked completely around the car, giving it his full attention. "The paint, old-school black lacquer I think, is really faded, almost to a flat matte finish. But it's so even a fade that it appears almost deliberate." He took several steps back. "And, what little chrome there is . . . Look at the grille! It's painted, too, flat black!"

Mark opened the hood. "Oh man! Hawk, is that what I think it is?"

Hawk's jaw dropped. "Whoa! It's a *409*, I think. In '62 the factory *high performance 409* came with two four-barrel carbs. Those are *two fours;* so, it's gotta be *that* 409!"

"Yes indeed, you boys certainly do know your cars," observed Armand dryly.

"I've always been a *gearhead*," admitted Hawk with a broad grin. "It sounds like Mark got it from his dad."

Mark opened the driver's door and looked inside. "Yeah, he taught me a lot. He loved to work on them; he used to say it was *therapeutic.* He'd have really loved this!" He stroked the front seat upholstery. "Black vinyl and cloth, and *seat belts?* That's not right, is it?"

"Nope, not standard until '64," Hawk agreed. "The belts are probably aftermarket."

Mark nodded. "It's a floor-shifted standard transmission. Hey, this is a Hurst shifter! That's not stock either, is it?"

"No," Hawk answered. "It would have been a GM stick, round and thin. Yeah, that's a Hurst all right; it should be mounted to a Borg-Warner T-10 four-speed. I can't tell for sure without looking under the car. Anyway, let's check out the suspension." He dropped to the stone floor by the rear bumper and shimmied beneath the car.

"Be careful," warned Armand. "Do you trust those jacks?"

"Yeah," Hawk responded. "I can see they're old, but they're pretty heavy duty. I'll be fine."

Mark squatted near the left front wheel well. "Hawk, this thing has disc brakes up front; that's not stock, is it?"

"No, I don't think so. It's got drums in the rear . . . Hey Mark, this thing is set up with anti-sway bars, extra leaf springs, helper coil springs, and air shocks. It looks like an old NASCAR setup. Hold on." Hawk crawled farther forward. "I can see what looks like twin electric fuel pumps, and some aluminum cross-bracing on the frame."

"Uh, you'd better come out from under there and have a look at this," said Mark softly, looking into the open trunk.

Hawk crawled out, stood and dusted himself off, then joined Mark and Armand at the trunk. Inside he saw a large tank, roughly the width of the trunk between the wheel wells and about half its fore-to-aft length. The remaining space between the tank and the lower trunk lip held four old milk crates, each holding half a dozen empty Mason jars.

"What do you think this means?" Mark asked.

Hawk stood there in silence for a minute. He picked up one of the jars, gripped the top and twisted. It didn't budge. Straining, he grimaced as the reluctant cap finally succumbed to his efforts. "Wow, that's been on there a while."

One sniff of the jar, and he began chuckling. "Well, I'll be damned. Now this is starting to make sense."

Armand just smiled and winked at him.

Mark scratched his head. "Okay, what?"

"Mark," Hawk responded, "I think this is an old *tanker car*, a rumrunner's hot rod, used to transport moonshine, or some other illegal spirits, from a hidden still to a secret distribution point. That's one reason why the suspension is so beefed up; the extra liquid was heavy. Plus, this car had to *run!* I mean *really run* because it was liable to be chased by *revenuers,* you know, tax agents."

"Oh yeah, I get it!" Mark beamed. "You mean like in that old movie, *Thunder Road!*"

"Yeah, a classic film! I mean, just *look* at this car!" Hawk urged. "It appears to be a plain, unremarkable two-door sedan at first glance, but it's actually fairly lightweight and very high performance for its day, a real road racer, or would have been in the sixties. That would also explain the car's appearance; no visible chrome and flat black paint, so at night it'd be hard to see. Why, I'd even bet we find a switch that shuts off all the rear lights, illegal as hell!" Hawk grinned unabashedly. "Gentlemen, what we have here is an early example of *applied stealth technology*."

"But, wasn't all that *Thunder Road* stuff over by the sixties?" Mark asked.

"Not by a long shot, young man," interjected Armand. "Moonshine production continues today; and it still must be transported and distributed, perhaps no longer by such unique machinery as this. Nor is it as dramatic and exciting as it was years ago.

"However, the comparison to NASCAR is most apt. That's how NASCAR got started. Drivers would compete against one another with their *hot rods* on flat beaches and early racetracks when they weren't running illegal alcohol. It seems I can remember some very well known NASCAR drivers getting into trouble for still 'moonlighting the shine' as late as the seventies."

"You know," suggested Hawk, as he looked around, "it wouldn't take too much to get both of these vehicles running. Whoever put them in storage knew what they were doing. Replace any dry-rotted belts and hoses; get new batteries; change all fluids and lubes, and get new tires."

"Yeah, and you know what?" Mark grinned. "Ellen's going to need some transportation here. Can you just see her tearing around in this Biscayne?"

Laughing at the image, they re-covered the vehicles and closed the garage.

THE WOMEN WERE IN THE kitchen, seated around the table, drinking tea and enjoying their own spirited conversation punctuated with periodic peals of laughter. A blanket of quiet settled over the smiling women when the men entered.

Armand stopped short, feigning surprise and mild shock. "Oh dear me, I fear we were being talked about!"

Of course, the women again erupted in laughter, which only served to confirm his amused suspicion.

Mark and Hawk just shrugged and shook their heads.

Madeline scolded her table-mates in mock severity, "Now ladies, please remember the fragility of the male ego." More laughter ensued.

The men served themselves iced tea, and joined them.

Each group was eager to share the results of their explorations. The men graciously deferred as the women discussed their discoveries. Stacy and Madeline described the herb garden in detail; and Millie discussed recipes and menus that could benefit from a ready source of fresh herbs. Mark and Hawk described the barn, pump house, carriage house, and finally, with the barely restrained enthusiasm of teenage boys, the Ford truck and Chevy sedan.

As the unusual details of the sedan were described and discussed, Ellen acknowledged the unspoken question that hung about like an unwelcome guest.

Just what was Maude doing with such a vehicle?

She was also surprised that she had not given any consideration to her own transportation needs. "Gosh, I hadn't really thought about it, but I guess I really am going to need some wheels if I'm gonna stay here."

"Yeah, your L.A. bus pass isn't going to cut it," teased Stacy.

"What? I've still got my little car!"

"Oh yeah, sure, the rattletrap that hasn't run for the past two months, that car? Girlfriend, please!"

In truth, Ellen had gone through a succession of high-mileage *clunkers* living in Los Angeles, but it seemed that the maintenance costs nearly rivaled that of a monthly car note. Her last car, the compact in question, had an odometer that stuck at 159,000 miles a year ago, and hadn't run reliably since, despite her mother's mechanic boyfriend, Earl, and his increasingly futile efforts at vehicular life support. Not being in a position to acquire another car, she had little choice but to rely on friends like Stacy, or public transportation.

Ellen realized that wouldn't work here, not out in the country where a local bus service didn't exist. The car and truck, assuming they would run, might represent the solution.

The pickup truck sounds pragmatic, especially for a farm. But the old Chevy, that sounds like fun! Definitely have to at least get the truck running. Shouldn't be too hard, since both Mark and Hawk seem to know a great deal about cars, and they seem eager to help. Of course, having Hawk hanging around doesn't sound too terribly unpleasant.

THE REST OF THE AFTERNOON was focused on checking out of the hotel and grocery shopping. Armand offered to shuttle the luggage from the hotel to Delafaire Farm in his minivan; that would free Millie and Mark to go grocery shopping unencumbered. Stacy offered to ride with Armand; Madeline and Hawk would stay at the house with Ellen.

After helping to clean up the kitchen, Ellen wandered out to the front porch where Madeline and Hawk sat in rockers, sipping iced tea.

"Oh, here's Ellen," Madeline announced. "Would you like to sit down?"

"Oh, no. If y'all don't mind, I'm a little tired so I think I'll lie down and try to nap."

"Of course, dear, you go right ahead, and don't mind us."

With a small tired smile Ellen entered the house. At the foot of the staircase she found Max and Sophie waiting for her, and Smokey already loping up the steps. He paused and looked over his shoulder as if to say . . . *well, come on then.*

Ellen chuckled and ascended, with Max and Sophie at her heels.

She went right to the far corner bedroom, Maude's room, without conscious thought; it just seemed appropriate. She realized that she'd keep this room as her own. She sensed that Maude would approve.

She plopped down on the bed, kicked off her shoes, and willed herself to relax. Just being horizontal helped, but she couldn't get her mind to slow down.

If my brain doesn't relax, sleep is not in my immediate future. I can at least rest, but there's so much to do. The tax problem is a big issue; I could lose all this. Now I just want to drift softly, free of worry, free to daydream . . .

At first she wasn't sure she heard it. But there it was again, a soft crying sound, and yet again.

Who else is in the house? Madeline and Hawk are downstairs on the front porch. Should I call out for them? No! I've got to start doing things on my own. This is now my house, and I will investigate all of its secrets, to include any little unidentified noises. I have to! I will not always rely on someone else; that's a weakness I can't afford!

She sat up on the bed, swung her feet over and startled herself; she had almost stepped on a sleeping Sophie. Ellen had never even heard her lie down next to the bed; that dog was very quiet.

Ellen stood carefully and retrieved her shoes. She noticed that Max lay sleeping in the open doorway, effectively blocking it. She carefully stepped over him and into the hall. She stood there quietly, just listening.

A soft scratching sound seemed to come from behind a door about midway down the hall to her left. She looked back at the dogs, but they showed no reaction. She went to the door, listened but heard nothing. She grasped the doorknob and twisted, *locked!*

Ah, but I have the keys! Digging them out of her jeans, she tried several before the right one clicked in the lock.

She looked down to see Max and Sophie at her side. *Well now, it seems I have some backup after all. Boy, you guys can really move quietly.*

Slightly emboldened, she turned the knob and pushed on the door; it didn't budge. She checked for hinges which might indicate the door opened *out;* but none were visible. *So, this door definitely opens in.*

Now she was determined. Conscious of her recent injuries, she put her hip into it, and using her legs, carefully *shoved.* The door squeaked fully open to reveal the first few steps of an ascending staircase; the rest were shrouded in darkness.

She felt along the inner wall and found a light switch. The sudden flare of a bare bulb held in an old sconce illuminated the staircase and a landing. There sat Smokey, grooming the fur of his shoulder.

The cat looked at Ellen, blinked slowly, turned and bounded up the next set of steps.

"Smokey, how did you get in here? That door was locked and stuck! There must be some other way in."

She heard him *mew.* It must have been him she had heard before.

She trudged up the stairs after him; at least her curiosity would be appeased. She came to another door, unlocked and yielding at a touch. She had found the attic.

Sets of windows on the east and west walls, and a series of incandescent bulbs easily illuminated the entire space. Ellen surmised that the light bulbs were on the same circuit as the switch she found at the base of the stairs.

The attic was warm, but not yet uncomfortably so; in high summer, that would likely be another matter. Broad pine planks nailed perpendicular across the joists served as the floor. Wisps of insulation hovered in nooks and crannies between the boards. Dusty trunks, old furniture, and assorted boxes covered most of the floor space. Hanging baskets, carved gourds, and an old set of wooden chairs hung suspended from the exposed rafters.

Smokey sat on an old steamer trunk, flicking his tail until he had Ellen's attention. As she approached, he jumped to the floor and pawed the trunk's clasp.

"So, you want me to open that trunk, do you? Hmm, no good, I think it's locked."

Ellen peered at the small keyhole centered in the clasp. On a hunch, she started looking through her key ring again; sure enough, she found a small brass key, patinated with age. It fit and turned easily with a soft *click*. She gently released the clasp, and using both hands, lifted the lid.

As it opened, she felt a slight chill and a moment of disorientation, but it quickly passed. At first glance, the trunk appeared to contain mostly an assortment of loose sheet music, books, ledgers, and old photo albums.

She lifted a handful of sheet music, revealing a soft velvet bag, dark blue with a snugly knotted yellow draw-tie. The bag was in a recess between two thick photo albums. She lifted the velvet bag; it obviously contained a book, and something else.

Carefully untying the knot, Ellen eased the mouth of the bag open and peered inside, but it was too dark. She reached in and withdrew a smaller velvet bag of identical color and construction, and set it to one side.

She then removed the book. Slightly smaller than a modest ledger, it was obviously a journal. Thumbing through a few pages confirmed it to be a handwritten journal, but not in any language that Ellen recognized.

Somewhat disappointed, yet intrigued, she set it down and reached for the smaller bag. Upon opening, she found a delicate pair of spectacles, thin wire-framed *granny glasses* with light blue lenses. However, there appeared to be no prescriptive curvature or distortion of the lenses.

Are these just plain glass? Maybe they're just old sunglasses? Whatever, they are really quaint and quite lovely.

The old photo albums drew her eye; she took one from the trunk.

Madeline's voice called from the floor below. "Ellen! Ellen, are you up there?"

Smokey spun about and disappeared down the stairs.

"Yes, I'm here, Madeline. Be right down!"

Ellen closed the trunk. She slipped the glasses and journal back into their respective bags, tucked the photo album under her arm, and made her way down to the second floor.

Madeline stood smiling with the dogs in the hall. "I thought you went to lie down, but when I saw the dogs here, I figured you went exploring."

"Well, yes," Ellen responded somewhat chagrined. "I heard a noise, but it turned out to be Smokey. Somehow, he got into the attic. Do you know of any other way up there, besides these stairs?"

Madeline shrugged. "No, my dear, I don't."

"Well, I found some old books, a photo album and maybe an old journal, or at least I think that's what it is. Oh, sorry, did you need me?"

"Our young detective needs to speak with you," she confided. "He got a call on his cell phone; I think he's been called in to his work. He wants to see you before he goes."

"Okay, give me just a second." With that Ellen returned to her room and placed the books on the bed. She slipped the spectacles, still in their bag, into her shirt pocket. Pausing at the mirror she fluffed her hair, inspected her appearance, and with a wry smile shrugged her shoulders. *Oh well, this is me; that'll just have to do.*

Hawk was standing in the front hall, at the base of the staircase, looking just a bit anxious. When he saw Ellen descending, his face brightened and then assumed the countenance of concern.

"Ellen, I'm sorry. I didn't really want to bother you, but, I couldn't just leave. And Miss Madeline didn't think you were asleep yet. But I have to go. Trey, my partner called; I have to go in to work."

"Is he all right?" Ellen asked, mildly alarmed.

"Oh, he's fine. We caught a case—er, I mean a case has come up, and he needs me."

"I understand," she assured him. "Do you think you'll be able to come back for supper this evening?"

"Much as I'd like to, I seriously doubt it," he confessed, and then confided in her. "A body has been found on tribal land at the casino; it looks like a homicide. Unfortunately, we don't wrap these cases up as fast as they do on TV. So, if it's all right with you, and your mother, of course, I'd love a rain check on supper."

"You've got it, Detective." She smiled and added, "Please, Hawk, be careful."

CH 14

SALIDAR SLOWLY REGAINED consciousness, his mind adrift in a fog. The last thing he remembered was the Sidhe reaching out to him as his awareness dissipated like steam from a drowned fire. Groggily, he realized he was no longer in the Baron Von Kestel's fortified manor. The Lady Leanan had taken him *somewhere?*

Near the foot of the bed, a sole candle flame flickered upon a small, but elegantly crafted, marble-topped table.

Bed? Indeed, I do find myself upon a sumptuous bed, and still in my traveling attire. Apparently, no harm has befallen me, yet.

He sat up and gaped at his surroundings. The chamber was of good size, opulent beyond expectation. Polished wood panels, gilt-framed portraits, and rich narrow tapestries adorned the walls. Tiny motes of reflected candlelight danced about the room, flitting like frolicking sprites amongst ornate fixtures and silent statuary.

Salidar slowly stood, his boots sinking into the nap of plush sheepskin. He rubbed his temples in an effort to banish the remnants of woolly befuddlement from his mind.

Careful! No doubt I am watched even now.

He approached the guttering candle, his shadow looming ever higher, swallowing the wall behind him. For some reason he was reluctant to touch the taper; instead he grasped a nearby candelabrum, and was stunned at the weight. *Remarkable! This must be solid gold!*

Tilting its three candles in turn to the struggling flame, he effectively brightened the chamber. Returning the candelabrum to its place upon a mantle above a cold hearth, he could now see much more of the room.

Two chairs of burnished leather and carved ironwood flanked the dark fireplace. Upon one chair leaned his staff, his traveling pack nestled in the seat. A single tall window, its wavy panes of thick glass mullioned in diamond shapes, was deeply set in the massive rough-hewn stone blocks of the outer wall. Drapes of heavy brocade, pulled to the side, could easily stifle any incursion of daylight. However, full night now reigned and entered the room with impunity, barely tolerating the modest illumination.

A soft knock caught Salidar's attention.

The stout oaken door swung inward. The face of a pale woman hesitantly peered into the room. As her gaze found him, she nodded and kept her eyes averted from his.

Salidar realized she was young, perhaps twenty or in her late teens, yet her hollow eyes and subservient demeanor belied her youth and hinted at a resigned sense of hopelessness, or perhaps despair.

She stepped into the room, and was immediately followed by another who balanced a tray of wines and glasses. Salidar stared in amazement—the two women were mirror images of one another, even to the level of their despondency.

They must be twins, in thrall to an elder vampire? Hmm, or perhaps vampires themselves? No, I think not, more likely slaves, or familiars?

As one set the tray on a serving table, the other bent to the hearth and laid a fire. Both women went about their duties in silence.

As the light of the small fire strengthened, Salidar looked more closely at the woman so engaged. In truth, he hoped to espy her neck and wrists for marks of a vampire's feeding, but her long sleeves hid her arms.

He glimpsed a small mark, a tattoo of an emblem or glyph, on her neck, just below her ear. It was certainly not a wound.

He watched the other woman as she poured a glass of wine, and offered it to him upon a small serving tray. As he accepted the drink, he noted that similar long sleeves covered her wrists as well. She kept her head bowed; he could not readily view her neck.

As if responding to an unheard command, both women finished their tasks and came to stand, side by side, before him. They broke their silence; one would begin speaking, and the other would finish the thought.

"If you please, sir . . . "

". . . be at ease, enjoy the wine . . . "

". . . and the gracious hospitality of Her Ladyship . . . "

". . . who will be pleased to join you, presently."

Even their voices were identical. Had not Salidar seen them speak separately, he would have sworn only one person had spoken.

He had been observant as well. As they curtsied and turned to leave, he noticed that each shared the same mark on the neck, below the ear. However, there was a subtle difference; one bore it on her left side, the other on her right.

Aha! Of course, as would be the case of a true mirror image. What might this portend?

ALONE WITH HIS THOUGHTS, Salidar quietly rummaged through his traveling pack, taking a quick inventory. As he suspected, only the sealed scroll was missing.

"Looking for this, Salidar?"

Lady Leanan stood in the center of the room; the sealed scroll lay in her outstretched hand.

He had neither heard nor sensed her entry.

Hopefully hiding the icy chill that crept up his spine, Salidar executed a graceful bow. "Ah, Lady Leanan. Indeed, that very scroll is the object I seek."

"Be seated, Salidar, and let us have an amicable conversation." She gestured to the chairs.

He removed his pack from the near chair, setting it and his staff aside, and waited courteously for her to sit. As she settled in the other chair, he gestured to the wine bottles on the serving table.

"Why, yes," she acknowledged. "Please pour for me from the black bottle. Feel free to refresh your own glass."

The black bottle was warm to his hand, too warm for wine. As he poured the dark contents into a goblet, the coppery tang of fresh blood assailed his nostrils. He held his breath. Into his own glass, he gratefully poured a bit more wine from a different bottle, pale green and properly chilled.

Mustering his composure and his wits, he returned to the hearth, his façade firmly in place, and presented the tepid goblet to Lady Leanan.

Watching him with a raptor's piercing gaze, she accepted the drink, a small smirk betraying the fact she was likely savoring his discomfiture, notwithstanding his effort at feigned indifference.

"Be seated, Salidar. Assume I was not told of your coming. So, let us begin there. Why are you here, in Shadow?"

"M'lady, as you know, I am in service to the Lady Diere. I am here upon her instructions." He smiled, tilted his head, and displayed his open palms.

She gently tapped the scroll against the palm of her hand. "Lady Diere, indeed? I sense the truth of that. And those instructions were?"

"Merely to deliver a message, specifically that very scroll, to Boltar at the Inn of the Crying Cup, m'lady." He took a generous gulp of wine.

"Is that all?" Her smile was feral. "You have no interest in the whereabouts of Padraic the Rogue?"

His survival instincts were shrieking in silent alarm. *She knows! Or at least she knows something. This is no time to quibble, for she is far too dangerous. On the other hand, perhaps she can somehow be of help. She may be allied with Lady Diere, but there is no love lost there.*

"On the contrary, m'lady, I am very much interested in his whereabouts, as are many within the Council Realms."

He watched her carefully, but she betrayed nothing, casually sipping from her goblet, licking an errant spot of crimson from her full lips.

"Salidar, I know Lady Diere sent you here to find Padraic. Do not lie to me; you would not enjoy the consequences. What are her plans for him?"

She placed the goblet on the hearthstone and leaned forward.

He felt the full power of her gaze, and was strongly compelled to answer truthfully. *Ye gods, she's strong! I'm under a truth compulsion as strong as any such spell. Unfortunately, I haven't a clue what the answer might be.*

"M'lady . . . I-I know not . . . Lady Diere does not . . . share her plans . . . with me."

She held him transfixed with her gaze for another long minute, and then released him. He crumpled in his chair, his breath coming in ragged gasps.

"It would appear, Salidar, that you are not as well-informed as I had hoped."

She retrieved her goblet and stood. After a second thought, she picked up his glass as well, went to the serving table and prepared refills. She returned and handed Salidar a glass full of wine. She sat and sipped pensively from her ensanguined goblet.

He found the silence most uncomfortable, and resisted the urge to squirm.

"Salidar, do you know this 'Boltar'?"

She had asked softly, but he was well aware of the importance she attributed to the question.

"No, m'lady, I do not. I know of the inn, but there was another innkeeper, Elwood, I believe; but, that was long ago."

"Yes, I remember Elwood," she mused aloud, "but I know naught of Boltar, for the moment." She lifted the scroll. "Are you aware of the spell upon this scroll?"

"I was not, until the Baron Von Kestel warned me. He said it would only do harm if the scroll were opened by another, rather than the intended recipient."

She smiled, but the sentiment never reached her eyes. "That's not entirely true, Salidar. Oh, the baron spoke truthfully, but he could not see deeper into the binding of the spell."

Salidar's instincts alarmed once again, he dared to ask, "M'lady, is there a greater danger?"

Lady Leanan sighed and considered him. "Salidar, we are going to have to trust one another. It may well be to our mutual benefit to do so, at least for now. Do you understand?"

"I think I do, m'lady, I think I do, indeed. Please continue."

"First of all, the spell on this scroll can be activated remotely, and at any time, presumably by Lady Diere. Fear not, for within these walls a very old magic negates any such activation. The scroll holds a very strong spell of incandescence and intense heat. Actually, I suspect it is a type of reverse transit spell that allows intense light and flame, no doubt from the bowels of some hell, to enter a considerable area in the vicinity of the scroll. It may be fatal to any for some distance beyond as well."

Salidar was speechless. *I've been carrying that, unknowingly? Just what is the Mad Elf up to?*

Lady Leanan sighed and confided, "I doubt the Council, or either of the Courts, know of this."

"M'lady, I would not know. But what am I to do? My instructions were quite specific. I am to deliver the scroll; and, I am certain that I am watched." Salidar was torn; he feared the scroll and Lady Diere. And more immediately, he feared Lady Leanan.

"For the moment, you will do nothing. Remain here as my guest. Understand this, Salidar, I do not yet know what Lady Diere intends. However, should it upset the balance among the realms—*that shall not be*."

The steel in her voice surprised him. He wisely remained silent, coming to his feet as she stood.

"I have something I must do. So, enjoy my hospitality until we speak again. I bid you good night."

She slipped quietly from the room, gently closing the oaken door.

The lock softly clicked into place.

CONSCIOUS OF THE INEXORABLE passage of the night, the dawn a mere hour away, Lady Leanan made her way to her own chambers, the scroll an ominous weight in her grasp. She would have to secure it in a safe place, adequately warded and shielded from any attempted remote activation of the spell.

She had been somewhat candid with Salidar, but she had not emphasized the potential scope of the destructive power she sensed within the spell. It could possibly be devastating on a massive scale.

She would have to consult with a very powerful entity, discreetly.

As she reached her chambers, she saw two of her guards escorting a third person hurrying down the hall. Stopping before her, the trio bowed deeply.

She recognized Gunther, the familiar of a younger vampire, the Lady Sabrina.

Leanan was immediately concerned. She had sent two vampires, Sabrina and Stirling, to the Realm of Man to keep watch on the human, George Papadolis, and the Were, Ling—*at the request of Lady Diere.* That thought darkened her visage.

Of course, it was to be expected for Sabrina and Stirling to have familiars accompany them. After all, one needed to be guarded while in repose during the hours of daylight. And, of course, continuous surveillance of the subjects could be maintained.

That the familiar Gunther was here, now, boded ill, indeed.

"Speak," she commanded. "What has happened?"

"M'lady," Gunther groveled nervously, and dropped to one knee. "I have come on the instructions of my mistress, Lady Sabrina, to inform you of the death of Chloe, favored familiar of Lord Stirling. She was killed, m'lady, *savaged—dismembered . . .* " His breath caught in his chest; he could hardly go on.

What is this? Shock? Has he seen too much? "I understand. Now calm yourself," Lady Leanan soothed, "and tell me of Lord Stirling."

Gunther took a deep breath. "Lord Stirling, he is *furious*, m'lady, in a horrible rage! He has vowed vengeance. My mistress suspects that he has already made a kill. But she is not certain. He has not responded to her call."

"Does Lady Sabrina know who is responsible for the death of Chloe?"

"M'lady, I-I know not for certain, but I think she suspects *Ling*." Gunther seemed somewhat more in control of himself, but he was far from calm.

To be assured of his compliance, Leanan formulated a simple obedience spell in her mind, narrowed her eyes, and spoke firmly. "Gunther, you are to return to your mistress and tell her to await the arrival of an Elder Lord.

Should Lord Stirling contact her, he is to hold himself available. The night grows late and the dawn approaches, so go now."

Gunther rose, bowed, and hastily departed.

The guards bowed and returned to their posts as she entered her chambers.

The twin familiars awaited her within, as was their custom, to prepare her for the day's repose, and then secure the chamber. She waved them off with a gesture. "Leave me for now, but return before the coming dawn."

She settled herself on a divan and set the scroll to one side. Willing herself into a meditative state, she focused on establishing contact with another of her kind.

. . . Lamia, Mother of Night, it is I, Leanan of the Sidhe, your Celtic daughter, hear me, Mother . . .

. . . I hear you Daughter . . . The night wanes. Your need must be great to seek me this close to the onset of day . . .

. . . I fear it is, Mother . . . I invite you into my mind, that you may know what I know, see as I have seen, and hopefully understand that which I do not. I feel the winds of fate freshening beyond the horizon. I sense that time grows short . . .

. . . Very well, I come. Prepare yourself . . .

With that, Leanan felt a forceful presence invade her mind, probing, assessing, evaluating. It was uncomfortable, but not quite painful. In a matter of minutes, she sensed the presence depart her mind. She felt curiously empty—and thirsty. She would have to feed heavily within the next few nights; this sharing always left her ravenous.

. . . Daughter, you have just cause for concern . . . I shall not command, for I see no need for my involvement, but I will offer suggestions. Send Vlad to deal with Stirling—the young one is too impetuous for his own good. It appears the Dark Elf, Diere, has decided to test the bounds set by the Unseelie Court—if

not those of the Council itself. Release Salidar on the morrow and let him deliver the scroll. We must watch carefully. This Boltar is thought human, but is not native to the Realm of Shadow. You will need to learn more. I have every confidence in you . . .

. . . Mother, I am grateful for your insight. All shall be done as you suggest. Now we must both rest . . .

. . . Daughter, you have my blessing . . .

Lady Leanan rose, placed the scroll in a jeweled box, and whispered a containment spell which would serve as both lock and distraction should curious eyes take notice. She then sent a mental message to Vlad, her colleague, asking him to come to her upon his awakening at nightfall.

A soft knock upon her chamber door announced the return of the twin familiars, who proceeded with preparations for her ladyship's daylight rest period. The large curtained bed served the purpose adequately. Windows shuttered and heavy drapes drawn, the room was dark but for a single candle that would be extinguished in a moment.

Satisfied with the preparations, Lady Leanan nodded approvingly. The twins bowed in unison and departed, locking the door behind them.

A WEAK SUN SLUGGISHLY rose above a bleak horizon, failing to burn off the sickly mists that huddled in low places and shadowed hollows. Night predators sought the shadows; wizened prey stayed hidden, for even the daylight presented unsavory dangers to the unwary.

Salidar had managed a few hours of restless sleep, but worry gnawed at his gut and forced him to waken. He lay in the timid light of the morning sun, the bedclothes disheveled and rank with the sweat of his fear. He felt helpless and powerless; that frustrated him.

A small knot of determination was born from his frustration. *I must leave this place—now, while the vampire sleeps.* After that, he had no idea; but he had to be free of this place.

He dressed and collected his staff and pack. He checked the window and door; both were locked. He pressed his ear to the door but heard nothing in the adjoining passage. Satisfied that no one was near, but still uncertain that he was not being watched, he decided to chance a transit spell.

He stood in the center of the room, dropped his pack at his feet, and closed his eyes. He cleared his mind, and began the process of gathering energy to form the spell. He thought he felt a slight tug of disorientation. His concentration was shattered!

"Stop immediately, you fool!" thundered throughout the room.

Salidar spun around, the staff clattering to the floor. He grabbed his throbbing head with both hands. Sudden vertigo sent him to his knees; he collapsed across his pack.

It took several moments before the pain began to ease and his sense of balance settled; his stomach still threatened to revolt.

Through squinted eyes he saw the dull ruddy glow, still fading along the intersections of ceiling, walls, and floor, retreating into the corners, reluctantly withdrawing like an ill-tempered salivating carnivore denied its prey.

Damn the gods! Another elfin counterspell? Or something worse?

Only the shouted warning had saved him from the counterspell's full impact. *Ah, but then, who warned me?*

He looked up from the floor to see the twins standing there and scowling at him.

"That was a very foolish . . . "

". . . and dangerous thing to attempt!"

He struggled to stand, his equilibrium barely cooperating, and faced them. "Wh-why did you warn me?" Surely it had been they who had done so.

The twins looked at one another, then at him.

"You will come with us . . . "

". . . and you will be silent . . . "

". . . for the danger is great . . ."

". . . and your continued services are needed."

With that, the twins turned in unison and faced a panel in the wall. One of the twins touched a piece of carved trim in a succession of places and the wall panel slid aside; a dark passage yawned. The other twin lit a small candle and beckoned him to follow.

It was then that he realized that the door to the room remained closed, and was presumably still locked. Salidar was not trusting in the least, and was not about to walk into another trap.

"Hold! Why should I trust you? You are servants—*familiars* to the Lady Leanan, are you not?"

The twins stepped up to within a hand span of his face and leaned in, one to either ear, and whispered.

"You will trust us . . . "

". . . *Grimrald* . . . "

". . . because you are overdue . . . "

". . . at *Storm Haven*."

"We will show you a place . . . "

". . . from which you may safely transit . . . "

". . . but you must return before nightfall."

"This is not negotiable."

"Do you understand?"

Salidar was stunned; they knew his true name! They knew of Storm Haven; and, that he was expected there! He now knew he had little choice but to trust the twins. He nodded and followed them into the dim entryway.

They carefully traversed a series of narrow passages, some through rough-hewn rock, and others between timber-braced smooth stone walls. At last, they emerged upon an open balcony below the tumbled ruins of an ancient watchtower. The broken balustrade and moss-covered stones indicated centuries of disuse and abandonment.

The twins faced him once again.

"You may safely cast a transit spell here . . . "

". . . but you must also return here . . . "

". . . before nightfall, this day . . . "

". . . or much will be lost."

"One of us will await you here . . . "

". . . in the hour before dusk."

"You must be back in your chamber . . . "

". . . before her ladyship arises."

Salidar nodded in understanding; but he had reservations, and his own questions.

"You know me, by my *true name;* but, I do not know you. May I know your names?"

The twins looked at one another and smiled.

"Certainly, I am *No One* . . . "

". . . and I am *Nobody*."

Salidar just smiled and shook his head in resignation. Quite clever, like an old Greek myth, he mused. Even under the influence of the strongest truth spell, he could honestly say that *no one* and *nobody* had aided him.

The twins smiled in return and spoke again.

"You will see the Guildmaster, to whom . . . "

". . . you must convey that Sabrina and Stirling . . . "

". . . are in the Realm of Man . . . "

". . . and Vlad, an elder, will soon join them."

"Two deaths occurred there . . . "

". . . the familiar, Chloe . . . "

". . . and a human female of that realm."

"Advise the Guildmaster that you must return . . . "

". . . before nightfall, because . . . "

". . . aside from the obvious . . . "

". . . the Lady Leanan intends to . . . "

". . . return to you the scroll . . . "

". . . and release you to complete your task."

Salidar was indeed surprised once more; but not so surprised that he cared to delay his imminent departure. He thanked No One and Nobody and set about casting his transit spell. As the globe formed and the scene inside stabilized to depict an empty, yet brightly lit room, he nodded once to the twins.

They merely nodded in return, stepped back, and disappeared into the bleak passageway.

Salidar turned his attention to the sphere, this time walking all the way around it to see what awaited him. He saw nothing but the empty room, with a single large wooden door set into one wall. Reasonably satisfied, he pushed into the globe, and into the room within.

IT HAD BEEN MANY YEARS since Salidar had visited Storm Haven; so, he expected to see some changes. He was not disappointed.

The entire ceiling of the square room in which he stood flared with a harsh light; the only place for a shadow to hide would be beneath the soles of his boots.

He noticed horizontal and vertical slits staggered at various heights in the stone walls to either side.

Ah, arrow ports for crossbows, no doubt.

However, as he peered closer, ominous black tubes could be discerned within the ports, easily tracking any movement throughout the room.

What the—gun barrels? They're using firearms now? Likely muzzle loading flintlocks, I'd guess.

Clearly, this chamber would be a death trap should anyone uninvited get past the wards and spells that protected access to this realm.

He calmed himself, lowered his pack, and stood still, waiting.

"State your name." The metallic voice seemed to come from all around him.

He knew the ritual; the correct answer was his true name.

"I am Grimrald, called Salidar. I am expected."

He suddenly remembered that he had to also give a simple silent sign. He had almost forgotten; that would have surely been fatal. He touched the right side of his nose with his right index finger, then his left earlobe, and finally drew his finger across his throat from left to right.

After a moment, the voice announced, "Welcome, Salidar, to Storm Haven. You are expected. You may enter the next chamber."

The thick door opened and Salidar passed through. He found himself in a much larger chamber, but otherwise identical to the first. However, he was not alone.

Four large black-clad guards, anonymous in helmets that covered their faces, silently awaited him. One relieved him of his staff and pack, and proceeded to empty his belongings into a neat line on the smooth stone floor. Another waved a curious paddle-shaped device that emitted a low warbling tone over his person and his property.

Salidar glanced over his shoulder at the remaining two guards, who stood slightly behind him and to either side, at least three paces away. Their black garb reflected none of the overhead light. Their easy yet alert stance suggested well-trained competence. But it was what they casually cradled in their arms that momentarily unnerved him, short-barreled pump shotguns.

Ye gods! Shotguns! Not antiques, but Man's current technology! Devastating weapons, especially at close range. I have seen firsthand the gruesome results of their use on more than a few of my previous travels in the Realm of Man.

The hulking guard nearest him stepped back and announced the results of their search in a strangely metallic voice. "He's clean."

The air before Salidar warped; a distinct form shimmered and solidified.

A tall man in a hooded grey robe, holding a traditional mage's staff, now stood amongst them. He gestured to the guards and stepped forward. Tossing back his hood, the grey-haired man stroked his silvered beard and focused his gaze. Ice blue eyes of startling intensity peered into Salidar.

Chilled for a moment, Salidar felt like an onion, layers of his very being peeled back and inspected. The man seemed satisfied; the chill slowly ebbed.

"Welcome, Salidar, you are overdue. I am called Gallenius, a mage of the college." He smiled. "That just means that I teach at our College of Magic, and of course, serve a rotation with the Security Forces."

"Thank you, Gallenius, I was, uh, delayed a bit. Circumstances require that I pass on certain information to the Guildmaster and return to the Realm of Shadow before sunset. Of course, I also have some inquiries of my own to make while I am here." Salidar raised both his palms and his eyebrows in a display of well-intentioned earnestness.

Gallenius smirked. "We are aware of the 'circumstances' and your need to return before the fall of night, and we will see to it. You are to have an immediate audience with the Guildmaster. Please follow me."

The mage's longer legs and brisk stride had Salidar scrambling to keep up.

Salidar tried several times to ask a question; the lanky mage deflected each attempt.

"You should hold your questions for the Guildmaster. Come along now."

Within a few minutes, they stopped before a set of plain wooden doors. Gallenius knocked firmly and pressed the doors inward.

The room was a combination of a fair-sized library and a simple office. Bookshelves lined the walls and bright sunlight poured through large windows and overhead skylights. A long table of a strongly grained wood darkened with age was centered in the room, its surface covered in open books, large sheets full of diagrams, blueprints, and assorted notepaper. A number of chairs surrounded the table.

Near the head of the table, Salidar could see a large mahogany desk and the back of a tall office chair. A row of metal file cabinets stood incongruously along the far wall.

As Salidar walked closer, he realized the chair was occupied. The occupant appeared busy, intensely focused with something on a credenza behind the desk.

The occupant slowly swiveled around to face him.

Salidar saw a man of average size in a hooded grey robe identical to the one worn by Gallenius. However, no face was visible within the hood, only a subtle display of shimmering light and shadow. *What's this? A masking spell? The serving Guildmaster's identity is a closely guarded secret? A formidable mage as well?*

As surprising as that was, it paled in comparison to what Salidar saw upon the credenza that had occupied the Guildmaster so intently a moment ago, *a laptop computer*.

Gallenius made a small bow and announced, "Guildmaster, this is Salidar, a member in good standing. He comes now from the Realm of Shadow. He bears a message."

Salidar mimicked Gallenius' bow and spoke deferentially. "Guildmaster, I was instructed to inform you that the vampires Sabrina and Stirling are in the Realm of Man and will soon be joined by an elder vampire, Vlad. Chloe, a familiar of Stirling, has been slain there, as has a human woman of that realm. There may now be other deaths, in retaliation. Furthermore, I must return to Shadow before nightfall. I am tasked by the Lady Diere, yet held by Lady Leanan. Neither knows of my presence here. I was told that I am to be released by Lady Leanan to complete my task."

"Thank you, Salidar. This information confirms that from other sources. But this is not your sole reason for your sudden visit to Storm Haven, is it?"

The Guildmaster's voice had a strange metallic quality, obviously a deliberate alteration to further obscure his identity. It was similar to the tone Salidar had noticed when one of the security guards had spoken; and yet, it was somehow vaguely familiar.

"No, Guildmaster," admitted Salidar, knowing that complete candor would be required if he was to learn anything useful. "I have a number of puzzling questions. May I provide some background?"

"Indeed, please proceed," directed the Guildmaster.

"I am currently bound in service to the Dark Elf, the Lady Diere, a member of the Unseelie Court. Initially it was a normal, uh, mercenary contract, payment in gold and bonuses of enhanced magical knowledge. Admittedly there were some, uh, more sinister aspects of such service. But as we all know, that is often to be expected when dealing with members of the Unseelie Court.

"At any rate, I am not privy to all her plans, only those tasks she sets before me. But I grow unsettled and worried that she plans something that will prove catastrophic and fatal, at least to me. I have too little information; and, information has become a lucrative commodity for our guild. So, I have come here in the hope that I will learn something useful, and, of course, enhance my personal safety."

The Guildmaster clasped his gloved hands before him on the desktop and asked, "What do you know of the ensorcelled scroll you've been carrying?"

Salidar sighed; of course, they would know about the scroll and realize it was dangerous. Complete honesty was his only option.

"At first, nothing, that is until the Baron Von Kestel warned me of a spell against opening by any other than the intended recipient. However, Lady Leanan believes it to be far more than it appears; and is capable of remote activation. Knowing Lady Diere, I am certain it is very dangerous, and no doubt very powerful."

"Who is the intended recipient?" asked Gallenius.

"The innkeeper, Boltar, a human, I think, at the Inn of the Crying Cup. I know him not, nor his role in her plans. She said he possibly has information for me."

The Guildmaster changed the subject. "Why do you seek Padraic the Rogue?"

Since Salidar had discussed with no one, save Leanan, his intention to find Padraic, this surprised him, but he answered honestly. "On Lady Diere's instructions. I have no personal desire to seek him, notwithstanding the price on his head offered by the Light Elf, Duke Briar of the Seelie Court. I was to make inquiries, ostensibly for the reward, but in truth only to report his location to Lady Diere. I have no idea as to her intentions."

The Guildmaster sat in silence and studied him.

Salidar stood at ease, comfortable in the fact that he was being completely honest. It occurred to him that he might be under the influence of a subtle, yet powerful, truth spell, but he really didn't care. He would never knowingly lie to, or betray, the Thieves Guild; it was his ultimate bolt-hole, and optimal survival strategy. As far as he knew, it was the most protected realm in all the known universes, and the best-kept secret.

"What role did you play in the death of the Steward, Maude Delafaire?" the Guildmaster asked in an even tone, but the subtle undercurrent was cold and brittle.

Salidar hung his head; he had no choice but to answer. "I was present, at the direction of Lady Diere; she told me where and when. Lady Diere and others, Lord Addecus of the Were and a human named George Papadolis, had been planning this for years, and crafting certain spells to debilitate and drain the Steward slowly, without her notice. Ultimately she was hospitalized. In her diminished and addled state, I was supposed to converse with and listen to the dying Steward. I think Diere intended to manipulate the transfer of the office to someone of her choosing. I don't know who, or how. Instead, I attempted to get the Steward to bestow it upon me; I even used a powerful amulet in an effort to coerce her. But the attempt failed, and she died. In truth, I think she decided to depart this plane and willed herself through her passing. I later learned that she had already made arrangements for an heir to assume the role of Steward. Of course, the three, Diere, Addecus, and George, were furious with me."

"What role did you have in the attempt upon the life of the heir, Ellen Doyle?" asked Gallenius as the Guildmaster sat immobile, stoically observing Salidar.

"Lady Diere told me to set a watch on the heir and observe her. In the course of that task, George sent me three of his henchmen, and the suggestion that if the opportunity presented itself, the heir should be eliminated if it could be made to appear as an accident. The men he sent came with such a plan; and, while I did accede to it, I did not participate. The plan failed; one man died, and the other two disappeared. The heir was severely injured but survived, and is recovering.

"I was severely punished by Lady Diere. In fact, I still lack sight with my left eye." Salidar paused. "But, now that I think about it, George took no responsibility." Another memory surfaced, something about George wanting the elimination of another *problem,* one Fenton Brewster, to *look like an accident*, but Salidar remained silent as he digested what this might suggest.

The Guildmaster stood and strolled in silence over to a window. At his beckoning gesture, Gallenius joined him. Heads together, they conversed quietly.

Salidar remained standing before the desk, trying to appear relaxed and composed.

"Salidar," called the Guildmaster, "join us at this window, and tell me what you see."

"Of course, Guildmaster, as you wish."

Salidar strode to the window and took a minute to gaze at the rich tableau before him. His view, from slightly above treetop height, included a number of brightly colored rooftops sporting large black panels, and a host of large thickly leafed trees shading streets and pathways. The air appeared clear, the sky cloudless. In the distance a number of tall narrow windmills spun thin arms in lazy revolutions. He could hear a woman's voice calling nearby and the bright laughter of children playing in the street below.

"My perspective suffers somewhat being sighted in only one eye, but I see a realm at peace, secure. However, I do not understand, are those windmills? And what is on the roofs of those buildings, the black panels?"

"Ah, very observant," acknowledged the Guildmaster. "Those rooftops support solar panels, and the windmills spin turbines which generate electrical energy. We also have dammed the nearby Azure River and installed hydroelectric power generators. Indeed, much has changed since your last visit. We have taken considerable advantage of certain technology developed in the Realm of Man."

Salidar nodded and mused aloud, "I see. That would explain the attire and weapons of the security force I met upon my arrival."

"Indeed," added Gallenius. "The twelve-gauge shotgun has proven to be highly effective in close quarters. The shells are loaded with a mixture of iron, lead, and silver pellets, something potentially fatal for all the known races. Should any bypass the diversion spell, they would not survive an encounter in the portal room. You may have noticed the excessively bright ultraviolet ceiling lights; they are quite deadly to the nocturnal denizens of Shadow."

Salidar gestured to the laptop on the credenza. "Electric power would explain the computer."

The Guildmaster chuckled. "Actually, it is battery powered; but, I can easily recharge the battery when its stored power wanes."

Salidar was impressed, and made no effort to hide it.

"But, I digress." The Guildmaster sighed. "More to the point, how do you think we acquired all this technology? By which some might argue that we have equaled or even surpassed the standards of the other known realms. Care to speculate?"

Salidar began to sense a sinking feeling, and chose to withhold comment, in the hope that the question was intended to be rhetorical.

"Ah," intoned the Guildmaster coolly, "I take it by your silence you may have deduced that we had an *arrangement* with Maude Delafaire, Steward of the most powerful permanent transit portal within the Realm of Man. We were quite disappointed and inconvenienced by her untimely debilitation and demise. It was most distressing to learn that a member of our guild might even be involved."

Salidar winced and dropped his eyes. To run afoul of his guild was very bad; his life could easily be forfeit. He could only mumble, "Guildmaster, I had no idea . . . "

"We believe you," said Gallenius. "I suspect that nothing you could have done would have much altered the Steward's fate. Lady Diere worked her evil far too well.

"However, your *interference* appears to have seriously disrupted Lady Diere's plans and frustrated her attempt to gain control of the Grand Portal. You may rest assured that was her goal.

"Now, an heir has been named by Maude, but not yet acknowledged by the Council. So, we should expect something unsavory from Lady Diere, an attempt at manipulation at the very least. I doubt another attempt upon the life of the heir is likely."

"It is ironic indeed," noted the Guildmaster, "that your continued 'interference', specifically the *attempt* upon the life of the heir, that plan to which you 'acceded', failed so publicly, thereby generating an official investigation creating a documented record in the Realm of Man. That will assuredly proscribe any further attempts on her life. The subsequent scrutiny would surely result in discovery of the portal. And that could potentially bring the Realms of the Council to their knees, if not to *oblivion*."

"*Oblivion?*" Salidar gasped, sincerely confused. "I do not understand."

The Guildmaster nodded. "I'm sure you don't. Would it surprise you to learn that our guild membership has increased dramatically? It is quite true. We, originally an association of thieves and smugglers, now have members who have never stolen or smuggled anything. They have found their way to us because they are crafty, stealthy, curious and creative. These very traits are suppressed, to varying degrees, in all the known realms, but for two, the Realm of Man and this realm of Storm Haven.

"Consider this, for you know it to be true. In any other realm, every time a being, especially a human, is perceived to demonstrate any initiative to create or improve something, or to even rise above his station, he is tested for possible training in magic, or he just disappears, slain most likely."

Salidar nodded in agreement, for it was so.

The Guildmaster motioned for the senior mage to continue the explanation.

Gallenius nodded. "Part of our *arrangement* with Maude Delafaire was to accept many of these refugees as new members of our guild. She established what she called 'a sort of Underground Railroad', an appellation I initially did not understand, but came to consider quite appropriate upon further explanation. She assisted in smuggling many out of their repressive realms and into Storm Haven. This went on for many years; it was all very clandestine.

"We do not know how she found them, but she carefully screened all such candidates. We were never infiltrated by any undesirable elements or agents of any realm. New arrivals were assessed for certain skills and offered appropriate training. Without exception, they have all integrated quite well into our community. The diverse array of skills available became quite impressive. This allowed us to devote efforts to the *interception* of useful information, which, as you know, is now one of our most lucrative commodities.

"In consideration of our efforts to support and maintain Maude's *Underground Railroad*, she arranged the transfer of considerable technology, and the necessary knowledge for its application and use. She was of great assistance in recommending appropriate selections of specific technologies; some were capable of more harm than good, and thus avoided. Unfortunately, everything ground to a halt about three years ago."

"That would have been," Salidar calculated, "about the time she was hospitalized."

"We agree," said the Guildmaster. "However, the salient point is what we learned, and what Maude consistently warned us about. There exists a level of technology within the Realm of Man, such that total oblivion of the realms as we know them is quite possible. I know that sounds like the legendary magic of the Old Ones as told in the lost fables of the dim past; but this is no magic, rather weapons of mass destruction, born of mankind's mastery of technology. Aside from a host of potential chemical and biological threats, what Maude referred to as *nuclear options* we found most harrowing. To be candid, it boggles the imagination; however, we found ample reason to believe her."

Salidar was speechless.

"Now she is gone," observed the Guildmaster solemnly. "We have lost much more than a valued friend and conduit in the Realm of Man; we may have lost the ability to stave off chaos and final entropy."

Gallenius pulled Salidar around to face him. "Listen to me. Some among the races, especially within the Unseelie Court, hold the Realm of Man, and humans in general, in disdain, and have proposed to return there for occasional sport." Gallenius scoffed. "However, of those who do venture there, few return. In truth, wiser heads would give humanity a wide berth. Mankind learns and adapts quite well. If the seven billion or so inhabitants of the Realm of Man were to learn of the other realms and decide to invade, nothing can stop them."

"But why should they *invade?*" asked Salidar. "I have traveled there extensively and there is little, save an abundance of true magic, that they lack."

"A fair question, Salidar," the Guildmaster conceded. "May I ask, in your travels in that realm, did you learn much of their history? Some perhaps? Then tell me, what would they do if they were to learn that other *innocent* human beings were being held in virtual slavery, and routinely slain by those considered *monsters* according to mankind's own folklore? And furthermore, that these monsters had spent millennia amassing the wealth of that realm, to say nothing of its untapped natural resources? Does the concept of *crusade* strike any familiar historic notes?"

Salidar whitened in shock. "Ye gods! I see. Their technology is not to be underestimated. They would be formidable, indeed. I have learned that they will not desist if they feel their cause is just, or should their greed be sufficient."

"Indeed," remarked Gallenius soberly. "There must be a balance maintained; and the Realm of Man dealt with most delicately. Should even as few as one percent of mankind muster against the known realms, for any reason, all would be doomed."

The Guildmaster returned to his desk, sat down, and sighed in resignation.

"Salidar, for whatever reasons, fate has dropped you into the middle of this maelstrom. As you know, it is guild policy not to interfere, except in matters of guild interest. The guild is *very interested* in coming to a mutually beneficial arrangement with the new Steward. So please, no more *interference* in that regard.

"We are concerned, of course, as to whatever Lady Diere is up to, so we will help you. However, we do expect to be kept informed. Considering that we now operate the most efficient intelligence gathering and analysis network in the known realms, you may find that periodic communication with us will be to your benefit.

"For example, you should be aware that at the most recent Council meeting, the representative from the Realm of the Dark Elves proposed a native human of the Realm of Man, George Papadolis, for the vacant Chair of Man on the Council. Yes, the *same man;* he must possess a trace of the old blood to be eligible. I have little doubt that Lady Diere sits at the center of this web."

The Guildmaster placed both gloved hands flat on the desk. "As of this moment, Salidar, you know what we know, and what we suspect. Now, as I recall, you indicated that you had some questions?"

"Um," Salidar stalled; he had expected neither this much assistance nor this much information. "Actually, only two. Do you know of this Boltar? And have you any information on the whereabouts of Padraic the Rogue?"

The Guildmaster held up a lone finger, spun in his chair, and tapped a few keys on the laptop. "One moment. We have nothing on Boltar. Now, as for Padraic, he will attend the Fertility Rites on the Mother's Island in the Realm of Mer twelve days from now."

"My thanks, Guildmaster, and to you Mage Gallenius." Salidar bowed in sincere respect. "I shall not let our guild down. But I must return before nightfall as requested, lest friends are placed in jeopardy."

"A wise and commendable strategy, Salidar. You have a few hours yet at your disposal. I suggest you attempt to rest; it does not appear that you have slept very well lately. Gallenius will show you to a rest chamber near the portal room. He will call for you in ample time. I wish you good luck."

After Salidar bowed once more, Gallenius led him from the room, closing the doors.

THE GUILDMASTER SAT in silence for a time considering new facts. He spun to his computer and tapped a few keys. A ruggedly handsome face appeared on the screen and nodded in deference.

"You heard all?" asked the Guildmaster.

"I did."

"He was honest, at least as far as he believes in the truth."

"I sense so, as well. It was, nonetheless, disturbing. Do we know any more about this George Papadolis?"

"We do not, regrettably. But we will make the appropriate inquiries and keep you informed."

"Excellent. Regarding this innkeeper, Boltar, I seem to remember an agent of a secret cabal, rumored to have existed within the Unseelie Court, who used this name, an alias, of course. The whispered tale held that this cabal tried to foment a *coup d'état* almost two centuries ago."

"Oh yes," the Guildmaster acknowledged. "It did happen; but they failed. Queen Mab crushed them mercilessly. Anyone even suspected of involvement was summarily executed; the whole affair was hushed up. You don't suppose this is the same?"

"No, *that* Boltar was a Dark Elf, and was supposedly executed. Salidar expects to meet a human. But, I am intrigued by the use of that particular name. This situation would bear watching closely. Have you any assets in place?"

"Close enough. Can you be in Mer for the festival?"

The face broke into a grin. "Am I not always?"

The Guildmaster laughed aloud. "My word, you are ever the rascal! Have you any more questions?"

"Just one, what of Queen Mab? I find it hard to believe that Lady Diere could orchestrate such a broad scheme, to include engaging certain resources of the Unseelie Court without Mab's knowledge, if not her tacit approval."

"Hmm, that is true; yet we have heard nothing. This latest Queen Mab, the fifty-fourth I believe, has not ruled the Unseelie Court for two and one-half centuries without considerable craft and guile. She has proven to be devious and quite Machiavellian within her own court."

"Indeed, that court is a hotbed of intrigue and petty vendettas. Lady Diere is hardly her favorite. It seems they respect one another for their respective deadly skills, like a tiger and dragon sharing the same jungle. There is certainly no love lost there."

"Please correct me if I am mistaken," cautioned the Guildmaster, "but are not this Queen Mab and Lady Diere of the same House, the current Administration of the Dark Elves?"

"Ah, such a good memory, my old friend. They are indeed distant cousins within the House of Hawthorn. This Queen Mab is the former Lady Celeste, and Lady Diere was once a rival. Perhaps she still is?"

"Be careful, we do not yet know Diere's game. She has ever been unpredictable, vicious, and vindictive!"

"Oh, fret not, Guildmaster. You know that I know her, uh, rather well. Now, I really must go. I will need to conserve my strength for the Fertility Rites. Be well, old friend!"

"And you—you incorrigible *rogue!*"

At the tap of a key the screen went blank. The Guildmaster leaned back in his softly creaking chair, steepled his fingers, and savored an unseen smile. *Ah, good friends warmed the heart.*

He had successfully led his guild for more than a century, through times of slow and steady growth, to a point of comfortable prosperity. His discreet association and collaboration with Maude Delafaire had been a significant factor in the improvement of the quality of life for his people.

He had known her well, better than most knew, and perhaps best kept secret. She had proven to be a fine person and a true friend; he missed her terribly. He was torn with mixed emotions when he considered Salidar's role in the course of her demise. But that was a demon with which he would wrestle at another, more appropriate, time.

Sighing, he rose and stood before the window, considering current developments, and what perils or opportunities for his realm and his people might be imbued therein.

He was not so naïve as to believe that the very existence of Storm Haven was as closely held a secret as it once was; but he would do his very best to keep it so.

He couldn't help but feel like the fates had turned a page, closing a chapter in this tale of ages, and now contemplated a blank sheet, the unwritten future, unknown and unfettered. Whatever was to come would do so on its own terms, in its own time, and for its own reasons. The Guildmaster could only hope that he, his realm, and most of all, his people were up to the challenge.

CH 15

HAWK HAD GONE HOME to the rustic cabin he shared with his grandfather. Upon his arrival he had the slightest sensation that he was being observed, but he knew Wendell was at his office at the casino.

What the—? Was that movement in the woods?

He saw no one, but couldn't quite shake this unsettling feeling.

His cell phone rang. Trey's number was displayed on the caller ID screen.

"Hawk here, what's up, Trey?"

"Where are you?"

"Home. It's gonna rain, so I thought I'd better park the bike and get the cruiser."

"Get a move on. The lieutenant's off today and the captain's already called. He's going in to the office. I'm at the casino. We have two crime scenes now."

"Two? At the same site?"

"Close enough. Listen, one's pretty bad, *old boots*, partner."

Trey's voice was devoid of emotion, but Hawk knew his partner was disturbed. *Old boots* was an in-house warning that the scene was particularly messy. It referred to old precinct lore that seasoned cops never wore good shoes to a bad crime scene, not if they could help it.

"I'm on my way. Ten minutes, tops. Later."

Hawk hung up. Checking out any movement in his woods would have to wait. He made sure the house and garage were secure and took one last look around before leaving.

As he drove the cruiser down the driveway, he made a mental note to mention the movement in the woods to his grandfather. Wendell was among the finest hunter-stalkers of his generation, or any to follow. Nothing would happen in his forest that he could not discover, or track, despite his age.

TEN MINUTES LATER, Hawk parked his cruiser next to the departmental CSI unit van. He nodded to the sheriff's deputies and tribal police officers on the outer perimeter as he passed under the yellow crime-scene tape.

He took a moment to look around. A recently arrived news crew was busy unloading their camera gear. A few casino patrons slowed their pace to gawk as they passed the area en route to the casino entrance. Overhead clouds continued to build and darken. Rain was inevitable; Hawk hoped the scenes would be protected from the imminent weather.

The entrance to a newly constructed parking garage had been further cordoned off. CSI techs were dusting the stairwell door and handles for latent prints. He nodded in greeting and slipped past them without disturbing their work.

Trey met him just inside the stairwell doorway and handed him a set of latex gloves and plastic booties. "Here, Hawk, you're gonna need these. It starts upstairs on the third floor."

"It *starts?*"

Trey just nodded and headed up the stairs.

Hawk fumbled the booties on, snapped on the gloves, and followed.

Trey kept up a monologue as they climbed the steps; Hawk just listened.

"This parking garage is new, five levels. Construction is almost finished; all that's left is to paint stripes and number the parking spaces. Oh yeah, the single elevator hasn't been inspected yet, so it's powered off. There's a glass enclosed walkway between the second level and the casino, but it's not open yet, still locked, no access either way. The usual surveillance cameras are installed, but not yet linked or powered.

"The painting contractor sent his site boss, Paulie Buffett, here this morning to see if the other contractors had cleared their gear out so the painting could begin first thing Monday. Buffett found the first body, or rather the body parts. He then ran downstairs and called the Tribal Police. They called us, and here we are."

The third level landing was awash in the harsh glare of klieg lights arranged to illuminate the scene. Gloved and masked CSI techs were busy taking photographs and digital videos, while another CSI team identified items of evidence and placed plastic numeric markers.

A few flies buzzed past the detectives' heads as they stood at the edge of the landing. The smell was almost overpowering, a pungent mixture of the rancid coppery tang of blood, acrid urine, and feces.

Hawk also noticed an underlying subtle musk that simmered in the sinuses and seemed to flirt with some primitive fight-or-flight response reflex. And yet, it suggested an involuntary arousal, almost like a pheromone. He found it slightly disorienting.

Trey pulled him to one side, closer to the safety fencing atop the short side wall, and into a cleansing breeze. Hawk took a deep breath; his head felt a little clearer.

Trey just nodded. "Yeah, I know, it's a real stinker. Stay by this wall where the air is better. The M.E., Dr. Pritchard, is up on the fifth level, the roof, at the other scene. He's already examined this one. This victim, *Jane Doe Number 1*, is an unidentified white female, 20-30 years. The body's eviscerated, and completely dismembered. However, the head is intact, the largest single piece; even the pelvis is broken in half." Trey paused, looking out over the nearby treetops, and took in a few deep breaths through his nose.

Hawk made notes in silence as they watched patrons trickle in and out of the casino some distance away. He whispered, "I don't think I've ever seen one this bad, all this blood, tissue, and the smell. There's something about the smell."

"I know, but I don't know what it is. Neither does the Doc, so he had the techs take air samples, too. By the way, the Doc thinks she, our victim Jane Doe 1, is all here. Nothing is apparently missing; it's just *distributed* around. He'll know for sure after the postmortem. No ID, but the techs got some fingerprints. Doc said she's got good dentition, so maybe we can get lucky with the identification.

"The Tribal Police have accounted for all casino employees on the job today, and they're checking on those who worked yesterday and last night. I called the captain and he's got Billy and Gordon checking the missing persons reports. But I think that's probably a long shot."

Hawk shone his flashlight up at the low ceiling. "Not as much overhead blood spatter as I would have expected, considering the rest of the scene."

Trey shook his head. "It didn't start here; it ended here. Follow me, and watch your step."

They slipped carefully past the CSI techs still working in the upper stairwell. Copious amounts of blood and tissue were there as well. On the fourth level landing the techs were almost done.

Trey pointed. "The initial attack appears to have happened here. The techs tell me there's much less tissue to recover and the blood spatter is consistent with arterial spurting."

Trey and Hawk carefully examined the area from several different perspectives. Hawk did a scene sketch in his notebook, and borrowed a tape measure from a CSI tool box to record certain reference point details. He grunted as he stood from a squat, rewound the tape measure, and made some final notes.

Trey waited patiently, then asked, "Done? Let me hear your analysis."

"Okay, I agree the initial assault was here. The victim was either pursued or was dragged down to the lower landing. I think she was still alive, at least at first, while on the third level and probably expired there. What's weird is I'd expect some sort of footprints, considering all the blood, but there's nothing I can make out. "

"Yeah, I know." Trey sighed. "Too many unanswered questions. We have no definitive cause of death yet, no apparent weapon, no victim ID, no suspects, and no motive; so, it can only get better. Are we through here? Ready to see the other scene?"

"May as well. Do you think they're linked?"

"I don't know; but I don't think we can rule it out. Let's discard these gloves and booties in the CSI hazmat bag down here and get some fresh ones upstairs before we go out to the other scene on the roof. Then you can see for yourself."

Trey turned and trudged up the stairs.

THEY FOUND THE MEDICAL Examiner, Dr. Pritchard, reading from a notebook and talking on his cell phone. Noting their arrival, he nodded to Trey and Hawk and returned to his phone conversation. He was standing to one side of a decapitated female body that was propped in a sitting position. The victim's back was leaning against the wall of the elevator shaft housing. There was surprisingly little blood, a mere trickle from the gaping wound of the neck stump.

Hawk nudged Trey. "Note the lack of blood. Think this might be a *dump job?*"

Trey shrugged. "Well, I suppose it's possible that *Jane Doe Number 2* may have been killed elsewhere and the body deposited here, but I don't think the Doc or our CSI guys think so. Take a good look."

He did. The body was fully clothed in a dark blue pantsuit and lighter blue blouse; the clothing was intact, in disarray, yet barely bloodstained. The feet were shoeless; the soles of her hose were torn and tattered. The hands lay on the thighs, covered by brown paper bags closely taped to the wrists, a CSI technique to preserve any trace evidence, to include defensive wounds, any foreign tissue under the nails, and gunshot residue.

Tearing his eyes away from the body, Hawk made a deliberate effort to see the entire scene, which for the moment was the entire rooftop level of the parking garage that lay open to the darkening sky.

A small pistol the color of dull silver lay centered in a white chalked circle about ten feet to the left of the body. Strewn to the right of the gun, a series of smaller chalked circles marked the spent brass casings that were scattered about on the concrete surface. A CSI tech was patiently placing a numbered plastic marker and a short ruler in each of the chalked circles as another tech followed, taking photographs.

Trey nudged Hawk toward a chest-high side wall. He looked over the edge and pointed. "We found a pair of shoes down there that might be hers. They've already been recovered."

Hawk could see a grassy area cordoned off by yellow crime-scene tape fifty-some feet below. Two small spray-painted orange circles were visible within. "Interesting, if they're hers. Who found the body? And do we have an ID yet?"

"Nope, no ID yet, nor do we have Jane Doe 2's head. Hold on." Trey opened his own notebook and rummaged through a few pages. "A tribal cop found the body. He was part of the response to the initial call on the third level scene. He ordered an immediate search of the entire garage. Here it is; Sammy Caldwell, a rookie with the Tribal Police. He's been on just under two years, but he did everything right; noted the time and weather conditions, preserved the scene, and called his sergeant."

Hawk grinned and nodded appreciatively. "Well, you can't ask for more than that. You've already taken his statement?"

"Yeah, he's downstairs on the perimeter with the patrol deputies. He's a good kid, eager but not in the way. I'm thinking about asking Captain Miller to see if we can get Caldwell detailed to us for this investigation. We're facing a mountain of paperwork with two victims and two scenes. You know they're going to ask for a 'cooperative' investigation."

Hawk pursed his lips. "It's your call, Trey, but you know the Tribal Police Department really does little more than security for the casino and its patrons. The investigations they conduct are usually pretty routine stuff; petty theft, vehicle burglaries, and cheating the house. This is homicide."

Trey's eyebrows rose.

Hawk winced and stammered, "I'm not sure that came out right. I don't mean to, uh, I meant—"

Grinning, Trey interrupted. "I know what you meant, and don't worry. This Caldwell is pretty sharp; he's already suggested checking all the other parking lots for a car that doesn't move for the next day or so. Here comes Sgt. Melancon."

The graying CSI sergeant stowed his notebook under one arm as he walked in their direction. Seeing that he had their attention, he altered his course, pointed to the nearby pistol, and waved the detectives over.

Squatting down, he pointed with his pen. "Gentlemen, I draw your attention to this recumbent stainless steel, Sig-Sauer P230, semi-auto pistol, in .380ACP caliber."

Trey and Hawk squatted as well.

Gesturing to the scattered chalked circles, each of which the detectives could easily see held a spent brass cartridge case, Sgt. Melancon continued. "You'll note that eight spent .380 shell casings are very likely in the locations they fell after being fired and ejected. The pistol is empty; don't assume otherwise just because the slide is fully forward in battery. You may already know this, but when using the P230 with the factory supplied magazine, the slide does not remain open after the last round is fired. I suspect it was fired *dry*. I think that our victim, Jane Doe 2, fired the weapon. Of course, we'll take prints and do a GSR test to confirm. Dr. Pritchard advised me that his cursory examinations of this victim and the dismembered one on the lower level did not reveal any gunshot wounds."

"I noticed that your techs had bagged this victim's hands," said Hawk.

"We're going to bag her feet, too. There are some scrapes and contusions on her feet that are consistent with the brushed concrete of this parking surface. We also found a few traces of blood; *smudges* is an apt description."

Sgt. Melancon rose; Trey and Hawk followed suit.

"So you think this is the actual site of the killing? It's not a *dump job*?" asked Hawk.

"The physical evidence seems to confirm this as the site." The CSI sergeant hesitated. "But I would have expected more blood. Finding the head would help. We'll have to wait on the M.E.'s report, of course, but that neck wound looks more torn, rather than cut. We found some hair; long, straight, and very dark, maybe black."

Trey and Hawk shared a glance, but remained silent.

Sgt. Melancon opened his notebook. "We found a pair of woman's shoes on the ground below, which we suspect belong to this victim. The grassy area on which they were found was mowed and raked yesterday, no shoes then. My gut tells me that they were dropped from this level. Of course, I'll know more when I get the shoes to the lab." He closed his notebook and slipped it into a pocket.

"Of course, Mel," drawled Trey, "but I have a question. I haven't seen, or been told, that any spent rounds were found. If our victim got off eight rounds, where did they go?"

The CSI sergeant held one hand flat slightly above his shoulder, and pointed with the other to the wall that surrounded the rooftop level.

"Having consulted with Dr. Pritchard, I'm estimating the victim was approximately sixty-four inches in height—please, no comments about her missing head. That wall is sixty inches high; yes, we measured. Let's assume our victim is the shooter, and she fired while standing, using a two-handed grip in an isosceles or 'Weaver' stance. Now let's further assume a six-foot target."

He paused and held his hands together forming an oval with his index fingers and thumbs. He placed this oval over the center of his chest. "A marksman is typically trained to aim for the center of mass, here, which is about fifty-two inches high on a six-foot man, who, if he knows he is being shot at, typically and instinctively hunches forward in a crouch, effectively lowering the CM further." He hunched in a crouch to demonstrate and returned to his erect posture.

"I get it," said Hawk. "If our victim went for center of mass, the rounds would have been at about four feet or under, and should leave impact marks on the wall."

"Only if she missed," noted Trey grimly.

"Aye, there's the rub," quoted a grinning Sgt. Melancon.

"Wait a minute," Hawk cautioned. "We're making a lot of assumptions here, not the least of which is that our victim put eight rounds into her assailant—"

"Of course," interrupted Trey, "a lone assailant is another assumption."

A muted rumble of distant thunder failed to draw their attention; the persistent breeze grew ominously still. However, the other CSI techs did not ignore the capricious nature of the ever-darkening sky. They began gathering their gear and equipment in careful but practiced haste.

"Right," agreed Hawk, frowning in concentration. "But let's assume one assailant for the sake of argument. So, finding no spent rounds means no apparent misses? Eight rounds didn't even slow him down? Then he kills her by beheading?"

"Actually," intoned the M.E., Dr. Pritchard, as he walked up and joined the conversation, "I suspect the decapitation occurred postmortem, as the lack of bleeding suggests. I can't yet hazard a guess as to methods or any weapons used on either of the two victims. Of course, I'll know more after the autopsies."

A CSI tech holding a clear plastic evidence recovery bag approached Sgt. Melancon. "Excuse me, Sarge, but we found this gold colored plastic card in the left jacket pocket of the victim, Jane Doe 2. It bears a hologram, a three digit number on one side, '721', and a magnetic strip on the reverse. It's likely some kind of security card." The tech hefted the bag for all to see.

Hawk recognized it immediately. "It's a proximity access card; a security card that permits the bearer access into restricted areas of the casino. The hologram is the Tribal Gaming Board logo, and the gold color indicates that it accesses an executive suite or office. My grandfather serves on the board, and he has a similar card. They're all individually numbered."

"So, Jane Doe 2 had access to an executive office or suite?" asked Trey.

"So it appears," admitted Hawk.

"Only one way to find out if she's an executive or employee," said Trey. "Hawk and I will visit with the casino manager. The number is '721', is that right?"

The tech nodded. "Affirmative, '721', Sarge. We can't do any more with the card here, but we can scan it and download any data in our lab. It has to be kept away from magnets and strong electrical fields."

"Trey, let me make a quick call," suggested Hawk, reaching for his cell phone. "We might get lucky on that card."

Trey nodded. "Do it, Hawk."

A few solitary raindrops teased the warm parking surface.

Sgt. Melancon cast a wary glance to the sky. "Gentlemen, my CSI team is almost done here; and, not a moment too soon, considering the impending weather. Doctor, we're ready to remove the body whenever you are."

"Very well, let's proceed." The M.E. and CSI sergeant turned and walked back to the body.

Hawk pulled his partner aside. "Trey, I just talked to my grandfather. He's here, in his office; he can make time for us right now. He probably has access to more information than the casino manager anyway."

"Great! The more we know before we have to brief the captain, the smarter we look. And right now, I'm afraid we don't have enough to look *sentient*."

They discarded the gloves and booties in a CSI hazmat disposal bag and left the scene.

THE CSI TECHS HAD FINISHED processing the stairwell and waved the detectives on.

As they made their way down the stairs, Hawk wrestled with the differences and the similarities of the two scenes. The location and timing of the two crimes made it highly likely that they were somehow related. Both involved dismemberment, yet the conditions of the scenes were dramatically different.

One seethed with raging violence, savage carnage distended over a wide area; such gross evisceration and complete dismemberment are actually something quite rare. In contrast, the other scene was contained and neat; although, beheading is a rather specific type of dismemberment.

Was the body posed, perhaps? In fact, both scenes could have been deliberately staged, each to send a message, but to whom? Both victims were women. Was that of significance, or merely coincidence?

It appeared that one victim, Jane Doe 1, tried to flee; and the other, Jane Doe 2, stood her ground and fought. Or did both fight? Was this the work of a single killer, or more? How much time was taken with each victim? Had a single killer been preoccupied with Jane Doe 1, only to be surprised by Jane Doe 2? Which crime happened first? Or were they simultaneous?

Hawk chewed at his lower lip. His gut didn't like the single killer theory; the overall scenes were too different, despite both featuring beheading. Different styles and patterns usually meant more than one perpetrator. Of course, there were the rare exceptions, for example, multiple personalities in a single serial killer. However, that just didn't seem to be the case here.

He had the feeling he was missing something, but *what?*

As they passed the third level landing, he caught a whiff of that cloying under-scent of musk that he'd noticed before. He realized he had not smelled it on the fifth level, another difference. Could it be important? Maybe so, but how or why?

TREY POINTED TO THE sky. "Look at those clouds! Let's move! It's gonna dump on us!"

They walked briskly up the landscaped walk toward the casino entrance, about fifty yards away. A series of big irregular raindrops intermittently splashed to the ground around the detectives, who increased their pace accordingly.

They were about halfway to the doors when Hawk caught one on his left shoulder; it felt like he'd been smacked with an egg. He knew what was coming; giving up all pretense at dignity, he laughed aloud and broke into a run. Trey just chuckled and trotted after him. A peal of angry thunder ruptured the sky directly above.

They almost made it. Ten yards from the doors, the celestial dam broke.

They staggered into the lobby, drenched and sputtering, mostly from their own laughter. A few casino patrons stopped to smile and laugh as well. They were quite a sight, soaked, dripping puddles on the marble tiles of the lobby floor.

"Hey, Trey," teased Hawk, "you're a regular meteorologist!"

"Damn straight, *Aquaman,*" Trey wheezed between guffaws, "I told you it was gonna dump on us!" He slapped a dripping hand on Hawk's equally wet shoulder.

Rain pummeled the lobby doors in thick silvery sheets as rolling crests of thunder punished the atmosphere. The parking garage had vanished in the deluge; ghost-like hints of walls and landscaping appeared and disappeared as the spasmodic downpour lurched in the grasp of erratic winds.

Hawk knew the ferocious storm would not maintain this intensity for long; its energy would soon diminish. A more moderate rain would no doubt follow, bringing a sense of cleansing, as if Mother Nature herself could not abide what she had seen today.

Trey pointed to a nearby men's room. "Come on, maybe they've got those heated hand dryers in there. Let's try to clean up before we drop in on your grandfather."

TEN MINUTES LATER, in Wendell Small Owl's office, Trey and Hawk, still somewhat damp, sipped hot coffee while Hawk's grandfather checked a computer database to ascertain whatever information was available regarding the security card.

"Card 721 was one of four issued to 'Mr. George Smith and staff' last week. That's unusual," commented Wendell. "Standard procedure is to issue access cards to specifically named individuals, not to unidentified staff members. One moment. Ah, 'Mr. Smith' is with *Moonglow Financial & Holding Company*. That firm recently acquired the outstanding construction loan on the new parking garage, the same one you were in this afternoon. There's an addendum to the file that MFHC would exercise the option to take temporary on-site office space prior to completion for the final inspection, acceptance, and certification phases of the project. We have a balloon note due sixty days thereafter. The board is already in initial negotiations to wrap that residual into a new loan to expand the casino hotel. We'd like to have another hundred rooms. Oh, you probably don't need to know all that. Sorry."

"That's okay, Grandfather, I already knew most of that. And now Trey doesn't have to play *catch-up*. After all, he's not as quick as he used to be," teased Hawk.

"Not true, young apprentice," responded Trey wryly, as he raised his cup. "I stay saturated in ample quantities of caffeine, and am thus nimble of mind."

"And dry of wit," Wendell observed, tongue in cheek. "Although *dry* is an ironic turn of phrase under the present circumstances."

Trey and Hawk could not help but laugh.

"Seriously," interjected Trey, "what more can you tell us about Mr. Smith and his staff?"

"Nothing, I'm afraid, other than that they occupy a large suite on the seventh floor, number 720. There are only ten suites on that floor, 700 through 790. The access card numbers are a simple code; the first digit is the floor, the second is the suite, and the third is the sequential number, 1 through 9, of a card programmed for access to that particular suite. So card 721 is the first card issued that will access suite 720; 722 would be the next, and so on. I've personally never met George Smith or any of his staff. I'll find out who arranged the suite and checked them in, but—"

Wendell was interrupted by a feminine voice from his desk intercom. "Sir, excuse me, but are the sheriff's department detectives with you?"

"Yes, Diane, they're in my office. What is it?"

"Sgt. Broadfoot is here and needs to see them right away, please sir."

"Fine, send him in, please."

Wendell and the detectives stood as a truly massive man in a Tribal Police uniform, a wet raincoat in hand, ducked his head to clear the doorway lintel as he entered the office. Upon seeing Trey and Hawk, the hardened sunbronzed face broke into a wide grin. Trey and Hawk grinned as well and were soon shaking hands with their old friend.

Sgt. Jim Broadfoot was a part-time defensive tactics instructor at the Sheriff's Department In-Service Training Academy. For two weeks every year, he and other instructors put law enforcement personnel from agencies parish-wide through the required annual recertification process for the use of batons, pepper spray, compelled compliance and defensive techniques. He also served as an assistant firearms instructor.

"Sir, I apologize for the interruption," boomed the smiling Sgt. Broadfoot as he nodded deferentially to Wendell Small Owl, "but we may have a break. We had a team checking the roof of this building and one of our men spotted something on the balcony of a seventh floor suite. We've gotten no response at the door."

"Seventh floor?" asked Hawk. "Let me guess, 720, the 'Moonglow Financial' suite?"

"Uh, right, according to the front desk," Sgt. Broadfoot acknowledged. "There's no other access to that balcony except through that locked suite."

"What, exactly, did the officer see?" probed Trey.

Sgt. Broadfoot leaned forward and spoke quietly. "He reports what appears to be a human head, with long black hair. Actually, he saw the hair first, being blown around by the wind. That side of the building is leeward of the storm."

"And he saw it from the roof? Five floors further up? In this rain?" pressed Trey.

"Yes. The rain's easing up a bit. I went up there with a pair of binoculars to confirm the report. And I agree; it looks like a human head."

"Well, it sounds like we have *exigent circumstances* to enter the suite to get to a possible crime scene," Trey announced. "I'm going to call our captain and advise him. We're gonna need CSI back here, too." He pulled out his phone and stepped to one side of the office.

Wendell picked up his phone and buzzed his secretary. "Diane, please have the manager on duty meet me at suite 720; and have him bring a master passcard . . . Yes, as soon as possible. And see who checked in the *George Smith party*. Thank you."

Sgt. Broadfoot held up a hand the size of a dinner plate. "There's no need to rush. I have four men on the seventh floor and two on the roof. We'll get photographs from there as well."

Hawk nodded and explained for his grandfather's benefit. "Photographs of the head taken from the same vantage point as when first sighted could be quite valuable at a subsequent court hearing should the *exigent circumstances* become an issue. Any shrewd defense counsel would most certainly challenge the admission of such damning evidence as the decedent's severed head."

"I see. Please, follow me, gentlemen." Wendell took them via a restricted access elevator to the seventh floor. One of those gold security cards was required to operate it.

In fact, Hawk noted, the holder of such a card could come and go undetected; there was no CCTV camera in the elevator car.

They found the four uniformed officers at the suite entrance, the door secure.

A man of slight build hurried down the hall. His horn-rimmed glasses kept sliding down his nose, despite the repeated push-back of a nervous finger. A gold nameplate pinned on his camel blazer declared "Howard Simms, Manager".

Sgt. Broadfoot pointed to the master passcard in the hand of the fidgeting manager. "I'll take that, Mr. Simms."

He balked, initially reluctant to surrender the passcard, until a nod from Wendell Small Owl relieved him of that concern. Mr. Simms gratefully faded to the rear, his back pressed to the wall opposite the suite entrance. Hawk thought the poor man looked to be torn between wishing he could disappear within the textured wallpaper and straining to see around the uniformed officers, his curiosity flaring.

The huge sergeant whispered to Trey, "If you don't mind, my men are *entry trained* and know the layout. So, we'll enter, clear, and secure; if you've got our backs?"

Trey grinned and nodded. "Done deal, Jim; we're good. Whenever you're ready."

Sgt. Broadfoot didn't need to say a word to his men. Through a series of succinct hand signals, he made the assignments. He slipped the passcard in the electric lock and removed it smartly. A small green light glowed on the lock housing.

An officer, squatting to one side of the door, pressed the lever fully down and gently pushed the door open. Another officer *quick peeked* into the room, and tapped the squatting officer on the shoulder. In the next instant all four officers and the sergeant had silently entered the room. Weapons drawn, they went about securing other rooms in the suite.

Within a minute, Sgt. Broadfoot returned to the suite's entrance. "It's clear and vacant."

Trey and Hawk entered a large office space, fronted by a receptionist's desk. Six doors, three to either side, stood open; a kitchenette and bedrooms were visible.

The rear wall of glass door panels was shrouded by floor length curtains; however, the fabric did a poor job of holding the muted flash of capricious lightning at bay. A few feeble gusts of diminishing rain, remnants of the storm's spent fury, impotently lashed the glass. The muffled thunder was reduced to a more distant rumble.

At a nod from Trey, Hawk snapped on a pair of latex gloves and started for the curtains, but Sgt. Broadfoot stopped him.

"Hawk, the curtain controls are electric." The big man pointed. "See the buttons at the side of the receptionist's desk?"

"Oh yeah, I got it." Hawk used the tip of his pen to press the outermost edge of the *open* button, a little trick to preserve any latent fingerprints.

The curtains slowly opened as a soft whirring sound hummed from the ceiling. The balcony slowly came into view. The rain had stopped, a few tardy drops punctuating the wet tableau; a chaise lounge, a set of white plastic chairs, and a round glass-topped table near the far railing.

There upon the table, in a brown crusting pool, sat the severed head of a woman. Wet ropes of long black disheveled hair were trying to flee upon the undisciplined eddies of the wind while other strands tugged and flailed, stuck in the muck of pooling fluids. The glazed eyes stared vacantly into the room, the lids at half-mast. A large iridescent fly lazily landed on one ashen cheek, meandered towards the small chin, and disappeared inside the agape mouth.

Trey broke the silence. "No, don't open the balcony doors. Preserve the scene for CSI. In fact, we need to treat the entire suite as a crime scene, so if anyone touched anything, make notes to that effect."

"There's no problem there, Trey," assured Sgt. Broadfoot. "My people are all gloved, and we only touched the front door. All other doors were open."

Trey was still staring through the glass when he uttered, "Oh my God . . . "

"What?" Hawk asked.

"Gimme a minute!" Trey held up his index finger, grabbed his cell phone and hastily made a call. "Hello, this is Sgt. Bassett from the Sheriff's Office.

Is Dr. Pritchard available, please? That's fine, I'll hold . . . Doc? Yeah, it's Trey. Listen, have y'all started on Jane Doe 2 yet? No, no problem. Listen, we may have found her head. Yeah, we're waiting on CSI now. Okay, can you have someone check the body for extensive tattoos, especially on her back? With the clothing she was wearing I don't think any of what I'm looking for would have been visible at the scene. I'll hold."

The room had gone dead quiet once more. All eyes were on Trey, who was almost electrically alert. He never took his eyes from the half-lidded sleepy gaze on the balcony.

"Yes, I'm here . . . Okay, thank you very much, Doc. Yeah, I do believe we can make an ID; you ready? Okay, I know her as *Suzi Origami;* first name S-U-Z-I, last name O-R-I-G-A-M-I. Yeah, I know, like the Oriental art of paper folding, probably an alias; but, she is Japanese, dual citizenship. We know there may be a possible *Yakuza* connection. Okay, we'll see you later. Thanks again, 'bye."

Trey turned to the rest of the group. "Gentlemen, allow me to introduce Miss Suzi Origami, formerly known as Jane Doe 2. She is known to us from another investigation." Trey paused. "In fact, that Wilkerson case is still open."

"Wilkerson?" asked Hawk. For him, the name, *Suzi Origami*, didn't ring a bell.

"It was that lawyer, Perry Wilkerson. You know, the same lawyer that ripped off all his clients, gambled their money away, and then just disappeared."

Hawk made the connection. "The same lawyer who ripped off Maude Delafaire, Ellen Doyle's aunt?"

"Right! *Perry Wilkerson* was actually a *missing persons* case that we suspected was probably a homicide, but we never found a body."

"Okay, so that's how you know her by sight?" Hawk probed.

Trey pointed towards the balcony. "Yeah, I interviewed Suzi Origami in New Orleans when we did some follow-up on the Wilkerson case. She was supposedly on the executive staff of a now-defunct casino, where Perry Wilkerson blew a lot of money. That establishment was suspected of being a major money laundering operation. And guess who was the behind-the-scenes power broker—'Papa George' Papadolis! We didn't know it at the time, but the feds were looking very closely at 'Papa George' and some of his operations. I'll get into the details later, but the bottom line here is that Suzi is, or rather *was,* a suspected contract hitter, among other things, for 'Papa George' and some other unsavory groups. We knew she had some vague organized crime connections overseas."

"Okay, I get it," Hawk acknowledged. "So, the question is, what's she doing here?"

Trey looked intensely at the others in the room and asked, "Has anybody ever seen this 'Mr. Smith' or any of his staff members?"

The tribal police officers and their sergeant shook their heads.

Wendell Small Owl held his chin in a pensive moment. He suddenly looked up and walked to the suite's entrance. Looking down the hall, to the left and right, he shrugged and returned to the room. He took his cell phone and made a quick call. "Hi Diane, it's Wendell. Would you please have Howard come back upstairs to the suite on seven? Oh, he is? That's excellent! Just have him find me. Thank you."

Turning to Trey, Wendell said, "It seems that the on-duty manager, Mr. Howard Simms, was the manager who handled the Smith party at check-in. He should be on his way back up here now."

While they waited, Hawk pulled Wendell to one side and said, "Grandfather, I almost forgot. Earlier, I stopped by the house to get my cruiser, and I had the feeling somebody was watching the house. I didn't actually see anyone; I didn't have time to check it out. Have you noticed anything?"

"No, not that I can think of at this moment." Wendell pondered. "Wait—you don't think there's a connection to this matter, do you?"

"No, not this. It may be nothing, Grandfather. I just remembered and wanted you to know."

"Oh, well don't worry. I'll keep an eye out."

"Yeah, it can't hurt," Hawk agreed. "Grandfather, you said that Mr. Smith's first name was George, right? I've got an idea, but I'll need a minute. Listen, when your manager gets here, don't let him leave." With that he stepped away, his phone in hand.

Trey nudged Sgt. Broadfoot. "Jim, let's close the balcony curtains. The fewer *civilians* seeing that aspect of the crime scene from this vantage point, the better. When Simms gets here, lets be sure he touches nothing."

Moments later, Howard Simms politely knocked on the door of the suite and was ushered in by Sgt. Broadfoot.

Wendell greeted the manager warmly. "Howard, thank you for responding so quickly. We need your help. Can you describe the circumstances surrounding the arrival and check-in of Mr. Smith and his party?"

Simms was nervous but his memory was quite good.

"Ah, as I recall, two men and two women comprised the George Smith party. Mr. Smith was a somewhat brusque, white, middle-aged businessman who seemed in a hurry. The other gentleman was younger, tall, muscular, and silent. He carried a large gym bag that he refused to allow the porters to handle."

"I see. Go on, Howard," Wendell urged.

Simms had obviously paid a bit more attention to the women.

"The ladies were both lovely, rather striking Asian beauties, actually. One was quite tall, her long black hair woven in a single braid, and held herself somewhat aloof. The other woman was shorter, more petite, almost delicate by comparison. She wore her long black hair free, to her waist. She was very friendly and asked me a lot of questions. I'm afraid I was a bit distracted with her during the check-in procedure. I didn't realize until later that I had failed to get individual names for the suite access cards. I'm so sorry."

"Not a problem, Howard," Wendell assured him.

Trey and Hawk exchanged a knowing glance.

"Mr. Simms," Hawk asked, "do you think you would recognize 'Mr. Smith' if you saw him again?"

"I should think so; although, I only saw him the one time." Simms nodded earnestly.

Hawk held up his cell phone so Simms could see the digital photograph displayed on the screen. "Mr. Simms, do you recognize this person?"

Howard Simms squinted a bit through his glasses, rocked his head upward and pulled back. He looked directly at Hawk. "Yes sir. That is Mr. Smith."

"You're certain?" asked Hawk mildly.

"Absolutely, there's no doubt in my mind."

"Thank you very much, Mr. Simms, you've been a big help," added Trey sincerely.

"Well done, Howard!" Wendell beamed as he clasped Simms' hand and patted him on the shoulder, all the while maneuvering the manager into the hall. "Please feel free to return to your duties. Of course, keep this matter confidential until you hear otherwise from me."

Hawk had engaged in a quiet conversation on his phone while the manager was escorted from the room. As he bid his caller good-bye, he looked up to be certain that Mr. Simms had gone and the door was closed. He gestured for everyone's attention and held up his cell phone.

"This is the most recent photograph of 'Papa George' Papadolis, from the OCDETF investigation file, complements of Deputy Willis Hebert of the U.S. Marshals Service."

"Well done," approved Trey. "Y'all take a good look. Does anyone else recognize him?"

The tribal police officers shrugged and shook their heads; no one else had seen Papa George while he was here.

"Well, needless to say, if anyone does, please call us. We'll try to get you some better pictures. And thanks very much for your help today. Nice entry, by the way."

Sgt. Broadfoot beamed with no small sense of pride in his team. "Trey, we'll secure the scene now, and during the CSI procedures, if you'd like."

"That'd be great!" Trey gladly agreed. "There's something else, Jim. We'll be asking for some of your guys to help us with this one. We're looking at a lot of staff and patron interviews. We might ask for someone to be assigned TDY for the duration. Of course, I gotta run it past the captain first, but I wanted to give you a *heads-up.*"

Sgt. Broadfoot's smile couldn't get any bigger.

Hawk, still on his phone, tugged on his partner's sleeve and drew him aside as he concluded the call. "Trey, listen, Willis wants to talk to us. He checked, the investigation is still open but there are no current active warrants for 'Papa George'. Unfortunately, they'd lost track of him; resource constraints mandated only intermittent surveillance. Willis said that the rest of the OCDETF crew will be very happy to know that we've found him, or at least where he's most recently been. And, if we need anything, anything at all, from the task force, all we have to do is ask."

That was Trey's cue to smile. "Oh, I like the sound of that, and so will our boss. We'll probably need their help in trying to identify the other man who was with Papa George."

"He's probably muscle, you know?"

"Yeah, but if he's *known* muscle and has a rap sheet, that'll make the captain even happier."

Hawk pocketed his phone, mimed straightening an invisible tie, and mimicked Capt. Lou Miller's signature deadpan stare, almost a scowl with a single raised eyebrow, and flat monotone delivery that seemed to manifest whenever he dealt with the media.

"Ahem . . . At this time, I am authorized to confirm that in the course of the investigation, recent developments point to *persons of interest* in this case."

"Don't start practicing for a commander's job until you've mastered this one," Trey cautioned with a wry grin. "Although, I must admit this intel is the kind of positive information one should have on hand when briefing one's captain. You are learning, *grasshopper*."

CH 16

AS ELLEN EXPECTED, Armand and Stacy returned to Delafaire Farm by mid-afternoon, the minivan hardly burdened by the luggage from the hotel. Within the hour, Millie and Mark returned from grocery shopping. As everyone gathered on the porch to help shuttle the bags of food to the kitchen, Ellen explained that Hawk had been called in to work and would not likely be back for dinner.

Mark gazed up at the gathering clouds. "I bet he'll be getting wet if he's still on his bike. Look at that thunderhead. We're in for a storm before the day is out."

"I think you're right," agreed Armand. "After we get these groceries unloaded, I suggest putting our vehicles in the garage. Hail is quite possible in a strong thunderstorm, especially in late spring."

Mark nodded. "Good idea. I want to take another look at the old Ford, anyway."

"So get to it already," Stacy teased. "Make yourself useful and get Ellen's new truck up and running as soon as possible." A mischievous smile on her face, she hip bumped Mark off the porch, spun about in laughter and disappeared into the house with fistfuls of plastic grocery bags.

Mark couldn't stop grinning. Armand just smirked and winked at him.

Stacy followed the other women into the kitchen, where they began putting the food away and planning the dinner menu. Ellen had seen the front porch antics, and catching Stacy's eye, they shared knowing grins. Madeline and Millie hadn't missed anything either; they just shook their heads and rolled their eyes.

The first few raindrops fell unnoticed, stealthy scouts riding a freshening wind. An eerily still calm followed, as if the sky were gathering its breath in an ominous pause, determined in its purpose.

Armand and Mark had unknowingly chosen that moment to depart the secured garage and walk back to the house. Armand looked skyward, saw the impending threat, and grabbed Mark's arm. "I think we'd better hurry to the house, and I mean now!"

Tugging on Mark's sleeve, Armand broke into a trot.

As Mark loped towards the house, a grey blur streaked past his legs, Smokey. The cat made a beeline for the front door, leaving Mark and Armand in his dust. Ellen appeared on the porch and swung the screen door open at just the right moment; Smokey, never breaking stride, disappeared inside.

Just as Mark and Armand reached the porch, lightning flashed to earth close by; robust thunder crashed overhead. The brief whiff of ozone surrendered to the heavy scent of rain. A deluge commenced; sheets of driven rain swept up the drive, pummeling gravel and dust into a craggy paste that melted within churning puddles. The wind picked up, sending occasional bursts of rain across the porch. Armand and Mark followed Smokey's example and ducked inside.

The storm eventually settled into a steady rain as everyone gathered in the dining room for dinner, or *supper* as Millie insisted was the proper terminology, in the South at least, for the evening meal.

She had prepared stuffed rolled steaks; marinated boneless beef round steaks with sautéed chopped onions, bell peppers, carrots, and mushrooms, simmered in a wine-based browning sauce and topped with new potatoes, celery, and caramelized onion rings. Freshly baked drop biscuits and an assortment of jams and preserves further enticed the diners. A modest California claret complemented the main course nicely. Warm rice pudding topped with a lemon glaze tempted all for dessert.

Ellen had a momentary flash of guilt when she remembered the pets, but a quick look around the kitchen put her mind at ease. Millie had prepared their dinner as well; a sampling of round steak, carrots and potatoes mixed in with dry pet food and covered with a few ounces of browning sauce gravy. The two Chows looked up at her; Ellen could swear they were smiling!

Smokey, on the other hand, was casually blasé as he nibbled at the repast, as if he ate this way all the time, and expected no less a sumptuous feast on a regular basis.

Ellen smiled, remembering an old saying about the feline species.

Cats were once worshiped as gods by man—and they have never forgotten.

DURING THE MEAL, MARK brought up the matter of the stored truck with Ellen.

"All things considered, it's in pretty good condition. I think that a battery, a tune-up, an oil change, and a set of tires might be all you're going to need, at least initially. I'm not planning on returning to New York until sometime next week, so I should be able to finish the truck project within a few days, barring any unforeseen problems."

Mention of returning home prompted Millie and Stacy to discuss their options; both had jobs to return to. After some debate, they decided to return to Los Angeles together by the end of the week, assuming they could get the appropriate flight connections.

"Now Ellen, don't you worry, because you know I'll be back to visit," Millie assured her daughter.

"Me, too," echoed Stacy, "maybe sooner than later; you never know."

Amused, Ellen noted how closely Mark followed their conversation, and wondered what he was thinking—*about Stacy, no doubt.*

In the background, the hypnotic patter of the rain softly diminished to a near-silent misting. The dismal grey of the overcast began to visibly lighten.

After dessert, Millie produced a round of Irish coffees. "Now, this is how to properly cap off a meal, right?"

Judging by the smiles and bobbing heads, no one disagreed.

Conversation soon returned to the grounds and gardens. Mark and Armand, savoring the excellent coffee, were content to just sit and listen.

The rain stopped; soft sounds of dripping leaves, the mirrored puddles, and the lingering coolness marked its passage. Rents in the cloud mass allowed cracks of blue to peek through; occasional bursts of slanting sunlight splashed upon patches of wet earth. Tattered clouds shredded on the wind and the lowering sun slowly reclaimed a western slice of early evening sky.

The garden conversation seemed to wind down as well; a long moment of contemplative silence ensued.

Finally, Stacy broke the spell. "Well, there's something I just don't get. These gardens, they're all overgrown of course, not having been tended; but, there's not a weed in any bed, anywhere! How is that possible? I mean, what's supposed to be growing there *is* overgrown, as I said. However, there are no weeds of any kind, no pests either, not that I could see. I just don't get it."

No one else could explain it either.

As the setting sun tried fruitlessly to assert a lingering trace of celestial dominance, but managed only to tease longer shadows from the western trees, Armand and Madeline stood and announced that they had to depart.

"Thank you so much for the wonderful meal and warm hospitality," effused Madeline. "It's not the company; it's the hour. At my age, I'm actually quite content to be in my own home before nightfall."

Armand smiled and scoffed. “My dear wife is being kind. The truth is that I prefer not to drive in the dark, my night vision isn’t what it used to be.”

Madeline patted her husband’s arm. “Don’t be silly, you’re still my knight. I’m just a bit tired.”

Ellen caught Madeline’s surreptitious wink and understood completely; Madeline could have driven, but she graciously deferred to Armand.

Saying their good-byes from the front porch, Ellen, Millie, Stacy and Mark watched as the minivan idled down the drive, disappearing in the deepening shadows of the forest.

Stacy leaned into Mark’s shoulder and murmured, “They’re really each other’s better half, aren’t they?”

“Yeah,” he breathed as he draped his arm across her back and gave her shoulder a quick squeeze.

“Stacy, I didn’t notice about the weeds before. Could you show me? You know, take a bit of a walk in the gardens,” Millie suggested, “before it gets too dark?”

“Sure, it’s still light enough. Mark, you and Ellen should come, too. A little walk after supper would do us all some good.”

That elicited a few theatrical groans and chuckles. However, everyone generally agreed they could use the exercise after such a good meal.

It did not surprise Ellen in the least that the dogs acted like this was a wonderful idea. However, the nonplussed cat refused to leave the porch.

Ah, Smokey, I know what you’re thinking . . . Wet paws? No thank you.

THE AFTER-SUPPER STROLL didn’t take too long. Within a few minutes of returning, Ellen began to realize just how tired she was. “If you will all excuse me, I'm going to call it a day." As she trudged up the stairs, the dogs followed at her heels.

In her bedroom, she sat in one of the armchairs to relax and unwind. Max and Sophie settled in their favored spots.

The dogs had the uncanny knack of being in the room, yet never being in the way. One of them would always be in the vicinity of the hall door, almost as if guarding the entrance, and the other near her. Even the cat had made an appearance and took up residence on the bed. Ellen had a hunch that this scenario might turn out to be a permanent arrangement.

The photo album and the velvet bag containing the journal drew her attention. As she retrieved them, she suddenly remembered the small spectacles and had a moment of concern; but a glance at her dresser assured her that they had come to no harm. The delicate glasses sat atop the small dark blue bag, right where she'd put them when she'd changed for supper.

She returned to the low armchair by the fireplace, turned on a reading lamp. Books in her lap, she began to examine the pages in the album. Thick black pages held numerous photographs, some tucked at the corners by delicate paper chevrons, some held by old yellowing tape, and some pasted by a sort of homemade adhesive that crumbled to grey dust if touched—*flour paste?* The photos in the front of the book were old and yellowed; many were faded. Most were of people in stiff formal poses wearing clothing reminiscent of the nineteenth century. A few were of street scenes from an unidentified town or city; horse-drawn conveyances and electric streetcars were common.

Ellen wondered if she'd find any photos of Maude; she hoped so. She remembered Maude as a very old woman; but that was almost ten years ago. How Maude would appear as a much younger woman would be just a guess. Now Ellen was intrigued; she was determined to find a photograph of a younger Maude.

Page after page held photos that snagged her interest. It was like traveling through time, decades slipping past with the soft fall of brittle pages. She found that some photographs held her attention. Some scenes and faces seemed uncomfortably familiar, but she didn't know why.

It was near the middle of the album that a slightly yellowed black-and-white photograph stunned her; a woman in a rocking chair, who wore her hair piled up in what Ellen always thought of as a *Gibson girl* style. She wore a high-necked, long-sleeved, cinched-waist dress; its crinoline skirt flared at her high button shoes. Her age was indeterminate, neither young nor old, her expression calm and placid as if a smile had lingered on her lips but a moment before. She sat in a rocking chair on a porch, a porch that looked very much like the front porch of this very house.

Ellen had no doubt that this was Maude; she sensed the truth of it intuitively. As if any further corroboration were needed, the woman was flanked to either side by dogs, a pair of Chows. In her lap, lay a large grey cat considering the camera with mild disinterest.

Ellen plucked the picture from the clasp of its paper chevrons and examined it more closely. The stiff photo paper felt old and bore scalloped edges, something she had not seen for years on any photograph. She flipped it over, but there was nothing on the back.

Maude appeared to be a much younger woman than Ellen last remembered her. Of course, that was to be expected; but when was this taken? The animals certainly resembled Max, Sophie, and Smokey; but, how could that be? Was this one of those staged *old-time* photographs? It did not seem so. Perhaps these were other pets, from long ago? Somehow, that didn't seem right either.

Ellen glanced at Max asleep at the hall door, and Sophie stretched out on the rug in front of the fireplace. Smokey, snuggled on the bed, returned her gaze with an inscrutable smirk and soft purr. She smiled.

There's more to you guys than meets the eye, isn't there?

She sighed, returned the photo to the album, and continued her perusal of the rest of the book. As Ellen turned the pages, the photographs depicted scenes from later periods; and personal attire altered with the times. One photo portrayed three smiling women in a nightclub setting, all dressed in the *flapper style* of the 1920s. Several pages later, she found the same three women, not smiling this time, dressed in the more conservative fashions of the early 1940s and standing beneath a theater marquee. The film was *Casablanca.*

Flipping back and forth between the two photographs, Ellen was convinced of two things; these were indeed the same three women, and none of them seemed to have aged a day.

On a hunch, she retrieved the photograph depicting Maude on the porch and compared it to the other two pictures. One woman in each photo bore a strong resemblance to Maude, but different hairstyles and clothing left her vaguely uncertain as to the woman's identity.

As Ellen neared the album's final pages, she found only one more picture of Maude. In this photograph she appeared to be much older, more like the image held in Ellen's memory. The grey-haired woman, seemingly oblivious to the camera, was seated at a small desk, writing in an open book. She seemed intent and focused, squinting behind her narrow tinted glasses. The two dogs lay at her feet apparently asleep. The grey cat lounged atop one side of the desk, his large head propped indolently over a foreleg. He lay to the right side of the open book apparently watching the motion of her pen on the opposing page, as if debating the entertainment value of a playful paw swipe.

Ellen looked more closely at the photo, trying to determine where it was taken, but she recognized nothing. The room in which Maude sat at her modest desk did not resemble any part of this house. A wall of coarse wood paneling, a woven round rug, and a simple window were the only other clues in the photograph. Ellen studied the dogs and cat. It had to be somewhere else, a place where the animals were comfortable, a place they were familiar with; but it was no place Ellen knew.

Another question arose; *who had taken the photograph?*

That thought gave Ellen pause. *Who indeed?*

She scrutinized the rest of the album but found no more photos of Maude, and only a few more photos of the dogs and the cat, usually in or about the main house and grounds. Sighing, she closed the album in her lap and let her mind wander.

The photographs had certainly intrigued her, but had answered no questions. To the contrary, only more questions seemed to have been raised. She remembered that this was only one of several albums she had found in that trunk. Her curiosity flared, but she was too tired for another foray into the attic this evening. The albums would still be there tomorrow, as would other books she seemed to remember seeing.

Other books . . . of course—the journal!

Placing the album on the floor, she settled the journal in her lap and opened it. For just an instant she felt mildly disoriented, but she was so tired she attributed the sensation to simple weariness.

The binding was somewhat stiff and the unlined pages felt like parchment. Ellen thought it was an old book, but in remarkably good condition. Curiously, it bore neat cursive handwriting on only the front of each page, the back was left blank. It was as if the writer did not care to chance any ink bleeding through and obscuring the words on the front of the page.

Hmm, when I first looked at this in the attic I didn't think I could read it, like it was in a strange language. But now it seems I can. Maybe it was just the poor lighting?

She skimmed the first few pages, just to get a sense of the entries. She was growing sleepy and did not intend to read much. Her eyelids felt like they were developing small soft knots in their surrounding muscles; keeping them open was taking some effort.

Unlike a daily diary, the entries were in blocks of time, weeks and months reduced to a few paragraphs. Any reference to the year of the particular entry was conspicuously absent. Weather, plantings, and crop yields of flowers, fruits, vegetables, and nuts were carefully notated. Occasional comments about events happening in LaBorde, and people, whose names she didn't recognize, seemed to comprise the rest of the entries.

Ellen was losing the battle to fend off sleep; she could fight it no more. She closed the journal and placed it upon the album, *my stack of things to do tomorrow.*

Her bed beckoned, and she wasted no time in making her final preparations. She tried not to dislodge Smokey as she snuggled deep under the covers; he merely stretched and took up residence on her other pillow.

Her breathing slowed, and the cat's soft purring lulled her into contented sleep.

But, it was not to be a dreamless sleep. She knew some people dream in color, some in black and white, and some never remember dreams at all.

I wonder if that might be a blessing in some cases . . .

ELLEN SENSED THAT SHE was dreaming, but not in color, yet not exactly black and white either. It was more like shades of grey, deep shadows and glints of silver—*night?*

She was following Smokey as he trotted down a wooded path in the old growth forest of Delafaire Farm. She had no trouble keeping up with him. She could see the cat plainly, but everything in her peripheral vision was fuzzy, out of focus. Somehow she knew that Max and Sophie were nearby, somewhere to either side of her as she made her way through the darkened forest.

The wide path wound easily through the wood, bright moonlight accentuating the depth of shadows. At one point it seemed that the path narrowed and stopped abruptly at the face of a steep bluff, thickly overgrown with privet and honeysuckle. Peering through the growth Ellen sensed an opening, a cave; but, there was something wrong about it.

She unaccountably felt a strong inclination to be away from this place; but, it seemed to be more of an external suggestion rather than her own idea. Her reaction, however, was one of curious defiance. Was this not now her land, and her home? It was! She would not be intimidated or afraid of anything on her own property. She started to step forward but Max stepped across her path and leaned into her legs. Facing the cave, he growled in a low tone, the vibration of which she could feel in her knees, pressed against his ribs.

Sophie pawed Ellen's calf and moved off to the right where Smokey stood, tail twitching. Once he had her attention, Smokey moved off on another path Ellen had not seen. Sophie followed and paused, casting a look over her shoulder at Ellen and tossing her head with a subtle whining growl.

. . . *Come on, this way* . . .

Max nudged her in that direction, so Ellen acquiesced, reluctantly turning from the cave to follow Sophie.

Ellen was next aware of stepping from the forest into a large clearing by the edge of a small lake. A number of large standing stones ringed the grassy clearing. On the far side, a rustic cabin sat nestled in the deeper shadow of the forest. Nearby, a small dock reached out into the lake, its black surface speckled with floating stars. The low moon and its wetly stark reflection flooded the night with cold silver light, painting a surreal landscape before her.

Ellen seemed to float across the clearing, onto the porch, and into the small cabin. The single room held a potbellied stove, cabinets and a sink, a bed, a table with two chairs, and the desk that she had seen in the photograph. In the moonlight she could see a cold hearth and several oil lamps. This was evidently the place Maude had come, perhaps for the solitude, perhaps to write. Ellen could easily understand having a special place to write; she often fancied having such a place herself.

Her mind drifted. The sense of being somewhere faded and she slipped deeper into dreamless sleep.

IN THE MORNING, ELLEN recalled her dream rather clearly; quite a surprise, since she rarely remembered her dreams.

As she dressed, she noticed the album and journal near the chair, and remembered that she intended to revisit the attic this morning, after her ritual morning coffee. The tantalizing aroma wafting from the kitchen would prove a significant distraction; Millie's bacon, eggs, and pancakes would not be ignored.

After a sumptuous breakfast, Ellen retrieved four more albums from the attic and brought them to the library. Millie and Stacy joined her in thumbing through the pages of photographs. The three shared a second pot of fresh coffee while taking a leisurely tour through the annals of frozen time.

"I can't seem to find that picture I told y'all about. I know it's here somewhere," Ellen groaned, thumbing through an album.

"This one?" Stacy asked, pointing out the photo of a younger Maude with her pets on the porch.

"No, that's the first one I found. The one I'm looking for depicts Maude, *an older Maude,* sitting at a small desk."

Millie picked up the journal and the missing photo slipped out and fluttered to the floor. "Oh, is this the one you mean?" she asked, handing the photograph to Ellen.

"Yes, that's it, I think." Ellen studied the picture for a moment. "I'm not sure. Something's different. This must be another, because the cat's looking the wrong way. At least I don't remember him looking right at the camera."

Stacy leaned over her shoulder. "What are you talking about? He's looking right at Maude's right hand, the one with the pen."

Stacy plucked the photo from Ellen's fingers and held it up for Millie to see; Millie nodded in affirmation.

Taking it back from Stacy, Ellen said, "Let me see that again, maybe it was a trick of the light." She walked over to the window.

Sure enough, the cat was looking to the side, at Maude's right hand. Ellen stood there confused, certain of what she had seen, or perhaps of what she *thought* she had seen. Had she hallucinated? Was this some residual manifestation of her head trauma, her concussion?

Or worse, would everybody think so? Would this mean a return to the hospital and more damned tests?

Staring at the photograph as her mind wrestled with these unsettling thoughts, Ellen's eyes relaxed their focus. She felt a passing moment of disorientation and watched in fascination as the cat in the photograph turned his head to look right at her, then up at Maude, back towards Ellen, and finally at Maude's right hand.

Ellen dared not breathe . . . *It is Smokey—it has to be!*

"Ellen," asked Millie, "are you all right?"

"Oh, uh, sorry," Ellen stammered. "I was just, uh, daydreaming. I'm fine, just fine." She was far from *fine;* but she'd keep that to herself. She handed the photo back to Stacy. "Yeah, it must have been the light. This is the right picture, the one I found yesterday."

"Well, it fell out of this diary, or whatever it is," Millie said as she thumbed through the journal in bewilderment. "I can't make sense of this writing. What language is it?"

"Hmm, not English," Stacy mumbled, looming over Millie's shoulder, "that's for sure!" Stacy refocused her attention on the photograph. "Whoa, *tres chic!* Look at these glasses Maude's wearing! Aren't they darling? They're little granny glasses. I love `em!"

Millie smiled as Stacy handed her the photo. "Oh, yes. These were quite in vogue in the sixties, especially as sunglasses."

Ellen stared into the cold hearth. She'd had no difficulty reading journal entries last night, but thought it best for the moment to keep her own counsel. Her confusion was giving way to caution. Too much strangeness, too many things she didn't understand, and too many questions were percolating in a confused stew; she didn't feel the urge to stir the pot.

A serendipitous distraction, Mark strode into the room. "My apologies, ladies, for the interruption, but I have good news! I believe I may have the truck running today, but I need fresh oil, new spark plugs and of course a new battery. I called Hawk; he told me I could get oil, plugs, and a battery at the truck stop out by the interstate. That's the closest place with parts that's open on a Sunday. So, I'm going there. Can I pick up anything else for anybody?"

Millie shook her head. "Not for me. But, don't you want to have dinner, or what you probably call *lunch*, first?"

"No thanks, Aunt Millie, I'm still stuffed from that fine breakfast. Skipping lunch would probably do me some good."

"Actually, that sounds like a good idea," said Stacy. "I could pass on lunch, too; then I'll be really hungry for dinner! Oops, sorry Millie, I mean *supper*. Maybe I could ride along with you, Mark?" Stacy dipped her chin to her shoulder and glanced at Mark demurely, apparently so only *he* could see her bat her eyelashes; but Ellen saw as well, and hid her own smile.

"Sure!" Mark grinned. "I'd appreciate the company."

"Ellen," asked Millie, "what would you like for your lunch?"

"You know what, Mom?" Ellen sighed. "I think I'll pass on lunch, too. Actually, I'd rather lie down for a while. I hope you don't mind."

"Of course not, dear," Millie assured her. "I can use the time to organize the kitchen. You get your rest."

As Millie collected the coffee cups and headed toward the kitchen, Ellen heard her mother mumble, "My goodness, I've slipped right into *work mode*. It's not like I'm running a *bed and breakfast* around here."

Ellen smirked, collected the loose photographs, and closed the albums.

As Mark and Stacy prepared to leave, Ellen gave them a half-interested wave, slipped the photo of Maude at the small desk into the pages of the journal, and, tucking the book under her arm, made her way to her bedroom.

ARRANGING HER CHAIR so that sunlight would stream over her shoulder, Ellen retrieved the photograph and studied it once more. Something nagged at her, something she was missing.

Then she saw it; the cat was laying to the *right* side of the open journal, and Maude was writing on the *left* page. Ellen opened the journal to confirm that only the right pages bore script; all the left pages were blank. There was no doubt that the photo depicted Maude writing on the *left* page that appeared to be blank.

What else was different? She stared at every detail; the cat, the open book, the pen, Maude's glasses—*the glasses?*

Ellen went to her dresser and picked up the spectacles, delicate wire-framed glasses with a slight blue tint to the lenses. Returning to her seat, she perched on the edge of the chair and examined the glasses in a sunbeam. They did indeed resemble those retro granny-style sunglasses from the sixties. She slipped them on and looked about the room. The light blue tint had a novel effect on the quality of light but did not really darken the room that much at all.

Max, Sophie, and Smokey had silently joined her. Now, they were all seated patiently before her, almost expectantly, watching her.

Ellen picked up the journal placing it flat in her lap. The book felt warm and slightly heavier, but both sensations were hardly noticeable. She opened the journal and experienced an instant of disorientation followed by a blissful calm. Her breath stilled in her throat as a subtle play of light and shadow swirled in small patterns on the left page, coalescing into a delicate script—script that she could *read!*

These are the chronicles of my tenure as Steward of the Grand Portal of the Realm of Man, meant only for the eyes of my successor. As I have kept this record, so also shall you, Steward of the Grand Portal of the Realm of Man.

Stunned, Ellen removed the glasses; the page was blank. She put the glasses back on, and the script swirled into being once more. She thumbed through a few more pages, and found neat handwriting on the formerly blank pages. Removing the glasses rendered the pages blank once more.

She sat in silence, and admittedly a little in awe at what she perceived to be happening. She realized that she accepted it, and was prepared to believe it.

A vague recollection of Maude's words floated to the surface of Ellen's memory. They were dreamlike in their essence, but Ellen sensed their importance.

. . . I've left you some help . . . a journal . . . spectacles are important . . . named you my successor to the Stewardship . . . a lot to learn as you go . . .

A lot to learn, indeed.

She looked up to find the pets still patiently staring at her; she smiled.

"You guys were just waiting for me to find this, weren't you?"

Both dogs wagged their tails, something she now realized they rarely did. They turned and sought their favored sleeping spots, Max in front of the door, and Sophie at the side of the bed. Smokey simply stretched, leapt upon the bed, and curled himself into a ball. Within minutes, all three appeared asleep.

A sense of peace and calm settled over Ellen as she gazed at her pets.

Somehow, I know you guys are special . . . and I'm lucky you're with me . . .

Nestled comfortably in her chair, Ellen began to read. She was drawn into the journal with a comfortable and familiar ease. Written in the style of a first person narrative, the information was couched in a candid and factual tone. It seemed fairly obvious that the writer had anticipated a degree of skepticism on the part of the reader. Such restrained caution was tacitly acknowledged by a subtle undercurrent of a seemingly benign tolerance, as if to say, *doubt if you must, but please be patient and you will see.*

Even if it were merely a work of imaginative fiction, Ellen found it quite entertaining. The book was multifaceted; a business record of the farm, considerable historical information, and related personal anecdotes.

Curiously interlaced throughout was a fanciful, yet scholarly, account of the capricious nature and speculative workings of *magic*. Far more intriguing were the rich descriptions of the most wondrous, and sometimes disturbing, other realms, veritable worlds unto themselves.

Ellen found it all fascinating, especially the most interesting aspect; how to go to these places, traveling through portals. In fact, one of these, a *major* portal, was supposedly here, on Delafaire Farm, and under the control of the Steward.

The Steward? That would have been Maude; and now, that's supposed to be me? This still doesn't make any real sense. I just don't get it.

She read until she just couldn't keep her eyes open any longer. Her thoughts slowed, grew befuddled, and lost cohesion. She had only covered a bit more than a third of the journal before she admitted defeat and surrendered to the call of Morpheus. With a tired smile, she put the book and the spectacles in their respective bags and placed them on her dresser.

Yawning, she crawled into bed, snuggled under the covers, and let her mind wander. In mere moments, she drifted off into a restless sleep.

CH 17

AS THE DYING SUN SANK below the horizon, dusk swept inexorably across the dismal forests and barren fields of Were. Mere shadows lost definition and bled a dark tide that soon lapped upon the lower stones of the castle tower.

A servant bearing a smoldering brand scurried among the ramparts to ignite a series of torches held in robust iron sconces evenly spaced about the rough stone walls. A sickly breeze teased the flickering flames as errant shadows danced amongst the ancient crenelations.

Adder Castle may have been one of the oldest within the realm, but it was nonetheless well maintained. Its master, Lord Addecus, was conscientious about its upkeep, and personally oversaw any renovations or improvements.

The torchbearer rounded a corner to find the master in quiet conversation with a quite striking, tall woman. The servant quickly averted his eyes and bowed deeply. Upon receipt of a nod of acknowledgment from his lord, the menial silently resumed his assigned task.

Ling waited until the servant was out of earshot before responding to Lord Addecus' question. "Perhaps I was too *enthusiastic,* but I wanted to send a message. I only wish it had been the vampire instead of a mere familiar. *Stalking us!* How *dare* they!" She still seethed with anger.

Addecus sighed and cautioned the intense assassin. "Calm yourssself, and think thisss through. The presssence of vampiresss and their familiarsss in the sssame place and time asss your asssignment isss no coincidence. Thisss hasss the ssscent of Lady Diere'sss doing. I sssuspect tisss more becaussse ssshe doesssn't trussst *George.* I doubt we were sssuspected of any duplicity . . . perhapsss until *now.*"

Ling bowed her head. "Forgive me, m'lord, I acted rashly. I thought we were in danger. The two goons you sent me, *Bubba* and *Iggy*, were of little help. They were almost discovered by the familiar—the bumbling fools!"

"Did you not ussse them asss I sssuggesssted; to monitor the activitiesss of the only sssignificant potential threat, the ssshaman, Wendell Sssmall Owl?"

"I did, m'lord, and they were barely adequate for that task. But they seemed to demonstrate a certain level of, uh, I am not sure how to describe it—*criminal initiative*? When not specifically watching the shaman, one or both of them would engage in petty crimes; stalking women in and around the casino, stealing from the hotel rooms and unattended vehicles. They were at it again when I caught the vamp—forgive me, m'lord, I mean the *familiar,* stalking *them*."

Ling paused, but Addecus gave no reaction, so she continued. "They stayed away from George, as you instructed. But, m'lord, in truth, they may be more of a problem than they are worth. Perchance the mind-wipe spell was insufficient; perhaps they should have been reduced to the level of *drones* rather than that of *goons*."

"I sssee," said Addecus. "Where are they now?"

"They returned here with me, after George responded to Lady Diere's summons. I had them wait in the Guards' Barracks. And, I suggested that the Sergeant of the Guard keep an eye on them."

Lord Addecus paced slowly along the ramparts, his forked tongue flicking, tasting the air. Ling fell into a measured step with him.

"Be patient, my dear Ling. We may yet have further need of your goonsss and their dubiousss ssskillsss. I did not wisssh to have them bessspelled to the near-mindlesss level of dronesss becaussse they would have been of no ussse to you in monitoring the activitiesss of the ssshaman. Remember, we have ssso few asssetsss who can operate unfettered in the Realm of Man, and thessse two men, Bubba and Iggy, are of that world. In fact, they were once lowly ranked minionsss in a criminal enterprissse controlled by George. That isss why it isss bessst that he doesss not sssee them. Regrettably, we are compelled to take advantage of sssuch raw material where and when we find it."

Ling bowed her head in submission and remained silent.

The Were Lord looked askance at the stoic assassin, intuitively sensing that she was still not satisfied with the inherent constraints of the situation, but would nevertheless endeavor to comply with his instructions. That might well be all he could hope for, knowing her proclivities. *Perhaps it is bessst to change the sssubject.*

"What can you tell me, Ling, about the other woman, the vampire'sss victim?"

"Ah, Suzi Origami." She hesitated, and seemed to order her thoughts. "She worked for George, and I suspect, in a similar capacity to what services I can render. I sensed her as a killer immediately; however, I think *unimaginative,* yet capable and experienced. She was on the balcony, drinking a glass of wine, around midnight. That was the last I saw of her, alive. I found her head on the table there just after dawn. Moments after that discovery, George received Lady Diere's summons."

Addecus stopped walking and faced Ling. "Did George sssee the sssevered head?"

Ling shrugged and nodded affirmatively. "He did, m'lord. It was unavoidable. But I must say, he lost some of his bluster and was very cooperative when I suggested relocating once again."

"Doesss he have any idea that ssshe wasss killed by a vampire?"

Ling shook her head emphatically. "No, I seriously doubt it. I did not tell him so, nor did he venture onto the balcony to examine her head. He seemed anxious. He sent his driver, Vito, back to New Orleans with instructions to await his call. George responded to Lady Diere's summons shortly thereafter. I immediately returned to you, with my *native assets*, per your previous instructions."

Addecus resumed walking along the ramparts, deep in thought. "Tell me, Ling, what do you know about thessse vampiresss and their familiarsss?"

"Not very much, m'lord. I know there were two *bloodsuckers*, a male and a female; but, I do not know their identities. There were at least two familiars, including the one I killed. Of course, I thought she was the female vampire when I caught her skulking around that empty building after sunset; but, dealing with her was no real challenge. I took my time, but all I got from her was her name, *Chloe*."

Addecus stopped, and leaned against the wall. "Actually, that knowledge may be mossst helpful. Chloe isss, or rather *wasss,* a familiar to Lord Ssstirling. Do you know of Lord Ssstirling?"

"I do not, m'lord."

"Lord Ssstirling isss not an *elder* vampire, being lesss than three centuriesss old; but, he is nonethelesss rasssh and quite dangerousss. Harming a vampire'sss familiar can bring ssseriousss consssequencesss. Killing a favored familiar will asssuredly merit retribution, ssswift and sssevere. I sssuspect he took vengeance on Sssuzi Origami thinking ssshe was you—"

"Me?" exclaimed Ling, clearly shocked. "How could he mistake her for me? We are nothing alike!"

Addecus was momentarily taken aback, but soon amused. *Ah, the feminine persssspective—no two femalesss ever think they look "alike".*

"Ling, Diere knowsss of you and your misssion. In fact, it wasss, to sssome degree, her idea. Ssstirling doesss not know you, nor do you know him. However, he may have been told about you, perhapsss by Diere. I believe ssshe isss sssomehow ressspponsssible for the vampiresss being there.

"You are a renown asssasssin; and consssidering your sssignature techniquesss, Ssstirling would have little doubt that you were ressspponsssible for the death of hisss familiar. However, he hasss never ssseen you. Ssso, he would vent hisss rage on the firssst perssson he ssseesss who approximatesss your dessscription—Sssuzi Origami."

He raised a hand to forestall the protest the fuming assassin was about to lodge, and spoke soothingly. "I will grant you that any who know you would never make sssuch a missstake. Remember, Ssstirling knowsss neither you nor her, and he isss known to act quite rassshly."

Smarting from the perceived insult, Ling's anger smoldered, her righteous indignation obvious; but to her credit, she held her tongue.

Addecus knew her well. Considered the finest assassin in the realm, she typically did not make mistakes. Her pride was sorely tested; she hated to lose face, under any circumstances. He watched her carefully, easily sensing her anger and frustration. Normally, he would let her simmer, for as long as necessary, until she was fully in control of her emotions. But time was a luxury they might not have; and he needed her to be at her best.

"Ah, Ling, my pet, be calm and centered. Our plansss are fluid and we can easssily adapt."

When in control, she was focused and deadly, a lethal instrument of surgical precision; however, her emotions at a boil, she was unpredictably dangerous. Or worse, she could shape-shift unintentionally. He knew that was a distinct possibility.

Some of the Were were still subject to the lunar cycle, particularly younger, less experienced individuals. However, most mature Weres developed a disciplined control over their shape-shifting, and could do so at will. Maintaining such control was critical to all Weres. To lose it was more than an embarrassing *faux pas;* it could be fatal under the wrong circumstances. Extreme emotions, including stimuli that triggered the instinctual *fight-or-flight* response, could initiate an unintended shift if the individual had not mastered the personal discipline of control.

Considered a last resort, there were, of course, drugs and certain spells, enchantments that forestalled the metamorphosis, holding one's shape in stasis. However, there were side effects; loss of one's memories, sense of purpose, and personal identity, all to varying degrees. No Were willingly sought such remedies.

After a few deep breathing exercises, Ling seemed to be at ease, so Addecus resumed walking.

"No doubt the authoritiesss in the Realm of Man are eager to quessstion George. For the moment, that isss Lady Diere'sss problem. At sssome point he will have to return; resssidency in his realm isss required by the Council. Ssshe hasss gone to great lengthsss to have him nominated for the vacant chair. Her plansss are often frussstrated, but it ssseemsss never completely foiled."

"M'lord, if I may? I know Lady Diere aspires to amass more power, perhaps even to the throne of Dark Elves; but, why are we assisting her?"

Addecus stopped and faced Ling. "From anyone elssse, I would consssider that an impertinent quessstion. But you have a role to play, ssso I will indulge your curiosssity, thisss one time. Sssome thingsss you will need to know, sssome you will not."

He sighed and wondered how much to tell her. Just enough, he decided, to make her understand.

"Sssuffice to sssay, it isss in our bessst interessstsss to accommodate Lady Diere'sss ambitionsss at thisss time. I believe that you are correct in your ssspeculation that ssshe covetsss the throne of the Dark Elvesss. And there are thossse who would sssee the current Queen Mab removed for other reasssonsss. I learned asss much when I ssserved asss *regent pro tem* at Court decadesss ago.

"You are, of coursse, aware of the Council'sss prohibition againssst all hunting, and the harvesssting of unwilling émigrésss, in the Realm of Man?"

"Yes, of course, m'lord. Although I know those rules, as well as the prohibitions of poaching prey in other Council Realms, are frequently broken."

"Too true," acknowledged Addecus, "and the penaltiesss are sssevere. Neverthelessss, it happensss that beingsss from other realmsss are quite willing, or are compelled, to sssecretly violate the prohibitionsss, primarily becaussse their home realmsss are ssslowly diminissshing in population, or *prey*, if you prefer.

"The inhabitantsss, or prey, of their home realmsss ssseem to be dying off at the normal rate, but birth ratesss have dropped in sssteady decline. Thossse who hunt notice the ssscarcity of game. Sserfsss who till the land have diminissshed in number, and raissse fewer and paltry cropsss.

"Thessse problemsss and related isssuesss are evident to sssome, and yet ignored by othersss." He sighed in resignation.

"Begging your pardon, m'lord, but, I don't understand what this has to do with Lady Diere."

"Ah, the Lady Diere . . . Ssshe would have usss believe that ssshe could arrange to ressscind the prohibition, thusss opening the Realm of Man for hunting and harvesssting once again."

Ling's eyebrows rose in surprise. "Indeed, m'lord?"

"You mussst underssstand, Ling, that prohibition exissstsss only becaussse a Council majority ssso voted over a century ago. Queen Mab of the Dark Elvesss and Queen Titania of the Light Elvesss reached a mutual agreement and sssupported the ban. The realmsss of Dwarvesss, Mer, and Man alsso voted *aye*; only the realmsss of Ssshadow and Were voted *nay*."

Ling smiled, a predatory gleam in her eyes. "I see Lady Diere's strategy now. If she were to supplant the current Queen Mab with herself, and put a puppet in the Chair of Man, she could effectively control the Council through a majority of votes. That assumes, of course, that the realms of Were and Shadow vote with her. She could indeed rescind the prohibition; the Realm of Man would be open to hunting once again."

Addecus raised a cautionary finger. "To hunt freely once again would ssseem to be wonderful; many among our nobility are sssussceptible to ss-such ssshort sssighted folly. But we mussst take a longer view. We need to replenisssh our dwindling populationsss with an infusssion of fertile breeding ssstock. Our immediate needsss are for ssservantsss, ssserfsss, vasssalsss, men-at-armsss, and lessst we forget, magesss. Thusss, capture mussst take precedence over ssslaughter. Do you not sssee?"

Ling did not respond; puzzlement clouded her face as the Were Lord continued.

"Nor would it be an easssy tasssk. You ssshould be aware; you have been in that realm. Mankind hasss come a long way, without magic, in the lassst century. Mind-wipe ssspellsss would be in high demand, lessst their innate belligerence and predilection for independence asssert themssselvesss."

"Indeed, you are correct, m'lord. It will be challenging. I look forward to it."

"Be not too eager, my dear Ling," Addecus warned as he rested his elbows upon the parapet wall, and stared into the hungry night. "The activitiesss of which we ssspeak, hunting and harvesssting, are known in the Realm of Man asss *murder* and *kidnapping*."

SALIDAR RETURNED TO the Realm of Shadow from Storm Haven as planned, well before sunset. He had even managed several more hours of needed rest in his room before the anticipated summons arrived. In fact, it was almost two hours after nightfall before the twin familiars announced that Lady Leanan required his presence.

As he followed the twins through the castle halls, he thought it unusual that she had waited so long in summoning him. *Something has happened, otherwise she'd have dealt with me sooner. I must be careful.*

Upon entering the Great Hall, Salidar found Lady Leanan standing near the grand hearth, staring stoically into the heart of glowing coals. The twins bowed and backed out of the room, softly closing the great doors.

Salidar slowly approached Lady Leanan, who appeared preoccupied and did not seem to notice his presence.

She disabused him of that notion with a casual gesture to a nearby set of chairs and small table, upon which several familiar decanters and two crystal goblets caught the dancing firelight.

"Ah, Salidar, would you be kind enough to pour? I believe you know my preference."

"My pleasure, m'lady."

Cautiously glancing askance at her while filling the goblets, he noted her severe black and grey gown, a somber image enhanced by her pursed lips and clouded brow. She seemed deep in thought, and concerned.

Clearly something disturbs her. Whatever it is, I have this feeling that it would disturb me as well.

As if waking from a dream, she delicately shook off her reverie and strode toward Salidar, her face blank of expression. Taking the offered cup from his outstretched hand, she smiled and sat down. She took a long draught of crimson from her goblet, and licked an errant drop of bright red from the lip of the cup.

"Please, Salidar, be seated." She gestured to the other chair, on the other side of the small table.

Slightly unnerved, Salidar bowed. "As you wish, m'lady."

From within the folds of her gown, she withdrew the sealed scroll and placed it on the small table between them. He just stared at the scroll; he made no move to touch it.

Leanan wryly noted his reluctance and smirked. "I return this scroll to your safekeeping. I suggest you exercise the utmost caution in its carriage."

"My grateful thanks, m'lady." Salidar managed a small bow while sitting. Slightly emboldened, he asked, "I presume that I am to continue with my task, as directed by the Lady Diere?" He sipped his wine, fighting the urge to gulp it down in nervous haste.

"Indeed," responded the Sidhe. "However, I would recommend that you avail yourself of my hospitality another night, and continue on your way in daylight. As you may know, travel in this realm during the hours of darkness can be potentially eventful. No doubt it would be *unfortunate* if something untoward should befall you before you had fully complied with Lady Diere's instructions."

"My dear lady, I would consider it most unfortunate indeed, should some ill befall me, notwithstanding my compliance with Lady Diere's instructions. I shall, of course, graciously accept your kind offer of extended hospitality."

She smiled, the effort never quite reaching her eyes, and sipped from her goblet.

"Salidar, sometimes you demonstrate wisdom beyond your years; and, I am well aware that you are older than most halflings. Tell me, are you wise enough to answer a forthright question, without benefit of a truth spell, or any other compulsion or constraint?"

"Ah, m'lady, now that would entirely depend upon the question, I should think."

"Very well," she said, seemingly somewhat amused. "It is a simple question. Do you trust the Lady Diere?"

Salidar sensed that absolute candor was appropriate, notwithstanding the absence of a compulsion, so he responded without hesitation. "No, m'lady, I do not."

Lady Leanan nodded and softly repeated, "Wise beyond your years . . . "

She drained her cup and placed the empty goblet on the table. Salidar gestured as if to refill her glass, but she merely placed her flattened hand over the cup and gently shook her head.

"Thank you, but no. I have other business to conduct this night. I have made arrangements for you to sup in the kitchen. After which, I must ask you to return to your chambers. You have a long day's journey before tomorrow's sunset; you will need your rest. You must reach the Crying Cup before nightfall."

She stood, and Salidar followed suit. The great doors swung open, revealing the twins awaiting their mistress.

Nodding to them, Leanan said, "My servants will take you to the kitchen and see to your meal. It would be in your best interest not to mention our conversation—*to anyone*. I see that you understand. I will not likely see you before your departure in the morning. So, I now bid you farewell and safe journey."

Salidar bowed deeply. "My humble thanks, m'lady, and I bid you a good night."

Slipping the scroll into his doublet, he joined the twins, who closed the doors after him. He followed them to the kitchen, his mind frantically analyzing the Sidhe's terse and strangely cryptic comments.

Damn the gods! I know nothing more of consequence; she betrayed nothing of value!

HE SMELLED THE FOOD before he entered the kitchen. A trencher of steaming boar meat, boiled potatoes, a warm loaf of hard bread, and a flagon of mulled wine had been laid upon a rough wooden table. Salidar realized that he was starving. He sat upon a wooden bench and drew his small knife.

He hesitated. Had the Lady Leanan wished him any harm, she certainly had ample opportunity before now. However, a trusting soul, he was not. He settled his breathing and allowed his eyes to relax out of focus. He took in his surroundings, and the repast spread so invitingly before him. But he neither saw nor sensed anything to alert or alarm him.

The twins sat opposite him at the table, and observed his pause. One spoke, almost a whisper, No One or Nobody; he didn't know which.

"Grimrald, there is nothing ill or ensorcelled about this food; you may eat in safety."

He smiled, nodded, and began to eat with gusto.

The other twin left the table and slipped behind a cupboard. Within a few moments she returned. He looked at them for an explanation, and they began to speak softly.

"Finish quickly, and take nothing from this table."

"You will follow us, and . . . "

". . . you will make no sound."

"Something is about to transpire, which . . . "

". . . would be to your advantage to observe, but . . . "

". . . you will maintain complete silence . . . "

". . . Grimrald, for your guild oath binds you."

"You will divulge neither the method nor the means."

"Do you understand?"

The use of his true name both assured and concerned him. Nonetheless, he knew he had little choice, so he nodded affirmatively. Within a few moments, he had finished his meal. They were alone in the kitchen.

The twins stood and beckoned. He followed them behind the cupboard. They came to a halt before a wall of mortared stones. One woman pressed a series of stones in a rhythmic pattern, and a portion of the wall silently swung inward. She stepped inside and stopped, cocking her head to listen. After a moment, she nodded to her twin, looked directly at Salidar and placed her right index finger to her lips. Her sister lit a small candle and proceeded into the passage; Salidar followed. The wall closed softly behind them and darkness surged about. The small lonely flame was the only illumination.

He followed them through a series of narrow passages, doing his best to move silently. The twins moved like ghosts. In contrast, Salidar was acutely conscious of his own soft footfalls. Try as he might, he could not match the twins' stealth.

Eventually they came to a fork in the passage.

Silently, the twin holding the candle placed it in a recess at about shoulder height in the rough stone wall. Each woman took one of his hands in theirs, and with a warning glance, proceeded to lead him into the darkness of the left passage.

The twins moved surely in the stygian space; one before him, leading, and one behind him, following. But for the contact of their hands, he was lost in a void. He wondered briefly if his racing pulse was perceptible to his invisible companions. As if in answer to his unspoken question, both women squeezed his hands simultaneously; but they were only bringing him to a stop.

As he concentrated on lowering his pulse rate, he thought he could hear voices.

The twins gently turned him in one direction and held him still. He *could* hear muffled voices. One twin squeezed his hand twice and let go; her sister did not release his other hand. There was a slight sound, almost a *wisp;* dim light shone in an oval at chin height. He leaned down and peered through the spy-hole.

He was looking into the Great Hall, the same room in which he had met with Lady Leanan, but it was as if he was looking through gauze or a light fabric of some type. He could see five people in the room. Lady Leanan stood in quiet conversation with an older man, well dressed and distinguished, who carried himself with authority.

Assuredly a vampire, perhaps an elder?

Another man, younger than the first, stood to one side. He looked harried and distraught, but was still a commanding presence.

Another vampire, I'll wager.

A woman, quite beautiful, sat nearby. A fawning male servant poured a scarlet trickle from a familiar decanter into her crystal goblet.

And yet another vampire, and her familiar?

With another soft *wisp*, the sounds from the room were more easily heard; no doubt another panel had been deftly opened. He tried to concentrate on the conversation.

Lady Leanan was not pleased. "No Vlad, you did precisely the right thing. I cautioned you before you left that any further confrontations were to be avoided. Stirling has created a problem—"

A stifled shriek of rage and indignation slipped from the throat of the disheveled younger vampire—who, at a sudden flick of the wrist from the older man, found himself sprawled flat on his back on the cold stone floor.

"You will be silent, Stirling," seethed the icy voice of the elder Vlad, "whenever our mistress speaks."

"If I may, m'lady?" asked the seated woman, as she gestured for her familiar to refill her drained cup.

"Yes, Sabrina?" acknowledged Leanan.

"Thank you, m'lady. Please understand that Chloe was more to Lord Stirling than mere familiar. He intended to share with her the Dark Gift. They were to share a life together. Her brutal murder, at the hands of such a *beast,* left him unhinged, obsessed with slaying her killer."

"Aye, therein lies the problem," spat Lady Leanan. "The fool killed the wrong woman!"

Stirling groaned from the floor, and began to sob quietly.

Vlad grumbled, "I, too, would have killed whomever I thought was responsible. I would have made the same mistake. My apologies, m'lady."

"I am not unsympathetic, Vlad." Leanan sighed. "I am concerned how Lady Diere will react to this development. I am certain it has disrupted her plans in some fashion. How it will impact our realm, I do not yet know." She made a small gesture to Vlad in the direction of the prostrate Stirling.

Vlad stepped over to the softly sobbing form and extended a hand. "Rise, Stirling, and return to your manor and lands. I will accompany you."

As Vlad and Stirling slowly left the room, Sabrina stood and started to speak, but Leanan held up a hand to forestall her.

As the doors closed, Leanan looked to Sabrina and cautioned. "I know you care, but Stirling must heal on his own, in his own time. Vlad will see to his welfare, so you need not concern yourself. Your presence, especially with your familiar, Gunther, will only remind him of his loss, and his ill-advised reaction."

Sabrina bowed her head. "Of course, m'lady, I understand."

"Good," Leanan said with finality. "I have another assignment for you. Salidar is my guest this night, and departs for the Crying Cup tomorrow. He serves Lady Diere. I am not informed of his mission, but I know he is to deliver an ensorcelled scroll to the innkeeper, Boltar. I intend to discover what Lady Diere is up to; but that presents a problem. Salidar is to be monitored. He knows neither you nor Gunther. Salidar must make this delivery unimpeded. I will need to know with whom he speaks, and anything else you can learn. Be discreet, and if possible, unobserved."

"It shall be done, m'lady," Sabrina assured, bowing.

As Sabrina and her familiar left the Great Hall, Leanan returned to the hearth and stared pensively into the amber glow of the flames. Her furrowed brow betrayed her growing concerns.

Salidar felt a slight tug on his clasped hand as the open panels were silently slid closed. Without a sound, the three eavesdroppers retraced their careful steps in the dark, recovered the guttering candle, and made their way through a warren of passages.

Salidar was quite lost; he recognized nothing. Consequently, he was quite surprised to pass through a sliding panel and find himself in his assigned chambers.

The twins arranged his bedclothes and bid him good night, dryly wishing him pleasant dreams.

The irony was not lost on him. He would now have a vampire, somewhere over his shoulder, watching his every move—*pleasant dreams, indeed.*

LADY DIERE'S SUMMONS did not bring George to their usual isolated meeting place. Instead, he found himself before her in the reception hall of her palatial castle in the Realm of Dark Elves. He was astounded at the obvious wealth and casual opulence of her domain. Gleams of avarice and envy shone unfettered behind his eyes despite his best efforts to appear unfazed.

Lady Diere, resplendent in a purple diaphanous gown threaded with spun gold, welcomed him. "George, it is time to begin tutored sessions in preparation for your anticipated examination by the Council—"

"Okay, but first I gotta tell you something!"

George had the effrontery to interrupt her, earning an icy glare. Lady Diere's frosty demeanor did not thaw, but she listened intently to his account.

Her brow furrowed. *So, another complication?* "You have no idea who is responsible for the death of your minion, this Suzi Origami?"

"No, but I will find out," George assured her.

Diere considered him for a moment. "George, I asked you once before if there were any potential problems that could impact our plans, anything related to your enterprises or associates. Need I remind you of *Fenton Brewster*? No doubt you have neglected to keep us as well informed as you pledged; or perhaps you have merely forgotten something of passing importance?"

George faltered at the chill recrimination in her voice.

"No-no, Lady Diere! I admit I've made some enemies, who hasn't? But nobody else knows I've relocated to the casino in Chantilly Parish. No one I know of would willingly take on Suzi Origami. She's, er, she *was* a fearsome *cleaner* who excelled at *wet work*. I can think of no one who'd have dared do what I saw, nor anyone who'd have even tried."

"You are absolutely certain?" Her gaze burned into his soul. "You've forgotten nothing?"

"Lady Diere, t-to the best of my knowledge, I have forgotten nothing. I know of no one; but, when I return, I'll make it my business to find out."

Diere signaled for a nearby servant to attend her, and watched George's face blanch as she asked, "Has it occurred to you that the authorities in your home realm may desire to speak with you in this regard?"

"But I didn't do anything!" George protested. "I have witnesses! Vito and Ling were with me. See? I have an alibi; they were with me the whole time!"

Lady Diere shrugged. "It is not I whom you will need to convince. Be that as it may, it is time for you to begin your preparations for your anticipated Council summons. You will accompany this servant to chambers prepared for you; your tutors will join you there. You must understand that I have issues that require my attention, but I will look in on you from time to time, of course."

George nodded and started to follow the young man in silver and scarlet livery, but turned and asked, "Lady Diere, how long will this take?"

She made no effort to disguise her disdain. "As long as it takes. The Council meetings are scheduled to conform to aspects of the lunar cycle; you will have several weeks. You should be fully prepared by that time. Now, do as I instructed. You would do well not to try my patience."

George nodded once again and without further comment followed the servant.

LADY DIERE STRODE TO a dimly lit hall. Whispering a small incantation, she stepped through what appeared to be a solid wall and into a hidden chamber. With another gesture, she let a heavy velvet curtain drop closed behind her. At a word, pale candlelight flickered to life and softly glowed where darkness held sway but a moment before. A heavy silence muffled the room.

It was empty but for a large crystal globe, its diameter a bit wider than her shoulders, delicately held in the fingers of a large golden hand, its arm thrust up from the polished marble floor. The bright orb seemed to hover on the fingertips at chest height.

Clearing her mind she focused on collecting ambient energies, and sent them coalescing into a spell intended to channel a link within the crystal into the recent past. If successful, she could observe past moments and events, or more accurately, those impressions left by the attendant energies expended during the event, almost like a sepia-toned memory.

Knowing the exact time and place, within any realm she had physically visited, was required for the spell to work. The farther back in time and the more physical distance involved, the greater the energy requirement. To view events of the past twenty-four hours within the Realm of Man should be well within her capabilities, notwithstanding the considerable energy drain.

Nonetheless, she knew this was dangerous. Whosoever cast this spell was somewhat vulnerable during the actual viewing. Tides and eddies in the stream of time could confuse and trap the unwary. And worse, an unshielded mind could fall prey to something else, something unknown, something that left the body a vacant shell, bereft of intelligence, initiative, and instinct—a soul stealer.

Diere was no fool. She knew the crystal globe was not of elfin origin; it was far older. Dim rumor held that it was a repository of ancient thaumaturgy, darkly obscure sorcery, and perhaps even a scrying device of the Old Ones, forgotten gods from a time far beyond most memory. More arcane tales held that the glass had enabled the Old Ones to view the future as well as the past. But according to ancient elfin folklore, none but the most powerful of elfin mages had ever seen anything but ghost-like images of the most recent past.

Diere smirked smugly. How pathetic those bumbling fools would now seem in comparison to the level of mastery she had developed over this ominous orb. Not that she was truly its master—no, more likely that she fancied herself the most accomplished adept in its use in all the known realms. Her ego could settle for that accolade, for now. After all, she had used it to locate much forgotten lore and thus ascertained the appropriate sorcery to apply to the scroll intended for Boltar before entrusting it to Saldar.

Diere also found it comforting that in current times, very few even knew of the globe's true existence; it had passed from legend into myth millennia ago. As far as she knew, not even Queen Mab was aware of the orb.

Feeling rather pleased with herself, Diere concentrated on her casting; the dark spell slowly grew in strength. Tiny points of iridescence began to glow within the depths of the crystal and soon began to swirl, accelerating in frantic patterns. She intensified her will, focusing on the time and place she desired to view. The orb clouded and the dancing lights slowed their mad whirl.

As the scene within began to resolve, she sensed that something was wrong. Not only was the scene of a strange landscape of rocky crags and barren heights, but she was shocked to sense that her mental shields were being probed. The incursion was subtle, even deft. She could begrudgingly appreciate such skill; but, she resented and reasonably feared such power.

She considered initiating a probe of her own to ascertain the source; after all, something had caused her spell to go awry. However, that would most likely alert whomever, or whatever, was behind the questing probe. Deciding that discretion was the wiser course, she began to diminish the energy supporting the spell in an attempt to slowly minimize her exposure and withdraw from the contact completely.

It did not work as she hoped. As soon as the drop in energy became perceptible, the spell faltered, a sort of metaphysical *hiccup*.

Immediately, her shields were assaulted! Virulent energy slammed into her defenses, bringing her to her knees! She fought back, reinforcing her mental barriers and struggling for a balance of energies to resist the attack. Slowly regaining her feet, Diere saw that the crystal had gone black, as if it held an obsidian sentience, a roiling mass of dark energy. She was looking into the heart of chaos, and sensed it pulling at her very essence—*the soul stealer!*

Diere mustered her remaining strength and deliberately severed the energy flow. The spell sputtered and collapsed. The orb held the ferocious darkness for a long moment in which she felt its frustration and rage at her narrow escape. A heartbeat later, the crystal cleared of any trace of the formidable entity.

Diere leaned against the wall until her ragged breathing slowed and her pulse calmed. She stared at the quiescent globe and pondered in awe.

By the gods, nothing like that has ever happened before, at least, not to me. Whatever that was, it is very powerful. I wonder if it can be controlled?

Her composure once more intact, but nonetheless still shaken and drained, Diere left the hidden chamber and made her way to her private rooms.

Without the use of the orb, she knew she would have to summon Lord Addecus and the Lady Leanan to sort out what had happened in the Realm of Man. If George wasn't to blame, she was all but certain Addecus and Leanan, or their respective minions, were involved. She could summon Addecus now, but Leanan, a Sidhe Nosferatu, could not respond before nightfall.

A wry smile briefly slipped across her face as she considered that it might be interesting to have them both present for the inquiry. But her lips drew into a tight line as she recognized that the mutual animosity they harbored, which she found sufficiently entertaining under normal circumstances, was becoming annoying and most certainly detrimental to her plans.

Sighing, she realized dealing with Addecus and Leanan would have to wait. The incident with the orb had nearly exhausted her, and sometime in the next few hours she expected a summons from her house guest, the Dark Elfin Queen.

Mab had arrived at Castle Diere earlier that morning, before George had been summoned. She had been expected, of course, but her presence, as always, tended to heighten the tension and stress of all in her vicinity.

Diere knew that she needed to rest before an audience with the queen; such meetings were always strained, and potentially dangerous.

THE SUMMONS CAME SOONER than Diere expected, about an hour after she had retired to her rooms. She had rested, but felt less than refreshed. No matter, one did not keep the Queen of the Dark Elves waiting. Diere made her way to the royal guest quarters, and was immediately admitted.

Queen Mab stood in the reception area, reading a scroll. A personal servant stood to her side with several more scrolls tucked beneath his arm. As Diere executed a deep curtsy, she noted the queen's rather drab green and brown traveling attire, and her silent personal bodyguard, a large warrior-elf of the queen's own House, almost invisible in the spare shadows.

Mab only trusted closely related guards from her own House, and for good reason. A corrupted personal guard, turned assassin, had been the means by which she herself had risen to the throne in a palace *coup d'état* two hundred and fifty years ago.

The queen acknowledged Lady Diere with a nod and gestured for her to rise.

Returning the scroll to the servant, she waved him off. "Thank you, Cedric. Please leave us now, and see that we are not interrupted."

The servant bowed and withdrew; but the stoic bodyguard remained, as immobile as the furniture.

Mab gestured to a pair of soft chairs. The two most powerful Dark Elves sat and considered each other.

Both stunningly beautiful, in the way that elves infuse a certain effortless elegance and grace in all they appear to be and do, they had always acknowledged each other as competent, intelligent, and truth be told, rivals.

When Lady Celeste, a distant cousin to Diere within the House of Hawthorn, plotted to usurp the then reigning monarch, *Queen Mab the fifty-third*, Lady Diere, like most of the Unseelie Court, stood aside and merely observed. Celeste had taken a terrible gamble; failure would have been fatal. Diere had naturally expected failure. She was surprised at Celeste's success, and jealous.

For two and one-half centuries, the fifty-fourth Queen Mab had ruled shrewdly, and when warranted, ruthlessly. Lady Diere had been careful not to offend Queen Mab. Both knew they were still rivals.

"I understand your pawn has arrived and prepares for his *performance* before the Council." Mab made it a statement, not a question.

"That is correct, Majesty," responded Diere carefully. "He studies as we speak."

"I have granted you considerable latitude in this matter, and I expect your further discretion as your plan comes to fruition. I will not have the throne implicated, or sullied, in any way," cautioned the queen. "Are we clear?"

"You have nothing to be concerned about, Majesty. All is proceeding as planned. By two moons from now, you will control the vote cast by the Realm of Man." Lady Diere held her open palms up as if in offering. "*De facto* control of the Council will be yours."

Mab smiled, but the expression was more predatory than pleased.

"Majesty, if I may? I am certain you didn't plan your visit merely to observe the tutoring sessions. Is there another purpose of which I should be aware?"

"Ah, very perceptive as always, my dear Diere. I received an emissary from the Seelie Court yesterday, to be specific, from Duke Briar. You are no doubt aware that he seeks Padraic the Rogue, to answer for besmirching the honor of his consort, the duchess. He has even placed a price on the Rogue's head."

"I have heard the same, Majesty." Diere kept her eyes downcast.

"Then can you explain why you are seeking Padraic? You see, I have my doubts that you are greatly concerned for the reputation of the Duchess Briar. I am well aware that you and Padraic were, at one time, quite close."

"Actually, Majesty, I have only made certain inquiries out of curiosity. I do not deny that I would like to see him again; but, what we once had is long in the past." Diere stared demurely into her empty lap. "I feel no urge to rekindle that which has been but ashes for decades."

Mab smiled, her insincerity blatant. "I am so pleased to hear that. It would simply not do for the Rogue to be seen or apprehended within this realm; especially since I have assured the Seelie Court that he is not among us. You are aware that bounty hunters from realms of both courts actively seek him, are you not?"

Diere shrugged, clearly unconcerned. "I am not surprised, Majesty. But I think we both know they will not likely find him, unless he wants to be found."

Mab clapped her hands and laughed aloud. "Ha-ha! Indeed, that is certain! He may be a rascal of the first order! I have no doubt that he seduced the duchess right off her prim and proper pedestal. His escapades are at least entertaining. You are right, of course; he is a wily old fox, and not easily cornered. I have often thought it a great waste that he refused to swear fealty to the Unseelie Court."

"He refused the Seelie Court as well," Diere reminded the queen. "He once said that his allegiance was to Faerie in general, and that was sufficient for him. He did not care for the general rules of comportment observed by both courts." The barest trace of wistfulness tinted her remark, a trace that her cousin did not miss.

"Be careful, Lady Diere," admonished the queen. "I will not have the delicate balance of the relationship that Queen Titania and I have maintained for the last century disrupted, nor our current plans upset, by a distraction over the incidental actions of a rogue fey. Dispense with any such thoughts and focus on your work. Are we clear?"

"Absolutely, my Queen." Diere dropped her eyes in apparent acquiescence. It took an effort not to clench her jaw muscles, as a knot of ire began to smolder deep in her soul.

"By the way," mentioned Mab casually, "I was thinking about the passing of Maude, the Steward in the Realm of Man, another fey who declined fealty to either court. I rather liked her. We often disagreed; but I found her interesting. As I recall, you and she were friends. You have my condolences."

"Thank you, Majesty," acknowledged Diere, her eyes still downcast. "I had not seen her in decades. I was nonetheless saddened to learn of her passing."

The queen stared at Diere. "I'm sure you were. I was surprised; I would have thought Maude easily had another century or so in her lifespan. Perhaps she was older than she appeared?"

"Perhaps so, Majesty." This topic of conversation was making Diere decidedly uncomfortable.

"What of the heir, the new Steward?" asked the queen.

"I am aware of her name, Ellen Doyle, but little else, Majesty," responded Diere as placidly as possible.

"Indeed? Little else?"

"Quite so, Majesty. Do you wish me to make inquiries?"

"No, do not. I think it best to stay out of that issue entirely."

"Of course, Majesty, it shall be as you wish."

"I must return this afternoon to my duties. Before I go, I would like to briefly observe, unnoticed of course, your pawn during his tutoring. Is this possible?"

"Yes, of course, Majesty. I shall make the arrangements immediately." Lady Diere rose, curtsied, and took her leave, careful to maintain a bland smile despite her clenched teeth.

LATER, IN A HIDDEN room that provided a view of the tutoring chamber, Lady Diere stood to one side a pace behind the queen. The ever-present bodyguard hovered nearby.

Diere allowed herself an inaudible sigh. This consistent portrayal as the loyal retainer, a mere façade that hid her racing mind, was taxing indeed. Keeping the queen focused on the plan in which George was to play an essential part was critical to her overall strategy. However, the references to Padraic and Maude had shaken her. What did the queen know, or *suspect?*

I stand here now, so close, so very close. Yet, I must wait, biding my time in patient silence.

THE QUEEN DID NOT LEAVE Castle Diere until an hour before sunset. Despite her announced intention to travel earlier that afternoon, she took a keen interest in her observation of George and his interaction with his tutors. She watched carefully for several hours. The obvious depth of her contemplation disturbed Lady Diere. Had not the queen indicated that she wished to observe the tutoring *briefly?*

As Mab was about to depart, she spoke in a low voice, audible only to Lady Diere. "Cousin, it seems you have chosen your pawn well. I wonder if perhaps you may have chosen *too well?*"

"Majesty?" Diere's confusion was evident.

Mab's voice was laden with condescension. "This man, George, assimilates knowledge quickly, and I sense that he is quite shrewd. He would merit close scrutiny and supervision more than trust. Do not forget that he is human, and therefore dangerous."

"Of course, Majesty. He will be watched."

The queen paused in thought. "I have decided to assist you in his period of indoctrination. I will send my alchemist as a tutor to oversee a portion of his training, and to assess his loyalty. I would have suggested an appropriate mind-spell but for its certain detection by the Council. This is *your* plan, so use your pawn carefully, and watch him closely. You know I will hold you responsible."

"Of course, Majesty," Diere responded, her face bereft of any expression. "I bid you a safe journey."

Queen Mab nodded imperiously and departed without further comment.

IN COMPLIANCE WITH the expected custom, Lady Diere remained on the ramparts long enough to see the royal escort pass through the outer gates. As the portcullis came down, she spun on her heels and stormed to her chambers. Servants hastened out of her path; she bore her wrath like a thundercloud before her.

In the privacy of her chambers, she fought to control her fury at the queen. She realized her anger was, in part, because she reasonably feared the queen, and what Mab might suspect about her plans. Intuitively she knew that she could not allow her emotions to influence or dictate her actions. The cold and ruthless logic that she strove to employ with focused skill was her secure bastion, her strategic fortress, weathering ever steadfast in a sea of fear and anger.

Seeking it now, she shunted her emotions to one side and focused on the next few steps of her plan, weighing each in light of the latest developments and compensating for potential alternative results. It was much like planning a strategy in chess. It steadily calmed her to the point where she could consider how to deal with Lord Addecus and Lady Leanan. She would hold that meeting this night, elsewhere, in her special and private place. To have either of them at Castle Diere was out of the question, especially so soon after the queen's visit.

IT WAS JUST BEFORE midnight when Lady Diere summoned Lord Addecus and Lady Leanan to the vast hollow chamber where they typically conducted their meetings. Diere, attired in a form-clinging gown of iridescent greens, stood in the broad cone of soft light, her arms folded and lips pursed in displeasure. An indignant Lord Addecus, in his usual shapeless hooded robe, and an angry Lady Leanan, in a severely cut grey and black gown, stood before her, their seething mutual animosity so palatable that small sparks danced at the edge of darkness.

Lord Addecus had arrived first, and launched into a heated complaint without preamble. Lady Leanan had arrived in time to hear his vitriolic accusations of vampiric interference. She interrupted his tirade with a curse, and commenced an equally vile bombast of her own.

Lady Diere let it go on for several moments and then demanded, "Silence!"

She let them stew in the dearth of sound until both were calm and composed. When she spoke, she had their full attention.

"Listen carefully, I shall not repeat myself. Each of you had a task to accomplish, albeit through your respective minions. It is obvious that neither of you had adequate control of your own people. That, I cannot tolerate! This petty animosity that you and your respective kind bear for one another has now seriously hampered my plans. I am most displeased."

Lord Addecus could not remain silent. "Lady Diere, I wasss not informed that vampiresss would be in that realm *ssspying* on my people. I—"

"Enough!" Diere declared, as a sudden violent energy crackled around the cone of light. "I alone determine what you need to know!"

In the deafening silence, Lady Diere stared above their heads, as if focused on a distant thought. Angry and unrestrained power radiated from her in waves. She took a moment to reinforce her control and regain her composure.

This blatant slip, this unanticipated loss of control, however brief, was a crack in Lady Diere's façade of competent omnipotence. It did not—*could not*—go unnoticed by either Lord Addecus or Lady Leanan.

Addecus narrowed his eyes, the tension in his jaw and shoulders was evident, and with obvious effort he refrained from speaking, or even flicking his tongue.

Her glance subtle, Leanan watched him closely. She could see the evident rift, however slight, now developing between Addecus and Diere. The Were Lord and the Sidhe locked gazes for an instant, but remained silent.

"It is not your concern what the other is tasked to do. It obviously matters little now, since both of you have failed. You both disappoint me," muttered the disgusted elf.

Scowling at one another, the Were Lord and the Sidhe did not offer any response.

Diere's voice now took on a cold and threatening edge. "Leave me, now. Return to your realms, and await my pleasure. Your minions are to have no further contact, unless I authorize it. Shadow and Were are not to engage in argument or strife. Are we clear?"

Addecus and Leanan nodded as one. Lady Diere waved a hand in dismissal.

As they silently turned to depart, they caught each other's eye once more, a stroke of chance unnoticed by Lady Diere. Something had changed. With the barest of nods, they clandestinely acknowledged the moment and stepped into their own separate darkness.

IT TOOK CONSIDERABLE effort for Lady Diere to reach that state of pragmatic calm where cool logic and calculated risk were clear to her once more. The conflict between Were and Shadow had left damning traces in the Realm of Man, a real problem should someone in that realm recognize the true meaning of such evidence.

The added complication was that George had to return there; the Council would not be dissuaded from the residency requirement. George would just have to deal with the authorities. And now Queen Mab had added her alchemist as a tutor—a spy, of course. But just who was to be watched, George or herself? What would Mab do should George be deemed insufficiently loyal by this alchemist?

Diere had too much time and effort invested in George. She shuddered at the thought of losing her pawn. Starting over was unacceptable. Timing was critical. There was no doubt now that her strategy would have to be adjusted; plans, already in play, must be accelerated.

She considered the implications, and smiled. The heightened anticipation of a death that she had so carefully and patiently orchestrated, she found almost intoxicating—especially this death, this long awaited death.

Now, she thought, just one more thing . . .

Where is Salidar?

CH 18

SALIDAR TRUDGED ONWARD along the worn road that would take him to the Inn of the Crying Cup. Untended fields, long fallow, lay to his right and left. The dark shadow of an unkempt forest hovered on the distant horizon. The land about him seemed barren and empty. It was midmorning, yet he saw no people or animals; even the sky was devoid of birds.

No great surprise, I suppose. Life is spare and cheap in this Realm of Shadow.

The sickly sun had banished the cooler mists and dew; sparse grey clouds lingered, spent actors reluctant to leave the celestial stage. He sighed knowing the rest of the day would be appreciably warmer. The first beads of sweat appeared upon his brow, mute testament to the lingering humidity.

It would take almost eight hours of walking to reach his destination. He grimaced at the memory of Baron Von Kestel's offer of a mount and an escort. Lady Leanan had not been so generous, allowing him to continue on his way, without benefit of either.

But wait, that's not quite true, is it? I do have an "escort" of sorts—that is, if being under surveillance by a vampire and her familiar qualifies. Methinks I would rather have the horse.

He resisted the temptation to turn about and look for his *watcher,* no doubt the familiar, Gunther, at least during the daylight hours. However, it would serve no purpose, other than to potentially alert the hidden observer. So, he ignored the itch between his shoulder blades, shifted his pack, and walking stick in hand, resignedly plodded forward.

COMFORTABLY NESTLED in her bed at Delafaire Farm, Ellen awoke late, almost mid-morning. Groggy remnants of slumber tugged at her half-opened eyelids as she slowly stretched her arms above her head. She was still somewhat tired, having stayed up way past midnight reading Maude's journal. She felt less than refreshed and more than a bit confused.

Nonetheless, she shook off her malaise and prepared for her day. She laid out a new pair of jeans and an oversized grey T-shirt bearing the likeness of a grizzled Albert Einstein. She took the time to snip the store tags from both. After learning that Ellen had lost her luggage in the accident, Stacy had bought some clothes and a backpack for her while she was hospitalized. Ellen would be forever grateful—especially since Stacy knew her taste and sizes.

As she descended the stairs, the aroma of freshly brewed coffee drew her on.

Entering the kitchen, Ellen caught the tail end of Stacy's speculation about Mark's physique—absent his shirt. Millie smiled uncomfortably and rolled her eyes.

"Really, Millie! I mean it stands to reason; he's gotta work out! Most of the lawyers I know are *desk-jockeys,* you know, kinda soft."

Ellen smirked. *Uh-oh, Stacy has it bad; and vice versa, I suspect.*

Reaching for a mug, she poured herself a hot cup of coffee.

"Oh, good morning, Ellen," greeted Millie. "How are you feeling? Are you hungry? Would you like some breakfast? Pancakes and sausage? Is the coffee still hot?"

"I'm fine, Mom. The coffee's fine; and maybe just a couple pancakes and sausage links. Your cooking's too good and I've been eating too much. You know, I'm thinking about taking a walk in the woods today."

At the word *walk*, both dogs looked up alertly to Ellen.

"Hey, that's a great idea!" Stacy exclaimed eagerly. "And I know what you mean. I swear if I keep eating like this, I won't get into my jeans. Hey, speaking of—how do those jeans fit?"

"Fine, thanks so much! Hmm, a minute ago it didn't sound like it was *your* jeans you're worried about getting into!" Ellen teased. "So, where is Mark, by the way?"

"He's out in the garage working on the truck," Millie answered, as she slid a plate of pancakes and sausage in front of Ellen. "Are you going to ask him to go, too?"

Ellen paused and reflected. "No, I don't think so. He seems to really like working in the garage, and I don't want to pull him away. Say, why don't you come with us, Mom? It'll be just us girls, and the dogs, of course."

"Oh, thank you, sweetie. But, I have too much to do around here, so you two go. I'll fix you a picnic lunch; sandwiches, snacks, and some bottled drinking water."

"This is gonna be fun! Oh, I love the woods," Stacy declared. "Can we take something for the dogs, too?"

Millie smiled. "I don't see why not."

"When I finish eating I'll get the backpack from my room," Ellen offered. "It'll be the perfect tote for our lunch. I think I'll get a long-sleeved shirt, too, in case the mosquitoes get bad."

During the preparations, Ellen took the opportunity to slip the blue velvet bags containing the journal and spectacles into a wide zippered pocket in the backpack.

TEN MINUTES INTO THEIR hike, Smokey seemed to just appear on the path some distance ahead of them. The dogs trotted up to the cat; the pets went through a sniffing and tail-wagging greeting ritual. By the time the women reached them, the animals were waiting patiently, ready to continue the forest adventure.

Ellen smiled at their attentiveness. "Okay, guys, let's go!"

The three pets were off, bounding down the trail, only to periodically spin around to see that the women still followed.

As they walked, Stacy took several deep breaths and gazed up at the leafy canopy. She was obviously quite comfortable in such a sylvan setting, as one with the woods. So, Ellen found it a bit ironic when Stacy tucked a set of wired earbuds in her ears and dialed up a song on an old MP3 player she had stashed in one of the pockets of her green *hoodie*. Stacy just smiled at her and shrugged.

Ellen recognized the MP3 player; it was a gift she'd given Stacy a while ago. It'd been a private joke between them that Stacy was never without music; Stacy cherished the gift ever since. Ellen smiled. *You can take the girl out of Los Angeles, but you can't take Los Angeles out of the girl.*

Some time later, Ellen experienced a strong sense of *déjà vu* and stopped. The path in the woods, the dogs and the cat—too much mimicked her recent dream far too closely.

Stacy removed her earbuds, and asked, "Ellen, what is it? Is something wrong?"

"No, not exactly, it's just that this is all so familiar. I mean like from a dream I had." She resumed walking.

Stacy fell into step. "A dream? Really? Too cool! Tell me everything!"

Ellen shrugged and shared the gist of her dream. When she finished her description, they walked on in silence for several minutes.

"You know," Stacy offered, "I think dreams really do have meanings, or you know, mean things to most people, sometimes important things."

"Yeah? Like what?" Ellen pressed, truly curious.

"It's like your subconscious is working on an issue that your conscious mind, for whatever reason, can't devote adequate time and attention to, or doesn't really *want* to. Do you know what I mean?"

"You mean, like *unconscious avoidance* or *denial*?" asked Ellen, as the gamboling pets disappeared down the path.

"Yeah, maybe in some cases, but in this one, I don't think so." Stacy paused and cocked her head. "Take your dream; you were walking in the woods, with the dogs and Smokey, but I wasn't there. So here we are, walking in these woods—which, by the way, is something anyone could have predicted or expected. I mean, these are *your* woods now; so, of course you'd eventually walk in them. You probably had this trip in the back of your mind to do at some point. You were probably even looking forward to it a little; and your subconscious just took the idea and ran with it! See, isn't this all excellent raw material for a dream?"

Ellen stopped walking, stood very still, and pointed. "Yeah? How would you explain that I dreamt that as well?"

They had come to a break in the trees, a large clearing surrounded by a series of standing stones. To the right of the grassy clearing, a small cerulean lake placidly mirrored the early afternoon sky. A modest dock jutted out upon the lake surface. Across the clearing, close to the nearby trees of the deeply shaded forest thickening beyond, sat a small cabin.

Ellen recognized her dream painted in daylight.

Max, Sophie, and Smokey reclined at ease on the cabin's front porch, as if this had been the expedition's destination all along.

"Okay, now this is getting a little strange," admitted Stacy.

"Let's check out the cabin," said Ellen, moving forward.

"Okay! How can we not?" Stacy chuckled, following.

Standing stunned in the opened doorway, Ellen declared, "This *is* my dream; the little desk, the rug, everything!"

"I didn't have a dream; but I saw the photograph. This is where it was taken, here, in this room," Stacy concluded.

"Oh yeah, you're right," Ellen breathed.

"Let's see what else is here!" Stacy pushed past her.

A wood-burning potbellied stove centered the room, a small table with two chairs to one side, and a single bed by the wall. Affixed to the rear wall, they saw a set of cabinets supporting a countertop and sink with a hand pump.

A pair of doors to either side drew Stacy's attention; she opened each in succession.

"One's like a storage closet or cupboard, and the other's a bathroom. It's even got a claw-foot tub!"

Ellen stepped to the sink and tried the pump handle; after a few strokes a pulse of fresh water gushed forth. "It works! This cabin must have its own well and septic system."

"Oh, that explains the hand pump by the toilet—you pump to flush! This is so cool!" Stacy spun about, catching herself with a sudden thought. "Do you think this was like Maude's secret retreat, a private place of quiet and solitude?"

"Yeah, I think so. It *feels* right." Ellen stepped to the small desk and gently ran her hand across its surface. Lost in thought, she was slightly startled when Stacy broke the silence.

"Well okay! That's one mystery solved. Come on, let's sit and eat something."

They sat at the small table. Ellen rummaged through the backpack and doled out lunch; tuna sandwiches for her and Stacy, and dog biscuits for Max and Sophie. Smokey was treated to shared bits of tuna.

As they ate, Ellen got up the courage to show Stacy the journal. "Here, take a look at this, and tell me what you think. I've read some very interesting stuff in there."

Examining the book, Stacy's face became a study in confusion. "Are you putting me on? I don't understand; I can't read any of it. It's like an unknown language to me."

"Really? Try it with these on." She handed Stacy the delicate spectacles.

"Oh, I remember these from that picture. Are they the same ones? They are so cute! Where did you find them?"

"I found them with the journal in the attic. Go on and try them."

Stacy put them on and resumed looking in the journal. She became very quiet—too quiet.

"What?" Ellen demanded. "What's the matter?"

Stacy dropped her chin and looked over the glasses at her friend. "Okay, now I am officially freaked out. I can read what is on the right side, but the left is still blank. Hold on."

Ellen fought the urge to smile; she could rarely surprise Stacy.

Stacy removed the glasses and flipped through several pages. She put the glasses back on, and stared at the same pages. Finally she looked up to Ellen. "*With* the glasses, I can read it, but just the right side, not the left; it's blank. But I can't read *anything* without them. It's all just gibberish."

She rose from her chair and walked to a window. Ellen watched in silence.

"They do seem like sunglasses with light blue lenses." Stacy looked through the pane. "Have you tried them outside yet?"

Ellen just shook her head and shrugged. "No, I haven't. Go ahead and try it."

Stacy stepped onto the front porch and stared across the clearing at the lake.

Ellen leaned against the doorjamb and watched her friend.

"Yeah, they are just like sunglasses." Stacy stepped off the porch and began to slowly turn about; suddenly she stopped. "OMG . . . "

"What? What is it?" asked Ellen from the porch, mildly alarmed.

Stacy was facing the nearest of the old growth trees to the rear of the cabin, a massive white oak. She slowly walked toward the tree. Stopping about ten feet from the trunk, she spoke very softly, but Ellen could hear the awe in her voice.

"I can see lights, well, more like a slow pulsing glow around—no, coming *from* the tree. They're different colors, kind of soft and soothing, like an aura? Oh my, that's it! I can see the tree's aura!"

Stacy started forward, carefully stepping over several gnarled and humped roots, until she was within an arm's length of the broad trunk. She slowly reached out, placing her palms gently on the rough bark of the old oak.

"The colors of the aura, they're soft and changing. I can sense strength, great age, and wonder. There's more, like recognition, and welcome. Wow, you just gotta have deep respect and reverence for this magnificent tree. It's like the tree *knows!* It's hard to explain."

"Stacy, are you all right?" Ellen asked, growing concerned.

Stacy smiled up at the great oak, dropped her hands, and returned to Ellen. "I don't know how to explain it; but that tree knew I was there. I knew *it,* and the tree knew I knew *it,* and, you know it just felt, uh, well, *right* somehow."

Her hands waving in frustration, Stacy was uncharacteristically at a loss for words as she handed the glasses back to Ellen. "Here, you've gotta try it! Put them on and stare at the tree."

For a fleeting instant, Ellen suspected that Stacy might be merely mocking her, but her friend radiated such palpable waves of blissful awe and innocent sincerity that she dismissed any lingering hints of such childish suspicion.

Ellen complied with Stacy's request, but sadly she saw only the tree, no aura.

"It doesn't seem to work that way for me. Here, try them on again and let's see what else you can see."

Stacy took her time, walking all around the perimeter of the clearing, just inside the tree line. Occasionally she would touch a certain tree for a few moments, a blissful smile on her face.

Ellen and the dogs watched patiently from the shady front porch; Smokey was nowhere to be seen.

Finally Stacy returned, sat with Ellen on the porch, and handed her the glasses.

Ellen just looked into her friend's peaceful smiling face and raised her own eyebrows in an unspoken question. *Well?*

"It was incredible. I could see the auras of all the trees, some I could even feel, without touching them, I mean. They're individuals, you know." Stacy sighed and stretched out her legs. "There was something else, too. It seemed to help if I sort of relaxed my eyes, let them go out of focus a little bit; the auras were easier to see that way. I'm not sure that makes sense, but it's true. When I looked back at the cabin I could see these soft lines of reddish light, along the lines of the walls and roof, kind of like highlights."

"Highlights?" repeated Ellen looking around, but seeing nothing unusual.

Stacy cocked her head. "Yeah, kinda like mood lighting. Does the cabin have electricity?"

"No, no electricity. Are you sure you saw something?"

"Yeah, I'm sure; trust me. Try with the glasses on; take another look."

Ellen slipped the glasses on, strode into the front yard, and turned to look at the cabin. She still saw no lights. She removed the spectacles and gently wiped the lenses with the dangling tail of her shirt.

"Try letting your eyes slip a little out of focus," Stacy called out.

Ellen glanced up while cleaning the glasses and let her eyes relax. She slowly perceived *something.* Subtle red light flowed along the structural lines of the cabin. Flowed? *Yes, moved!* More specifically, something flowed within the core of ruddy light. She stepped closer and realized there were figures, or rather letters, some sort of script flowing along. She backed up and blinked; as her eyes focused, the lights paled and disappeared. Deliberately relaxing her focus brought the red lines back. She stared for several long moments, before returning to the porch and resuming her seat.

"You saw it, too, didn't you?" asked Stacy softly.

Ellen could only nod an affirmative response.

"And you did it without wearing the glasses." Stacy pointed to the spectacles still in Ellen's hand.

"Oh, man, I guess I did."

"I think it's time," Stacy urged, "that you told me more about what's in this journal of Maude's."

THEY SPENT THE NEXT hour discussing the contents, inferences, and implications of the enigmatic journal, at least to the extent that Ellen had read. What held the greatest fascination for Stacy was the concept of alternative worlds, and the ability to instantaneously access them through specific portals.

"Let me see if I've got this straight." Stacy prepared to count off discussion points on her fingers. "There are other worlds or *realms.* There are other beings or races living there. Anyone can instantly travel there through these *portals.* You are now the Steward. The Steward has control of a portal; and that portal is here on Delafaire Farm property? I am going to run out of fingers."

Ellen smiled. "Yes, according to the book, there are other *realms* populated by other beings. But it says that some 'races' can use *some* or *specific* portals, but *anyone* can use a Grand Portal, which is why Grand Portals have Stewards. I think that's to somehow control access or use. I admit it's somewhat vague. And supposedly, I'm now the Steward, theoretically in control of a Grand Portal; and, yes, it's supposed to be here, on this property. Actually, I think—no, somehow I *know* it's in this clearing."

"Okay, let's say that's true," speculated Stacy. "How do you, uh, you know, make it work?"

"Arrgh!" groaned Ellen. "I knew you were going to ask me that! Well, I'm not sure. The book doesn't give specific instructions, or at least I haven't found any yet."

"Well, that sucks!" Stacy grinned, reaching for the journal. Without the spectacles, she couldn't begin to read any of the script, so she sheepishly handed the book to Ellen. "So, put your glasses on, and look it up."

Ellen chuckled. "Yes, ma'am, right away, ma'am, will that be all, ma'am?"

Nonetheless she did as Stacy suggested. Leafing aimlessly through the pages, she was startled when Smokey leapt into her lap. He placed a paw upon a page and softly purred. Once Ellen began to read the script, he leapt down and began licking the fur on his forepaws, oblivious to the world.

Ellen's breath caught in her throat. That was exactly the passage she sought.

She paused to look at Smokey. *Thank you, dear cat. I don't know how you knew what I needed, but I am very grateful for your help.*

Smokey returned her gaze with a languorous and knowing blink and resumed his grooming.

Ellen spent several moments studying the page before her. "Well, according to this, I need only draw upon the ambient energies around me and *will* the portal into tangible existence. Ha! Wouldn't *that* be easy?"

The sarcasm was not lost on Stacy. "Don't knock it, Ellen. I had a yoga teacher who was very much into the concept of energies being all around us. Look at electricity, magnetism, even gravity; they exist all around us. Isn't that energy?"

Ellen shrugged, mutely admitting that her friend had made a valid point.

In a much softer voice, Stacy continued, "I don't understand how I could see the auras of the trees, much less feel them. But I am prepared to believe that energy exists all around us. And it's not that great a leap to think there may be a way to focus it to accomplish something."

"I'm sorry, I only meant . . ." Ellen faltered. "I just don't see how I could do any of this."

"Well, I can tell you one thing for certain," fumed Stacy, "you won't accomplish anything if you just sit there and whine. You have to at least try!"

Ellen winced; Stacy had struck a nerve. They'd had similar discussions many times in the past, but the topic was usually dating, or more specifically, Ellen's lack of enthusiasm for playing the *dating game*. She was just more conservative, and less self-confident, in counterpoint to Stacy's spontaneity and annoying predilection for blind dates and speed-dating experiments.

In the present case however, Ellen thought that Stacy was pushing too hard, too fast.

Ellen was not the least bit comfortable making decisions or taking action whenever she didn't have all the facts, or at least as much information as possible. Too much was happening that she didn't fully understand. Now, she was supposed to gather *ambient energies* and *will* something into existence?

As if Stacy had read her mind, her friend reached out and took her hand.

"Ellen, listen to me. There's a lot we don't know, and a lot we have to learn. We are not going to acquire new data without trying to search for it; you know that. This journal is the key, but we have to use it. We have to act.

If nothing happens, at least we'll know what doesn't work. But right now, there is no more information available; so, let's test the information that we do have. That's a rational approach."

"*Rational?"* Ellen spouted in exasperation. "There's nothing *rational* about any of this!"

Stacy just smiled and shrugged. "So? Chill out! Besides, what have we got to lose?"

Ellen nodded and mumbled, "Well, I suppose at worst we could look a little silly."

"Who's going to see us? The dogs?" Stacy chortled. "I'll get them to promise not to laugh! But, you know, I'm not too sure about Smokey; cats have always laughed at us behind our backs!"

"Okay, okay!" Ellen surrendered with a chuckle. "But I have no idea what to do."

Stacy shrugged and pointed. "Come on. Let's go to the clearing, and try something, anything, okay?"

At the clearing's edge Ellen stood quietly. Stacy and the dogs stood behind her and to one side. A soft breeze off the lake teased the long grasses. Late afternoon shadows inched incrementally from the forest. Ellen tried to clear her mind like she used to do when meditating, but it was nearly impossible to banish the incredulity she felt when considering the concept of *creation* from *ambient energies, by an act of will no less.* She could not seem to accomplish anything; sometimes she felt like she never had.

Looking over her shoulder at Stacy, she noted the obvious. "Uh, nothing's happening. Sorry, I don't think I can *create* anything."

"Hmm, maybe we need to move closer to the center of the clearing," Stacy suggested. Matching deed to word, she grabbed Ellen's hand and pulled her forward.

The dogs followed, taking the time to sample numerous scents of varying interest. Smokey rejoined the women as well, entwining in sinuous figure eights around their ankles.

"You know," Stacy mused aloud, "all this stuff about other worlds reminds me of what that physics professor, you remember, your doctor's husband, um, Zack? Yeah, Zack! What he was talking about that night at the bookstore, do you remember that?"

"Yes, I remember, but I'm not sure I understood everything he said."

Smokey began nuzzling Stacy's leg, and she dropped to one knee to pet him. She looked up to Ellen. "It's like I'm getting this idea. For the sake of argument, let's say Zack's point about different universes, worlds, or whatever, *actually touching* in some places, according to that *something-or-other* theory—"

"*Membrane* or *M-theory*, I think," interrupted Ellen.

"Yeah, okay, M-theory. Anyway, suppose it's true, and this is one of those places where the walls of the different worlds, universes, or whatever, are *thin*?"

"Okay, I'll play for the sake of argument." Ellen sat down on the soft grass. "Let's assume that's true, okay? How am I, or anyone for that matter, supposed to *create* a portal, doorway, passage, whatever you want to call it, out of thin air—oh, excuse me, I mean out of *ambient energies*? The concept of *creation, out of essentially nothing* is just too *godlike* for me."

Stacy sat and crossed her legs; Smokey promptly crawled into her lap, the better to enjoy being petted by *both* her hands. She was quiet and pensive for a few moments, gently stroking the purring cat.

Her face brightened; she looked to Ellen and smiled. "Oh, I get it. You don't consider yourself capable, or worthy, of this type of *creation* despite the fact that you are *creative* in your own right. But that's not the point here. In fact, I think we missed the point; you're not supposed to *create* anything."

Stacy sighed, handed the cat to Ellen, and stood.

Ellen watched as Stacy began to pace back and forth. The dogs watched from where they lay, mildly interested. Smokey just purred in Ellen's lap as she absently scratched behind his ears.

Stacy stopped pacing long enough to say, "Bear with me a minute, Ellen, I think I understand." She resumed her pacing and mumbled to herself, her fingers waving about.

Ellen smiled in recognition of the unconscious gesturing and pacing as sure signs that Stacy's sharp and sturdy intellect was in full analysis mode. A minute later, Stacy stopped pacing and collapsed back into a sitting position facing Ellen.

"Okay, that's it! You don't really *create* anything. You don't have to, because the portal already exists! We just can't see it! It's merely a matter of perception. We can't see air, unless it contains something we *can* see, minute particles like smoke or fog, right? It's like an encrypted or protected computer program running in the background; without the proper access codes or password, we can't perceive it."

Smokey nestled deeper into Ellen's lap, looking up at her in obvious contentment.

That phrase, *merely a matter of perception,* seemed to echo in Ellen's mind. She looked deeply into the eyes of the cat. *So you agree, do you?*

Yes, I do . . .

Startled, she looked up, catching Stacy's eyes. In that moment, all the pieces seemed to fall together in a simple, yet elegant, design. Somehow, she just *knew*. All she needed to do was to slightly alter her perception, much like she had done in order to see the red lines of light at the cabin, but in a different way. Now, she knew not *how* or *why*, but she understood what she had to do. Standing, she let Smokey spill from her lap.

Stacy watched for a moment and then stood up as Ellen closed her eyes.

Rather than trying to get her mind to go blank, as she had before, Ellen opened her mind, her perception, to everything around her. The more she relaxed, the more she perceived. She became aware of the subtle energies in constant flux around her; the breeze, the flow of a nearby stream, the ebb of simple currents in the lake, the straining plates of the earth, and life, the life energy of the grass upon which she stood, the stoic, yet majestic, energy of the forest, and the strong energy of insects, animals, and people. All became apparent to her.

She could sense the bright energy of the dogs and Smokey; each was quite pronounced, and unique. Stacy's energy was also a strong and comforting presence.

Ellen could sense the portal now; she could almost see it in her mind's eye. She visualized assembling a small mass of tiny amounts of energy from sources around her, although she was careful not to take energy from any living creature; somehow, she intuitively knew that was neither necessary nor desirable. She applied this mass of accumulated energy to the conceptual portal she carefully held in her mind, shaping it as needed. Finally she had a firm image in her mind, and she decided she was satisfied.

"Uh, Ellen," said Stacy, "I think you might want to open your eyes."

Ellen slowly opened her eyes, and beheld . . . *a big bubble?*

For want of a better description, Ellen thought it looked like a large, clear, soap bubble just sitting there in the middle of the clearing. She could see the grass inside, and the trees behind it. In her mind she had visualized a sphere; but this was, at best, half a sphere, a hemisphere. Much like a soap bubble, prismatic light reflected off its surface; pale iridescent blues, reds, and yellows oozed in lazy patterns flowing into one another, yet never quite losing their chromatic identity.

"So, that's the portal?" asked Stacy, restrained excitement sparkling in her voice.

"I guess so," said Ellen, reservedly. "Funny, I thought it'd be bigger, you know, like the size of the clearing."

No sooner had she uttered the words, than the bubble began to expand. Slowly at first, it accelerated outward, passed over them with only an instant's sense of disorientation, and stopped right at the clearing's edge, just inside the standing stones. Ellen, Stacy, and the pets were now inside the bubble. Their initial surprise paled in comparison to the impact of their new surroundings.

They were no longer in the center of the grass-covered clearing bordered by standing stones, no cabin, no forest, and no lake. They were somewhere else.

It was a huge place, far larger than the bubble appeared from the outside; no ceiling or walls were evident. They stood among a host of pale globes, each about the size of a basketball, floating at waist height above a smooth stone floor. One nearby was larger than the rest, a pale golden glow about it. Ellen approached and clearly saw, within the orb, the clearing, the cabin, lake and forest, where they had been an instant before.

Stacy went from one globe to the next, staring deeply into each one. "Ellen, look at these! Look at all of them! There's a different scene in each one; and I think it's live! You know, real time!"

Ellen turned and started toward Stacy, but had to step around Max, who was busy sniffing at some errant scent on the stone floor. Looking around, she saw a seated Sophie scratching at an ear with her hind foot, and Smokey sitting nearby, appearing mildly bored. The pets certainly looked at ease, as if they were familiar with this place. No doubt they had been here with Maude, Ellen surmised, perhaps in happier times.

Joining Stacy, Ellen peered into globe after globe. Each held a different landscape. Most were from an overhead perspective, a bird's-eye view. Movement was evident in some, grasses and trees swaying in response to breezes and wind. Another held what appeared to be cultivated fields, and cattle grazing in a meadow.

Ellen looked up and about her; there were hundreds of these globes, perhaps thousands, as far as she could see, in any direction.

"Ellen, come here!" squealed Stacy in delight. "I can see a person in this one!"

As Ellen looked into the orb that held Stacy's fascination, she felt a little *put off* as if the globe itself was somehow unsavory, but the sensation passed. As Stacy said, there was the figure of a hooded man, bearing a simple pack and staff, walking along a rutted dirt road. He seemed to be hurrying, his shadow long and his strides purposeful, as if his destination was nearby and he was eager to end his traveling.

"I wonder where he's going?" Stacy mused aloud.

As if in answer to her question, the figure shrank as the view zoomed out to show a much larger landscape. The worn road continued into an area of dense forest and emerged not too far from a crossroad. Near the intersection, several connected buildings sat surrounded by a stout palisade wall.

"No doubt, that's his destination," observed Ellen. "You know, when you 'wondered where he was going' the view shifted. So, let me try something; I'd like a better look at those buildings."

As she suspected, the view shifted once again, zooming in to show the settlement and its wall in detail. The buildings were constructed of rough wooden planks with shake roofs; only two were taller, perhaps two-storied. One appeared to be a stable and the other a dwelling. The rest were much smaller, their purpose undetermined until Stacy pointed out what appeared to be chickens scratching and pecking in the yard.

"Look! Some sort of farm? No, I don't think so," Stacy pondered aloud, and gestured to the surrounding land, snarled in thick brush and stunted trees. "There would be planted fields or at least a large garden, wouldn't there?"

As they watched, a line of horsemen, riding two abreast and armed with lances arrived at the outer gate. From one of the buildings came a man who swung the gate open. The dozen men-at-arms filed in, disappearing into the stable.

Before the gate could be shut, a black horse-drawn carriage appeared at the entrance and was admitted amidst much bowing and scraping by the gatekeeper.

"I think it's an inn, or the equivalent," Ellen deduced. "But what's really interesting is the way the view changes according to our requests."

"Yeah," agreed Stacy. "And we can both do it! I feel like I'm playing with one of NASA's surveillance satellites, zooming in and out. This is so cool!"

"It is that," Ellen agreed. "And I think you mean NSA, not NASA. But you're right; both of us can do it. But we still don't know how to get from point A to point B. So far we're just observing. I wonder if we can do the same with the rest of these globes."

"That's easy enough to test," Stacy reasoned. "Try a few other globes. While you run your experiments, I'm going to check on my hooded traveler, now that I've got the hang of this thing."

Ellen chuckled and moved off to another globe that depicted a mountainous landscape, with sparkling motes of sunlight glistening on snow-clad peaks. With a little practice, she had the *zoom in and out drill* down cold. *Cold, indeed—ouch, terrible pun, just look at this frigid wasteland.*

She moved on to another globe, and another, and another.

STACY, STILL FASCINATED by the globe in which she had seen a person, had managed to zoom back out to view the road and forest, but the traveler was nowhere to be seen. She speculated that he must have already entered the forest, and was still walking upon the roadway.

She tried zooming in on the forest but it was difficult to see through the thick canopy. Wondering if it was possible, she tried to change the perspective from overhead to almost ground level; to her surprise, it worked! However, her field of view was correspondingly restricted; she could see the entrance to the forest, where the road wound inward, but the trees blocked any view of the interior.

Trees of another world . . .

She felt a thrilling chill. Could she see the auras of these trees, too?

It never even occurred to her that she didn't have the spectacles. She concentrated, then let her eyes relax, losing their focus. Ever so slowly, she became aware of the subtle colors of multiple auras. But, this was different, not peaceful and soothing, not welcoming, but defensive, assertive. She was confused; she wanted to understand, to help. She needed to touch the trees, to feel their life, to give them assurance, and the respect all trees deserve.

Leaning closer without thinking, she placed the palms of her hands on the globe and gently pushed, as if she could reach the trees. Without warning, the globe began to quickly expand and envelop her.

Stacy jerked in surprise. Her MP3 player fell from her pocket, tugged loose from the earbuds wire, and clattered to the stone floor.

ELLEN SPUN AROUND AT the incongruous sound.

Stacy had vanished.

Calling out for Stacy, Ellen made her way among the globes to where she had seen her but a moment ago. The dogs and Smokey converged on the same spot. Max and Sophie sniffed at the MP3 player and the nearest globe.

Smokey looked up at Ellen as she stood there wide-eyed. He made a low guttural *row-w-l-l-l* sound. In the next instant, the cat leapt upon the floating globe and stared at Ellen.

Do not follow. Get help first . . .

Slowly his paws made deeper impressions in the surface of the globe, almost as if he was sinking into it. The globe expanded just enough to encompass him; he was gone.

Ellen stared into the globe, but she could see nothing; for the moment, it had gone completely opaque.

What the—? Where did he—? Wait! Stacy surely has her cell phone; I can call her!

She grabbed her phone.

A warning tone sounded and an error message declared *NO SERVICE.*

Arrgh! What was I thinking?

Knowing she needed to act, she made her way to the large globe emitting the pale golden glow; she was already thinking of it as her *home* globe. Without hesitation, the dogs at her heels, she pressed into the surface of the orb; and promptly found herself and the dogs standing once more in the clearing before the cabin.

The *bubble* was nowhere to be seen, but Ellen instinctively knew it was there.

Hastily gathering her backpack, the journal, and spectacles from the cabin, she set out at a run for the main house.

She would return, with help! And do what?

Somehow find Stacy, and bring her home . . . somehow.

CH 19

HER SENSE OF BALANCE completely jumbled, Stacy plunged through the globe and fell about five feet to the surface of the dusty road. She instinctively tried to land on her feet, but barely managed to get her hands down in time to divert the energy of her fall into an awkward shoulder roll. Her years of aerobics and simple martial-arts-based exercise programs now proved their worth, preventing any serious injury.

She stood, brushed herself off, and looked around to get her bearings. Somehow, she had fallen into the world depicted in the globe. To her chagrin, she realized that *fallen* was an apt description. Her arrival may have been accidental, but she'd have to remember to bring the globe all the way to ground level next time. A fall from a greater height could have been far more serious.

A bit of white on the ground caught her eye. As she squatted, she recognized her earbuds and their white wiring. Unfortunately, they were no longer connected to her MP3 player. A quick check of her hoodie pockets revealed that she had lost it; but, where and when?

At least she still had her cell phone; but *NO SERVICE* appeared on its screen.

Well, that figures!

Retrieving the earbuds, she stood. Hearing a soft *thump* behind her, she spun to find the cat, Smokey, crouched in the road, his tail twitching and eyes quickly scanning the immediate area.

"Smokey! How did you—? Never mind, I think I already know. The real question is how do we get back?"

Stacy looked about in vain; there was no globe to be seen.

"Ellen! Can you hear me? Can you get us home? Yeah, Smokey's here, too. Is there anything I can do? Ellen?"

Silence was the only response.

Stacy looked around. The open fields to either side of the old dirt road were weed choked and clearly long abandoned. There was no sign of any inhabitants, but for a set of indistinct footprints in the pervasive dust, and narrow crumbling ruts, no doubt lingering testament to the passage of old wagon wheels. She forced herself to remain calm and patient, alert for any sort of response from Ellen, or any signs of indigenous life.

Time seemed to pass with agonizing slowness, and nothing changed. The late afternoon sun was slowly losing ground to lengthening shadows.

Stacy was reluctant to leave the location of her entrance to this realm. Surely she would be missed and someone would search for her. However, waiting here, with darkness perhaps a few hours away, did not feel wise. Shelter for the night seemed very appealing; after all, she could always return to this spot in the daylight.

But how would she find this particular spot?

After a moment's thought, she gathered up a handful of stones and built two small cairns on either side of the road, several paces from the road's edges. She reasoned that they would go unnoticed unless someone was deliberately looking for such markers. Next to each, she placed a few stones in the pattern of an arrow in the direction she intended to travel, just in case Ellen came looking for her.

She stood to review her handiwork, *slip-slapped* the dust off her hands, and noticed Smokey quietly watching her.

She considered the cat for a moment, and looked down the road toward the nearby forest. "I don't think we want to be out here after dark, so let's see if we can make it to that inn before sunset."

As if he had understood every word, and approved, Smokey turned and trotted down the road toward the shadowed forest. Stacy followed, easily keeping the cat in sight. If she avoided the ruts, walking was not difficult.

The road narrowed once it entered the woods. To either side, the forest was exceptionally thick; she could not see much beyond the first few rows of densely packed trees. The underbrush was almost impenetrable. Stacy resisted the temptation to try and view the trees' auras for fear of losing track of Smokey.

AFTER HALF AN HOUR of walking, the forest had become perceptibly darker. Sparse enough sunlight penetrated the thick canopy.

Smokey suddenly stopped and crouched. Stacy froze and scanned the nearby shadows for any threat. She neither saw nor heard anything; but clearly, Smokey had.

Flowing like liquid muscle as only a cat can, Smokey stealthily stalked forward a few paces and came to a crouching stop. Ears pinned back, he stared directly upward and let out a long warning hiss.

Stacy quietly moved to join him. Peering up into the dim canopy, she gasped.

Suspended above was a man; the man she had previously seen in the globe, the traveler on the road.

He appeared helpless, tightly wrapped in a mass of rope-like growths. Small vibrations and sudden shaking within the constraining vines were proof of his continued resistance. He hung out of her reach, and yet they could see one another. His eyes were wide, wild with fear.

As she looked around and above him, she saw other bundles of vines, but these held only skeletal remains, animals and beings whose bone structures she did not recognize. However, some were undoubtedly human.

There was movement along the tree's limbs, subtle and difficult to discern in the poor light; but, she saw it nonetheless—ants. Each nearly the size of her thumb, the insects moved in a slow single file along the limbs in the general direction of the entangled traveler. They had not yet reached him; but that was only minutes away.

Suddenly, he shook violently and his eyes grew even wider as he stared at something over her head.

Without hesitation she flung herself backwards and rolled into a crouched defensive position. A dangling mass of sticky vines dropped and writhed vainly in the space she had been occupying an instant before.

Smokey had moved quickly as well, so quickly that she barely saw his prodigious leap to the other side of the road.

Noting that the cat was safe, or at least out of range of the tree's grasp, Stacy felt it critical that she assess this tree's aura. She did so without conscious effort, as easy as breathing.

The tree was emitting a series of confused colors within its aura, but she didn't sense anything particularly dangerous or inherently evil. She cast about and viewed the auras of several nearby trees; none were of the same variety as the sticky-vine tree. She found nothing very unusual about them; admittedly, they were certainly different from what she had experienced at home.

That ought to make sense; after all they had evolved in a different ecology, a different world.

She had to touch this tree. She wasn't thrilled with the idea, but she had to try something. She could see the ants were much closer to the trapped man; his muffled screams were escalating.

She approached the trunk, carefully dodging any remaining vines that had not fully receded into the canopy. Seeing no ants nearby, she carefully placed her palms on the smooth bark and relaxed. She deliberately evoked a soothing sense of peace from the very core of her being.

At first, there was no change in the tree's aura. Then the confused flow of colors within began to settle, and a slow rhythm, almost a dull pulse, became apparent.

She sensed a curious acknowledgment of her presence, and a vague sense of recognition, like a dim ember stirred from the ashes of distant memory.

Somehow she knew that the tree bore the man no personal malice. He had become ensnared as prey by mere happenstance.

Over the gulf of time, this tree and its kind had evolved, perfecting this method of acquiring sustenance in a symbiotic relationship with the ants. The tree provided the colony a home and enjoyed the protection of the insects. The tree could trap food. The ants would flay the entrapped victim, and the resulting sustenance would be shared by the insects and the tree.

Stacy sensed the tree becoming more comfortable with her, accepting her. So, in her mind she asked a boon of the tree . . . *Stop the ants and release the man.*

The ants paused in their relentless march, the leading insects stopping mere inches from the bound captive's frantic face.

The tree's aura seemed to flare slightly and Stacy had the sensation of actual communication, slow yet articulate.

. . . It has been very long—perhaps too long—since any of thy kind has deigned to grace this forest. No blood oath has existed in long memory. We are not bound . . . Perhaps we would comply with thy request, but know this—the price would be a blood oath.

Confused, intrigued, but not the least intimidated, she probed . . . *And just what does a blood oath entail? What is required and expected of the parties?*

. . . How is it that thou knowest not, Nymph? Has memory faded amongst thine as well?

. . . I—I've uh, been away . . . Please, answer my question, noble tree.

. . . Very well. By the Tree of Life, and a drop of thy blood, we are bound to thee, and thou to us . . . We pledge mutual support, respect, and honor one another. We exchange true names.

Stacy considered the implications . . . *I see . . . You should know that I travel—a great deal, even to other worlds, er, realms . . . I will not always be present, in truth, for most of the time.*

. . . Ha! Is that not always the way of nymphs? I know it is impolite to ask, but how many forests dost thou serve? Canst thou find a sliver of time for one more?

Stacy thought this over, and decided on a carefully worded response . . . *It is indeed impolite to ask—so, we shall proceed as if you had not . . . Yes, I can find time for one more. Therefore, I accept the offer of a blood oath.*

. . . It shall be done, m'lady. Mine avatar will prick thy thumb; press then thy blood unto my bark.

An ant, much larger than the rest, scurried down the trunk and stopped at Stacy's left hand. It waved its antennae at her and turned to her thumb. She raised her thumb and presented its tip to the ant's pincers. It quickly bit, raising two drops of bright blood. She squeezed her thumb to get larger drops and pressed her bleeding thumb into the smooth bark.

. . . On behalf of the Forest of the Damned, I, Marmon Bloodroot, pledge support, respect, and honor to thee.

Somehow, Stacy knew to respond. She hoped her first and middle names would suffice as her true name . . . *And I, Stacy Elizabeth, do pledge my support, service, respect, and honor to the Forest of the Damned.*

. . . So be it, Lady Stacy Elizabeth . . . Call me Tangle. How shall I call thee?

. . . Oh, call me Stacy.

. . . Thou doest me great honor to permit the use of thy true name. It will greatly enhance my ability to call to thee in times of need.

. . . Let us hope that times of great need are infrequent. Now will you release this man?

. . . It is done.

The tangled bundle slowly lowered to the ground and the vines began to unwind from the exhausted traveler. A walking staff clattered to the ground, followed by the spent man collapsing in a heap. He was panting for breath, as his chest had been constricted. He could barely speak.

"Th-thank you . . . m'lady . . . I ken not . . . what . . . you have done . . . or how," he gasped, "but, I am . . . in your debt."

Her eyebrows rose. *Of course, he heard nothing because my communication with the tree was telepathic.*

She glanced at Smokey, who watched the man intently. *Hmm, I wonder . . .*

Smokey looked at her, blinked and nodded.

She smiled in surprised wonder, and returned her attention to the frazzled man. "Are you all right?"

"Aye," he wheezed, breathing somewhat better as he slipped his pack's straps off his shoulders.

"Who are you?" she pressed, watching him carefully.

"I am . . . Salidar . . . And you . . . dear Lady Nymph? Fear not . . . that I recognize your nature . . . I was . . . at the mercy of that . . . *vile tangletree . . .* before you charmed it. You saved my life."

"Vile?" snapped Stacy. "That tree was merely being true to its nature—there is nothing *vile* about it! And don't call me a *nymph!* You can call me . . . *Lady Stacy!*"

"My humble apologies, m'lady," Salidar whined and groveled, casting a glance at the imposing tangletree looming overhead. "I, of course, fully understand the need for, um, circumspection, as to your . . . *unique* nature."

She had no idea what he meant by that remark. She wasn't looking for an argument, so she let it slide.

It was getting perceptibly darker.

Salidar got to his feet. "I do not wish to appear ungrateful, Lady Stacy, but I am expected at a nearby inn, the Crying Cup, and I would prefer to be within its walls before nightfall."

She watched him shoulder his pack and retrieve his walking staff. Something about him did not engender trust. He seemed *slick,* in a *streetwise* sense, maybe *too* slick. His manner of speech was quaint and a bit archaic, but she realized that might be the norm here. Acting the part of a medieval lady might well be appropriate; but, *nymph?* She certainly had to think about that. Her impending need for shelter pressed; she made a decision.

Hands on her hips, she said, "You appear well enough to travel. One moment, Salidar, and I shall accompany you."

Stacy went back to the tangletree, placed her hands upon its bark, and called to it in her mind.

... Tangle?

... Yes, m'lady?

... The sun goes down and darkness follows. Am I safe within the Forest of the Damned after nightfall?

... Sadly, no, unless thou would care to take thy rest among my uppermost boughs ... There are denizens of this forest that thou would do best to avoid—a few roam in daylight, but a host hunt in darkness.

... I thought as much ... Thank you, Tangle. I must make other plans. I will go with this man to the inn. I'll bid you a good evening. I have no doubt we will see each other again.

... Touch any tree in this world, and I shall be so informed. May the Tree of Life shelter and shade thee, Lady Stacy.

. . . And you, friend Tangle.

She returned to Salidar, who was standing transfixed by Smokey. The cat merely stared at the man, who appeared to be frozen in place.

"Your, uh, familiar, m'lady?" he breathed, barely moving his lips.

Stacy looked at Smokey, winked, and fought not to smile as she faced Salidar. "He is my friend and associate. I've bid farewell to this wonderful tree. Shall we go?"

"Yes, m'lady, the day wanes, we should be off," Salidar managed to say as he tore his eyes from the cat. The feline unnerved him sufficiently to set him to mumbling under his breath.

Smokey rubbed against Stacy's ankle, and she heard an echo of Salidar's muted mumble as clearly as if he'd whispered in her ear. *"That is no mere cat—a nymph's 'associate' indeed. And when was the last time a wood nymph was known to be openly traveling in the Realm of Shadow?"*

Her eyes narrowed and she nodded imperceptibly to Smokey.

A bit louder Salidar asked, "Ah, shall we go, m'lady?"

Her lips thinned in a grim line, she felt she had little choice. "Yes, let's go."

Smokey led the way, Salidar and Stacy followed in silence. Neither man nor woman noticed that they were being observed. Of course, Smokey knew, but appeared indifferent, just like a cat.

SHARP EYES SQUINTED through the thick foliage deftly affixed to the rough weave of brown and green sackcloth covering the head and shoulders of the hidden watcher. Moments before, he had held his breath as the cat seemed to stare right at him, but the animal's gaze moved on. Breathing a slow sigh of relief, the man was confident that he remained undetected.

Before he had entered into the service of the Lady Sabrina, Gunther had been the best woodsman in his village, and one of the finest hunters of revenants in the region. His selection for the noble household of the vampiress had been his extremely good fortune, elevation from abject poverty, and his sole hope for a better life. He would never disappoint Lady Sabrina, especially since she had hinted that she might find him worthy of the *Dark Gift*.

She had tasked him with keeping track of a man who was no great challenge to trail, especially in daylight. But now, his subject was in league with a *wood nymph,* one with considerable skills. She had demonstrated control of a tangletree within the Forest of the Damned, a significant display of power by anyone's measure.

Her unexpected intercession had solved a perplexing problem for him as well. Gunther had seen the tree capture Salidar, but he had no way of effectively mounting a rescue, not that he would have revealed himself in the first place. No one escaped a tangletree.

He had been instructed that Salidar was to complete his task unhindered, but if the fool were to fail through his own carelessness and misadventure? Well now, that would not be Gunther's fault, would it?

But now that was no longer an issue, thanks to timely intervention by a wood nymph—*a wood nymph!* He had never even seen one before, and he had spent most of his life among trees and forests. They were creatures of *legend,* almost *mythical,* and now he *tracked* one!

Oh yes, his mistress would find this most interesting. He smiled as he silently made his way, almost invisible in the forest's dimming light, from shadow to shadow in patient pursuit.

SALIDAR, STACY, AND Smokey left the gloom of the Forest of the Damned just as the sun seared the tops of the western trees and their shadows stretched out before them. The rutted road wound on to where the crossroads met and the walled inn was visible just beyond.

As they plodded on, they could see a small cart drawing slowly southward on the other road, no doubt toward the same destination. At first, Stacy thought it was horse drawn, but as they closed the distance she realized the animal was a mule. Somehow, it was reassuring that they had mules in this world. She had always thought mules were under-appreciated and possessed of a certain dignity. Of course, some people thought *she* was stubborn, too.

Salidar softly spoke a warning. "M'lady, it might be best to cover your head with your hood. Your fair hair, shorn in a fashion of the Fey, might invite unwelcome questions or speculation. Did you not indicate your desire to be discreet?"

"Indeed," said Stacy as she flipped her hood up and zippered her jacket. *Stubborn perhaps, but not stupid. Time now to be low profile.*

At the soft sound of the zipper, Salidar's eyes went wide, but he continued to stare straight ahead.

"It'd be best," she added, watching her footing, "for you to do the talking as well."

"As you wish, m'lady."

They arrived at the crossroads at the same time as the farm cart. A man in simple homespun clothing led the mule; a petite woman in a patched auburn cloak rode upon the dray. Her hood hid much of her face.

The farmer waved and spoke first, his voice guttural yet firm. "Ah, good eventide to ye, good sirs!"

"And to ye as well, landsman," responded Salidar. "Make ye for the inn by chance, good man?"

"Aye, that we do, sir," the farmer replied, doffing his worn cap. "I be Wilhem, and this be m'wife, Frieda. We be bringing an early crop in; turnips, carrots, potatoes, onions and fat radishes. The inn buys our growin's."

"I see. I am Salidar." He nodded to the farmer and his wife, who kept her eyes downcast. "And this is the Lady Stacy. We would take lodging at the inn for the night."

Wilhem blanched at the introduction of *Lady Stacy* and bowed deeply to her. "Ah, beggin' your pardon, m'lady. I meant no disrespect."

Stacy smirked as she speculated that her attire, jeans and her oversize hoodie, had confused the old farmer into mistaking her gender.

"The hour grows late," observed Salidar, smoothly redirecting the conversation. "The light will soon fade."

"Aye, 'twill that, good sir." Wilhem straightened up. "We best be gettin' behind those walls afore yon sun goes. Ye might as well go ahead; move a tad slow, we do, this old mule `n' me."

Salidar acknowledged the suggestion and set off, but Stacy noticed that Smokey had not moved, nor taken his eyes off the farmer's wife. The woman had not budged either, nor would she meet the cat's eyes. Stacy unceremoniously scooped the cat up in her arms and followed Salidar.

WILHEM LINGERED AT the rear of his cart, presumably checking and shifting the load of vegetables as Salidar and Stacy walked on, out of earshot.

In a low voice, he whispered to his wife, "Tis him?"

"Aye, but what of her?" Frieda breathed.

Shrugging his shoulders, he sighed. "I know not. We can but watch, carefully."

"That cat . . . " Frieda shook with a sudden chill. "He seemed to look into my soul. I think he *senses me* . . . He has power—I felt it."

Wilhem's tone was of deep concern. "Can he—will he—betray you?"

"I . . . I think not. I cannot explain *why*, yet I feel that I am safe. No matter. Let us get within the walls; night comes. And, Wilhem?"

"Hmm?" he murmured, looking into her delicate face.

"I feel another set of eyes upon us, from within the forest; and these do *not* make me feel safe."

Wilhem nodded, resisted the urge to scan the tree line, and prodded the mule to resume its steady progress toward the rustic palisade.

THE GATEKEEPER HAD already admitted Salidar and Stacy, so he held the gate open and waited for the farmer's cart. Recognizing his friend, he smiled, and urged him to hurry.

"Ho Wilhem! That mule'll be the death of ye yet! Night is nigh, nag! Ha! His best pace has ne'er been more'n a walk, an' ye don' seem t' mind if'n he wants to crawl! Haw ha!"

"Keep y' peace, friend Amos! We'll make it by sunset. Have ye a crowd this night?"

"Aye, that we do," replied Amos as the mule finally broached the gate. "There be the baron's eastern patrol, a group of 'hunters'—four harsh men with the sly look of mercenaries, if'n y'ask me. There be the gentleman and lady y'spoke with, and an hour ago three strangers—came in a black coach, they did, w' a fine team."

Wilhem stepped closer. "Did ye get a close look at `em, f'm the coach?"

"Nay," whispered Amos, jerking his thumb over his stooped shoulder. "Took `em a room `n' stayed hooded—had the stink of magic about 'em, they did. I gives `em a wide berth, me. Now, what've ye brought us? I thought Boltar twas not expectin' ye for a sennight."

Wilhem turned to help his wife down from the cart, and gestured to the vegetables. "Twas the weather, mild winter `n' warmish spring gave us the early harvest. Turnips, onions, potatoes, carrots, aye, even some fat radishes. Y'know how Hilde likes `em."

"What ho!" Amos exclaimed as he secured the gate. "There'll be a fine feast tonight then! The patrol took a boar yesterday what wandered out the forest, more like twas chased, I `spect. And now we go' fresh vegetables! Oh yea! I'll tell the cook an' Boltar that ye be here. Early or no', I be glad to see ye!"

SALIDAR AND STACY PAUSED just past the inn's doorway to let their eyes adjust to the dimness. The common room was the largest on the ground level; the kitchen and pantry were squeezed toward the rear. The few candle lamps placed upon two long tables did little to brighten the dingy ambiance. The low brooding ceiling beams were smoke stained from decades of sooty fires like the one smoldering in the wide blackened hearth to their right.

To their left, a long slab of rough-hewn wood, its upper surface worn smooth and stained from a legacy of spilled drink, rested upon a row of old barrels, a rustic but functional bar. To the rear, near the kitchen entrance, a small alcove served as the innkeeper's modest office. A coarse cloth of stiff homespun hung across the alcove opening as the sole token of privacy.

Stacy wrinkled her nose at the stale and acrid smell of the place as Salidar asked the lone serving woman for the innkeeper.

With the toss of her head and a tired smile, she introduced herself. "Welcome, I'm Hilde." She indicated a swarthy man behind the bar. "Ye'll be wantin' Boltar, there."

Four swarthy hard-faced men in worn hunting clothing sat on benches at the end of one of the two long tables. Quietly drinking from wooden steins, they displayed little interest at Salidar's entrance, but Stacy had their attention.

She was still hooded, but jeans were not common attire. She carried Smokey in the crook of her arm balanced on her out-thrust hip, a pose that unintentionally accentuated her form.

Salidar noticed their interest and gestured for her to precede him to the bar, where he signaled for the innkeeper's attention.

"Be ye Boltar, good man?"

"Aye, and what of it?"

"I bear a message. Have ye somewhere private?"

The innkeeper shrugged and motioned for them to follow.

AS THE THREE STOOD inside the close quarters of the alcove, Stacy found the sour aroma wafting from the surly innkeeper reason enough to be brief. Smokey had gone very still in the crook of her arm and was totally focused on Boltar. She realized the cat was growling, a low rumble that she could feel through her hip; but she heard nothing. She had no doubt Smokey found something about this man unsettling.

"I am Salidar, and I bear a message from her ladyship." His voice was low in deference to their dubious privacy.

The innkeeper leered at Stacy. "Why this fair thing can speak for herself, surely?"

"Not her, you fool! I refer to the Lady Diere!"

Boltar stiffened in shock at the name; his face paled and his eyes glazed as if entranced. He leaned in toward Salidar and whispered, "I am her loyal servant! I meant no disrespect!"

Salidar reached within his cloak. Extending his hand, the scroll upon his open palm, he formally said, "I hereby deliver unto ye, Boltar, this scroll as instructed by her ladyship. I have completed my task."

Boltar initially hesitated. Then resigned, he accepted the scroll and tucked it into his tunic.

Salidar asked, "Have you any information for me? Anything regarding the *Rogue?*"

Boltar appeared to be confused. "What? Who? I know nothing of any rogue."

"You . . . never mind," Salidar said in exasperated disgust. His expression darkened. "Ye gods, I should have expected a twist of this sort."

Boltar scoffed and shrugged. He glanced askance at Stacy and smirked suggestively.

"Harken unto me!" Salidar demanded, jabbing a finger into the inkeeper's chest. "If anyone asks, we have only made arrangements for overnight accommodations, as required per her ladyship's instructions. Do ye ken my meaning?"

"Of course, good sir, a room for ye and thy . . . *companion.* Follow me."

HE LED THEM TO A NARROW staircase along the rear wall of the common room. The flight of steep steps led to a low hallway, dimly illuminated by simple sconces holding guttering candles in soot-streaked globes. The openings to rooms on either side were merely covered by pieces of hanging cloth, much like the rough homespun securing Boltar's alcove. At the end of the passage, the innkeeper pulled aside the tattered rags to reveal a small mean room with a low platform holding a mat of straw. More scattered straw covered the floor.

Boltar winked conspiratorially at Salidar and leered after Stacy as she entered the unwholesome chamber and took stock of the sparse accommodations.

Beaming as if he were displaying his finest suite, the unkempt innkeeper hoarsely whispered, "Of course, there'll be no charge for the room since ye be about her ladyship's business. But if ye care to partake of the supper meal, a fine boar's meat, tis ten coppers for two. I have to pay the cook and wench, ye understand? No doubt the cat can find a fat rat to feast upon, eh?"

Eyes narrowing, Stacy looked at Salidar and nodded imperceptibly. She was getting angry; the sooner Boltar was away from her the better. She found his leering disgusting, his manners atrocious, and his cloying body odor repulsive. *Jeez, doesn't anyone bathe in this world?*

Salidar counted out ten coppers from a money pouch and dribbled them into the innkeeper's grimy hand.

Stacy thought the coins looked suspiciously like pennies, but not quite round, kind of irregular, but about the same size. She wondered idly if she could have paid for their meal with a handful of her own pennies. *Now that might get interesting.*

The coppers tight in his fist, Boltar quickly retreated. The atmosphere improved slightly.

Catching Stacy's attention, Salidar held a finger to his lips and then carefully searched about the room. She watched patiently as he crouched in the middle of the room and slowly turned in a circle, staring blankly at the walls. Suddenly she understood what he was doing, letting his eyes relax their focus; but to see what?

She put Smokey down; he sniffed at the straw and began to explore the room's perimeter.

As she stood there, Stacy mimicked Salidar, using her own relaxed sight. To her surprise, she could see faint suggestions of auras about the wooden walls and fixtures. The auras were more like mere memories of the life energies of the former trees. But there was something else, something rather like a host of small echoes, lingering reflections of energies that had been impressed upon, and somehow absorbed by these walls. She would have to think about that.

Salidar straightened and focused on their present circumstances. "We are relatively safe, m'lady. I can detect no harmful spells upon this room. Although there are traces of old castings, crumbs of residual magic all around. This is a very old inn; it is built on an even older site rumored to have been a source of power in ages past."

Stacy placed a hand on the wooden wall. "I can sense something within the wood of these walls, great age, sadness, and fear as well."

Salidar nodded. "There is much to fear in this realm."

She raised an eyebrow, but remained silent.

Smokey returned to her, sat at her feet, and gazed into her eyes. A question formed in her mind.

"And what of tomorrow?" she asked. "I assume we will part company in the morning?"

"Quite so, m'lady. It is dangerous to travel by night. I would sooner leave this place on the morrow. I expect we are safe for now; we should rest." He sat on the floor, facing the doorway, his back to the wall. His eyes slowly closed.

She glanced at the straw mat and rustic pallet, and sniffed. *Whoa, that smells! I doubt the floor's much better. What the hell—I'm not gonna stand up all night.*

SALIDAR SURREPTITIOUSLY watched her spiral down into a crossed-leg seating position on the floor near the wall to his right. She threw her hood back, unzipped her jacket, and ran her hands through her hair, tousling it into shape. She didn't notice that her cell phone had fallen to the straw; but Salidar did.

His breath caught, but he kept his face impassive. He coughed, turned to his left and rummaged distractedly in the depths of his pack. His thoughts were turbulent.

I've had my suspicions . . . There can now be no doubt—a wood nymph who has traveled in the Realm of Man, and makes use of his "technology" and clothing . . . And worse, she knows too much—she saw me pass the scroll to Boltar. Ye gods—what a pig he is! In what capacity would Lady Diere employ him—or even stand his stench? Yet this nymph saved my life . . . Could she be in Diere's employ as well? That seems unlikely—especially with that cat. That damnable cat! Well, tomorrow I'll take my leave of her and the cat . . . That's probably for the best. I will leave this accursed Realm of Shadow in the morning, my task here completed, and return to Lady Diere with what little information about Padraic the Rogue I now have. I can only hope the Mad Elf will be grateful enough to return the sight in my left eye. Hmmph, I might have avoided that tangletree, had I full sight. Once whole again, I must do everything in my power to disassociate myself from her and her service . . . I trust her not.

By the time he turned around, Stacy had leaned back against the wall and closed her eyes. The cell phone had disappeared. The cat sat at Stacy's feet, staring unblinkingly at Salidar. Following Stacy's example, he leaned against the wall and drifted into a light sleep, his exhaustion catching up with him.

AN HOUR OR SO LATER, Hilde walked the length of the hall announcing that the evening meal was served in the common room.

Salidar and Stacy descended into a room far more crowded and warmer than they had anticipated. The same four hunters seemed not to have moved from their benches. Near the other end of the same table sat three robed figures, their faces hidden in the depths of their hooded cowls. The other table was occupied by the baron's eastern patrol; a dozen men well into their wine, ale, and food, who joked with one another in the camaraderie of seasoned soldiers.

Salidar acknowledged the seated farmer, Wilhem, and his wife, Frieda. He guided Stacy toward them at the only table with empty seats, between the hunters and the three hooded figures.

Hilde seemed to be everywhere, serving trenchers of roast boar meat with crude platters of boiled vegetables, and filling flagons as needed with wine or ale.

The food was simple but quite good.

Stacy had Smokey stashed in the front of her hoodie. She kept slipping him chunks of meat, an arrangement he seemed to be quite happy with, despite the temporary confinement.

Salidar kept stealing glances at the three robed figures. Silent, they ate sparingly and drank little. They seemed preoccupied and aloof.

All the while Boltar was becoming increasingly agitated, pacing between the bar and the kitchen, shouting at the unseen cook, and chiding Hilde as she served the patrons. His demeanor became increasingly frantic.

Salidar sensed that something was wrong. There was a hint of magic in the air; a very subtle questing spell was probing somewhere, or someone.

Boltar?

The innkeeper teetered near the edge of the bar, blinking his eyes in confusion. He shook his head irritably and reached out to grasp the bar; but, he lost his balance and stumbled into Hilde coming around the bar with two full pitchers of ale. She fell back, dropping into a seated position on the floor, without spilling a drop. Boltar was not nearly as graceful; he lay dazed, sprawled awkwardly on the floor, like a collapsed marionette.

Hilde recovered, still balancing the pitchers, and scowled at the prostrate innkeeper. “Ye gods, Boltar! Can ye not watch where y’ goin’? Boltar? Do y’ hear me?”

A muffled groan was his only response.

“Boltar, are ye all right?” she asked, her voice rising in pitch, tinged with concern.

Two of the nearest soldiers stood to assist Hilde to her feet. The three robed figures to Salidar’s left rose as well, but made no move toward the serving woman. Instead they stared at the disoriented innkeeper, who was now trying to gather himself and rise.

Boltar was barely to his hands and knees, his clothing in disarray, when a robed arm shot forth and a slender finger pointed to the innkeeper’s open tunic.

“He has the scroll! Seize him!” demanded a cold and commanding voice.

The four hunters to Salidar’s right sprang into action; two seizing the innkeeper by his arms and jerking him to his feet. The third snatched the scroll from Boltar’s tunic and tossed it to the fourth man. He in turn was about to present it to one of the robed figures when another voice boomed forth.

“Hold! In the baron’s name! No one moves!”

A tall soldier stood at the end of the long table. He made a few quick hand gestures; the rest of the soldiers took up alert-and-ready positions, prepared to confront the hunters and the robed individuals. The other two soldiers helping Hilde gently pushed her in the direction of the kitchen, but she retreated no further than the innkeeper’s alcove.

The tall soldier stepped forward two paces and pointed at the innkeeper.

“I am Captain Quinn of the Baron’s Eastern Patrol. You will release that man at once.”

He gestured and two more soldiers stepped forth from the shadows with crossbows drawn and aimed. The other soldiers stood poised and alert, well armed with short swords, cudgels, and knives at the ready.

Salidar's mouth went dry. He knew this could get very ugly, very quickly. He had seen firsthand just how well trained and efficient the soldiers of Baron Von Kestel actually were. He slowly stood and pulled slightly on Stacy's shoulder to get her to do the same. He glanced quickly behind him and saw that Wilhem had already left his seat and stepped back to the wall. Frieda, Wilhem's wife, was nowhere to be seen.

Salidar and Stacy joined Wilhem, their backs to the wall, their empty hands in plain sight. A soldier nodded approvingly at the three and returned his focus to the robed figures.

Wilhem gently pulled at Salidar's sleeve and began to slide along the wall, away from what was about to happen, toward the door. Salidar slowly followed, tugging at Stacy, who glanced down at Smokey, gone quiet and motionless inside her jacket.

The hunters held fast to Boltar, ignoring the captain's order. They looked as one to the three robed figures for instructions.

For a long moment nothing happened.

The guard captain was about to repeat his order when the three robed figures threw back their hoods and opened their cloaks.

Dark Elves!

Salidar's blood ran cold as he saw that one of them bore the mark of a mage, a dark inverted crescent tattoo on his cheek.

The other two were clearly elfin warriors, armed with short elfin swords of broad-leaved design and ornate silver-trimmed bucklers, no doubt bodyguards to the mage.

In a cool and almost musical voice, the mage spoke dismissively. "Stand down *your* men, Captain. We are on the queen's business. You will not interfere."

The guard captain bristled. It was clear he had no intention of backing off, his modicum of patience nearly exhausted. But before he could act, a chill feminine voice interrupted, dripping with condescension and derision.

"And what queen would that be, elf? No queen rules here."

The guard captain's eyes widened in recognition and surprise, but the elfin adept merely glanced casually toward the shadows.

"Ah, you would be the Lady Sabrina, a minor member of the ruling house." The elfin mage acknowledged the vampiress with feigned deference. He had clearly recognized her, but his demeanor remained assured and aloof. "I am Atrellan, mage in the service of Her Majesty, Mab, Queen of the Dark Elves, Monarch of the Unseelie Court. I should have said that we are on *Council* business, a slip of the tongue."

The Lady Sabrina stepped from the darkest of shadows. "Indeed? Council business, is it? I find that passing strange, since we were not so informed through the proper channels, nor were the required protocols observed. I think it more likely that you did not *misspeak;* that you are here either at the direction of your queen, or you are poaching in this realm. Which is it, Mage Atrellan?"

Her familiar, Gunther, emerged from the shadows armed with a crossbow.

The elfin mage gestured to the men holding the innkeeper; they released him.

Boltar stood unsupported, but he was still wobbly. Confusion clouded his face.

Atrellan held out his hand, accepted the scroll from the fourth hunter, and faced Lady Sabrina.

"Very well," he intoned imperiously, "I shall be frank. This man is a *traitor,* a vile and treasonous plotter, whom I have been tasked with apprehending. And *this,*" he hefted the scroll, "holds the proof of his guilt!"

Sabrina stared unblinking at the elfin mage, and shrugged. She did not appear the least bit intimidated.

Salidar did not like the way this was developing. Vampires were not unfamiliar with the use of magic, defensive or otherwise. A clash between an elfin mage and a vampiress of the Ruling House of Shadow could have far reaching consequences.

"Mage Atrellan, even if what you say *is* true," she smiled as he visibly bristled, "you have no authority here. I sense that you have used magic here, in this very room, against the innkeeper, perhaps? We have our own laws here; when you are here, you are subject to them as well. If your queen had sufficient reason for your 'task', she should have followed the proper procedures, those deemed appropriate by the Council as it relates to member realms, as you well know."

The elfin adept scowled.

Pointing her finger at the innkeeper, Sabrina continued. "This man, *Boltar* is it? This man is a vassal of the Baron Von Kestel and a citizen of the Realm of Shadow, and he shall not be taken without the approval of the Administration of the Ruling House."

"I see," said the mage. "Then you really leave me no choice."

"No, Atrellan," stated Sabrina firmly, "I most certainly do not."

"Time to go," Wilhem whispered to Salidar and Stacy as he gently tugged them to the outer door.

Without warning, the elfin mage made a sudden gesture; a blinding flash of light filled the room.

Outside, beneath the solitary lantern hung near the inn's door, Wilhem spun Salidar and Stacy to the right, placing their backs against the wall. His index finger to his lips, he quickly scanned their faces and whispered hoarsely. "Not flash-blinded are you? No? Tis good we faced the doorway! The soldiers aren't blinded either; they know to keep one eye squinted shut when dealing with a magic user. The flash of sudden light is an old and well-known trick!"

Nodding toward the interior, he added, "Listen now and learn!"

Chaos reigned in the common room.

A cacophony of thuds, shouts, screams, the clash of steel, and the smell of ozone had Salidar's hackles raised. The urge to flee almost got the best of him, but Stacy squeezed his arm so tightly in her own fear that he remained immobile.

He well knew the naked truth about short sword and knife work in close quarters. It was anything but graceful or elegant, but rather savagely swift and raw in its brutality.

The din lessened and a lull hung over the fighting; a strong voice could be heard.

"I call on ye to yield!" boomed the captain of the guard. "Your mage has deserted you and your prey lies badly wounded!"

"Aye," came the guttural response. "We must have his body, then . . . Ye lads are a tough lot, an' it's been a fine fight. But we canna' yield; twould be a fate far worse than a clean death at the hands o' the likes of ye."

Salidar peeked around the doorway and was stunned at the carnage. The tables and benches were overturned; broken clay pitchers, cracked wooden steins, and dented flagons littered the blood-slicked floor. The two elfin warriors, bodyguards to the mage, lay in bloody heaps, crossbow quarrels blossoming from their chests.

The mage had disappeared.

Two of the four mercenary hunters had been hacked to pieces, and three of the baron's eastern patrol lay unmoving. The captain and the remaining soldiers surrounded the last two mercenaries, who were both wounded and leaning on one another, back to back.

Lady Sabrina stood within the soft glow of a personal shield she had employed while counteracting the spells of the mage. Gunther stood to one side, the crossbow dangling from his hand, his quarrel quiver empty.

Hilde hovered, kneeling over the body of Boltar, softly sobbing, "He's gone . . . The great bloody fool is dead . . . This is over! No one else has to die!"

Lady Sabrina whispered an incantation; her shield shimmered and dissipated.

She looked to Hilde, not unkindly. "Regrettably, this is *not* over. They may not have his body. The Dark Elf Queen is rumored to have a necromancer in her service, so even in death, he would not be safe."

"Aye," gasped one of the surviving mercenaries, "your lady speaks truly . . . Now ye ken why . . . we rather die here, in failure, than return."

The captain turned to Lady Sabrina, "Your wishes, m'lady?"

Sabrina paused in thought. She pointed at the mercenary who had spoken. "I propose a temporary truce . . . How are you called?"

"Uh . . . Call me . . . Eric," he said, clearly puzzled.

"Very well, Eric," she said, gliding toward the desperate and confused mercenaries. "If you and your *associate* accept the truce, you may stand down without fear of further harm. Answer some questions, and it may come to pass that you may yet live out long lives."

"Ha! Trust a vampire? Well, what say ye, `Arry? A truce? Do we stand down and chance a longer life?"

Harry coughed, bloody spittle staining his lips. "Not yield? A truce, truly? Then, aye, accept the truce."

OUTSIDE AND SHELTERED by the wall, Wilhem urgently whispered to Salidar and Stacy, "We must be gone from here. Soon they will search for you."

Salidar balked. "Why? We've nothing to do with—"

"Silence *Grimrald!*" seethed Wilhem. "Follow me—now!"

Stunned at the use of his true name, Salidar blanched, but complied, following the farmer, who moved with deceptive grace in complete silence.

Stacy followed as well, with Smokey sticking his head out of her jacket. She had, of course, heard Wilhem command Salidar with the name *Grimrald.* She assumed that was his *true name*.

They wound around several outbuildings in the moonlit yard, stopping at a nondescript shed.

Wilhem signed for silence.

A moment later a sleek red fox stood before them, as if assessing their presence.

Stacy was fascinated, and surprised when Smokey leapt from her jacket to the ground.

Crouching slightly, his tail twitching, Smokey approached the vixen, who held her ground. They stood nose to nose in the moonlight for a few seconds.

Stacy realized that Wilhem was holding his breath.

Smokey stopped staring into the vixen's eyes and proceeded to walk along her side, rubbing his chin and shoulder along her flank and into the brush of her tail; then, he simply sat down. The fox turned, sniffed at him, and disappeared into the dark shed. Smokey leisurely followed.

A moment later, there was the faint rustle of cloth. A soft voice whispered, "Come inside, quickly!"

AS THEY SLIPPED INTO the shed, a small spark flared and a lone candle sputtered to life.

Wilhem caught Frieda up in his arms and embraced her. She smiled and urged him to put her down.

Stacy reached for Smokey and looked around the shed, but she saw no sign of the fox.

Salidar's pack and staff leaned against the coarse wooden wall. But what riveted Salidar's attention, and then Stacy's as well, was a grapefruit-sized globe hovering in the center of the room.

Frieda spoke softly, "Salidar, you must escape this realm; you are expected." She gestured to the globe, her eyebrows raised in an unspoken question.

He understood, of course. That Wilhem knew his true name could only mean that the Guildmaster had a hand in this.

Salidar looked at Stacy, with an uncharacteristic pang of conscience. He couldn't leave her here; she had saved his life. No, she did not deserve to fall into the clutches of the vampires. *Not to mention that she saw me give that damnable scroll to Boltar. Even if she tried to keep that a secret, how long would it take under torture for her to divulge whatever she might know, or suspect? No, she must escape as well.*

"The Lady Stacy must go with me, as should you both. The repercussions of this night will no doubt be severe, as you well know." He surprised himself with the scope of his suggestion; such consideration for the welfare of others was not typical for him.

Frieda considered Salidar for a moment, and then pulled Wilhem to one side for a private conversation. Wilhem listened carefully, added his observations, and nodded in agreement.

Turning to Salidar, Frieda whispered, "She is unknown, but since she travels with . . . *this cat* . . . it has already been suggested that she accompany you."

That brought Salidar up short, and he stared at Smokey. The cat, of course, ignored him.

Frieda faced Stacy. "Lady Stacy, you and your . . . *companion* are cordially invited to accompany Salidar to his destination. You are urged to accept; you will find sanctuary there, and most likely some answers to questions that you surely have."

No one missed that Frieda had spoken without accent or affected rural phrasing, much like Wilhem, who had shed the persona of the bumbling farmer at the onset of the melee in the common room.

"Well, I wasn't planning on staying here anyway," Stacy admitted, as Smokey began purring. "So, certainly we accept the invitation. But I do have a question. Where is the fox? It didn't come out, and there's nowhere to hide in here, is there?"

"The fox?" Wilhem chuckled. "I am sure she is around here somewhere. Now if I can draw your attention to this globe, I will explain—"

"Oh, I know what it is," interrupted Stacy, grinning. "But where does it go?"

"Sanctuary, m'lady, sanctuary indeed," intoned Wilhem. "However, there are certain protocols to be observed upon your arrival. Just follow Salidar's lead. Now you really must go—all of you, now."

"You're not coming?" asked Stacy.

"No, our *work* is here. We are in no real danger. Trust me; and ask no more questions."

Frieda hissed from near the closed door, "Voices! They have begun the search! Go!"

Salidar hefted his pack and staff, and pressed his hands into the globe's surface; it grew to envelop him. Stacy followed, Smokey cradled in her arms. The globe flared, went opaque, and shrank out of existence.

WILHEM NODDED AND WHISPERED to his wife who came softly into his arms, "Now, where were we, *my little fox*?"

She giggled and playfully slapped his arm. "Do not start, you randy old man, sometimes you act like a spry youth!"

"Well, you never complained before, dearest." Wilhem kissed the tip of her nose, earning a wry smile from his beloved. "They will find us in a minute or so; let us make it look good," he urged, grinning mischievously.

"Not too good, husband. We only need to appear a little embarrassed, not guilty."

"I am the soul of discretion, my vixen."

Frieda could only smile and roll her eyes as her husband lovingly nuzzled her neck.

SALIDAR, STACY AND Smokey found themselves in a small, brightly lit, empty room. Facing a closed door of stout oak, Salidar waited patiently; Stacy followed suit. Smokey dropped to the stone floor and began grooming the fur on the back of his paws.

"State your name," echoed within the room.

Stacy thought the voice sounded somewhat metallic.

"I am *Grimrald*, called Salidar. I am expected."

He turned to Stacy, but she needed no prompting.

"I am *Stacy Elizabeth*, called . . . um, Stacy . . . and I am *invited*."

She looked to Salidar, as if to ask *okay, what's next?*

He made a curious gesture, touching his nose, ear, and finally drawing his finger across his throat.

She carefully mimicked the gesture.

"Welcome to Storm Haven. You may enter the next chamber."

Once through the thick walled doorway, Salidar nodded to the black-clad guards, and whispered to Stacy, "Be not alarmed; this is the usual security check."

Stacy looked about in open wonder. She held her breath when she realized that some of the strategically placed guards, who watched them carefully, held short shotguns.

A guard announced, "All is well."

Two tall men, hooded in long grey robes, approached. One threw back his hood, exposing his smiling face framed in long grey hair and silvered beard. His voice was rich and clear, and his ice-blue eyes seemed to hold a power all their own.

"Welcome, m'lady. I am Gallenius, a Mage of the College. This is the Guildmaster."

The other hooded man nodded, but did not speak.

Stacy returned the nod, but Salidar bowed deeply.

She tried to look more closely at the Guildmaster, but his face was hidden; and no matter how closely she peered, no angle seemed to reveal his visage. *Oh, I hope I haven't offended him. But whatever—I'm new here.*

Smokey was not the least inhibited. He made several bounds and leapt up into the arms of the hooded Guildmaster.

"Oof," he exclaimed good-naturedly, a subtle metallic tone to his voice. "Smokey, welcome back, old friend. It is always good to see you." Hefting the cat, he teased, "Have you put on some weight?" He laughed and began to stroke the cat with his gloved fingers. "Now let us get to know our new guest. I am sure she has a few questions—as do we."

CH 20

ELLEN AND THE DOGS made it back to the main house in less than half the time she and Stacy had originally taken to get to the cabin.

Mark, on his cell phone, was in the kitchen. Millie was making a pot of tea and planning supper. One look at Ellen, panting and ashen, and both stopped what they were doing.

Mark spoke into his phone, "Hold on, Hawk. Ellen just came in and I think something's wrong."

"Ellen! What is it?" Millie asked.

"Stacy . . . " Ellen gulped down air, holding up her hand to forestall more questions and plead for patience. "She's missing . . . I think I know where she's gone . . . but I'm not sure how to get her back. I'm gonna need some help."

Millie ushered her into a kitchen chair. "Now what are you talking about? What happened?"

Ellen sat still and took a moment to calm down and catch her breath.

"Hawk is on his way," Mark said, pocketing his cell phone. "Now, what's this about Stacy? Is she hurt? Did she get lost in the woods? I just tried her cell phone; it goes to voice mail."

"Yeah, I tried that, too. Um, well, I don't think she's hurt—but lost, yes, something like that," Ellen stammered, as she realized how difficult it would be to fully explain—and worse, just what she would sound like in doing so.

She looked at Max and Sophie, her sole witnesses lying at her feet, and then to Mark, who stood over her, tense and primed to run to Stacy's rescue.

Ellen sighed and decided that only the truth would serve, notwithstanding that some might doubt her sanity. The priority was to find Stacy; right now, nothing else mattered.

"I know this is going to sound strange and unbelievable, but just hear me out. It's the only way to explain where Stacy went—where I *think* she went."

Mark and Millie looked at one another. Millie just nodded, and Mark shrugged.

Ellen considered her mother and cousin for a moment. She took a deep, resigned breath. "Listen, we can't tell anyone about this, at least not yet. I don't understand much of anything that's happening; but I do sense that it's powerful information, and best kept secret, for now anyway. Okay?"

Concern and worry marring their faces, Mark and Millie nodded their reluctant consent.

Ellen retrieved the journal and spectacles from her backpack. She placed them carefully on the table. She took a moment to reach down and pet Max and Sophie at her side. This simple gesture both calmed and reassured her.

And so, in the secure warmth of her kitchen, over a mug of hot tea, Ellen quickly told her story. She omitted only the descriptions of the *dreams* in which she and Maude had communicated; somehow, that was just too personal to share.

MILLIE SAT IN FASCINATED silence; her eyes widened in amazement as her daughter's tale wound on.

To no one's surprise, Mark made frantic notes, as was his habit in times of stress or anxiety. He fidgeted, apparently fighting the urge to interrupt. By the time Ellen had concluded, he had amassed almost two pages of scribbled notations, and appeared ready to burst with questions.

Ellen was temporarily spared Mark's interrogation when Hawk arrived. She hugged him without thought or hesitation.

The young detective unconsciously returned the hug, but then sheepishly held her at arm's length. "Are you all right? What's this about Stacy being 'missing'?"

Ellen retold the story, but this time Mark peppered her with questions.

Hawk found the frequent interruptions mildly irritating. Not all of Mark's questions were couched to elicit more specific information or clarify something already disclosed. Hawk sensed that a few inquiries were designed to elicit contradictory responses, an interrogatory technique frequently employed by trial lawyers. He knew this would be counterproductive right now. He was more interested in drawing as much information as possible from Ellen in a comfortable and cooperative interview. Interrogation techniques were better reserved for someone who was deliberately obscuring, shading, or omitting the truth.

Hawk wondered if Mark even believed his cousin. Her story was certainly unusual, if not bordering on the bizarre, but it had the ring of personal truth about it. At least *she* believed it.

When Mark started to repeat a series of questions, albeit worded slightly differently, Hawk called a halt to the process. "Okay, now I have a question. Ellen, is there any more information you can give us, that you've not already told us?"

"No, that's it," she admitted.

"I have a few more questions," interrupted Mark.

"I'm sure you do, counselor," chided Hawk. "But may I draw your attention to the fact that it'll be dark soon enough. Can't you ask them on the way to the last place Ellen saw Stacy? We need to go, now."

"Oh, yes, of course," Mark conceded with a wince. "I'm sorry, I only meant—never mind. Let's go."

"You all go on," offered Millie. "I'll hold down the fort here; you know, just in case she calls or finds her way home."

"Good idea," acknowledged Hawk. "Let me get some gear from my car. I've got some good flashlights. Bring your cell phones, too, in case we get separated. Meet me out back at the trailhead."

MOMENTS LATER HAWK handed Ellen a police-style flashlight as long as her forearm and as heavy as a rolling pin. She flicked it on and off, and stuffed it into her backpack. He gave Mark a hand-held spotlight attached by a coiled wire to a portable power pack with a shoulder strap.

"Mark, you have to be careful with this. It puts out almost two and a half million candlepower. You could do a lot of damage to someone's vision, perhaps even blind them, if you were to shine it in their eyes."

Ellen put a hand on Mark's arm. "Please be careful around the dogs with that. They'll be with us," she murmured under her breath, "at least to the cabin."

They set out briskly, the dogs in the lead followed by Ellen, Mark in her wake, and Hawk bringing up the rear. They hoped to reach the cabin and have plenty of daylight left to search the immediate area.

Looking over her shoulder without breaking her stride, Ellen asked, "Hey Hawk, don't *you* need a flashlight, too?"

"Actually, I have two; one is attached to the frame of my pistol, and this one."

Without slowing his pace, he fished a small black cylinder from one of the pockets in his vest and thumbed a rubber button on its base. A bright spot of light illuminated the ground at her feet. "This is a lithium battery LED flashlight, quite powerful for its size. It puts out almost as much light as that six-cell that you have stuffed in your backpack. The small light on my pistol is the same type; it just clips on to the front of the frame under the slide." Hawk returned the flashlight to a vest pocket, and gestured to the trail. "Let's pick up the pace, not waste daylight."

ADJUSTING THE SHOULDER strap for the spotlight power pack, Mark trudged after Ellen. It wasn't that heavy, just tiresome to lug along. He didn't think they would really need it. In fact, he thought the most likely scenario was that Stacy had just wandered off into the woods, and would no doubt find her way back to the cabin before dark.

Mark slowed slightly and dropped back. "Hawk, listen, man. I just can't accept Ellen's fanciful narrative. It might be a mere delusion, a residual effect of her head injury. I'm concerned for her well-being. Despite the fact that she appears to be functioning well and seems normal, this *delusion* is just that, no more or less. I expect to find Stacy waiting for us; and, *that* will be *that*. I might have to have a talk with Dr. Latrice-Johnson about Ellen's condition when we get back. I think—"

Hawk interrupted, "That your cousin's *lost it,* right?"

"Well," Mark waffled, "not exactly, uh, maybe. I'm trying to find out. I still have questions—"

"Stop right there, Mark," warned Hawk, not unkindly. "I like your cousin, a lot, so bear with me. You don't believe her; that was evident from your line of inquiry—*and she knows it*. Your questioning was taking on an adversarial tone, but I can understand that's your training. But I don't think you understand that Ellen can perceive your disbelief. And whatever is going on, she needs and expects your support. What she had to say was pretty strange, I'll grant you; but, I'm willing to listen and keep an open mind.

"I noticed that you didn't try the glasses or even look in the journal. You've already decided that it can't be true, any of it, because it's outside *your* frame of reference for *your reality*. Well, I have news for you, Mark; it's not outside the frame of reference for *my reality.* My people have lived here for untold generations; and, the folklore of this area, *my people's folklore,* holds stranger tales than the one I heard this afternoon from Ellen. So, I'm asking you to hold your disbelief in reserve, keep an open mind. Let's just see where the evidence leads us. Okay?"

"I'm sorry, Hawk, I meant no offense, okay? I agree, let's examine whatever evidence there is. I'm much more comfortable, on solid ground so to speak, when I'm dealing with hard evidence."

Hawk clasped Mark's shoulder. "No offense taken. And, uh, please, don't say anything about what I said about me liking her *a lot.*"

Mark couldn't help but grin. "Me? My lips are sealed! When are you going to tell her? You *are* going to tell her, aren't you? You're not shy, are you? Is that even allowed in *your reality?*"

Mark ducked a good-natured swipe at his head as he trotted forward a few paces and resumed his place slightly behind Ellen, who forged ahead unaware of the men's quiet conversation.

BY THE TIME THEY REACHED the clearing, Hawk estimated they had about twenty minutes until sunset. The scene was just as Ellen had described it; the clearing, the cabin, and the lake. He and Mark wasted no time in searching the cabin and its immediate vicinity. There was no sign of Stacy.

Hawk noted that Mark became more agitated, his cynical reserve eroding, as he paced around the perimeter of the clearing, loudly calling Stacy's name at the tree line. There was no response, not even an echo from the quiescent forest. It was clear that Mark had sincerely expected Stacy to be here. He grew mildly frantic, no doubt increasingly convinced that she truly was missing.

ELLEN AND THE DOGS had stayed in the clearing, not taking part in the hurried search. She merely waited until the men had exhausted their options, and then called out to them, a sad sympathetic smile softening her words.

"If you're both convinced she's not here, are you ready for me to show you where she went?"

Hawk and Mark looked to one another, nodded, and approached her in the clearing.

"Okay," said Mark, his voice slightly strained and hoarse. "Where did she go? Where do we look?"

"Easy there, Mark," Hawk cautioned. "Ellen, what do you want us to do?"

Ellen pointed to either side of her. "Just stand here with me and the dogs."

The men took the indicated positions.

In a softer tone she whispered, "I hope this works."

As she had done before, Ellen calmed herself and opened her perception to everything around her. This time she found it surprisingly easy. She sensed the bright vibrancy of the life energy of her companions and the surrounding forest. She found it easier to differentiate the energy signatures of the earth, air, and water, those subtle yet robust surges of elemental powers in a constant flow and flux. And yet, everything was in a harmonious balance.

She imagined gathering bits of errant energy from the surplus splash and overflow of the roiling surges, much like draining off the excess excitement of a burgeoning thundercloud. She realized that she was more competent and confident in her growing abilities. She would like to experiment further, but now was not the time. She had to focus on the portal.

At her very thought, the portal appeared. It was a dozen feet in diameter, but not quite resembling a clear soap bubble this time. It was more comprehensive, appearing as a shimmering golden hemisphere, reflecting the surrounding forest.

Mark's jaw hit his chest; he gaped, uncharacteristically speechless.

Hawk asked in a hushed tone, "That's the portal? That's where Stacy went? What do we do? How do we use it?"

Ellen smiled at him. "Think of this as the outer door; there are other portals, inside."

"O-o-okay. How do we get inside?" Hawk couldn't take his eyes from the portal.

A faint golden glow like a rippling mirage hovered over its surface.

Ellen grinned mischievously. "I thought you'd never ask. Stand very still."

In the next instant the hemisphere expanded to encompass them, stopping only at the standing stones on the clearing's perimeter. This time Ellen felt no sense of disorientation at all, and, of course, the dogs were unfazed. A quick glance at Hawk and Mark confirmed that they had definitely felt something.

Concerned, she asked, "Are you both all right? Mark, you're very pale; you should sit down."

"I-I'm okay," he assured her. "I'm just kind of shocked. I was a little dizzy for a moment there, but I'm fine now. Where are we?"

Hawk stared at the seemingly endless sea of floating orbs. "Are we inside the dome thing, portal or whatever? It doesn't look to be the right size."

Ellen paused. "Well, yes and no. I believe we passed through the portal to another *place*. I think it's like a pocket universe outside our own. Each of these other globes is another portal or doorway to other places, maybe other universes? I am reasonably sure this place is special, a kind of *Grand Central Station* for anyone who wants to go universe hopping."

Mark started to ask, "But how—"

Ellen cut him off. "Look, I'm going with my gut here! I don't pretend to understand the physics involved; so, don't even ask! Some stuff I got from reading the journal, but I haven't read even half of it yet."

Hawk interrupted. "We're here to find Stacy. We can deal with anything else later. Can you show us where you last saw her?"

"Sorry," said Mark, "but I was only going to ask, how do we get back?"

"Oh," said Ellen, slightly chagrined. "Sorry. See that larger globe that glows with a pale golden light? That's the portal that takes us home. You just press your hands on it, and it will sort of envelop you and deposit you in the clearing. It's easier to do than explain."

"Stacy's last location?" reminded Hawk.

Ellen looked around, trying to remember, but all the globes looked similar. A sharp bark in the near distance focused her attention, "That's Sophie! But where is she?"

Max nudged against Ellen's knee and led them off to the right.

Within moments they found Sophie sitting near a globe. Something small and white lay on the stone floor at the dog's feet, Stacy's MP3 player.

"This is Stacy's!" Ellen pointed. "I'm pretty sure she dropped it. I didn't touch it."

"Good thinking to leave it where you found it," Hawk assured her, squatting. "Did this have wired earbuds?"

"Yes, the plug-in type, but I don't see them."

He stood and pointed. "Is this the globe?"

Ellen carefully studied the scene depicted in the orb and announced, "Yeah, I'm sure this is the globe Stacy was looking into when I last saw her. She was watching a man walking on that road. I think she went into this world through this globe—maybe by accident, I don't know. All I know for sure is that after Stacy disappeared, I saw Smokey go in there; I think because she did. And I think he was going to somehow *look after her,* at least until I could bring some help."

Mark and Hawk exchanged a glance, but said nothing.

They studied the scene within the orb, but saw no one. Ellen showed them how one could change the point of view or perspective of the scene. However, the only sign of any civilization they could see was beyond the edge of the forest, at the collection of small buildings that Ellen and Stacy had seen before.

Ellen brought the globe's perspective back to where Stacy had left it. She paused, considered the view, and lowered the perspective a bit to ground level.

"I don't know how much daylight is left in that world," Mark said as he hefted the strap to the spotlight's power pack higher on his shoulder, "but if we're going to search for her, we need to start now. I'm ready."

Hawk nodded approvingly. "Let's do this. It's almost dusk there."

Ellen stooped to pet both dogs and said soothingly, "I want you guys to *stay, understand?* We'll be back as soon as we can."

Ellen stood and adjusted the straps of her backpack. "Okay! Mark, Hawk, watch and do as I do, one after the other."

She placed her hands on the globe and gently pressed. It glowed and began to expand; she found herself standing on a rutted and dusty dirt track with the setting sun at her back. She stepped forward a few paces and looked about; barren fields and gullies choked with bracken stared back, promising nothing. She turned at a shuffling sound behind her and found Mark catching his balance as his feet tripped up in a narrow wagon-wheel rut. Hawk appeared behind him and immediately assessed their surroundings.

"Are y'all okay?" she asked. Both men nodded in response.

Hawk began to slowly walk in a widening circle, his eyes on the ground.

Mark, disconcerted and unsure, looked around at the austere countryside. "This is pretty bleak. Hey, I don't see the globe!"

"Hold on." Ellen stepped to his side. "I know it's there. I can sense it, just can't see it." She concentrated and the globe shimmered into existence. She held it stable in her mind for a moment and then let it fade to nothing.

"Okay, now that's pretty cool, El'! Can you summon it anytime, or anywhere you want?"

"*Anytime?* Yes, I think so, if it's there, but *anywhere?* No, I don't think so. I mean, I don't really know, maybe. I think the locations of some portals are fixed somehow. Well, at least I sense that this one is. But I'm pretty sure I can sense their presence, even if they can't be seen."

"Hey!" Hawk waved from the side of the road. "Over here! I found something!"

Joining him, they looked down at a small pile of stones. Nearby, more stones formed an arrow.

"There's another, just like this," Hawk pointed, "on the other side of this road. I think they're cairns; the arrows are intended to indicate the direction of travel."

"Stacy?" asked Mark hopefully.

"Most likely, and here's what pretty much convinced me." Hawk squatted in the roadway and squinted at the dust. "Ellen, can I borrow your flashlight?"

She fumbled in her pack and produced the heavy six-celled torch.

Hawk held it low near the dusty surface, rotated the lens housing, and shined its broad beam across the tracks. "This makes the *sign* a little easier to see, more shadowed contrast and definition. It's not as harsh and focused a beam as my lithium lights. Look here; these are lug-soled boots, small for a man, and the track isn't pressed as deep as my tracks, with a man's weight. Ellen, what footwear was Stacy wearing?"

"Um, her hiking boots, I think. Are these her tracks?"

"I think so. They're fresh; the edges are sharp. There's no telling when it last rained here, but this road doesn't see a lot of use." Hawk pursed his lips. "There's another set of fresh tracks over there, wider and flatter, from a softer material, without lugs. This is just a hunch, but it's probably the man you and Stacy saw in the globe."

"So she went that way?" asked Mark pointing to the east where the road disappeared into the forest.

"That'd be my assessment. Look here; these are cat prints, faint, but right there in the middle of the road, probably Smokey." Hawk handed the flashlight back to Ellen.

"He followed her," she decided, shouldering her backpack. "Let's go!"

"Remember where these cairns are," cautioned Hawk, as they started walking. "They'll help us find the globe again."

"Right," Mark agreed, scanning the area. "There aren't many landmarks around here." Suddenly he pointed up, "Hey! What's that? *Birds?* There sure are an awful lot of them."

A stream of dark plumed creatures streaked overhead, widening into a virtual cloud of raucous ebony, thousands of birds, a wave flowing towards the canopy of the forest.

"Crows," offered Hawk, "on their way to their night roost. Maybe there's a rookery in there. Be dark soon; we need to cover some ground. Let's pick it up."

THE ROAD ENTERED THE forest. Hawk led, with one eye on the faint tracks in the dust. Ellen followed, trying to look farther into the gathering gloom, but the light was fading. Mark trailed her, equally aware of the diminished visibility. As they proceeded deeper into the woodland, he found the modest weight of the spotlight and battery pack to be comfortably reassuring.

The forest was unusually quiet as darkness stole over the horizon; even the air was still. The crows had fled the sky. The rustling and faint calls of daylight creatures were conspicuously absent. Now silent in their nests and dens, they would shelter through the night, hidden away from the tyranny of nocturnal predators.

All color had paled and bled away, leaving everything rendered in dim shades of shadow. A full moon would rise within the hour to paint argent highlights upon anything found by its sly beams through the porous canopy. But until moonrise, the forest would only grow darker, and bleaker.

Hawk raised a closed fist to indicate *stop*.

Ellen, not seeing him, walked right into his broad back and clenched at his waist to keep her balance.

"Oh, I'm so sorry, Hawk. I didn't see you." She quickly released him.

"No problem. Are you all right?"

"I'm fine," she insisted, although her cheeks felt flushed. She hoped he wouldn't notice in the dimness. "I'm sorry; I didn't mean to run into you. It's just getting too dark for me to see clearly."

"You're right," he confirmed. "That's why I called a halt. We need to start using lights. Can you reach your flashlight?"

"Sure, one second." She pulled the flashlight out and handed it to Hawk.

Hawk unscrewed the base cap and removed two colored lenses. He displayed them in his hand.

"These lenses, one red and one green, are for night work. One can be fitted over the clear lens, like this." He demonstrated by installing the red lens. "The colored light won't ruin your night vision the way *white* light can temporarily leave you blind when suddenly turned off. Also, it's worth remembering that many animals can't see red light."

"Really? I didn't know that," Ellen admitted.

"Yeah, *many* but not all," Hawk cautioned. "Remember that some *can* see red light."

Mark hefted the spotlight. "How about this one? Do we have lenses for it, too?"

"No, we don't, sorry." Hawk shrugged. "Mark, your light only emits white light, either as a wide spot or an intense beam, so leave it off unless we absolutely need it."

"Oh, so I rotate the lens to go from a spot to a tight beam?" Mark deduced, twisting the lens housing in either direction.

"Right, but it's white light, so keep it off for now," Hawk reminded. "I'm going to put a red lens on my light as well. The moon should rise in a little while and we'll have more ambient light, um, assuming that the lunar cycle here and on our world are on the same timetable."

"Hmm, I hadn't thought of that," Ellen mused aloud.

"But the premise is *logical*," observed Mark, "if we assume that this *is* a parallel world, or, um, universe."

Hawk and Ellen looked at one another with raised eyebrows, and then at Mark. Even in the ruddy light, he could see the wry amusement in their faces.

"Well, I do believe," said Hawk straight-faced, "that we'll have some 'hard evidence' in that case, oh, I'd say within the hour, as far as moonrise is concerned."

They set out once more, spots of reddened light skimming the path ahead of them.

While the forest seemed still, it was no longer silent. They heard small scratchings and scurryings beyond the thick growth on either side of the old road.

Periodically, distant sounds heightened their alertness; the crashing of something hurtling through the underbrush, followed sudden silence. A panicked squeal abruptly cut off was the most unnerving, until they heard the huffing and snuffling of something very large not that far away.

Mark's nerves were jumping. He kept glancing behind him, but he could no longer see more than a few yards back. He had the strongest sensation that something was behind them, stalking them, somewhere in the gloom. He nervously fingered the trigger switch on his spotlight, but he refrained from activating its strong beam in deference to Hawk's warning. Instead, he stepped up his pace until he was almost abreast of Ellen.

"Guys," he hissed, "I think something's following us!"

"Yeah, I think you're right," Hawk whispered. "Follow me, quick and quiet, now."

He moved forward silently in a crouched trot that rapidly ate up distance. Ellen and Mark trailed in his wake, although not quite as noiselessly. Hawk slowed to a brisk walk, his eyes scanning the brush on either side of the road. He signaled a stop and motioned them close.

"We're too exposed; we need to get off this road! Look here, see this? It's an old game trail. Follow me; we're going into the trees. Watch where you walk; be as quiet as you can. Ellen, keep your light low. Mark, keep yours off; it'll just give us away."

Hawk didn't wait, and slipped into the brush like a ghost.

Ellen followed without hesitation.

Mark cast a last look down the dark road, and pushed into the foliage after Ellen.

HAWK CAREFULLY PICKED his way along the old animal track with Ellen and Mark close on his heels. Much overgrown, it was difficult to do so quietly. On the other hand, Hawk knew it meant the track was no longer in frequent use, an equitable trade-off, as he did not want to meet any of the nocturnal denizens of this forest.

For about ten minutes, they wound their way in a northerly direction, generally perpendicular to the old road, and came to a shallow stream.

Hawk entered the ankle-deep water and grimaced at its frigid bite. "Whoa! Fair warning, it's cold. We'll have to tough it out and wade downstream for a bit to eliminate our tracks and disrupt our scent."

The three companions sloshed along the streambed for several bone-chilling minutes.

At Hawk's signal they gratefully left the water, their feet almost numb, and awkwardly climbed a series of rocks that offered a way up a brooding escarpment. Atop the bluff stood a massive willow oak, its gnarled roots gripping the earth like a clenched fist. The forest beyond thickened in an impenetrable gloom.

HAWK PUT A FINGER TO his lips for silence, pointed to the upper boughs of the old tree, and mimed *climbing*.

Despite the needle-pricks of renewed circulation in her wet feet, Ellen climbed without hesitation. Mark and Hawk followed.

Ellen ascended quickly, but carefully, grateful for the scant light from her flashlight.

She would have climbed higher, but a hand clasped her ankle. Startled, she bit back a scream, and looked down into Hawk's face.

He was slowly shaking his head, his index finger to his lips. Then he pointed above her.

She shined her reddened light straight up, and caught her breath.

Crows!

Hundreds of roosting crows blanketed the upper canopy of the massive tree. As Ellen cast her light about, she realized that even the nearby trees hosted an ebony mantle of drowsing corvids. They were in the midst of the huge flock they had earlier seen winging towards the forest. The birds seemed unaware of the three silent people seeking refuge in the boughs below.

Hawk squeezed her ankle again; this time, she froze.

She had heard it, too—a steady rhythmic splashing. Something was sloshing down the streambed, something large.

Their flashlights darkened, no one dared breathe.

The wet slogging grew louder and more distinct as something came closer.

Her eyes straining into the night, Ellen could see nothing. So she pinched her eyes shut as she had as a child when she played at willing herself invisible, and unconsciously expanded her perceptions. In much the same manner in which she sensed the ambient energies when opening the portal, she sensed the dark energy of the life-form sloshing through the stream.

It was of considerable size, but it was somehow corrupted, driven beyond its essential nature, almost mindless yet instinctively cunning. She perceived a strong sense of bitter rage, festering and simmering in the depths of a simple intellect reduced to a nearly irrational bestial mind. This beast felt perpetual torment, such that she almost felt sorry for it—*almost*.

The splashing slowed just past their hidden position, and stopped.

Ellen heard strong sniffing and snuffling from the stream bed. She instinctively shielded her mind, as if her empathic radar could be discovered and probed.

A pungent smell, stale and acrid, wafted up to their sanctuary. Within a few heartbeats, the splashing resumed and the odor diminished as the beast continued downstream.

A relaxed rustling of feathers above their heads betrayed the tension among the roost of crows, which had evidently been very much aware of the dangerous interloper.

Hawk hissed, "Time to move on."

Moonrise began to wash over the forest, rendering silvered highlights and obsidian shadows in ghastly contrast. Nonetheless, the pale light made the descent from the old oak considerably easier.

Once on the ground, Hawk cautiously led the way to a modest shelter offered by a clump of large boulders near the water's edge.

The stream was fully exposed in the surprisingly bright moonlight. Looking as far downstream as possible, they saw nothing of their recent visitor, but they were wary all the same.

"We'll wait here for a few minutes," Hawk whispered. "I don't know what that was; so, let's just take the time to be careful. I want to be sure that whatever it was is long gone."

He received wide-eyed nods of agreement, as they hunkered down amongst the rocks.

LONG MINUTES PASSED, and slowly the usual night sounds of crickets, small scratchings, and scurryings resumed.

Hawk motioned silently and pointed downstream; a doe had stepped from the forest to drink from a still pool at the edge of the watercourse. They quietly watched the poignant tableau in the silvery light.

Just as Ellen thought that this was surely a sign that it was safe to proceed, a broad shadow flashed soundlessly overhead. She looked up too late; the sky above her was empty. A startled bleat snapped her attention back to the deer. It was gone, ripples from its drinking still dissipating on the surface of the placid pool.

She looked to Mark and Hawk who were craning their necks and staring into the sky. "What?" she whispered impatiently.

Mark pointed up and softly breathed, "*What the—an owl?* That's the biggest I've ever seen! It just swooped down and snatched up that deer like it was a rabbit. That thing, it sure looked like an owl, was the size of a small car!"

"Keep your voice down and watch," Hawk warned. "That huge owl is circling to gain altitude. That deer is every bit of a hundred pounds or more. It's going to be flying close to the tops of the trees that we were just in, very soon. Just watch."

Its prey firmly clasped in its fierce talons, the owl made small gains in altitude with every beat of its mighty wings. As it neared the treetops, a disturbance like a rustling wave rolled over the dark canopy. A black tide of annoyed crows rose in raucous response to the presence of their natural enemy. The massive raptor ignored the first harassing sorties; but the sheer number of crows taking umbrage at its presence grew. The owl settled into level flight and made speed to the west, a murder of crows on its tail.

Ellen watched in fascination as the predator and its tormentors winged out of sight. The size of the owl staggered the imagination; Hawk's comment about the prey burden's weight only heightened her concern for Stacy. What other risks would a lone woman have to face in this world? What chance would she have?

Hawk snapped her back into the moment. "We need to move, *now!* Follow me."

He stepped into the cold stream and sloshed to the same small pool the deer had favored. A game trail, barely visible, led off to the southeast. Hawk signaled for them to follow.

THE TRAIL WOUND THROUGH the underbrush, generally taking them to the south, in the direction of the old road. They moved relatively slowly, doing their best to do so quietly. Much less moonlight penetrated the thickening canopy. The faint path, further obscured by encroaching roots and low brush, rose and fell with the hilly terrain.

Mark got distracted trying to avoid a thorny bush, tripped, and stumbled off the vague trail. Sliding down an unseen leaf-strewn decline, he yelped and flailed about, seeking any purchase to stem his uncontrolled descent. He finally came to rest at the bottom, near the base of a tree, splayed on his back upon a web of fallen limbs, and broken branches. He was essentially unhurt, but bruised and scratched from his fall. He looked up the dark incline to see two bobbing red beams playing along the hillside.

"Mark! Mark!" called Ellen in a hoarse stage whisper. "Where are you? Are you all right?"

"Here!" He sat up and waved a hand. "I'm okay! I just slipped."

"I see him, there," said Hawk, as a red beam found Mark's face.

"I'm fine, I just slipped," repeated Mark as he managed to stand amidst the forest detritus that had stopped his ungainly slide.

He pulled the battery-pack strap back up on his shoulder and noted that the spotlight appeared undamaged.

"Everything's okay. I'm coming up to you."

He took a single step and hesitated as a series of small cracking sounds beneath his feet escalated into a mighty *snap*. He felt an instant of weightlessness as he dropped into a stygian void—a jarring *thud,* then nothing, not even conscious thought.

CH 21

HAWK AND ELLEN MADE their way down the incline as quickly as possible without falling. At the bottom, Ellen tried to crawl over the broken limbs to the dark abyss into which Mark had disappeared.

"Ellen, stop! We have to make it safer first! It didn't support Mark's weight, so it might not support you either."

They pulled at limbs and tossed broken branches aside until they found bare earth at the lip of a roughly circular hole. Peering into its depths, they saw nothing but more broken branches on the muddy bottom about ten feet below.

There was no sign of Mark.

Removing the red lens from his flashlight, Hawk lay on his belly and studied the floor and sides of the pit in the harsh white light. He turned off the light, re-affixed the red lens, and rose.

"The hole's not that deep; there's a tunnel down there! I can see openings on either side near the bottom. There are gouge marks on the walls of the hole, like something with claws has crawled in and out. There's some debris down there, but I can see footprints—bare feet—going into the tunnel."

"Bare feet?" She shook her head. "That's not Mark!"

"I know— " Hawk began.

"We have to go after him!" Ellen blurted. "He could be hurt! He probably is!"

"We will," agreed Hawk, looking around, "but let's be smart about this and not get hurt in the process. We need a rope—a vine or something. We could hang from the edge and drop in without it, but it'd be easier to have some help climbing out—especially if Mark *is* injured."

It didn't take long to find a suitable vine. Hawk used a large pocket knife to cut a length several times the depth of the hole. Looping the middle of the vine's length around the nearest tree, he let the two ends of the vine dangle down into the open shaft. The ends reached to within a few feet of the bottom.

"Did you hear that?" asked Ellen.

"Hear what?" Hawk asked as he stepped away from the hole and looked about.

"I thought I heard something, a rustling and snuffling, up there." She pointed to the crest of the hill above them.

They realized the normal ambient sounds common in the forest night had gone quiet once again. Hawk put a finger to his lips for silence.

She watched him wet a finger and raise it to test the wind. She mimicked him and felt the coolness move from one side of her finger to the other as the barest breeze changed direction, now flowing down from the top of the hill. A strong odor followed, acrid, pungent—and familiar. They had encountered it once before, recently, while in the security of the old oak.

Ellen reached out with her perception and immediately recognized the energy signature of the beast from the streambed. It was somewhere on the hilltop above them.

"It followed us," she whispered in alarm.

"Yeah, time to go," Hawk breathed, pointing to the yawning hole. "You first, hold on to *both* vines; two are stronger and won't slip."

Tugging her shirt cuffs down to protect her palms, Ellen gripped the rough vines, quietly slipped over the edge, and lowered herself to the bottom.

As Hawk lowered himself, he grabbed at broken branches nearest the hole and pulled them over his head obscuring the opening. At the bottom, he quickly pointed to the open maw of the tunnel where the footprints led and nudged a stooping Ellen into the darkness. Once inside they could stand erect, although Hawk had to duck a few low spots in the crumbling earthen ceiling.

"Are you okay?" he whispered.

"Fine—now what?"

"We have to move." He pointed into the dark tunnel.

ELLEN LED. HER FLASHLIGHT'S red beam transformed the tunnel into the blooded gullet of a giant beast. She shook off the illusion and kept walking, determined to keep her imagination in check.

After they had covered a good distance, Hawk reached out to stop her progress. They remained motionless for a few moments. She watched him study the prints scuffed upon the well-worn floor of the tunnel.

"We're on the right trail." He gestured to the dirt. "There are three sets of fresh footprints and two appear to be carrying something heavy—probably Mark."

A muffled blood-curdling howl of rage shattered the silence behind them! A series of thudding impacts followed, shaking the very ground. Clods of earth and streams of sandy loam began to fall from the tunnel ceiling behind them.

Hawk grabbed Ellen's hand and they raced away from the destruction.

They stopped only when they could no longer hear the frustrated shrieks, nor feel any further vibrations from shuddering impacts or collapsing tunnels. Here the tunnel widened and branched off into three separate passages; one was considerably larger than the other two.

Hawk peered at Ellen in the ruddy gloom. "Are you all right?"

"Yes, I'm fine. What was that thing?"

“I have no idea, but whatever it was, it was big, too big, I think, to get into the tunnel—and it was angry. I also think that thing just might be what Mark sensed was following us. I certainly don’t want to meet it!”

“Me neither,” Ellen agreed, casting her light down each of the passages. “Now, which way do we go? Can you see any tracks? Wait—what’s that?”

Following Ellen’s light beam, Hawk stepped into the largest passage. Stooping, he picked up the object that had caught her attention. “It’s the spotlight and cord that Mark was carrying. It must’ve come unplugged from the battery pack.”

“Or,” she posited, “Mark’s leaving us a trail—you know, like bread crumbs.”

“Maybe, if he’s conscious,” Hawk allowed. Looking at the scuffed dirt floor, he pointed. “The tracks lead this way.”

Tucking the spotlight and curled cord into a large pocket on the back of his vest, he started down the passage. “I don’t think we’re too far behind them,” he cautioned. “We’ll have to move quietly.”

KEEPING THEIR LIGHT beams low and their footfalls soft, they made good progress. In several places the decline steepened only to level out once more. Overall, their path led steadily downward and the ambient temperature dropped perceptibly. The dusty dirt beneath their feet gave way to a worn rock surface, smoothed in its center by the passage of untold feet over unfathomed time.

The character of the debris to either side of the passage began to change as well, from loose rock and stones to small bits of bone and cloth. Within a few minutes they came upon another wide area, almost a small chamber. A truly macabre sight awaited, a stack of skulls and piles of disinterred bones. Many of the skulls were human, but not all. Some were generally humanoid but slightly elongated; others held pronounced teeth, especially the canines. One smaller skull actually sprouted small horns above the temples.

As Ellen cast her light about, something else lying askew among the larger bones caught her attention. "Hawk, isn't that the battery pack Mark was carrying?"

"Yeah, it is; and there's the strap. Hmm, I don't see any damage. It must've come unhooked." He retrieved the spotlight and cord from his vest. "Hold on, and I'll see if it'll still work. Just give me a second." He reconnected the cord, aimed the unlit light down the tunnel they had just traversed, and warned Ellen. "Look the other way and close your eyes. There's no sense in both of us ruining our night vision."

Hawk closed his right eye and squinted the left. He still managed to temporarily blind himself in his left eye when, just for a mere instant, the searing white light exploded down the tunnel.

"Damn! I should've closed both eyes! Well, the good news is that it works; the bad news is that it'll take a few minutes for my eyesight to fully recover." He grunted as he shouldered the battery-pack strap and rubbed his eye.

"No problem." She smiled, and teased, "I won't lead you astray—not too far anyway."

THEY HADN'T TRAVELED much further before they became aware of a faint odor, a sickly-sweet, fetid scent just below the threshold of offensive. They slowed in caution.

Hawk heard it first, the faint slap of bare feet, many feet, in the near distance ahead of them. He squeezed Ellen's hand and she returned the gesture; she had heard as well. They picked up their pace, and began to see a faint glow in the distant tunnel.

Hawk slowed to a stop, and finger to his lips, indicated that they should extinguish their lights before they approached any further. They crept forward in silence, ever closer to the edge of pale illumination pulsing beyond a curve in the tunnel. The cloying smell of corruption and decay lay about like piles of patient ash, poised to rise and cloud the senses if disturbed.

Hawk set the spotlight and battery against the tunnel wall, and crept as close as he dared to the bend in the passage. Holding his breath, he leaned forward to spy from the shadows.

Several candles guttered in a small cavern punctuated by a handful of stalactites and corresponding stalagmites. Water slowly dripped from the longest of the calcified cones and bled sluggishly through porous veins in the rugged stone walls to collect in a stagnant pool at the far side of the cave. Winking reflections flickered and flared on damp glistening walls as lean shadows pulsed in a slow circuit around the chamber.

Half a dozen thin shapes, hunched over and nervously gibbering like a pack of intimidated hyenas, moved about in deference to an erect hooded figure entering from another passage. The newcomer held a staff topped by a lone candle, a pale green tint to its unnatural flame. Stepping to the center of the chamber, the figure nudged something with the base of his staff.

A low groan issued forth.

Unable to see beyond a ridge in the floor of the chamber, Hawk was almost certain Mark had made that sound.

HAWK SLIPPED BACK TO Ellen and described all he'd seen.

"I don't think they're friendly, but I'm not sure they're hostile either. So, I think the way to play it is for me to just walk right in—like I own the place—take Mark and leave. You should stay out of sight, just in case."

"That's your plan?" she asked incredulously.

"Well, yeah. Of course, I'm always open to any better ideas." His peevishly wry smirk was wasted in the dim tunnel.

"Oh, really?" Ellen scoffed. "Then give me a minute. Let me try something."

With that, she settled herself into a calm state and stretched out her perceptions. It seemed to take hardly any effort at all. She was instantly aware of the energy sources around her. Hawk was an easily identified and comforting presence; Mark was nearby, too, his signature strong but quiescent. As for the others, she shuddered at their taint; they were of dark and corrupted energy, and barely identifiable as living things—*or were they?*

Another energy signature was very dark indeed, powerful yet somehow diminished, as if but a shadow of the intensity it once projected. Nonetheless, that entity intimidated the others . . . *and perhaps controlled them?*

Leaning into Hawk's ear, she whispered, "The hooded one is the real threat. I sense that the others are dangerous; but, I think he somehow controls or directs them."

"Okay, but I don't see how that should change my plan."

"I'm not done," she spat. "Be patient for a second!"

She focused again on the darkest energy signature and gently probed. She wasn't sure what she was looking for, something—anything that would give them an edge. As she concentrated she became aware that the figure was speaking to his minions. She didn't exactly *hear* his voice, as much as she *sensed* what he intended to convey to the others. It was more like eavesdropping on the energy he used to communicate his message.

. . . dare to defy me! You know well enough he lives! Therefore he is mine whilst his heart still beats! You will have the drained corpse soon enough. I will now prepare to feed. You will back off! I, Damien, command you!

She heard him in her mind as clearly as if he'd spoken directly to her aloud; but her ears had only caught a strained mumble. She turned to Hawk and gripped his arm in her whispered urgency.

"Listen! His name is *Damien!* I don't know if that's his true name or not; it may not matter. He's planning to *feed;* and I think he means *on Mark!* Then he's promised his corpse to the others! We have to *do* something!"

"I will!" Hawk insisted. "But, I need to get closer. I need to *see* Mark before I take any action. Look, I can work my way around to that large boulder. There's enough cover—well, to a point."

He chanced another peek around the corner, and then looked about the odd debris littering the floor of the tunnel. Picking up a random piece, he couldn't quite suppress a shudder, mumbling, "What the hell—a vertebra? Jeez, probably human—scored with *tooth marks? Oh man! Damn!* It'll have to do."

She had heard him, and almost balked in revulsion when he pressed it into her hand.

"Ellen, there's a pool of water on the far side of the cave. When I get behind that last big rock, I want you to lob this old bone into the pool. I'll need a diversion, and I hope the splash will do it. I have to get across that open space to those far boulders, and then I can get to Mark. Okay?"

"Okay," she acknowledged, trying to ignore the vertebra in her hand. "Then what?"

"Then, we're getting out of here," he said firmly. "I saw other tunnels—"

She suddenly shushed him with a finger to his lips and tugged her own ear—*listen!*

A groan, a cough, and the scrape of a boot on rock riveted their attention.

"What the—? Where am I? Uh, who the hell are you?"

There was no doubt that the voice was Mark's; and, he was irritated.

They stole a glance and saw Mark get to his feet and brush himself off. He appeared unhurt, just disheveled.

Hawk took advantage of this unexpected development. He nodded at Ellen in the dimness, silently mouthed *stay here*, and slipped soundlessly into the deeper shadows of the cavern.

MARK, NOW THE CENTER of attention, gaped at the ghastly appearance of the six gaunt figures in tattered rags that quietly encircled him. He shook off his initial shock and assessed his surroundings. His captors kept several paces distance, but periodically glanced up at a lone figure standing above them on a raised rock dais. Mark figured that this robed and hooded enigma was in charge, so he directed his questions to him.

"Can you understand me? What is this place? How did I get here? And damn it, who are you?"

Silence was his only answer.

Mark saw at least three tunnel entrances along one wall. The flame of a nearby candle flickered and tugged in the direction of the center opening. *Ah, fresh air, and the way out!*

Straightening his dusty clothes and mustering as much dignity as was possible under the circumstances, he announced, "Well, if we can't communicate, so be it. I'll be leaving now."

Before he could take a step, a parched voice rasped out from the depths of the shadowed hood. "Hold! Your speech is unfamiliar. Your *name?* What are you called?"

The tall hooded figure stepped down from the rock and stopped within arm's reach. Towering over Mark, he leaned forward, a gesture that Mark understood was intended to intimidate.

The inquisitor's imperious tone grated on Mark's nerves, but deep within the shadowed hood glowed twin motes of pale red, like the focused stare of a predator. A moment of innate wisdom tempered Mark's urge to retort and suggested that caution was well advised. He decided *not* to divulge his name.

"You may call me . . . um, *Counselor.* And *you* are?"

"I am the *Lord* of this place! You shall address me as *Master!*"

"Whatever, *Master,*" Mark begrudgingly acknowledged, unsure of the proper protocol. "I must go; I have something to do. So, if you'd please direct me to the exit, I'll be on my way."

"I think not, Counselor." The figure scoffed, flipping back his hood to reveal a pale face, angular and drawn; the patrician nose and prominent cheekbones overpowered the thin bloodless lips. But the eyes—the eyes smoldered with their own bloody light. He gestured with the flick of a wrist; Mark was seized and forced to his knees.

The hands that held him may have appeared to belong to emaciated and stooped old men, but their strength was surprising. Mark may have easily outweighed and outmuscled any one of them, but six controlled him without difficulty; he couldn't budge.

"As lord of this *domain,*" the Master sneered, "you are mine to do with as I please. And it *pleases* me to drink *your blood.*"

He smiled, revealing the elongated canines of the vampire, and suddenly grasped Mark's wrist, nearly pulling his arm from its socket. Holding Mark's arm fully extended, the Master sniffed at the inside of the wrist.

Mark shuddered in revulsion as the fiend licked the thin skin over the visible veins near the surface.

"Ah, but not too much, or too soon," the Master oozed. "I want you to last a few nights."

MOVEMENT CAUGHT ELLEN'S eye.

Hawk, hidden from the view of the others, pointed and mimed a throwing motion.

Ellen stepped to the mouth of the tunnel. She stood in full view, and could have been easily seen, but all of the focus was on the Master's victim. Her lob was perfect, and the resounding *ker-sploosh* instantly drew the desired attention.

THE MASTER LOOKED UP in surprised annoyance and then gestured to his minions. Four of them ran toward the black pool, while two remained to hold Mark prisoner.

The Master had not relinquished Mark's arm; instead he bit viciously into the wrist and sucked mightily. Pain and shock clashed as Mark's body went rigid and convulsed; mercifully, he lost consciousness. The Master's red eyes rolled up in oblivious rapture as the warm blood filled his foul mouth.

HAWK SPRANG FROM A shadowed cleft in the wall above the cave floor. He crashed into the two ghastly *things* restraining Mark, and they all tumbled to the floor. A few of the candles were knocked over and snuffed out, diminishing the light.

On his feet in an instant, Hawk scanned for movement while shifting into a tense crouch. He sensed the rush coming from behind on his left; he feinted forward and spun to his right. As he completed a full turn he drew and snapped open his collapsible baton, bringing it down sharply on the spine of his attacker. He dove and rolled to his left as the second assailant missed a two-handed grab for his throat and tripped over his fallen comrade.

Before the would-be throttler could scramble back up, Hawk stepped over him and delivered a crushing baton blow to the back of his neck.

Hawk quickly looked around, but neither Mark nor the vampire was anywhere to be seen in the gloom. A scraping sound from above drew his attention. Looking up, he saw a vague shape on the wall. Mark's boots dangled from the amorphous shadow.

Instinct caused Hawk to suddenly duck to his left, and a furious shape sailed past him. But another body struck him solidly from his right and sent him sprawling. He got to one knee and had to pitch to one side and roll as a rock came crashing through the space his head had just occupied.

Another candle had been knocked over and extinguished. A mere pair of guttering flames struggled to illuminate the cavern. Hawk could barely see; anything in shadow may as well have been invisible. Squinting into the darkness, he fumbled unsuccessfully with his free hand through his vest pockets for his flashlight, his baton held at the ready.

He never saw them coming.

They hit him from behind and both sides simultaneously, slamming him face down to the cavern floor and knocking the wind out of him. He lost his grip on the baton; it skittered across stony debris and disappeared into the darkness. Both of his arms were jerked fully extended from his sides and pinned by squirming weights. The small of his back and his shoulders were pressed down by bony knees and scabrous hands; horny nails dug into his knotted muscles. His vision was blurred and his chest heaved as he fought to suck in air. He was unable to free himself.

"So, another fly dares my web," creaked a dry voice from somewhere in the dark. "Bring him to his knees that I may examine my catch."

Hawk was wrenched cruelly to the supplicant position with his arms twisted behind his back. The face of the vampire became discernible in the gloom mere inches from his own.

The Master studied Hawk for a moment; he suddenly hissed and stepped back.

"You are marked!" His arm shot out, finger stabbing in accusation. "Her taint is upon you! Your *name?* Why are you here? Answer me!"

Hawk's mind raced. *What the hell is he talking about? I gotta stall for time—Ellen has to get away! What'd she say his name was? Damien?* He had no choice but to play the hand he'd been dealt, and continue stalling for as long as possible. He spat dust and tried to glare at the ominous figure before him.

"You do not need to know—*Damien!*"

The use of his *true name* clearly stunned the vampire; he literally backed up another pace. He stood in strained silence for a long moment; but his expression increasingly darkened as his anger rose.

"It matters not, you human fool!" Damien shrieked. "I will glean your intentions as I peel back the layers of your weak mind! All shall be revealed! You shall not leave, nor see another vaunted sunrise! Your mistress be damned! She cannot protect you here!"

As Hawk's vision cleared and focused, he could see Mark slumped against a stalagmite just beyond a guttering candle. He held his wounded wrist to his chest, but his other arm hung limply at his side.

Damien paced between them, finally stopping near Mark. In a sudden move, the vampire snatched Mark up and slammed him down on a chest-high slab of stone, which looked suspiciously like some type of Neolithic altar. Stunned, Mark lay supine, trying to catch his breath. Damien turned his back to him, and leaned casually against the altar stone. He stared at Hawk, and then seemed to come to a decision.

"I sense that you intend a rescue of this," Damien gestured over his shoulder to indicate Mark, "*meat.* But I know that is not the only reason she would send you. You must be shielded—a spell perhaps? Let us see if such a spell holds while my servants *attend* to you. Let us just say that you won't be needing hands, feet, arms or legs—"

"Release me immediately," demanded Hawk, "or suffer the consequences, Damien!"

"Again you dare to name me! And now threaten me? Your fate is assured! You are destined for the ghouls! I will see to it that it is slow, very slow!"

The fiends holding Hawk began an excited gibbering, hopping from foot to foot; but their grips did not weaken.

Damien reached behind him and jerked Mark's bloody arm over his shoulder. Facing Hawk, he contemplated Mark's limp hand and damaged wrist. He licked at the wound to stimulate the bleeding.

Hawk's stomach lurched and his revulsion rose; but he was held fast, forced to watch.

Damien smiled in hideous glee. "In fact, I will permit my hungry servants to begin with your appendages, your fingers I think. Oh, they are quite ravenous. I had promised them this one, your *Counselor,* once I drained him, but now we shall all sup together."

He brutally bit once again into Mark's wrist, satisfied to see Hawk wince.

At a gesture from Damien, two of the ghouls pulled Hawk's arms out, fully extended. They pried at his fists, trying to get at his fingers. The other two started to crowd them and shoved at one another.

In the off-balanced confusion, Hawk managed to get to his feet. He suddenly threw his weight backward, simultaneously stiffening his extended arms and slamming his fists together. The skulls of the two ghouls holding his wrists crashed together with a resounding *crack!* They dropped like sacks of desiccated bones.

The other two abominations lunged and grappled with him. They rolled across the rocky floor and Hawk managed to get one attacker in a headlock with his right arm and kick the other in the gut, sending him rolling away.

Damn! These ghouls are quite strong for their wiry size, but thankfully they're not trained fighters. I'm faster and more skilled, but they've got strength and numbers! I've got to fight smart!

Hawk twisted to the left, came up on one knee, and sank his left elbow into the face of the one trying to choke him from behind.

The fiend recovered quickly, despite his smashed nose, and wildly swung a rock, barely missing Hawk's right shoulder. Hawk released the headlock and *trip-shoved* the semiconscious ghoul into the rock-wielder; both went down.

The trouble was the ghouls wouldn't *stay* down. In the next moment both of them leapt up and attacked Hawk again.

MARK'S WRIST THROBBED; but surprisingly, he wasn't in any pain. He felt numb. A more rational part of his mind recognized symptoms of shock. As he caught his breath, he became more aware of his surroundings.

He realized Hawk was fighting for his life on the floor before him.

Trying to focus, Mark realized this *thing* called the Master was watching the struggle—*while chewing and sucking on my left wrist! Oh my God!*

That moment of panic was quickly replaced by flaring anger. Mark willed himself to fight back!

He tried to sit up, but his right shoulder flared with pain—the arm wouldn't work. He tried to roll away and pull his wounded wrist away from his assailant, all to no avail. He could not free himself.

In a moment of instinctive primal rage, Mark did the only thing left to him—he bit back. He clamped his teeth on the spine of his attacker and fiercely chewed.

The vampire choked in shock and frantically grabbed and fumbled at the back of his head.

Mark would not be torn loose! Jaws grinding, he relentlessly worried the back of Damien's neck like a terrier with a rat.

"NO!" ECHOED FROM THE walls as a searing white light exploded around the cavern; harsh reflections careened everywhere, sending shadows to oblivion.

The ghouls fell away from Hawk, their leprous skins steaming as they stumbled about in panic, beating at small flames erupting from their arms and legs. One by one, their bodies burst into flames and melted into noxious puddles of smoking ooze.

MARK, EYES SQUEEZED tightly shut, was oblivious to it all. The entire focus of his dazed universe consisted of his task of chewing through the spine of the monster that would kill him. He was even unaware that Damien had stopped struggling, or that his own wounded wrist had been released. Not until the bone between his teeth began to disintegrate and fill his mouth with coarse dust did he realize that something had happened. He coughed and spat.

Harsh light assaulted his squinting eyes and he slammed them shut once more. Exhausted, he lay back, and slipped into unconsciousness.

SOMETIME LATER MARK became aware of voices, solicitous and concerned. As he strove to rise above his murky confusion to full consciousness, his aches and pains breached the surface of reality as well. Hawk was propping him up in a seated position while Ellen tried to fit an improvised sling around his right arm. He moaned as his injured shoulder flinched in a sudden spasm and his clenched muscles shrieked in immediate complaint.

"Ah, I see you're back with us," Hawk commented dryly as he stuffed his recovered expandable baton into its compartment in his vest.

"How do you feel? Can you understand me? Look at me!" demanded Ellen tensely.

"Ooh, uh, I-I'm okay . . . just sore as hell." Mark winced, his voice hoarse. "What happened?"

"Well, the short version is that Ellen saved our butts," Hawk boasted with a grin. "We can get into the details later. Can you stand? We gotta get out of here."

Mark could see the entire cavern now awash in comparatively bright light, thanks to the spotlight illuminating the entire ceiling. The chamber seemed smaller now; they appeared to be alone. With Hawk's help, he stood, favoring his right arm suspended in the sling. He looked to Ellen and Hawk; his puzzled expression bespoke the question before he could find his voice.

"You were *out* for about ten minutes," Hawk explained. "Which was just as well, because we had to yank your dislocated shoulder back into place. Ellen bandaged your wrist. She has a small first-aid kit in her backpack. You've lost some blood, but we have no way of knowing how much."

"*Lost?* You mean *taken*, don't you? I know what he did to me, that *rat-bastard!"*

Hawk and Ellen shared a look, but kept silent. Ellen took a plastic bottle of water from her pack, opened it and handed it to her cousin. "Here, drink this. You need fluids; drink it now."

Mark swished some water around in his mouth and spat. "Sorry, I had this terrible aftertaste."

"I'll bet," Ellen murmured.

Mark savored a long draught. "Look, I'm okay. You don't have to worry. I'm just *pissed!* I feel like I've just donated at a blood bank and didn't get the orange juice and cookies."

He offered the water bottle to them, but both grimaced.

"Uh, no thanks," declined Ellen. "That's all yours. Drink up."

Hawk smirked and nudged Ellen. "I think he's gonna be all right. I bet he's thinking about suing the vampire—or his estate."

"Oh, Hawk, don't encourage him."

Hawk chuckled and looked around. "Okay, seriously, we have to get moving. Mark, you're going to have to keep up. If you can't, you have to tell us. Now we have to figure a way out of here."

"We can't go back the way we came," explained Ellen in a rush, "because we were followed by something big. We think it caved in that tunnel we—"

"I think I know the way out," Mark interrupted, as he pointed with the water bottle. "The center tunnel, there, fresh air. I saw the candle flame flickering in the air."

"Yeah? Well, that works for me," announced Hawk as he hefted the spotlight and battery pack. "We're going to have to use our smaller flashlights now. The battery pack charge is going down and we'll need to save what's left in case we *really* need it. It certainly has come in handy so far." He winked blatantly at Ellen just before turning off the spotlight and activating his small red-lens flashlight.

It took a few moments for their eyes to adjust to the reduced light levels. Then Hawk led them into the center tunnel and said, "Good call, Mark; it does go up."

HAWK STRAINED HIS EYES and ears for any sign of danger. But it was his nose, and the slightest waft of fresh air, that reassured him that they were moving in the right direction. In their trek they passed a number of side openings that offered alternative routes, a host of other tunnels that wormed in untold twists and turns; it was a virtual warren. But no other path offered the sweet scent of freedom. They pressed doggedly on.

Aching and a bit light-headed, Mark managed to maintain the pace. The frequent bends and corners were unnerving and tiring, but he pushed himself onward and upward.

Ellen followed, occasionally sending the reddened beam of her flashlight back down the length of the tunnel, at least to the last corner; but there appeared to be no pursuit. The floor was worn smooth; this passage was obviously frequently traveled. However, they neither saw nor heard another soul.

Suddenly Hawk came to a halt and clicked off his flashlight. Mark froze and Ellen doused her light. They could see a dim glow in the distance—the exit?

"I'll check it out," Hawk whispered.

Mark and Ellen watched as his shadowed bulk obliterated the muddled glow in his stalk up the passage.

A FEW AGONIZINGLY SLOW, creeping minutes elapsed before Hawk returned.

"Well, I've got good news and bad news. The good news is that the tunnel exit comes out among some large rocks in what looks like an old cemetery. There's some sort of a ruin nearby; I think maybe a church or temple."

"Okay, what's the bad news?" asked Ellen.

"Uh, do you remember that *smell,* when we thought we were being followed?"

"Oh no, you mean that *thing* is there, too?" Her shoulders slumped and she grasped his arm.

"Well, at least the smell is," he admitted. "I think it might be foolish not to anticipate that it might be waiting for us."

"Now what?" Mark asked. "Is there another way out of here?"

"I doubt it." Hawk sighed. "We haven't passed another tunnel for some time. I think this is our only way out."

"Okay, but," Mark cautioned, "you didn't *see* anything; you just smelled something, right?"

"Right, but . . . Oh, I get it. Hey, Ellen?" Hawk took her hand. "Can you do that thing you do? You know, sense what's out there, and maybe where?"

"I can try; give me a minute."

Ellen took a deep breath and cast her perceptive net. She ignored the obvious signatures of Mark and Hawk and concentrated on widening her receptive array. It helped to visualize her efforts as the expanding ripples in a placid pond, steadily questing in all directions. She sensed other life energies with an ease that she realized was truly becoming second nature to her. She was growing quite comfortable with her enhanced ability.

Ellen reached out and gently probed those other energy signatures, and found something familiar, unpleasantly familiar.

She touched both Mark and Hawk, immediately gaining their attention. "It *is* the same *thing* we were followed by. It's in the ruined building, somewhere below ground level, a basement, cellar, or something. I don't think it's aware of us—yet."

"Maybe we can just wait a bit and it'll leave the area?" Mark looked from Ellen to Hawk hopefully.

"No, there's more," she warned. "There's something, *several somethings* actually, coming up behind us, from the other tunnels we passed on the way up here. We only have a few minutes; they're moving quickly."

"Can you sense who or *what* they are?" asked Hawk.

"Not exactly. They're sort of like those *ghoul* things you fought; but they're like that vampire in some way. I'm sorry, I can't be more specific."

"I'd much rather avoid another fight right now," insisted Hawk. "Let's see if we can sneak out of here undetected, okay? Ellen, you're sure the *stinker* hasn't moved, or become aware of us?"

She paused. "There's no movement, no apparent awareness of us."

"Okay," hissed Hawk. "I'll lead. Complete silence. Communicate by touch. Let's go."

They slipped up the final length of tunnel and into the moonlit night. Several boulders near the tunnel's mouth offered a degree of concealment. They squatted in the shadows and peered across a small clearing punctuated by waist-high cairns, oblong mounds, and obscure monuments. It was indeed an old abandoned cemetery, long out of use judging by an overgrowth of rampant ivy and general condition of disrepair.

Opposite their vantage point, the roofless walls and distended piles of broken stone marked the last vestige of the presumed house of worship, now a despairing shell fit only perhaps for a long departed, spectral congregation. The remnants of a broken bell tower thrust up from the ruin; a sole squat gargoyle remained intact, clinging to a shattered cornice, as if resigned to its lonely vigil.

They watched the ruin carefully; there was no sign of life. All they could hear were the sounds of crickets and other night insects. To the right of the old church was the hint of a wagon road, overgrown to the point of resembling a mere path in the moonlight.

Hawk stealthily led the way around the cemetery, keeping near the tree line, reluctant to cross the relatively open expanse of the burial ground. There was little concealment, certainly not enough for the three of them together. The silvered light of the moon rendered everything in stark contrast.

The soft buzz of insects and the hopeful chirping of crickets suddenly stopped. The silence was unnerving, fraught with a sense of menace.

Hawk pulled Mark and Ellen into the shadow of the trees. Pointing to a stout oak, he mimed climbing. Mark and Ellen immediately ascended. With the use of only one arm, Mark had some difficulty; but, he managed with Hawk and Ellen's assistance. Perched upon broad limbs well above the ground, they parted the thick foliage and watched the drama unfold below.

HALF A DOZEN LOW SHADOWS streamed from the mouth of the tunnel like huge cockroaches and clambered over and around the boulders where the three companions had recently lingered. One ventured out among the graves in an easy lope and stood tall as if sniffing the air.

Ellen was shocked to realize it resembled a man's form. Its loping trot mimicked that of a four-legged animal; but its upright stance was humanoid.

The other creatures stopped in their tracks and rose to sniff as well. For an instant, they stood warily immobile, captured images in grey-scale, a moment suspended in time.

Ellen caught a sour whiff. The *stinker*, as they had been thinking of their bestial follower, was nearby.

In an explosion of gleeful fury, its roaring hulk was suddenly among the startled shapes in the graveyard. A huge fist smashed down upon one of the creatures, leaving only a bloody dent in the ground. A club the size of a tree trunk swished through the air, and a pair of the ghoulish creatures were rendered into bloody pulp. Two more simply panicked, running into one another with a resounding *thwock,* and lay unmoving.

Ellen gasped as another one ran for the tree line, right in the direction of *their* tree.

A tremendous *swish-THUD* abruptly ended that attempted escape. The business end of the huge club, darkly stained and dripping, slowly rose from the impact crater, and came to rest atop a massive shoulder.

Ellen tried to see more of the creature through the foliage, but the beast turned away, its attention drawn to the two dazed figures in the churchyard. One was moving, trying to crawl away.

With a low-pitched rumble, something between a growl and chuckle, the beast reached out with an oversized three-fingered hand and snatched up the flinching form.

Ellen saw the beast raise its clenched fist to its mouth and heard the captive shriek. The sound was suddenly cut off, followed by a sickening *ker-snick—pa-tooo.*

Something flew over the beast's shoulder, bounced and rolled, coming to a stop at the base of their tree. A pair of vacant red eyes stared upwards, then dimmed and glassed over in a pool of argent light.

Ellen gasped and quickly clamped a hand over her mouth; her mind was screaming.

A head! It bit off a head!

THE MASSIVE BEAST STOPPED chewing, and went still. It had heard something. Empty-handed it rose, silently turned about, and sniffed, testing the wind, listening and scenting.

Hawk had moved to another limb to get a better view; but he froze as the beast's gaze raked the tree line.

The creature stood much like a man, albeit about twelve feet tall, on bandy but powerful legs. Its huge arms were disproportionately long and its hands overly large; it could touch the earth while standing fully erect. Huge shoulders supported a small head that boasted a thickly ridged brow, broad nose, and a very pronounced lower jaw. There was no neck to speak of. As the monster slowly turned about in the pale moonlight, Hawk saw that a pair of tusks thrust up from that pugnacious lower jaw. It was male and wore a girdle of animal hides cinched with a bright silvered chain for a belt. Both wrists sported stout bracelets of tarnished silver with short dangling lengths of chain.

Manacles or restraints of some type? Had this thing been confined or imprisoned? And if so, by whom?

With a start Hawk realized that he no longer found the smell so offensive. It wasn't that he'd merely gotten used to it; *the wind had changed!* Sure enough, the beast had stopped turning about, and was now facing in their direction, nostrils flaring.

Hawk edged closer to the trunk of the old oak as the brute lumbered towards the forest, incessantly scenting the air and scanning the tree line. Hawk unconsciously let his right hand drift to the reassuring grip of his pistol, but he pragmatically dismissed its use as an option. A handgun simply would not stop anything this big. Remaining hidden was their best strategy.

The creature came to stand before the trees as the wind changed again, carrying their scents away from the searcher.

Hawk almost breathed a sigh of relief—*almost.*

Suddenly, the beast reached out and parted the lower tree boughs and looked up—right into Ellen's moonlit face.

She froze as the hulking thing smiled vacuously and began that low growling chuckle.

Hawk's mind reeled; *was she out of the monster's reach?* Crouched on a lower limb, he knew *he* wasn't. It didn't matter; he would not permit anything to harm Ellen. From his concealment he shouted, hoping to distract the monstrous thing away from her.

"Hey! Big guy! Back off!"

The beast jerked his head around. He couldn't see the speaker, but the sound came from his left. He reached up with a long arm, and another voice sounded off to his right.

"Hey! Ugly one! I'm talking to you!"

Mark had evidently decided to join in the distraction. Fortunately, he was out of the monster's reach as well.

The long arm shot into the foliage to the right, and found nothing.

"Don't waste your time, you oaf! Just go away!" Hawk called out and then deftly moved to a higher limb.

Its other arm reached into the foliage on its left, and found only the limb Hawk had just vacated. In a fit of frustration, it ripped the limb from the trunk sending a shudder through the entire tree. The brute couldn't find the source of the annoying voices; but it had seen Ellen.

"Ellen!" warned Mark. "It *intends* to leap up and grab you!"

"Damn," hissed Hawk. "We'll see about *that!*"

As Mark had predicted, the beast crouched and started swinging its massive arms, building momentum, and then furiously pitched itself upward.

It appeared that Ellen was doomed; but Hawk's arm extended from the foliage and a stream of fluid, like liquid silver, splashed right into the face of the creature.

For an instant, the beast seemed to hang startled in midair. It dropped to the ground and threw itself back, away from the tree, holding its tortured face in its hands. It howled and raged as it rubbed at its eyes and face, rolling haphazardly among the broken monuments and sunken graves.

"Down! Quickly!" urged Hawk. "We need to get away from here!"

Once on the ground, Hawk led them around the edge of the cemetery, giving the suffering beast a wide berth.

"What did you do? Was that stuff what I think it was?" rasped Mark.

Hawk held up a small aerosol can. "O.C. spray, oleo capsaicin—pepper spray! That shot took almost the whole can. Keep moving! We need to get to that old road and get out of here!"

"I think it heard us! It's coming!" Ellen whispered urgently.

The beast had recovered sufficiently to retrieve its huge club, but it continued to rub its eyes and snort great globules of mucus from its inflamed nose. It might be unable to see, and its sense of smell out of commission; but as Ellen had guessed, it could certainly hear them.

Bellowing in frustrated rage, it lumbered in their direction, swinging its club in murderous arcs.

As it closed the gap, they instinctively split up.

Confused, the creature blindly smote the ground wherever it thought it heard movement.

Ellen tripped and sprawled on the ground. Her fall had been heard; she dared not move.

When Mark looked back, he saw Ellen's plight and stopped in his tracks. "Hawk! Ellen's down!"

"Distract it!" Hawk cried as he spun about and ran toward her.

Mark called out and waved his good arm over his head, but to no avail.

Hawk tried screaming at the beast as he charged, but he too was ignored.

DEEP IN THE SMALL TORTURED mind of the brute, it decided it would not be fooled again by mere voices. It had a dim memory of elves playing similar tricks on it long ago—it *hated* elves. It had heard exactly where its quarry had fallen, and grunted in satisfaction. It would vent its pent-up fury upon these tricky elves.

ELLEN LOOKED UP TO see a massive shadow blocking the moon. She might not get far, but she would try. Run or fight—surrender was not an option, not now, not ever. As she gained her feet, she saw the shadow raise the club for a two-fisted strike.

The night exploded in white light as Ellen sprinted away, head down in anticipation of the crushing blow—that never came.

An arm reached out to her and clasped her about the waist to slow her headlong rush. Mark's familiar voice, close to her ear, calm and steady, caught and held her attention.

"Ellen! It's okay! Stop and look! Oh man, just look!"

The awe in his voice bordered on shock.

She looked over her shoulder and saw Hawk, the spotlight in hand, shining it upon the huge being. The creature's stiffened arms were held above its head, the huge hands gripping the massive club. No one moved. Ellen expected the cruel club to come crashing down on Hawk; her heart nearly stopped at the thought.

But nothing happened; Hawk and the beast faced one another in a frozen tableau.

Hawk slowly began to walk around the monstrosity, bathing it in the harsh light of the spotlight.

Sensing movement, Ellen cried out, "Hawk! Watch out!"

Hawk scrambled as the beast teetered.

The beast simply began to fall backwards in slow motion, barely moving, then accelerating until it slammed to the ground, its full length crushing an untold number of cairns and monuments.

Ellen and Mark, expressions aghast, ran to Hawk's side.

"Are you okay?" Ellen asked, gripping Hawk's arm.

"Yeah, I'm fine," he assured her.

Mark pointed at the downed beast. "What the hell is this thing?"

Hawk went forward and dared to touch it, then kicked it. He hopped away, mumbling something about being *stupid*, and turned to regard the supine monstrosity.

"Really?" Ellen scoffed. "Did you *have* to touch it?"

Hawk grinned. "No worries. I think I've got this figured out, or at least a working hypothesis." He rubbed the toe of his boot and explained. "I think this guy here is a *troll* of some kind; I mean that in the classical and traditional sense. And he's just been turned to *stone,* or *calcified,* by the application of this spotlight, which mimics daylight, or more specifically, that includes the *ultraviolet* aspects of daylight.

"Yelling at him as a distraction wasn't working, so I turned on the spotlight to get his attention. And he just stood there, all still, like he was surprised. As I widened the beam, by rotating the lens, he just seemed to stiffen. I think I caught him at the peak of his backswing; as he solidified he was off balance—that's why he fell over. Anyway, if I've remembered my fairy tales and folklore correctly, that's my theory. Yeah, he's a troll, gotta be."

Ellen stared at the supine figure. "You know, you may have something there. Back in the cave, that light sure did have an effect on the, uh, what were they—*ghouls?* And it just about disintegrated the vampire."

Mark nodded solemnly. "So, mimicking daylight, huh? That makes sense, at least according to the commonly accepted folklore, as I recall, too."

"More like according to the movies we saw as kids," Ellen reasoned. "Who knows? Maybe they had it right."

"Well, it appears to have worked," Mark observed.

Now Ellen ventured forth and touched the granite-like leg of the troll. "Will he stay like this, as stone I mean?"

Hawk shrugged and flexed his stubbed toes. "I don't know, but the way our luck's been running, I'd doubt it. Maybe if he stays like this until morning, when the real sun can get at him? Who knows?"

Ellen looked over her shoulder. "Those things that came out of the tunnel after us, shouldn't there be one left around here?"

Mark pointed. “It should be over there.”

Hawk washed the spotlight over the troll one more time, just in case, while Mark and Ellen used her red-lens flashlight to look for the last unidentified creature.

In a few minutes they located the partially eaten corpse; its head lay nearby. The body resembled a ghoul, but the dentition resembled that of the vampire. There was no mistaking the elongated canines.

“So, what is it?” Ellen asked.

“Hawk, try the spotlight,” Mark suggested.

Hawk brought it to bear and flicked the switch. The corpse aged, decayed, and was reduced to dust almost instantly under the glare of the spotlight. Only the charred canines remained.

“Perhaps it was a lower type of vampire?” Mark offered. “Hey, anybody want the teeth for souvenirs?”

Ellen scowled in distaste. “Really, Mark?”

“Just kidding . . . jeez.”

Hawk pointed. “There’s the old road.” He turned the spotlight off. “Let your eyes get adjusted to the moonlight; and let’s get outta here.”

Beneath the pale argent orb, they followed the old overgrown wagon road as it wound its way east.

They were tired, but in good spirits, ready to rescue Stacy, and, of course, return home.

FOR THE MOMENT, NOTHING stirred in the moon-washed cemetery. The fallen troll was no more than toppled statuary, an oversized stone monument lying amidst the rubble.

From his precarious perch high on the ruined bell tower, the crouching gargoyle slowly stood, stretched his limbs, and surveyed the scene below.

Satisfied that he had memorized the pertinent details, he flexed a broad set of leathery wings, tested the wind, and leapt into the night sky. He circled once to gain altitude, the subtle repetitive *whoosh* of his bat-like wings the only sound. He looked for, but could not see, the three companions on the thickly overgrown road below. It mattered little; there was likely only one destination to be found to the east, provided they managed to survive the night and escape the confines of the forest.

Those were grim odds indeed.

But, they had proven to be resourceful; that had been interesting.

He shrugged off such speculation; that was not his concern.

CH 22

THE WINDING ROAD NARROWED, becoming nearly impassable with thickening underbrush encroaching from either side.

Their progress was neither quick nor silent.

Hawk frequently consulted a small compass in his vest. Despite their convoluted track, he was satisfied with their general direction. Just when it appeared that they could proceed no farther, they broke through the entangled brush and found themselves back on the main road through the forest.

Hawk cautiously stalked a dozen paces in either direction to be sure they were in no immediate danger.

At his assured nod, Ellen and Mark shed their gear in relief and sat for a moment's rest.

Ellen shoved another water bottle at Mark. "Here, drink up; you need fluids."

Hawk accepted a water bottle from her as well, and squatted before them.

"Mark, I meant to ask you something earlier."

"Yeah, what?"

"When we were in the tree, trying to distract the troll from Ellen, you warned her that he 'intended' to leap up and grab her, remember?"

"Sure, I remember."

"Well, how did you know? I mean, were you deducing his next move from his body language or something? What tipped you off? Your warning gave me just enough time to ready my O.C. spray and get into position to give him a full blast in the face."

Mark stared into the darkness and sighed. "Truthfully, I don't know. It certainly wasn't body language; I could barely see him as it was. I just sort of *knew* what he planned, like it came to me as a *concept*. This is hard to explain; there was no logical reasoning involved. It was like I tapped into his *intentions*. I know that doesn't make any sense."

"Perhaps it does, in a strange way," Ellen mused thoughtfully. "When you were sort of out of it, that vampire, Damien, bragged that he could 'glean intentions' from Hawk's mind. He even demonstrated his skill by announcing Hawk's *intention* to rescue you. Now, when Damien died, you were in direct contact with him—trying to sever his spine with your teeth, as I recall. Okay, I admit that was disgusting enough—yuck! So, is it possible that you have somehow assimilated that same skill or power?"

"Come on, Ellen," Hawk teased. "It wouldn't have taken a mind reader to figure out what we intended."

"Perhaps not, but I don't think it was *mind reading* any more than what I seem to be able to do, sensing energy signatures, is miraculous. I think both are more like matters of passive perception. Maybe it's an innate ability in most people, but some are just better at it than others. And just maybe, under the right circumstances, this *power* or *ability* can be transferred or enhanced. After all, we have no real knowledge of how the laws of physics work in this universe. We're just learning as we go."

"Okay then, let's conduct a little experiment," said Hawk. "Mark, what are my immediate intentions at this moment?"

"Hmm, hold on, let me concentrate . . . Ah yes, it's coming through; I'm getting it now. You *intend* to tell us to get up off our butts and move out, right?"

Hawk's hands flew to his cheeks in mock shock. "Oh no! It's true! You've read my mind!"

"Wait," teased Mark, "there's more . . . Oh my, that's a bit personal. Don't worry, Ellen, it *appears* that his intentions regarding you are *honorable*!"

Snorting in slightly awkward laughter, Ellen playfully slapped her cousin's arm and chided, "Cut it out, Mark! Come on, let's get going."

Bright moonlight penetrated numerous gaps in the overhead canopy. The illumination was surprisingly sufficient on the forest road, prompting Hawk to make a suggestion.

"I can see pretty well in this light. If you can, too, it might be a good idea to try moving on without flashlights to save the batteries."

"That'd be good for our night vision, too, right?" Mark reasoned.

"It won't hurt. I'll carry the spotlight for a while. Come on, let's go."

THEY WERE MAKING MUCH better time on this main forest road. Hawk led with Ellen close behind. Mark brought up the rear, several paces behind Ellen. Consequently, he heard it first, the distant chaos of something crashing its way through the underbrush, well behind them.

Moments later, it sounded again, much closer this time—they all heard it. They picked up their pace, and were soon trotting.

Somewhere, just behind them, a frightening sound erupted from the forest, the ferocious rending of brush and small trees, accompanied by a series of enraged grunts and snorts.

The three companions broke into a headlong run!

Images of the rampaging troll played through their racing minds; but logic dictated that it was most likely some new threat. As if in proof, a large form crashed through the thick woods and tumbled onto the road a stone's throw behind them.

Mark stole a glance over his injured shoulder. But all he could discern was that it was large, ran on all fours, and had glowing beady red eyes carried low and forward.

He shouted in near panic, "Run! It's behind us!"

Despite their running at breakneck speed, the thunderous pursuit grew louder—pounding, snorting, and grunting in cadence like a runaway freight train. They ran as fast as they could, ducking low limbs and leaping over gnarled tree roots that had broken the surface of the road.

HAWK LOOKED DESPERATELY for any way off the road—a side path, a game trail, or a nearby climbable tree. But there was no such option, and no time. He could turn and fight; he had his pistol.

He looked for a place to make a defensive stand. If only Mark and Ellen could continue running, they might have a chance. He slowed as he ran past the bole of a large tree, as good a place as any for a fight, and waved them on.

Before he could stop and turn about, a twitching mass of vines dropped from the canopy of the tree, just missing Mark and Ellen as they sped beneath it. Hawk instinctively dodged to one side as another group of vines dropped right into the space he would have passed through in another instant.

Whoa—change in plan! Get outta here!

He sprinted after Mark and Ellen knowing the charging nemesis was almost upon him.

The thundering pursuit suddenly stopped!

A squeal of rage, frustration, and fear trumpeted into the night!

Chest heaving, Hawk stopped and turned to face their pursuer. He saw a squirming mass of shadow beneath the tree. He caught his breath and forced himself to calm. He drew his pistol and gripped the spotlight.

Hawk set the spotlight for a wide beam and switched it on. Before him, struggling mightily in a web of sticky writhing vines, was the biggest wild boar he had ever seen. It must have stood shoulder high to him, and weighed nearly a ton. Yet, it was totally ensnared, slowly being drawn upward by the awesome strength of the vines.

Mark and Ellen, panting and supporting each other, rejoined Hawk and stared in disbelief. They stood fascinated as a parade of large ants began to march along the tree's limbs in the direction of the porcine captive. The ants were clearly immune to the sticky substance coating the vines. The inevitable outcome became obvious.

"A symbiotic relationship, between the tree and the ants," remarked Ellen, taking deep breaths.

"What do you mean?" Mark gasped.

"Look up," said Hawk, holstering his pistol and aiming the light upward.

The various suspended skeletal remains were sufficient to answer Mark's question. He swallowed dryly and moved farther away from the tree.

Hawk panned the spotlight around. "We should leave this area; this might attract more predators."

"Hold on—what's this?" Mark toed something white in the dirt, and picked up a thin Y-shaped wire.

"Those are Stacy's earbuds to her MP3 player! She was here!" exclaimed Ellen. She instinctively looked up into the tree limbs, panic in her face.

Mark blanched. Suddenly reluctant, he looked upward. "No—no . . . "

"Easy, Mark—she's not up there." Ellen soothed.

"Hey, I think she's okay. Look at this!" Hawk squatted and played the light along the road's surface.

Holding their breath in hope, Mark and Ellen peered closely as Hawk pointed.

"Tracks, two people; this one is probably Stacy. See? These are her boot prints. I think these others are the prints of a man, probably the same guy you and she saw in the globe." He pointed. "And these belong to a cat."

"A cat? Gotta be *Smokey!*" Ellen declared. "Is he *with* her, or *following* her?"

"I can't really tell; no more than I can tell if she caught up with this man, or—"

"What do you mean?" Mark demanded. "Is she with this guy?"

"I don't know for sure," Hawk admitted, refocusing the light beam on the road. "But see for yourselves. Their tracks go east, away from here; and they don't overlap. They're pretty much side by side; so, it's a good possibility she's—"

"But she's *all right!*" Ellen interrupted, squeezing Mark's arm. "They went in that direction, Smokey, too."

"Yeah, okay. We should go now," Mark insisted, looking askance with a shudder, at the struggling mass of slowly ascending vines.

"Right," agreed Hawk. "We need to keep moving, quietly. We need to get out of this forest without any more incidents."

It was not to be.

IN A SHORT TIME, ALL three experienced the sensation that they were not alone. Ellen thought she'd felt a tug or two on her sleeves, almost as if snagged by passing brush or twigs, but there were none within reach.

Mark murmured, "I keep thinking I see, or just catch a glimpse of something, like from the corner of my eye, some ethereal wisp or shadow that disappears as soon as I look directly at it."

"Yeah? Me too," Hawk agreed. "I can't determine if it represents a threat." Hawk nudged Ellen. "Um, Ellen, I don't think we're alone. Could you, you know, do *your thing*, and maybe see what we're dealing with?"

"Sure." She opened her perceptions and immediately found a surprising number of energy signatures in their vicinity. They were similar to *life energy* signatures but somehow less intense, less cohesive . . . *spirits? souls? ghosts?*

As if in confirmation, many of the energy signatures glowed warmly.

A subtle and pervasive sensation came to her, one of compelled constraint. *What is this? A sense of entrapment or forced containment?*

Another warm glow confirmed her speculation.

Then she noticed, at the far periphery of these energy signatures, a few more that were somehow a little different. These were not emanating benign energy, but rather a darker, somewhat befouled presence tinged with traces of evil.

"Okay, Hawk, you're right; we aren't alone. There are a large number of, um, *spirits* around us. I think they're somehow trapped here. I get the sense that they died here and can't go on, like to whatever their respective faiths would prescribe. I think most of them are victims in some way."

Hawk leaned past Ellen and whispered, "Mark, can you pick up any intentions? Do they mean us any harm?"

Mark paused for a long moment, his eyes half closed. "I don't think so. I mean, I sense *something* all around us, but I think all they want is to leave this place. But there's something else, too—something that's not well intended toward anything. I don't know if that makes any sense."

"Actually, it does," Ellen remarked. "I sensed something else, as well; some energy signatures that are tainted and dark. I can't determine intentions. I think we need to be careful. I'm just guessing here, but I think these were *evil,* or at least *did evil* and were unrepentant when they died. Somehow they're trapped here, too."

Hawk walked in pensive thought for a few minutes. "You know, this reminds me of an old story told among my people; the circumstances seem similar."

"Can you tell us?" asked Ellen, a little hopefully.

"If I remember it all. It's kind of a sad love story; I wouldn't want to depress you, after all."

"A love story? Okay, Hawk, now you have *no* choice," Ellen declared. "You *have* to tell us!"

"All right, all right!" He chuckled. "Just bear with me; but, we have to keep moving."

"Deal," she declared. "You have our attention; so, tell!"

"A long time ago, a tribal chief had a beautiful young daughter who was secretly in love with the youngest son of the tribal shaman; and of course, that young man had a secret crush on her. Neither knew for certain that they shared a mutual affection; but they suspected as much from the stolen glances and playful smiles they exchanged. Now, both these teenagers were still too young, by one year, to be considering marriage. And as was the tradition, the families would arrange such a marriage.

"There was a place near the edge of their tribal lands that was forbidden, a forest rich in game and lush with fruits, nuts, and berries. It was an old tribal belief that those who wandered into that forest, for whatever reason, would never return. So, to hunt or gather food there was taboo—a taboo so old that no one even remembered how it began.

"Now, it was a popular tradition for a maiden, who desired marriage to a particular young man as a husband, to impress both the family of the young man and her own, by preparing a feast for both families, thereby proving her skills as a potential wife. If the young man wished to express his willingness for the marriage, and in turn impress both families with his worthiness and skill as a provider, he would hunt and provide the meat.

"The young maiden boldly decided to prepare a traditional meal for the families. She went to the young man and told him of her intention. His heart leapt, and he told her of his love. He declared that he would hunt a fine deer for the feast, the traditional gesture to please and honor the families."

Hawk cleared his throat and walked a few paces in silence.

"Keep talking," whispered Ellen. "*They* are listening—intently."

Hawk's eyebrows rose, but he continued. "Well, unbeknownst to the two lovers, the chief and the shaman, who were great friends, were well aware of their children's intentions, and they could not have been happier. They had all along planned to arrange such a marriage; and, that the children would observe tribal traditions swelled their hearts with pride. But, they had to appear aloof and impartial as the old traditions were observed.

"The young man went hunting on his tribe's traditional hunting lands. True to his word, he brought back a magnificent deer for the feast.

"The young maiden was very impressed. However, in her heart, she began to worry that she might not find any fruits, nuts, berries, or wild vegetables worthy of such fine venison. So, she decided to seek only the finest of such foods. That meant she would venture into the forbidden forest.

"Like many young people, she thought some rules were made to be broken.

"So, on the day before the feast, the maiden took her best basket, and set out to find the finest food. When she was out of sight of her village, she made her way to the edge of her tribal lands and slipped unnoticed into the forbidden forest.

"She did not return to her village at sunset . . . not that day, or the next, or the next. The young man was grief-stricken and prayed to his gods for help.

"His heartbroken pleas were heard by the Moon Goddess, who took pity upon him, and answered his prayers in a dream-vision. She told him that his love had broken the taboo by entering the forbidden forest, that she no longer walked among the living, and that her soul was trapped by a curse—to wander endlessly within that forest.

"This news ripped him apart. He begged and pleaded, but of course it was too late. Finally, he asked if there was any way his love's spirit could be freed from this curse to continue on its path of destiny.

"The Moon Goddess was touched by the selflessness of his request, so she asked her brother, the Sun God, for his help.

"The Sun God could deny his sister nothing. So, he took a tiny piece of himself, a mere mote, and put it in a silver box. He gave the silver box to his sister, the Moon Goddess.

"She in turn gave the box to the grieving young man, and then gave him very careful instructions. First of all, only he could perform this task because he was of the bloodline of tribal shamans. Secondly, it had to be done in the dark of night. Lastly, he could tell no one of what he did, nor speak of the involvement of the Moon Goddess and her brother, the Sun God. When he agreed, she told him what else he must do.

"Upon awakening the next morning, he found the silver box by his bedroll. The following night, deep in its darkest hours, the young man went to the edge of the tribal lands and faced the forbidden forest. He took the silver box from his deerskin shirt and placed it just inside the edge of the dark woods.

"He took a deep breath and cried aloud, 'In the name of all that is Light and Good, I crack the curse of this place!' He flipped open the lid of the silver box; a bright light, that tiny piece of the Sun God himself, shot up into the night on a column of light. A crack appeared in the wall of the curse. The spirit of the maiden and all the innocent souls who had been so cruelly trapped could now slip out; the curse could no longer hold the innocent.

"But the young man sensed that there were others, some who were not so innocent, who strove to pass through the crack but could not fit. He sensed their disappointment, their frustration, and in some cases—their anger.

"The spirit of the maiden hovered before him and spoke into his mind. She told him that she was very grateful for her freedom, and she would love him always. And as for those still trapped, they would remain so until they had shed all traces of evil, for only then would they fit through the crack and go on to their destinies."

Hawk grew quiet, his story concluded.

They walked on for several minutes in peaceful silence.

Ellen smiled and sighed. "That was beautiful. Thanks for sharing the story."

"Yeah, thanks," Mark echoed. "That was kind of a purgatory allegory, in the cultural myth sense. Have you ever told Armand, uh, Dr. Dupree, that story?"

"I haven't," said Hawk, "but, I'm sure he's heard it from my grandfather, who is a shaman among my people."

"Wow, cool! Your grandfather is a *shaman*? That's pretty interesting! Is it a traditional thing? I mean, did he have to train for it, like was it an elective decision, or is there some hereditary aspect?"

"Well, to be honest, Mark, it's supposedly a hereditary thing; but there was considerable training involved, a lot of cultural awareness, that sort of thing."

"Yeah, I get it. So, that means that you—"

"Not to change the subject," interrupted Ellen, "but is it just me, or are y'all finding it harder to walk, almost like we're going uphill, even though this is level ground?"

"Yeah, now that you mention it," observed Mark. "I thought I was just getting tired. Hey! Isn't that the end of the trees up there?"

"Uh, guys . . ? "

"You're right, Mark!" exclaimed Ellen. "I can see in this moonlight that the countryside opens up just beyond."

"Um, hey guys . . ? "

"I'll be glad to get out of these woods, if you know what I mean. Man, I'm getting really stiff," groused Mark, "from all this walking, I guess."

"Yeah," said Ellen, feeling extremely sluggish herself, "I know what you mean."

"HEY, YOU GUYS!"

Mark and Ellen spun to face a stationary Hawk, at least ten feet behind them.

"I can't move!" He grunted. "I mean my legs; they won't move. It's like I'm stuck in deep mud or something. Uh, Ellen, is something going on? You know, around us?"

Ellen paused, concentrated, and paled. "Oh boy," she groaned. "There are a lot more of those energy signatures—spirits, ghosts, whatever—around us now than ever before. I think they were drawn to us, or more importantly, to your story. The circumstances are just too similar."

"They don't intend to let us leave," added Mark. "They want you to '*crack the curse'* that binds them here."

"Yes," agreed Ellen. "That's it exactly! *Crack the curse* that traps the innocents."

Hawk looked toward Ellen and Mark in sheer disbelief. "Are you joking? *Mocking* me?" He fought to move his legs, in vain. "If I'm the butt of some joke; I don't think it's funny."

Mark shook his head. "Oh man, no joke, Hawk. These spirits expect an act of—what? *Magic? Sorcery?* And they don't intend to release you, or us, until you do so."

Ellen took a few careful steps toward Hawk. At least she could move, even if only in his direction. She motioned for Mark to join her; he too could comply without difficulty.

"Listen," she said softly, "I've been thinking, and I believe that you *can do this*. But more importantly, *you* must believe that you can do this. Mark and I will help; we'll lend our energy to the task. We know that Mark has gained some sort of power with his ability to perceive intentions. I can perceive energy, and apparently manipulate it to some small degree. All these spirits around us believe you can do this, in no small way because you are the grandson of your tribal shaman. You did mention that there is a hereditary aspect to that role. So, assume you have the right, and the power! And remember, you also have a little *technical assistance.*"

"Huh? What do you mean?"

She laid her hand on the spotlight. "Dial the lens for a tight beam and blast it straight up; there's your 'piece of the Sun God'! We *can—no,* we *will* do this!"

"But, there's only," Hawk studied the residual charge gauge on the battery pack, "about forty percent of a full charge left. I guess we can try."

Mark scoffed. "Come on, Hawk, that's still, what—one million candlepower? Do you think anything like that has been seen here before? Uh, discounting Mother Nature's occasional fits of fury, of course."

"*Believe*, Hawk," urged Ellen. "There is great power in faith—ours, too. Collectively we'll be stronger."

"Yeah," agreed Mark. "Hey, that gives me an idea! Ellen, all these spirits have a vested interest in the outcome, so why not ask them to participate? You know, lend the support of their combined energy to the task?"

"Good idea! Very well, I'll ask them."

She closed her eyes and envisioned the combined energies of the trapped innocents channeled through a focused beam of light and the subsequent *cracking of the curse*. She shared this vision with all the energy signatures she could reach; there seemed to be quite a lot of them. Were their numbers growing? She sensed a favorable response, and something else . . . *excitement? anticipation?*

"They will help," she announced, and laid her hand on his shoulder. "Listen, Hawk, whatever you do, be careful to articulate that only the *innocent* should attain freedom, like in your story."

"Oh yeah, I see what you mean."

Ellen stood to Hawk's left, with Mark on his right; each placed a hand on either of Hawk's shoulders. Mark held Ellen's free hand, completing the circle.

Hawk held the spotlight above his head, aimed straight up, a finger on the trigger switch.

Ellen had a sudden inspiration. "Remember, Hawk, you have to *believe*. Say something profound, like you would in an oath, and use your *true name;* then speak the final words."

He nodded and closed his eyes. Ellen and Mark did so as well. Each concentrated on calling forth their own power and melding it with that of the others.

Something was happening, building higher and higher, like an accumulated static charge. They all felt it. They rode it like a cresting wave until it seemed ready to burst.

Then Hawk spoke out in a clear, stentorian voice.

"Hear me! Powers that be! Air, Earth, Fire, and Water! I, Connor Redhawk, grandson of Wendell Small Owl, Shaman of my People, in the name of all that is Light and Good, do crack the curse of this place! No innocent shall be held! Those who shed all evil and reclaim their innocence shall be freed!"

He triggered the spotlight; a searing white beam streaked into the night sky.

A breeze began to twist around the three as they stood firm in their circle. A whirlwind formed from the swirling gusts and gained in strength, whipping around them, spiraling up in a dizzying dance with the blazing beam. Something ethereal—no, many such *somethings* began riding rampant up the ascending column of racing air. The companions' circle serving as a focal point, the amount of energy collectively funneling into this endeavor was staggering. Benign sparks danced across their arms and shoulders as their hair stood on end.

Just when it seemed like there would be no end to the tumult and chaos, there was a tremendous *CRAAAACK* across the heavens. A sound like a thousand crystal goblets shattering into diamond tears followed, echoing throughout the forest in softly tinkling waves.

The howling winds gradually abated and grew still. The ensuing silence was eerie; everything seemed held in a state of breathless suspension, waiting.

Hawk looked up to see that the spotlight's beam had softened to a diffuse golden glow, its battery was nearly spent. He switched it off.

They paused for a moment, and just stood there grinning at each other in the moonlight.

"It worked," announced Ellen. "Most of them are gone. They thanked us—you, Hawk, in particular. I told you! You just have to *believe*."

"There are still some here," cautioned Mark. "They couldn't leave; but, they bear us no animosity, no ill intent. Your incantation offers them a means to free themselves, should they choose that path. You've shown them the way, so to speak."

Hawk shrugged. "I'm not sure I fully understand what just happened, or how we did this; but I think—no, I *feel* that we did the right thing. I know that I'm finding this all very strange, and exciting. But I'm concerned," he admitted, as he gazed at the darkened forest, "that we'll have to face something we can't overcome."

Mark and Ellen remained silent. Despite the warm glow of the moment, they were well aware that the future was indeed unknown.

Hawk shook off his sense of foreboding, and took a few tentative steps without difficulty. "Hey! I can walk again."

"That's good! Now, can we get outta here?" Mark prodded.

Hawk shrugged. "You're right. We have to keep moving. I guess we'll just deal with anything else the best we can."

"Yes, let's go." Ellen stepped to his side and matched his pace. "But I want to point out a couple things. It's pretty clear we are acquiring some newfound abilities, right? So, it might be wise to keep that among ourselves, at least to the extent that we can. The other thing is that recent events seem to reinforce how significant *true names* are in this world. We should never tell anyone our true full names; not unless we trust them completely. Stick to nicknames for common conversation, okay?"

"Okay, that makes sense," agreed Hawk.

AS THEY LEFT THE CONFINES of the forest and followed the road onto the moor, Mark asked, "Uh, El', that thing about keeping our true names secret, did you mean like when we meet new and interesting people? For example, men who ride horses, carry torches, and wear armor?" He pointed into the distance. "Like those guys?"

In the bright moonlight, there was no mistaking the four horsemen fast closing the gap between the two groups. They covered the last several hundred yards with surprising speed.

Hawk looked around, but there was nowhere to go. They had obviously been seen; so, the best course was to stand their ground and brazen it out.

Ellen whispered, "Do you suppose they saw the light?"

"It would have been a little hard to miss, wouldn't it?" Hawk wryly noted. "Mark, determine their intentions, if you can. Let's listen more than we talk. And try to pick up on the local speech patterns."

Mark couldn't resist a bit of witty understatement. "Gee, I sure hope it's English."

SO IT WAS THREE SMILING, laughing people that the men of the Baron Von Kestel's Eastern Patrol came upon on the Forest Road during the hours of darkness, when the saner inhabitants of the realm would have been huddled in their homes behind locked doors. That alone made the baron's men wary, and courteously cautious.

The three companions found themselves loosely surrounded by the horsemen. Two bore torches. Each man was armed with a lance, casually pointed straight up, its butt braced in a lance bucket affixed to a stirrup. Sheathed swords and small shields were in evidence at their sides. They had the carriage of professional soldiers, comfortably at ease, yet alert.

One of the mounted men removed his helmet. "If ye please, your lordships, I am a sergeant of the Baron's Eastern Patrol, and I bid ye a good eventide. May I ask your business on this road at this hour?"

Mark looked to Hawk and Ellen; both shrugged. So he stepped forward and answered. "We bid you a good eventide as well, Sergeant. We are traveling, but have been delayed. We have become separated from a friend, a fellow traveler, whom we seek. Have you seen anyone pass this way in the past few hours, by chance?"

"Ah, I see, good sir. Might I have your name, sir, a description of your fellow traveler? Can you tell me how you came to be injured?"

"You may call me Counselor, and—"

Mark stopped speaking as Hawk laid a hand on his arm.

"Sergeant, you may address me as . . . Lord Hawk. This is neither the time nor the place for further questions. We are bound for yonder inn. We release you to continue your patrol. You may meet us there later that we might continue our conversation, or you can provide escort there now. You may choose."

The sergeant and Hawk stared unblinking at one another. It was instantly clear that neither man would back down. The building tension was palpable.

A guardsman stirred in his saddle, but the creak of leather did not fully conceal the hiss of drawn steel.

Ellen did not want a confrontation that was sure to escalate into something deadly, so she decided to act. Stepping forward she said sweetly, "My Lord Hawk . . . "

At the sound of a woman's voice the guardsmen were taken aback. In the dim light of the torches they had clearly mistaken Ellen for a boy or a small man of slight build; the jeans didn't help.

At any rate, her initiative broke the strained tension.

"My Lord Hawk," she cooed, "I can see it is evident that the good sergeant does not realize with whom he deals. May I?"

Surprised by her tactic, but not stupid, Hawk deftly played along. "Of course, er, my lady. Gentlemen, may I present the Lady Ellen?"

The horses stirred nervously; the riders gripped reins and touched protective talismans as they brought their steeds under control.

As his men bobbed their heads and mumbled "m'lady" in acknowledgment, the sergeant quickly dismounted. His eyes had grown wide.

"M-my deepest apologies, m'lady, we had no idea you were here," stammered the sergeant. "We will, of course, be honored to escort you to the inn."

Ellen glanced at Hawk, who discreetly shook his head.

"Thank you, Sergeant, but that won't be necessary," she said. "In fact, I think it best for you to continue with your assignment. We will proceed to the inn on our own."

"Begging your pardon, m'lady, but part of the assignment was to investigate the great light and noise in the near forest."

It escaped no one that the sergeant refrained from adding that *"the Lady Ellen"* and her two companions had obviously just come from there.

Ellen just smiled. "In that case, I can help you. That minor magic was merely a demonstration conducted by Lord Hawk, at my request. Does that satisfy your investigation, Sergeant?"

"Lord Hawk is a *mage?*" The sergeant could not keep the disdain, or the fear, from his voice.

Ellen noticed, so she tempered her response. "Not in the sense that you mean. He is something else altogether. You have not answered my question, Sergeant; does that satisfy your investigation?" She let her voice go cold. "I am not in the habit of repeating myself."

"Indeed so, m'lady, we shall be off, and resume our patrol assignment. I bid you a good night."

He mounted his horse and led his men toward the forest.

When the soldiers had ridden out of earshot, Hawk nudged Ellen. "Well, you sure impressed them, *Lady Ellen*. Who do you suppose they thought you were?"

She shrugged. "Some kind of nobility, I presume. I'm glad you picked up on the *lordship bit*; apparently titles are significant. And I have to admit I like the sound of *lord* and *lady*. Besides, it's good manners."

"Mark," asked Hawk, "did you get any intentions from them?"

"Intentions? Yeah, some, but not that much. For one thing, they intended to be away from you both, especially Ellen. It was pretty clear they were afraid of her; even their horses reacted."

"Well, horses are intuitively sensitive to their riders," Hawk acknowledged, "so, it's logical that they would react to their riders' fear."

"You know what?" Ellen mused aloud, "I sensed that, too, but I'm not sure how. Although we all heard it in the sergeant's voice when he thought Hawk was a mage. Did you pick up on anything else?"

"Yeah, all of them wanted to be away from you both, but they intended to stand fast until the sergeant ordered otherwise. As for the sergeant, his intention to do his duty was clear, despite his fear and experience."

"His experience? What do you mean?" Hawk pressed.

"Look, I don't know what he was thinking, of course, and I'm not real sure how I picked up on this, but his intentions were heavily influenced by his experiences. That makes sense, right?"

"Sure," Ellen agreed. "That makes sense for everybody. So?"

"Well," Mark hedged. "It seemed to me that in his experience, women bearing the title of *Lady* who went about after dark were nobility, *vampire nobility;* and one does not intentionally question the doings of vampires."

"What?" Ellen blurted. "He thought *I* was a *vampire?* What kind of world is this?"

Mark shrugged. "Hey, I don't know. I'm just telling you the impressions I got. We've seen ample proof that vampires exist in this reality, right? So, what could he have thought? I know this; he had no intention of staying here, near us, any longer than he had to."

"Well, it makes sense that his experience would have a strong impact on his intentions," Hawk reasoned, "and somehow you perceived it. Well done, Mark, but was that all you got?"

"No, there was something else; they intended to find somebody, two people actually, a man and a woman."

"Stacy?" asked Ellen.

"I don't know," Mark admitted. "It's possible."

Ellen furrowed her brow, her concern deepening, but kept silent.

"Hawk," Mark asked, "why did you interrupt? You know, stop me from talking to the sergeant?"

"Oh man, I'm sorry I jumped in like that. But I did because I recognized him, in a sense. Let me explain. That man may be a sergeant of the 'Baron's Eastern Patrol', but basically he's still a cop, and probably a pretty good one for this world. He maneuvered you into a field interrogation before you even knew it."

"No, he didn't . . . exactly," Mark stammered. "Oh, yeah, I guess you're right."

Hawk clapped Mark's good shoulder. "It's okay, no harm done. Right now we need to gather information, and not dispense any more than we have to. The more we listen, the more we learn."

"Point taken," Mark acknowledged. "I have to admit that entire encounter did provide us with useful information." He nudged his cousin. "Wouldn't you agree, *your ladyship?"*

Ellen smirked. "I would; and that's *your ladyship, Mistress of the Night,* to you, dear cousin."

"Oh, of course, m'lady." Mark groveled with an exaggerated sweeping bow.

"Actually, I find chivalrous manners quite acceptable," Ellen admitted, with an impish grin. "What say you, my Lord Hawk?"

"And here I thought I was always chivalrous." Hawk sighed heavily and shrugged. "Alas, so be it; when in Rome, I suppose. Wait, does that mean that hereafter Mark is to be addressed as the *Esteemed Lord High Counselor?*"

"Indeed, a most fitting title," Mark intoned, his nose in the air. "As I am a member of the bar, and due all respect pertinent thereto, I might find that connotation an appropriate appellation."

Hawk snorted in laughter. "And ever so humble!"

"Ha! Better than being called a *mage* in these parts; so, bite me!"

"Okay, my *childish lords,*" scolded Ellen. "That's enough; play nice, like *good vassals!*"

"Alas, m'lord Hawk," Mark bemoaned in mock-contrition, "we've been taken to task by her ladyship."

Hawk grinned. "Verily, m'lord Mark."

"Indeed," Ellen confirmed. "And besides, Mark, it's not wise to go around saying *'bite me'* in a world with vampires, now is it?"

"Ooh! M'lady shoots; m'lady scores!" Hawk teased, elbowing Mark's good arm.

"And the crowd," Mark groaned in his chagrin, "goes wild."

And so, smiling and laughing they approached the torch-lit gate of the Inn of the Crying Cup.

CH 23

"CORP'L!" CALLED OUT the guardsman on post at the gate. "Three approach afoot, on the road at half a bow-shot."

"On my way," responded the corporal, motioning to another guardsman. "Marcellus! Find the old gatekeeper, Amos. Look behind the kitchen; he was with the cook. Then notify the Lady Sabrina."

Peering through an eye slot in the gate, the corporal easily discerned the three strangers. "I see `em, but not well in this moonlight. No matter, anyone out in darkness is suspicious." He nudged the guard on post. "Have ye heard anything from them?"

"Aye, they be a-laughing `n' talking—havin' a merry old time. Methinks one be a woman, by her voice." He spat and wiped his lips with the back of a hand. "Y'know, Corp'l, tis not many would be so *easy* in the night, `specially this night."

"Aye, there is that." The corporal turned at the sound of footsteps. "Ah, tis Amos. Have a look, gatekeeper, and tell me if those yonder were here earlier this day. Be they the ones we seek?"

Amos had to rise up on his toes to see through the slot. He took his time studying the newcomers in the strong moonlight. Dropping down on his heels, he shook his head.

"Nay, tis not them ye seek, Corp'l. I ne'er seen the likes o' them afore." He rambled on in confusion, scratching his balding pate. "S'posin' they be wantin' rooms? What t' tell `em?"

"I will address that issue, should it arise," countered a cool female voice. Lady Sabrina and her familiar, Gunther, stepped from the shadows.

"M'lady," acknowledged the corporal with a brief bow.

She casually glanced through the eye slot, shrugged, turned to her familiar and nodded. Gunther moved to the slot and looked carefully at the approaching trio, then returned to his mistress' side and spoke so softly that only she could hear.

"M'lady, I've never seen them before. But their attire—"

"I know. Say no more," she cautioned. "Inform Lady Leanan at once."

She turned to the corporal. "Admit the travelers, and learn their names." She leaned forward for emphasis. "But above all, Corporal, do *not* let them leave."

AS THE THREE COMPANIONS arrived at the torch-lit gate, the gatekeeper swung it open and announced a greeting. "A good eventide to ye travelers." He bowed as gracefully as his years would allow. "Be ye welcome at the Crying Cup."

As Hawk started to step forward, a man in mailed armor blocked his path and spoke cordially. "Thy pardon, good sir, but I must ask thy name, and those of thy companions, before any are granted entry this night."

Hawk maintained a placid demeanor, but allowed his eyebrows to rise. "Indeed? Perhaps there is wisdom in such caution. No doubt you will extend the same courtesy by identifying yourself, and your authority to make such a request."

"Of course, good sir. I am Corporal Shivers of the Baron Von Kestel's Eastern Patrol. The inn is under our protection and control this night." The corporal examined the three as he spoke.

Hawk recognized and understood another professional, a man not lulled into a false sense of security. Such overt courtesy did not imply laxity. Their strange attire and lack of visible weapons could work to their advantage. So, Hawk smiled and responded heartily.

"The Baron's Eastern Patrol? Why, we just spoke to your sergeant and three of your fellows, on the road, within the last hour. We invited him to meet us here later. Oh do forgive me, I am Lord Hawk, this is the Lady Ellen, and this is, um, the Counselor."

"Thank ye, m'lord," acknowledged the corporal, with due deference, as he stepped aside. "Allow me to show ye to the common room. If ye will follow me, please?"

He led the party to the door of the inn where another guardsman stood a temporary post. At a nod, the door was opened.

Under the careful scrutiny of the guardsmen, they entered what Hawk immediately recognized as a graphic crime scene.

The coppery tang of spilt blood still hung in the air, mingling with the scent of a dozen or more tallow candles that illuminated the surreal sight. Four corpses, stripped of weapons and armor, lay in a row by one wall. Each bore horrendous wounds; two were barely recognizable as men. The other two, while not as severely mutilated, were something other than men. Pointed ears and elongated faces suggested *what? Elves?*

Another of the dead, wearing the mailed armor of a guardsman, lay upon a table in a position of honored repose. A drawn sword rested upon his chest, his stiffening hands folded around the hilt.

Two wounded guardsmen sat nearby. One's leg was splinted; the other's head was wrapped in a bloody bandage and his left arm hung in a sling. A tall, thin man, in a farmer's rough homespun, and a small delicate woman in similar attire, gently administered to the stricken men.

From the destruction of the furnishings and the evident blood spatter, it was clear to Hawk that a brutal and deadly brawl had happened in this very place a short time ago.

He could see that Ellen was shocked, no doubt having never before seen the immediate results of such deliberate violence. Like most people, he guessed, her experience in viewing the dead had likely been limited to the carefully orchestrated presentations of funeral homes and the comfortable illusion of peaceful repose, *an unconscious and unvoiced denial of the finality of death,* he thought grimly.

However, these bodies suggested nothing of peaceful repose, but rather anger, fear, and despair. Had he known, he would have spared her this. It was too late now.

ELLEN WAS NOT AS SHOCKED as Hawk feared, but rather *surprised.* Without realizing she had done it, she gazed at the lingering energy signatures of the slain, their auras, which were all but completely dissipated. As she watched the pale traces of luminosity dim and extinguish, she was unexpectedly saddened beyond description.

She gasped, and Hawk squeezed her hand in sudden concern and warning. Grateful for the timely support and distraction, she shunted the doleful vision from her mind and refocused on her more corporeal surroundings. Her wandering gaze rested on a covered bundle in the far corner. With a bit of a start, she realized it was another body.

A worn woman of middle years sat slumped nearby. Her tear-streaked face avoided the covered bundle; but an errant glance at the body betrayed her immense sense of loss. Her breathing hitched and shoulders flinched in mournfully mute spasms.

However, to Ellen's perception there was something unusual about the residual energy lingering around that particular corpse; it seemed contained or restrained somehow, not diminishing or dissipating. That this person was dead was not at issue; there was something else about the energy itself, as if it were affixed to the body rather than an innate component. Ellen caught herself staring and felt that she was intruding on the disconsolate woman's private grief.

Sharp voices arose from across the room and drew her attention. She sensed Hawk stiffen in response to the belligerence of tone; but the clamor was not directed at them.

On the other side of the large chamber, two guardsmen with crossbows stood guard over a pair of disheveled and slightly wounded men, restrained and seated on a rough bench. Four individuals, two men and two women, their backs to the three companions, were busy questioning the two prisoners. Voices were now low and indistinguishable, yet punctuated by angry outbursts and threatening gestures.

IT APPEARED TO HAWK that the prisoners were generally cooperative and compliant. Nonetheless, he wondered about the wisdom of simultaneously interrogating the two *what? Witnesses? Perpetrators?*

The two would occasionally look to one another as they responded to questions, as if mutually affirming their story as they went.

In Hawk's mind, it was generally a better investigative technique to conduct individual interviews, or interrogations, and then use the separate statements to corroborate or refute one another. Witness statements, even when completely candid and honest, always varied to some degree based on the perspective of the observer. Whereas, multiple witness statements that were patently identical, notwithstanding differing perspectives, were as equally suspect as blatant contradictions, at least to the careful investigator.

Hawk snapped out of his observational analysis as the outer door opened once more.

The sergeant, with whom they had previously met on the forest road, entered. For just a second, the sergeant seemed surprised to see the three travelers. He turned, ignoring them, and nodded to the corporal.

The sergeant and corporal approached the four inquisitors and made their report to their apparent superiors.

A STUNNING RED-HAIRED woman in black satin and a tall pale man in black evening attire turned and approached, flanked by the sergeant and corporal. Confronting Ellen and her companions, the aristocratic and self-possessed man spoke with just the trace of an accent, and more than a hint of condescension.

"I am Lord Vlad. I am told you call yourselves 'Lord Hawk', 'Lady Ellen', and 'Counselor'. I am unfamiliar with your house. You will please enlighten me. Be warned that we take extreme exception to *impersonation and pretenders.*"

Ellen sensed that Hawk bristled at the not-so-veiled threat as he stared unblinking into the taller man's face.

Suddenly, she realized that she was being stared at by the red-haired woman with intensely green eyes. Ellen had the uncomfortable sense that this person was somehow familiar.

The woman smiled wryly. "One moment, my dear Vlad. I believe I can help in this regard."

His brows rose as he deferred to her. "Of course, m'lady." He bowed slightly and took a step back.

Standing directly before Ellen, she spoke. "We have not been formally introduced. I am the Lady Leanan of the Sidhe, the House of Lamia, the Administrating House of the Realm of Shadow." Turning to Lord Vlad, Leanan continued, "Lord Vlad, allow me to present Lady Ellen Doyle, Steward of the Grand Portal of the Realm of Man."

Ellen was stunned into silence. This woman knew exactly who she was! *But who is this woman, this Lady Leanan? Why does she seem vaguely familiar?*

Leanan now stood before Hawk, who seemed equally stunned by her words, and looked up into his wide eyes. He appeared confused, like he was adrift, losing touch with the situation, as she began to slowly smile, a predator in recognition of a favored prey. "And this man," Leanan added, not taking her eyes from his, "who calls himself 'Lord Hawk', is indeed deserving of such a title among his own kind, in the Realm of Man . . . " Her voice trailed off as she studied his face. She took his right hand and considered the palm; her smile widened. "Furthermore, he bears my mark—and is mine!"

Ellen's gut twisted and her anger flared! She actually ground her teeth, but no one seemed to notice. That this woman had claimed Hawk as *hers* tripped an alarm deep in her subconscious. She sensed this was potentially far more serious than the immediate flush of jealousy she readily recognized, and somewhat reluctantly acknowledged. She fought to maintain a calm demeanor, lest she betray the depth of her feelings. Intuitively, she sensed that disclosure here and now could enhance her potential vulnerability, and perhaps endanger them all.

Lady Leanan stood before Mark, who appeared completely at ease, notwithstanding his surprise at hearing Ellen identified and Hawk so *claimed.*

MARK HAD IMMEDIATELY recognized Leanan, Vlad, and at least one more of the inquisitors, the other woman, as vampires, and therefore, as authority figures in this world. He had even *eavesdropped* on their intentions while they questioned the two prisoners. He now knew that they were genuinely concerned for the fate of their world; and that some significant, if unknown, event was feared to be at hand. Indeed, if they feared something, that gave him a potential advantage, however slight.

Leanan looked into his eyes, but she seemed puzzled, perhaps even conflicted. He simply stared back, smiling. Something registered within her and she drew her head back.

"You, *Counselor,* I do not know," she admitted, "but I know you are not *of the Council.*"

"I do not claim to be," stated Mark evenly. "You may consider me one who counsels, an advisor. I'm certain you can see the distinction."

"Oh, I am certain that you are more than that," she responded and stepped forward to within an inch of his face, and once again stared deeply into his eyes.

If her intention was intimidation, it did not work. He merely returned her stare, and subtly probed her intentions.

She suddenly hissed and stepped back.

"You *dare—*" she spat, and stopped abruptly. She kept her distance and studied him closely, sending her own probe forth.

He sensed her probe and tried to block it. His shielding worked, but not soon enough.

"So, you have slain Damien the Cursed, the only other who would, *or could,* dare such an incursion. And that would mean that you—no, all three of you, have traversed the Forest of the Damned, this very night!" Leanan was now the one stunned.

The room became as quiet as a tomb, and all eyes were on the three companions.

Pointing at Mark, she accused, "You are of the Realm of Man—and a *mage!*"

She spun to face the guardsmen. "Sergeant, did you not report that one of these three claimed responsibility for the display of sorcerous magic near the forest's edge this night?"

"Aye, m'lady." The sergeant pointed to Hawk. "Twas the Lord Hawk made the claim, not this *Counselor.*"

Hawk found his voice. "The sergeant speaks the truth. I was responsible for that, uh, bit of technical sorcery. But I make no claim to being a mage."

As Leanan looked from Hawk to Mark, in momentary befuddlement, Mark sensed an advantage in her confusion and deftly pressed.

"Lady Leanan," he began, "I am no mage either. We are here for the sole purpose of retrieving a friend who has come into this, um, *land* by accident. In our search, we were attacked by this *Damien;* we were compelled to deal with him. There were a number of other delays, but we dealt with them as well. That Damien was slain was perhaps regrettable, yet unavoidable. Bear in mind that he and his minions initiated the attack. We only defended ourselves." Gesturing around the room, Mark added, "We do not know what has happened here; nor have we any wish to interfere. We only intend to locate our friend and return home."

"Now this is becoming most interesting," observed Leanan dryly, a firm grip on her composure once more. "The loss of Damien the Cursed is of no real concern. He fell from power long ago, and his last known minions were mere *ghouls and revenants;* none would be missed. On the other hand, it may be that we share a mutual concern. I wish to locate your 'friend' as well; I have some questions of great importance for him."

"*Him?*" exclaimed Ellen. "Our friend is a *woman!*"

Hawk and Mark winced when she blurted that out. It was too late now.

Leanan looked back to the guardsmen. "Captain Quinn, was there not a woman with Salidar?"

"There was, m'lady; and so attired in trousers much like the Lady Ellen."

Leanan stood for a moment in thought, considering Ellen and her companions.

"Lady Ellen, it appears that your friend has fallen in with, ah, not the best of company. We indeed have a mutual interest in finding them. And I would speak with you further, in private, as this is a matter that may affect both our realms. So, please accept the hospitality of my House, in order that we might confer. I realize that you have the ability to transport your party anywhere at any time, but I ask that you, rather that *we,* help one another with our mutual task. You, Lord Hawk, and the Counselor will come to no harm, and shall enjoy the protection of my House while you are here."

Ellen looked to Hawk, who merely shrugged.

Mark looked intently at Lady Leanan for a long moment. He then whispered to Ellen, "You may accept her offer; her intentions appear to be as stated. But she is very worried about something."

"Very well, Lady Leanan, I accept your offer," Ellen said formally, "and will cooperate insofar as it is to our mutual advantage."

At that phrasing, Mark nodded approvingly.

"Excellent!" Leanan turned and addressed the guard. "Captain Quinn, commandeer the black coach and its team; these Dark Elves now have little use for it. Arrange an escort for my guests to my castle. I will meet them there, in time. Lord Vlad and I have some unfinished business here."

"At once, m'lady. Sergeant, see to it."

Lady Leanan smiled and nodded to the companions. "Before you go, I would like you to see something."

She stepped to the covered bundle and gestured for a guard to uncover the body. The sad woman sitting near the corpse stifled a quiet sob and averted her eyes.

"Look closely," Leanan urged. "Have you ever seen this man before?" She watched their reactions carefully.

All three shook their heads, and Hawk responded, "No, we haven't. Who is he?"

"That is not your concern," Leanan responded coolly.

At a glance from Hawk, Mark clearly bit back a retort. Obviously there was little to be gained by pressing the issue at this point.

Leanan arched an eyebrow and nodded, a slightly smug twist to her lips. Without another word, she and Vlad joined the other two inquisitors and resumed questioning the prisoners.

ELLEN HAD NOT MISSED a thing in that exchange.

And just what was that all about?

But before she could ask Hawk, the guard captain bowed before her. "M'lady, m'lords, if you would follow me?"

They stepped outside into the torch-lit courtyard, where the coach and an escort of four horsemen awaited. The elegant conveyance was painted a gloss black and was drawn by an equally sleek team of midnight-hued horses. The matched pair stamped and snorted, impatient to be off.

The captain introduced Corporal Shivers, who stood by the coach, as the officer in charge of the five-man escort. "Please do as the corporal asks; the journey is not without its potential hazards. Your cooperation is appreciated." The captain opened the coach door. "Now, if you would care to board?"

Ellen climbed in; Hawk and Mark followed.

The corporal scrambled up to the driver's seat and looked to his captain.

At his superior's firm nod, Shivers flicked the reins.

They set off at a brisk pace.

IN TRUTH, ELLEN FOUND the ride thrilling. As a child she had often dreamed of riding in a magical coach, on the way to some elegant royal ball; of course, she was the fairy princess, the envy of all, pursued by a charming prince.

But one look at Mark's concerned expression and her reverie dissipated as she was reminded of their mission, *to find Stacy*. Hawk's expression was no better; he seemed dislocated, like he wasn't all there, or something.

And what had Lady Leanan meant by saying that he bore *her mark,* and was *hers?* That still annoyed Ellen. In fact, the more she dwelled upon it, the more it irked her. Why did Leanan seem familiar? Well, there was nothing stopping her from simply *asking* for some answers.

"Hawk," she broached, loudly enough to be heard over the muted thunder of galloping hooves and iron-shod wheels. "Just what did Lady Leanan mean by saying you bore *her mark* and you were *hers?*"

"I have no idea." He shrugged his shoulders and idly scratched the palm of his right hand. "But, it's just that she's somehow *familiar,* like I've seen her before somewhere. But try as I might, I just can't remember."

Rocking with the pitch of the coach, Mark waved a hand to get their attention. "Listen, I think—no, I *know* that she intends to use you both; but, I couldn't sense *how.* Maybe she doesn't even know yet?"

"Well, she already said essentially that she intends to use all three of us in this search," observed Ellen. "It's weird; I can't shake the feeling that I should know her, too. She's familiar to me as well."

"Tell me about it," groused Hawk, frustration evident in his tone. "And by the way, what did she mean by saying that she knew you could 'transport your party anywhere at any time'? Don't you need a globe or something?"

"I don't know *what* she meant! I think I need to finish reading the journal. There's so much I don't know; it's getting *extremely* frustrating!"

Mark held up a hand for their attention. "Hold on. We're missing the obvious."

Ellen and Hawk stared at him in confusion, as glimpses of the shadowed night whisked by the open coach windows.

"Consider the facts. Lady Leanan identified you both; she *recognized* you. Neither of you, nor I, have ever been in this realm before. And yet, a native resident of this world, not to mention a vampire of the *ruling house,* knows you both. That suggests that *she* has been in *our* world, and in some proximity to each of you." He let that sink in. "Furthermore, it had to have been recently, within a few weeks. The two of you hadn't even met before that, nor had Ellen been named Steward yet. So, there appears to be evidence that there is either another way to transport between worlds, or someone else can access Ellen's portals. I think that discovering just how Lady Leanan knows you both may lead to that information."

Rocking with the motion of the coach, they looked at one another in silence. The logic was undeniable, and yet defied comprehension.

"This sucks!" griped Hawk. "I just can't remember. It's like I'm blocked."

"I understand, me too," agreed Ellen. "I think for me, it's like an old vague memory that won't quite come into focus, like a faded photograph . . . Oh, my gosh! That's it!"

"What?" Hawk quizzed her.

"A photograph! I think I've seen her in a photograph, an old one, with three women standing together. No, it was more than *one* photograph; it was several. I think one of the women was Maude; and one of the women looked just like Lady Leanan. I don't know who the other person was. The pictures were in these old photo albums I found in the attic at the house. Stacy, my mother, and I were looking through them yesterday."

"What else was in the pictures?" Hawk asked.

"What do you mean? It was just the three of them."

"What was the setting, the background?"

"Oh, I get it," announced Mark. "Where were the photos taken, in what *world*, you know, what *realm*?"

"Precisely, Mark," affirmed Hawk. "Ellen, what clues can you remember? You know, things that were in the settings or backgrounds that might suggest where and when the pictures were taken?"

"Oh yeah, I see. Well, I'd have to say home, *our* world, I mean. As I recall, one was in a nightclub, like an old speakeasy. Another was in front of a movie theater. Those are the ones I remember best. But as to time, *when,* I really don't know. I'd have to look again, much more carefully."

Hawk smiled and spread his hands. "It appears we may have corroborating evidence that would put Lady Leanan in our world, at a time or times yet to be determined."

"So, you think Mark's theory is right? She knows us from contact in our own world?"

"I believe so," Hawk acknowledged, "and those pictures may help to prove it. We now have a strong theory and a good lead. Well done, Mark!"

"Thanks, I do have my moments. But keep in mind that it'd have to be some pretty recent contact; those photos are likely to be much older. Nonetheless, we'll definitely examine them, when we get *home*."

"We're slowing down," noted Hawk. "Can you see anything on your side? There's nothing but dark fields and woods on my side."

"Yeah," said Mark squinting into the dark. "There's something . . . a palisade wall around some buildings, a few torches, but no other lights . . . and *no castle*. I don't think this is our destination."

The carriage slowed and came to a halt. The passengers heard a sentry challenge the escort. Shortly thereafter, the gate swung open and the coach rolled into a small courtyard.

The corporal jumped to the ground, pulled the coach door open, and announced, "Midway Station, m'lady, m'lords. We must water the horses and be on our way within the hour. There be a small larder and mulled wine inside, if y' fancy such. Please stay within the station walls; night is no time to be out." He caught himself, grinned and shrugged. "Of course, ye already know about that, do ye not?"

They alighted from the carriage and stretched their legs.

Mark and Ellen headed for the low building.

THE CORPORAL HUNG ABOUT, as if he wanted to talk but was reluctant to initiate a conversation.

Hawk could see his discomfort, so he offered a casual observation, a subtle effort to prime the conversational pump. "Well Corporal, it seems we are the only ones out here tonight, or at least I haven't seen anyone, or any *thing,* else."

"Aye, just because ye see them not tis no reason t' think such be not out there, and no doubt aware of us." He straightened his stance unconsciously as he peered into the surrounding night. "Not much would attack a mounted patrol; but, aye, some few, a basilisk or a troll, might try. But I ken not much else, not alone, anyway."

"A troll, eh?" Hawk chuckled. "About twice a man's height with arms as long as his body, a pair of tusks jutting up from his jaw, and ugly enough—"

"T' sour a cow's milk w' but a glance?" Corporal Shivers broke into a hearty laugh. "Aye, m'lord, that'd be the look o' the beastie! Seen one, have ye?"

"That we did, Corporal, that we did, had to deal with him as well." Hawk toed the loose dirt and let his voice drift as if reminiscing. "Nasty business, that . . . "

"M'lord, if I might be so bold," offered the corporal tentatively. "Would ye care to join me on the driver's bench as we complete our journey? We could continue our conversation. I be most eager-like to hear more of this troll y' seen."

"Why certainly, Corporal, I'd enjoy that. In fact, it happens that in my, uh, home, I have a job very much like yours, not dealing with trolls, of course, but to 'serve and protect', and conduct, um, inquiries."

"Excellent, m'lord," exclaimed the delighted corporal. "I canna say that I be all that surprised; I saw yer reaction to the carnage at the inn. Y' just sort of took it all in, like y' could figure it all out, in time. Y've done so before, I wager; an' it shows. I been at this a good while, longer than most, less than some. Aye, t' be sure, we've much to discuss."

IT TOOK LESS TIME TO reach their final destination than it had taken to arrive at Midway Station, or so it seemed to Hawk. Corporal Shivers assured him it was the same time and distance; it was just the fine company that made the travel time fly.

He and Hawk had spent the trip exchanging information. Hawk had learned a great deal about this realm and he was eager to share what he had learned with Ellen and Mark.

Corporal Shivers had enjoyed the tale of the companions' forest adventure immensely; and, had been subsequently indoctrinated into the secret mysteries of the *flashlight*. The corporal possessed a quick mind and easily grasped the concept of its operation, but was stymied by Hawk's futile attempt to explain electricity and batteries.

Hawk finally gave up, and promised to find a more comprehensible explanation for his new friend at his earliest opportunity.

It had become apparent to Hawk just how important it was to dispel any notion that either he or Mark was some sort of mage. The term was considered very negative, if not an outright pejorative, by men-at-arms in this realm.

The corporal explained that in past petty wars among the nobility, certain Houses had employed dark-magic users, *mages,* to bring havoc and death to opposing men-at-arms. To the soldier, this was considered dishonorable in the extreme; whereas the employing nobility considered it rather *expedient*. Of course, no one dared to question the doings of the vampire class, that upper crust of Shadow nobility.

However, Hawk could sense an undercurrent of resentment as Shivers spoke on. Over the centuries, internecine conflicts within the realm declined. In more recent times, disputes among the nobility seldom erupted into conflicts; the diminished population could not support such waste of humankind. Nonetheless, most noble houses still maintained and trained mages, as they did men-at-arms. And, as might be expected, this ingrained animosity toward mages was still a sensitive aspect of the military mindset.

THE COMPANIONS COULD see that their arrival at Lady Leanan's castle was obviously expected; a number of household staff were on hand to greet their Lady's visitors. Their guard escort, relieved of duty, retired to a barracks within the castle walls.

The three *guests* were shown to three adjacent chambers, nearly identical in size, shape, and appointments. However, Ellen's chamber had a balcony. Robust fires in each hearth brightened and warmed the rooms, but an incipient chill seemed to hover in forgotten corners, as if only temporarily held at bay.

Not confined to their rooms, they were invited to Lady Leanan's reception hall where they could sample some refreshments and await her imminent return.

Aside from the deferential servants, the castle had its own compliment of omnipresent guards, some of whom seemed to always be within earshot of the companions. As guests, they had been cautioned by the staff regarding limited access beyond designated areas, and seemed to be under constant, albeit casual, observation. While they may have been treated as guests, there was a subtle sense of custodial constraint.

As they waited, seated closely on a divan, Hawk quietly disclosed much of what he had learned about this realm from Corporal Shivers. Reasonably discreet, and pointedly nonjudgmental, Hawk described what was considered common knowledge, to include the local economy, property allocation, and governing infrastructure. Other details he would save for later.

GLANCING AT HAWK'S watch as he stretched and yawned, Ellen noted that it was almost 2:00 a.m. Mark's head had drooped once or twice as well. Clearly both men were starting to feel the drain on their energy reserves.

Only Ellen seemed wide awake as a pair of female servants swept into the room bearing a set of silver trays. She noticed that the two women looked remarkably alike.

Sisters, surely—perhaps twins?

The aroma of the dark liquid poured from the elegant silver pitcher demanded Ellen's full attention. "Hey! Is that coffee?"

The silent twins smiled and served each of them a deep china cup brimming with the roasted fragrance of select beans. The other tray held small decanters of cream and honey, in deference to personal taste.

"Oh man," Hawk moaned. "This is just what I needed."

"Yeah," Mark added. "Who knew they'd have coffee? Thank you, thank you, thank you!"

The twins smiled, curtsied, and slipped from the room.

The companions savored the delicious beverage, their fatigue fading in the wisps of succulent steam.

IT WAS JUST AS WELL that coffee had been provided, for Lady Leanan kept her guests waiting for almost another hour. She finally arrived accompanied by another noblewoman and her attendant, both of whom they had seen at the Crying Cup.

"Forgive me, I was needed elsewhere. I trust your trip here was uneventful and you have been made suitably comfortable, yes? Good. This is the Lady Sabrina. She has information you may find useful. Let us make ourselves comfortable and hear what her servant has to say."

The Lady Sabrina's attendant was a strapping young man who seemed to positively dote upon her, and anticipate her every need. He moved chairs forward for his mistress and Lady Leanan, and then stood by attentively.

At a nod from Leanan, Sabrina gestured to the young man.

"My servant, Gunther, has seen and observed your friend for several hours within the last day. He will now speak of this."

At his mistress' direction, Gunther told of his observation of Salidar and the timely arrival of the *wood nymph—the Lady Stacy.*

Mark and Hawk were equally stunned, but remained poker-faced when Ellen casually responded.

"Yes, well, she does have a way with plants. Now, can you tell us what happened after they left the forest?"

Gunther went on to describe the meeting on the road with the farmer and his wife, and their arrival at the inn. He did not see either the Lady Stacy or the man he was assigned to follow, this *Salidar*, again until the Lady Sabrina arrived and she and Gunther entered the inn.

They had intended merely to observe, but fate decreed otherwise and they were soon caught up in the chaos of the melee. When it was over, neither Salidar nor the Lady Stacy was anywhere to be seen. Guardsmen searched the inn and the grounds but found only the old farmer and his wife.

Lady Leanan interrupted. "I do not doubt that Salidar played a significant role in all of this; I am, in fact, aware of his mission. However, I do not understand what your friend, the Lady Stacy, had to do with it, or why she disappeared with Salidar."

Ellen almost bristled, but remained calm as she said evenly, "It could not be simpler; she had *nothing* to do with *this Salidar* and *whatever* he was doing. As Gunther has just described, she apparently got him untangled from a tree and walked with him to the inn. Chaos broke loose in the common room and she left. Nothing says that this Salidar and she are even still together. Perhaps it would be more helpful if you told us more about this Salidar character. I would be most displeased if he has forced her somewhere against her will."

Leanan considered Ellen for a long moment, and then seemed to come to a decision.

"Very well, but first I must be certain that you and your companions are not under the influence of the Lady Diere."

Puzzlement clouded Ellen's face. "Who? I've never heard that name before." Turning to Hawk and Mark, she asked, "Have you?"

Both shook their heads, their confusion obvious.

"Of course, you would say that," observed Leanan. "But rest assured, I have the means at my disposal to test the truth of such assertions."

Lady Leanan rose, compelling them to stand as well. She stood before Hawk, and studied him closely. Placing her hands to either side of his face, she gently pulled his head towards her. The gesture had a strong sense of intimacy, as if a prelude to a kiss.

Ellen stiffened, but was restrained by a touch and whisper from Mark.

"Easy, El'—she intends him no harm."

Holding his face mere inches from her own, Leanan looked deeply into his eyes. Hawk's shoulders slowly sagged and his expression went slack. She held him in a dazed paralysis for several moments, and then released him.

He stumbled in place and snapped his head around in confusion.

"What the—? You were in my mind!" he accused. "How the hell did you do that? And why?"

Leanan smiled as she resumed her seat. "As to *how,* I have that power over you because you bear my mark. Now, as to *why* . . . Simply because I must know the truth; whether or not you are in league with Lady Diere."

"What mark?" Hawk demanded. "What the hell are you talking about? I don't even know you! I don't know any Lady Diere either!"

Mark stepped forward, holding up a hand to forestall any further outburst from Hawk. "Lady Leanan, obviously we have many questions. But it might be more efficient if you were to explain just who these people are. Then we could likely be of more assistance to each other; and many of our questions may be satisfactorily resolved."

Ellen's patience was sorely strained. "We will exchange information, as we agreed, or our *mutually beneficial pact* ends now! And we will resume our search—alone. Now, who are Salidar and Lady Diere?"

Leanan stared at Ellen; a wistful smile played across the vampire's crimson lips.

"You remind me of someone . . . So be it. Salidar serves the Lady Diere of the House of Hawthorn, the Ruling House of the Realm of the Dark Elves. Lady Diere covets many things—powerful things, to include your Stewardship. I believe she is responsible for the attempt upon your life, and Salidar its architect."

Hawk's brows knit, but he kept silent as Lady Leanan continued.

"Salidar has played a sinister role in many of her plans, some of which I have seen first hand. Always, it is in the interest of furthering her power and influence. I am convinced that she is also responsible for the debacle at the Inn of the Crying Cup; and once again, Salidar was critically involved. He was to pass a cursed scroll to the innkeeper, Boltar."

Ellen saw that Mark was on the verge of a question, but a scowling Hawk caught his eye and subtly shook his head.

Leanan clearly noticed the interplay and smiled wryly. "That scroll was the catalyst for agents of Mab, Queen of the Dark Elves and Monarch of the Unseelie Court, to attempt to seize Boltar on a charge of treason. Her people have no authority here, and their presumptive actions precipitated the confrontation. You have seen the results. In the aftermath, as you have heard, neither Salidar nor the Lady Stacy was to be found."

"What did you learn," Hawk asked, "from the survivors you questioned?"

"They were hireling thugs, contracted by an elfin mage, who disappeared with the scroll in the ensuing confusion. The mercenaries were instructed to capture or slay the innkeeper and bring the body back to the Realm of the Dark Elves. They said that the mage was most insistent about them returning with the body. When they failed, they opted for death at the hands of the Eastern Patrol rather than return empty-handed. They rightfully feared the wrath of Queen Mab, who is rumored to have a necromancer among her mages."

Mark and Hawk balked at the mention of a necromancer, and would have inquired further, but Ellen forestalled them with a raised hand.

"Wait, the body? Was that the body of Boltar," Ellen asked, "wrapped in a bundle by the wall, that you had us try to identify?"

"Yes, that was Boltar."

"Who was the woman who was crying?" Ellen probed.

"That was Hilde, a serving woman who obviously bore him some affection, mourning his death."

"There was something strange about that body," remembered Ellen. "I can sense the *life energy* of a person, or the diminishing trace of it if they've recently died. But the energy around that body was different, like it was deliberately held in some sort of suspension or frozen state, almost like an outer shell around the body. Does that make any sense?"

"It may indeed; a spell may be on the body." Leanan looked to Sabrina and nodded. "We will investigate. If you will excuse us, I shall return in a few moments."

At that, Leanan and Sabrina rose and silently left the room. Gunther padded in their wake.

"WHY DID YOU TELL HER that?" Mark asked. "Could it be important?"

"I dunno, but somehow I think it is." Ellen shrugged and opened her palms. "Look, it's just a gut feeling, but I don't think there's any harm in telling her."

Hawk scowled. "You should've told us first. And what's this about a necromancer? We've gotta be careful about what information we share—and with whom. I don't trust her."

"Okay, I get it. I don't trust her either, but you said giving some information in order to get more in return is a good tactic, right? She knows more; that's for certain! And we need to learn more!"

Hawk winced. "Hoist with my own petard, eh?"

"Yeah, maybe a bit. Look, it might be nothing," Ellen hedged, "but I wonder what they did with the body? Think they may have moved it?"

"Probably, but we have no way of knowing." Hawk shrugged. "Maybe sharing what you told her will prompt her to share some more information."

"Well, it looks like you'll be able to put it to the test," Mark whispered. "Here she comes."

Lady Leanan swept into the room unaccompanied and resumed her seat.

"I apologize for the interruption. Lady Ellen, I appreciate the sharing of your perception. We shall know more shortly."

"If I may ask?" inquired Hawk. "You said Lady Diere was responsible for the attempt on Ellen's life, and that Salidar was the 'architect'. Which attempt were you referring to, the motor vehicle crash or the *overdose* attempt at the hospital?"

Lady Leanan merely smiled. "My dear Lord Hawk, there was only one attempt on her life, the 'motor vehicle crash'. The overdose attempt at the hospital was merely an attempt to ensnare her in a spell of manipulation, not an attempt on her life. But that also failed, as you well know."

Hawk stared at Lady Leanan in puzzlement. A pensive concern stole across his face as he squinted at her mocking smirk. Something was nagging at him, something important. He struggled within himself to find his calm center, to concentrate on the essence of his being, the very basis of just who he was, a complementary blend of his personal philosophy and the sum of his experiences.

In the synaptic corridors of his mind he found the anomaly. A nebulous wall of dark energy thoroughly obscured a memory. He sensed the hidden memory was his; but, the blockage was not.

In a moment of epiphany, he realized this sort of imaging was working for him, becoming second nature, and getting easier for him.

He focused on the foreign energy, envisioning it as a stone wall; odd shapes of ancient smooth stone stacked and mortared so as to contain as much as to exclude. He intuitively understood that this dark nebula was indeed a spell of some kind, one that would likely withstand a full-on frontal assault of his personal energy. But what of the cohesive mortar that held the component elements of the spell together? In his mind's eye, he began to chip away at the mortar, the implied intention of whomever cast the spell, to effectively weaken the wall. In what seemed like a matter of a few moments the mortar began to crumble, flaking away in puffs of metaphysical dust. The old stones grated upon one another and rocked off balance, tumbling aside like discarded debris.

His memory was no longer denied him.

From beneath knit brow, his piercing glare fixed upon Lady Leanan, his pointing finger accused.

"You! It was you at the hospital! You made the attempt to dose Ellen with whatever it was!" Hawk stared at the palm of his right hand, "And you *bit* me!"

Ellen blanched, her hand to her mouth, but kept silent.

Lady Leanan's laugh was almost musical. "Ah, ha-ha! Very impressive, my Lord Hawk! You should not have been able to know that without me allowing it. Hmm, there is more to you than I had thought. True, I was tasked by Lady Diere to administer the spell, a vile liquid concoction; but you prevented me from fulfilling that task. You chased me; but *I caught and tasted you.* That is how you came to bear my mark."

"Well," spat Hawk, "I *repudiate your mark!*"

"Hmm," she mused aloud. "It may be that you are strong enough to do so. But that is irrelevant at the moment."

He glared at her as she continued.

"What *is* relevant is that Lady Diere called upon many members of the Unseelie Court, myself included, to carry out certain missions and assignments under the pretext of *Council Business*, with the implied or inferred blessing of Queen Mab. It now appears that Lady Diere has had her own agenda for some time. Unfortunately, but for her blatant attempts to usurp the Stewardship in the Realm of Man, we are uncertain as to her goals. However, we have our suspicions. Suffice to say, I would oppose any disruption of *my realm*."

His composure once more in check, Hawk spoke in an even, yet ominous tone. "Tell us now; is Ellen in any danger, personally or in her capacity as Steward?"

Leanan sighed heavily. "I can only speculate. She is in no danger, in any capacity, from me. Lady Diere has ordered that no further attempts on her life be carried out. However, one would have to be very naïve to believe that Lady Diere does not plan some sort of manipulation strategy. She very much wants to control the Grand Portal in the Realm of Man."

Mark, who had been quietly listening, inquired further. "Lady Leanan, perhaps now you can tell us what you meant when, in the course of extending your offer of *hospitality*, you said that both our realms may be affected. What else are you aware of that has happened that may impact our home world?"

She paused before answering, as if organizing her thoughts.

"I do not know if you are aware, but with the death of Maude the Steward, the position she also held on the Council, the Chair of Man, is now vacant. The Dark Elves have proposed a native human as the representative of your realm, a man named George Papadolis."

"Papa George?" exclaimed Hawk. "That low-life *wise guy!* He's one indictment away from a prison cell! He's wanted right now for questioning in a *double murder* that I'm working. He's here? In this realm?"

"No, he is not here. He is most likely with Lady Diere in the Realm of the Dark Elves. It appears that he is to be her pawn. The Chair of Man could become the *swing vote* on the Council if he were under her control. Yes, this is exactly the sort of plot she would weave."

"Damn," Hawk muttered and turned to Mark and Ellen to explain. "We almost had Papa George! Well, the feds almost had him, when another crook, Fenton Brewster, was supposed to roll over on him. Now Brewster's dead, an apparent jailhouse suicide; but my gut doesn't buy it."

"Fenton Brewster did not take his own life," said Lady Leanan softly. "At the request of this man, George, Lady Diere ordered him killed."

"I see," said Mark, "and how is it that you know this, Lady Leanan?"

She smiled and folded her hands in her lap. "Salidar arranged it; I killed this Fenton Brewster on the rooftop of a building. I let his body fall to the street below. I was told that it was important that his body be found, otherwise I—"

"What?" Hawk interrupted. "You do realize, do you not, that aside from other offenses you have admitted, you have just confessed to *murder*?"

Leanan simply sighed and shook her head. "My dear Lord Hawk, I have killed many over the centuries; it is my nature. I tell you about this death because it appears to be relevant to matters at hand, and to demonstrate the scope of Lady Diere's intentions and treachery."

Hawk fumed. He now had the answers to open cases, solutions to crimes! Yet there wasn't a damn thing he could do about it. His mind raced, but he could fathom no pragmatic way to bring the perpetrator to justice. "Trey's never gonna believe this," he murmured.

Ellen heard him. She laid a comforting hand on his arm. "It's gonna be okay, somehow."

"Hawk, consider this," Mark suggested. "Lady Leanan could be considered a *cooperating witness* who could potentially negotiate immunity in exchange for exposing the overall conspiracy."

"Yeah, but," Hawk countered, "cooperating witnesses almost always have to *testify* in court against the co-conspirators. I just don't see that happening here."

"Well," remarked Ellen, "we are in a bit of a unique situation. And we're getting bogged down in legal issues that can be considered or debated later. Remember, our primary goal is to find Stacy. So, let's clear this other stuff up quickly and get back on point, shall we?"

"Right," Mark agreed, and looked to Hawk.

Hawk sulked in frustration, sighed, and bobbed his head.

"Lady Leanan," Ellen probed, "just to clarify, you said that Maude's death created the vacancy on the Council. So, she occupied the Chair of Man *and* she served as Steward?"

"That is correct," Leanan acknowledged. "You must understand that the two roles are entirely separate, not dependent upon one another."

"You knew her; in fact, you were friends, at least for a time." It was not a question.

Lady Leanan dropped her gaze and a sad smile slipped across her lips. She looked up at Ellen. "Yes, we were good friends, for longer than you can imagine."

"You've told us that Lady Diere covets the Stewardship, and I surmise through this man George, control of the Chair of Man, both of which were held by Maude." Ellen paused and leaned forward. "Did Lady Diere have anything to do with Maude's death?"

Lady Leanan responded in a cold voice tinged with equal parts anger and loss. "I have no proof; but neither have I any doubt."

His tone still cool, Hawk interjected, "Lady Leanan, do you know if George Papadolis had anything to do with Maude's death?"

"Again, my Lord Hawk, I have no proof, and yet, little doubt. Perhaps you can now see the depth of our concerns, in that Lady Diere would somehow upset the balance among our realms, and perhaps many others as well."

Mark nodded. "So, far more may be at risk than anyone knows."

The Sidhe raised her eyebrows. "Indeed, Counselor."

Lady Sabrina returned, but stayed by the door at a gesture from Lady Leanan, who went to her. They spoke so softly that none could hear.

"Hawk, are you okay?" Ellen whispered. "You got pretty angry."

"Yeah, sorry about that. But how do we know this *Lady Leanan's* not playing us? We never heard of her or *Lady Diere* before tonight. She's given us nothing that we can corroborate or refute at the moment."

"True, for now," agreed Mark. "Even if we assume she *is* playing us, what else can we do? We're here to find Stacy, right?"

"Right," Ellen agreed, "and Lady Leanan is giving us information that may be of use to us in our search. Hawk, you can check out the other information later, okay?"

Once Sabrina stepped back, Leanan knit her brow, pursed her lips, and nodded once to Sabrina. "I understand. You should return. I will join you shortly."

Leanan addressed Ellen. "Your perception, Lady Ellen, is indeed acute. There most certainly *is* a spell on the body of Boltar, a casting that has just been discovered by my mage. We now know that this *Boltar*, if that is his name, is not human. He is Were! This is an ominous development."

The companions knew not what to make of this.

Lady Leanan abruptly stood. "You must excuse me, the night flies and there is much that requires my immediate attention. Please enjoy my hospitality and get some rest. I will rejoin you at sunset."

As she departed the room, Hawk dropped his gaze to the pink scar tissue on the palm of his hand and muttered, "Hospitality—yeah, right."

CH 24

LADY LEANAN SWEPT INTO the torch-lit chamber in a swirl of black lace.

Lord Vlad and Lady Sabrina acknowledged her entrance with slight bows and downcast eyes. They stepped back from the rough table upon which the body of the innkeeper lay.

On the other side of the table, two figures in the dark red robes of the sorcerous arts bowed deeply; a tall grey man of advanced years, whose lined face bore a number of small tattoos, and an unmarked young man of slight stature, barely out of adolescence, yet clearly an acolyte to the aged adept.

Lady Leanan nodded to her favored senior mage. "Ah, Magus Jalash-el, what can you tell me?"

"With deepest respect, m'lady, I am certain that this body is ensorcelled, and has been for some time, years perhaps."

"Go on."

"I can identify the specific aspects of the spell, and speculate as to its intent, but . . . " He shrugged, hesitated, and chose his next words carefully. "I suspect that this spell was cast in such a way, almost as if it were *intended* to be easily discovered. I cannot be certain, of course."

Vlad, his impatience plain, scowled and interrupted. "Get on to the other spell! We don't have all night!"

"Other spell?" Leanan asked. "What *other* spell?"

"M'lady, if I may explain," the mage began. "There are *two* spells on this corpse. The first one, more easily apparent, holds the body in this form, a stasis spell. Common enough among the adepts of the Were, it is intended to prevent shape-shifting, whether the shift would be intentional or uncontrolled. The other casting is far more subtle and quite well hidden, a very comprehensive *mind-wipe* spell of arcane elfin origin."

Lady Leanan gestured to the body. "So, this individual is actually a Were. He has been bespelled to prevent his shape-shifting, to maintain this shape and appearance; and, his mind has been wiped. Very interesting. May we assume that 'Boltar' is not his true name?"

Magus Jalash-el was decidedly uncomfortable. "Ah, m'lady, therein lies a problem. Both spells are old, cast some years ago; yet, they are quite strong. The stasis spell is such that this corpse may not even decompose. But worse, this particular mind-wipe spell, if it is as I suspect, is among the darkest of the black arts. It robs the individual of his *true name,* possibly leaving the soul in thrall, at the mercy of the sorcery's author."

"So," Lady Sabrina reasoned, "this Were has been someone's puppet, *for years?* Who is responsible for this treachery? Is there any way of tracing the origin of these spells?"

Turning to face her, Jalash-el held his hands open in a gesture of frustration.

"We have indeed tried to do so, m'lady. We can identify, with relative certainty, that the stasis spell is of *Were* origin, and that the mind-wipe spell is of *Elfin* origin. However, that does *not* mean that the spell caster is of either race. We can find no trace of his hand, no way to identify the sorcerer. This is the work of a first-ranked mage, one who would have had the appropriate knowledge, the time for proper preparation, and the dark intent to perform such sorcery. I must point out that such knowledge is exceptionally rare. Even I, the Primus of Shadow Mages, could not cast such a deep mind-wipe spell. My acolytes could find no reference to a spell of this magnitude within our records and resources."

Lady Leanan raised a slim finger and pondered a point. "Jalash-el, you said that it appeared that the stasis spell was 'intended' to be discovered. Exactly what did you mean?"

"M'lady, I believe it would be no great task for a mage, or even an advanced apprentice, to recognize the stasis spell, or to identify this individual as a Were. However, the underlying mind-wipe spell is far too well hidden to even be suspected, much less found by most practitioners of our art. It was difficult enough for me to find. Therefore, I suspect the stasis spell was intended to be discovered; but the mind-wipe spell was not."

Lady Leanan frowned pensively, and finally gave voice to an ominous question. "Tell me truly, Magus, could a *necromancer* find the hidden spell, and perhaps learn of its caster?"

"N-Necromancer?" Jalash-el sputtered in shock. "M'lady, forgive me; you surprised me. As we all know, necromancy is forbidden throughout the Realms of the Council. As to your question, yes, it is possible that a necromancer *could* discover the existence of the spell, although he would have to be powerful indeed.

"However, he would learn nothing of its caster, because the corpse no longer has a *true name*. Without knowledge of the true name, a necromancer can hold only modest dominion over the dead, certainly insufficient to identify the original sorcerer. Now, if the necromancer were to deal with a corpse whose true name *were* known, all aspects of the deceased, to include the author of any attendant spells, even mere traces of sorcery, would be laid bare by the *Darkest Art*."

Lady Sabrina pondered this development. "So, if the mercenaries had returned to the Realm of the Dark Elves with this body, Queen Mab's necromancer would have discovered only that it is a Were without a true name?"

The old adept nodded. "Quite so, m'lady."

"Then Queen Mab would have grounds," concluded Vlad, "to accuse the Realm of the Were of participation in a treasonous conspiracy."

"Not only Were," cautioned Leanan, "but our home realm of Shadow as well. Have we not played an unwitting role in this *incident?* We have shed the blood of Dark Elves in open conflict this very night; the reason may not matter. Queen Mab's mage, Atrellan, escaped with that damned scroll! Who knows how he will spin his tale?"

The room grew quiet as the potential gravity of the situation became evident.

"M'lady, if I might ask a question?" begged Jalash-el.

At her nod, he continued.

"Is it confirmed that Queen Mab has a necromancer in her service? I knew there had been vague rumors, but nothing more than that. If it is true, I fear we must take certain precautions."

Leanan sighed. "Ah, Magus, I believe we have little choice but to treat such information as very likely to be true. I did not intend to keep this from you; it was thought to be only unfounded rumor. However, it is now fairly well confirmed by the two captured mercenaries, who survived the fight at the inn, but would choose death rather than return to Mab. We must assume there is some truth to these whispers of necromancy. So, yes, it would be wise to take appropriate precautions."

"At once, m'lady!" Jalash-el acknowledged and bowed briefly, but hesitated as something occurred to him. "M'lady, if I may? It may be most helpful if I were to question these two mercenaries further for more specific information about this necromancer. Would that be possible?"

Lady Leanan looked to Sabrina. "They still live, do they not?"

"Indeed, m'lady," Sabrina acknowledged. "They are held in the lower level dungeon. Their fate awaits your attention."

Lady Leanan nodded. "Magus, question them as you will; but waste no time. Lord Vlad will accompany you. You are to prepare our defensive measures and our specific precautions with due haste. We must be prepared for any eventuality."

Lord Vlad bowed and strode from the room.

Magus Jalash-el bowed deeply and followed the vampire lord. The silent acolyte scurried after his master.

Lady Sabrina was also about to depart, but Lady Leanan stopped her with an upraised finger.

"Sabrina, you've done well in this matter. I have a further task for you, but first seek out the captain of the guard and arrange for a guard on this corpse. I believe we have yet more to learn about this body. In half an hour, join me in my chambers and we will discuss this new task."

"As you wish, m'lady," said Sabrina, as she combined a delicate bow with a slight curtsy.

ALONE WITH THE CORPSE, Leanan stared at the pale slack-jawed face. But her mind contemplated another image, from another time and place; it sent a shudder the length of her spine.

Shambling grey forms in the night, staggering and shuffling, yet steadily making their inexorable way through a sick fog toward a sleeping village. The walking dead, empty of soul and free will, blindly enslaved by necromancy, were intent only upon slaying all within the unprepared hovels, their own unprotected families and kin; a chilling horror kept secret for millennia from all but a select few.

There had been no survivors that night.

Alerted to the imminent attack, two vampires of the early nobility, the lord and lady of that region, accompanied by a small band of their retainers to include some men-at-arms, had come rushing to the defense of their vassals, but to no avail.

The dead could neither be slain nor stopped; there were too many. Limbs hacked free by slashing swords still crept forward undeterred, inching and grasping.

A junior wizard among the retainers exhausted his repertoire of spells and incantations; nothing had any effect. Spent and defenseless, he perished in a pillar of malignant green fire that seemed to come from within his own body.

The lord and lady fought ferociously, laying corpses about them like splayed cordwood; but, the numbers were too great. The dead kept getting up, kept coming, and coming. The outnumbered defenders fought valiantly, but were ultimately overrun and torn apart, a fate from which not even the most resilient of the Nosferatu could recover.

It was a lesson that the most senior elders among the vampires of the Realm of Shadow would never forget.

Similar scenes of mind-numbing horror were repeated in almost every known realm before the aloof Dragon Lords deigned to intercede, and ruthlessly hunted the rogue necromancer, this self-proclaimed *Lord of the Dead.*

The necromancer was responsible for the deaths of thousands; victims who were in turn reanimated to slay more innocents, a self-perpetuating cycle of death and destruction. Evil incarnate roamed the realms, infecting all with fear and despair. It was a time of such terror, mistrust, and simmering panic that shook the very foundations of the alliance of realms. The crisis almost sundered the delicate balance of powers so assiduously maintained by the Council.

The Dragon Lords ultimately prevailed in a battle of epic proportions fought in their home realm, in which many of the soulless met oblivion. As for the dark necromancer, this *Lord of the Dead*, his identity and his fate were known only to the Dragon Lords. His seemingly senseless rampage stopped with his capture, and, as most speculated, his unconfirmed death.

Thereafter, the Dragon Lords insisted that the Council forbid the practice of necromancy in any realm within all spheres of Council influence. Compliance had been eager, complete, and consistent, at least insofar as Leanan knew.

Had been . . .

That thought gave her pause. The Dragon Lords had not been seen in over five hundred years; the Dragon Chair on the Council remained empty.

Did Mab, Queen of the Dark Elves, secretly flaunt the prohibition? And if I suspect so, might not others? Rumors abound. Would it not be foolish to ignore the potential danger?

It would be equally foolish to assume the Queen of Dark Elves was unaware that vampires have an enhanced aversion in particular for necromancy. Being *undead* renders them particularly sensitive, if not unduly *susceptible,* to its influence.

There was another twist; the recipient of the *Dark Gift*, a new vampire is thereafter only known and addressed by his or her *true name*.

What appeared to be an obvious vampiric vulnerability was in fact a counterintuitive, yet intrinsic, aspect of the Dark Gift, and a closely kept secret. Few knew that a null field would permeate the new vampire's true name, thus providing reasonably effective shielding from more common sorcery. Consequently, most spells directed at vampires, even the newest fledglings, through their true names, simply wouldn't work.

However, the dark sorcery of necromancy was another matter altogether.

Leanan frowned and considered the facts. It was no secret that most residents of the Council Realms were well aware that the knowledge of the true name of a person or thing is often an important element in crafting magic that will affect that person or thing. That is why, among other reasons, all vampires become reasonably accomplished magic users, to establish and maintain some form of metaphysical defense. Many, like herself, become quite powerful; some are so skilled as to be compared to *mage level adepts*.

However, notwithstanding the mastery of quite advanced sorcerous skills, none would *dare* to dabble in necromancy. It would invite—no, it would most likely guarantee, a horrible fate; possession by demonic entities, or worse. For it is well known among the wisest and most skilled of magic users, that there are dark forces beyond this time and place that would endeavor to take advantage of any such opportunistic opening, with potentially disastrous results.

Leanan heard approaching footsteps. She shook off the mantle of fear that had settled about her shoulders. Once more composed, she faced the door.

Two guards she had ordered stepped into the room and bowed to their mistress.

She acknowledged them as they took up their posts.

"Maintain your vigilance. No one touches the body."

"Yes, m'lady," they replied.

LEANAN MADE HER WAY to her chambers. Sabrina would be there within a few minutes, and there was yet one more person to consult before this night was done.

The twins were waiting for their mistress. Tending a small fire at the hearth, they rose and curtsied in unison at Leanan's entrance. Their twin shadows dipped and rose as one on the candle-lit walls like the trough and swell of a deep ocean wave.

"M'lady, if you please . . . "

". . . the Lady Sabrina waits without . . . "

". . . at your request, she so advises."

"Shall we bring refreshment?"

Lady Leanan thought for a moment, and considered how much of the moribund night remained. She could not afford to linger too long with Sabrina; they would forgo any refreshment for the moment.

"No, send her in, and leave us. Return to me within the hour, before the dawn."

They bowed silently and filed from the room.

Lady Sabrina glided in as the door closed quietly behind her. Leanan gestured to the tapestried chairs by the hearth, and they both sat by the small flickering fire.

"How may I serve you, m'lady?" inquired Sabrina politely.

"Oh, I think you may enjoy this task, my dear." Lady Leanan smiled as she settled more comfortably in her chair and smoothed an errant thread back into the woven cloth of the armrest. "You are, of course, aware of our three guests from the Realm of Man; Lady Ellen the Steward, Lord Hawk, and the Counselor, are you not?"

"Of course, m'lady," Sabrina responded with a smile that suggested she saw where this was going.

"As you know," confided a grinning Leanan, "I have had occasion to taste Lord Hawk; he consequently bears my mark. But this *Counselor* is unknown to me; and, I would know more about him. He admits to having slain Damien the Cursed; and I sense the truth of that. So, we must assume that he is potentially dangerous. But I also know that he is human and a man. So, I want you to *taste* and *mark* him. *Seduce* him if you like; make him yours. Do you understand?"

"Absolutely, m'lady," Sabrina, smiling eagerly, assured her mistress. "Do you think Damien may have tried to mark him?"

"No. I think Damien, ever the fool, meant to slay him," Leanan reasoned. "But that is moot; any such marking would vanish with Damien's true death. Of course, I hope you are more successful."

"Of course, m'lady," Sabrina snickered. "But, did you not pledge that no harm would come to them while they are your guests?"

Lady Leanan smirked. "I did indeed. Surely he would not consider any harm in a little seduction, now would he? Would any man? I understand that in some cultures, it may be considered the *height of hospitality*. But be careful; do nothing that might antagonize the Lady Ellen. Indeed, a seduction may be the best strategy."

Sabrina burst into a positively coquettish laugh, laced with just a hint of lust. "Oh, m'lady, this is indeed a task I shall enjoy! It has been ages since I tasted such a one from the Realm of Man. How soon would you like him wrapped around my finger?"

"Oh, that shall be at your discretion. You can be such a wanton tart," Leanan teased. "I think we have some time, a few days perhaps. I doubt that we shall find Salidar still in Shadow; he likely took their friend with him. That should mean at least two days of searching. Surely, that is sufficient time. Of course, if you are that eager, there is almost an hour of darkness left this night."

Sabrina grinned widely, a predatory gleam in her eyes and the tips of her canines emerging. "Why, m'lady, I am never one to waste such an opportunity; and as you say, there is almost an hour left to this night. By your leave, I shall be about my task."

Leanan laughed and waved a hand in dismissal. "Go then. Try not to enjoy this task too much."

"Ha-ha! We shall see, m'lady, we shall see." Sabrina giggled as she rose to take her leave. She tugged at the bodice of her saffron gown, emphasizing her cleavage. With a last nod and wry smile for Lady Leanan, Sabrina spun about, flared skirt billowing, and departed.

As the door closed, Leanan felt her smile fade. While she enjoyed Sabrina's company, the lightness of the moment they had just shared waned as the more ominous portents of this night clamored for her attention.

LEANAN PREPARED HERSELF for her final task. She went to her bedchamber, and sat upon a large cushion in an alcove. Assuming a position of meditation, she closed her eyes, opened her mind, and composed her plea.

... Lamia, Mother of Night, it is I, Leanan of the Sidhe, your Celtic daughter, hear me, Mother.

... I hear you, Daughter ... Again you seek my counsel as the night wanes. Share with me your concerns—quickly for the hour is late.

... Too true, Mother ... I invite you into my mind, that you may know what I know, and see as I have seen.

... Prepare yourself ... I come.

Leanan's mind was flooded with the familiar and powerful presence. All that she was and knew was laid bare. For long moments Leanan struggled to remain placid and receptive. This was an invasive violation of self that she tolerated at great cost to her ego and pride. However, the protection of her realm was a most powerful motivation; so, she acquiesced. Soon enough, it was over; she was drained, almost listless.

The spectral voice of Lamia echoed in her mind.

... These are disturbing developments, indeed. It is likely that a far more sinister plot is afoot than you suspect, Daughter. The throne of the Dark Elves may indeed be in jeopardy, from within as well as without. That "Boltar" is a Were is intended to focus suspicion on that realm, and that the "conspiracy" is discovered here in Shadow is equally accusatory. The shedding of elfin blood is a further complication. As you know, the Lady Diere is certainly capable of orchestrating such treachery—and Queen Mab herself is not above crafting such a scenario in order to create circumstances to rid herself of a rival or threat. The thought of a necromancer in her service is indeed cause for concern. Do not overlook that it is entirely possible that a genuine coup attempt by one of the elfin Houses is underway; remember that "Boltar" was the name of a rebel elf who unsuccessfully challenged Mab for the throne over two centuries ago. Use of this name is no coincidence.

. . . Mother, I do remember. He was slain, was he not?

. . . True, Daughter. However, I suspect that other events are developing much more quickly than we may know. Above all, we must resist being drawn into any conflict among the Elves—neutrality is our path. Whoever is spinning this web of intrigue will likely have to take a more active role soon. I suspect that someone may come with an offer or request that would serve to further involve us. Beware—that being has likely already betrayed someone, and would assuredly betray us as well. However, we are in a very strong position to negotiate, for you now hold the Steward of the Realm of Man and her associates.

. . . Mother, they are my "guests" and I have pledged that no harm would befall them while they enjoy that status.

. . . Indeed? Does that include your sending Sabrina to "taste and mark" one of the Steward's party?

. . . A small strategic tactic, Mother. No real harm would come to him.

. . . I will not debate your ethics, Daughter, do what you must. But do not think that your presumed honor supersedes your obligation to defend our realm. Until we are better prepared to deal with whatever is happening, you will hold the Steward and her associates as your prisoners—guests, if you prefer. Treat them well, keep them safe—but hold them you must!

. . . I understand, Mother. It is late and the sunrise will be upon us. We both must rest.

. . . Of course, Daughter. Consult with me when you have learned more.

With that thought, the rapport was broken. Leanan stood, a bit unsteadily, and stepped to her bed. She gripped a bedpost as she sat heavily upon the mattress.

Seeking her mother's guidance at this time may not have been the wisest move. Lamia's command—no, her *suggestion,* was not a good development. Keeping the Steward and her friends as hostages or prisoners would surely backfire. She would have to think about this. In fact, she would *sleep* on it;

a new night would be here soon enough. She rationalized that she could do nothing about it now, for daybreak would be upon the land. She would let her subconscious mind mull over the issue as she took her rest; a rather passive yet effective technique of problem resolution she had perfected over the millennia.

As she found comfort in her decision, the twins swept into her chambers to make the preparations for her repose. She allowed her mind to wander as the twin familiars went about their routine, but a sudden thought intruded and prompted a question.

"Has the Lady Sabrina retired for the day?"

The twins looked at one another and shrugged identical shoulders.

"We know not for certain, m'lady, for . . . "

". . . she went to arrange a meeting with the Counselor, and . . . "

". . . Gunther told us . . . "

". . . that she was not to be disturbed . . . "

". . . unless summoned by your ladyship. So . . . "

". . . do you wish to do so, m'lady?"

Leanan considered aborting Sabrina's mission for only a brief moment.

"No, I think not."

So be it. Let us see how this plays out.

IN AN OPEN SITTING area to one side of the Great Hall, the Lady Sabrina was becoming quite frustrated. She had spent the last forty-five minutes in what she thought was stimulating conversation that literally dripped with *innuendos and double entendres*, being as provocative and flirtatious as she dared, and she hadn't yet gotten inside the Counselor's bedchamber.

At her request, Gunther had roused Mark from a sound sleep under some pretense that a lady needed some immediate advice.

Sabrina had no way of knowing that Mark would read Gunther's true intentions so readily.

Begging a few moments to dress, Mark had insisted on meeting the *lady* in the open reception area of the Great Hall rather than in his chambers.

Sabrina hadn't thought that would even matter. Such confidence had she in her wiles, that she didn't even consider the location a challenge. She would deftly render him as eager as a besotted youth, a quivering moth to her enticing flame, thoroughly ensnared in her lustful web, and panting in his bed, in no time at all. It was what vampires did best.

He was maddeningly polite, and listened attentively; but, he asked *so many damned questions!* And she had to answer his each and every inquiry with such a façade of sincerity that she thought her face would crack. She couldn't even clearly remember the details of the fiction she'd initially spun to get him to see her in the first place. She was losing her patience. *Seduction be damned! I am ready to tear his throat out!*

She was near her breaking point when Gunther appeared, and knelt before her.

"M'lady, you asked me to keep you apprised of the hour."

She glanced up at the eastern windows, and was shocked to see the first gray hints of a pale dawn.

Mark noted the quickening of the day with feigned surprise. He stood—no, practically *jumped,* as she gracefully rose to take her leave.

"I regret that I must retire, dear Counselor. I found your company quite *interesting*. I so look forward to *finishing* our conversation, after sunset."

"I cannot imagine how the time slipped away. This was so *stimulating*." Mark gallantly executed a small bow. "Until this evening, then."

She smiled delicately, but embers of frustrated anger flared in her eyes.

Mark smiled blandly in return.

She flounced from the hall with Gunther in her wake.

MAINTAINING A BLASÉ expression, Mark made his way back to his chambers; but, he didn't enter. Instead, he went on to Ellen's door, glanced up and down the deserted hallway, and knocked softly. To his surprise, she responded almost instantly.

"Who is it?"

"El', it's me, Mark. We gotta talk."

The door opened and he slipped in.

"What's wrong? Oh man, what time is it?" asked Ellen, still fully dressed and looking like she hadn't slept a wink.

"It's late, or maybe early. Did you get any sleep?"

"Not really," she groaned, stifling a yawn. She pointed to the two wooden chairs facing the fireplace. "Sit. Now, tell me what's wrong."

"I think we need to get out of here." He described Sabrina's attempted seduction, and his chilling interpretation of her motivation and intentions.

"Oh, hell no! That bitch!" Ellen spat and winced. "Uh, sorry. Seriously? No way you're gonna be alone with her again! We gotta come up with a better strategy, something that gets us all outta here. We gotta think; there's some things I've learned and I think I understand better now." She paused, fighting a yawn but losing. "Ahhhh-umph! Sorry, look, bear with me. I wanted to read more of the journal, and I'm glad I did. Although, I gotta admit time got away from me; I pretty much read through the night." Ellen glanced at the balcony doors. "I can see daylight starting." Shifting in her chair, she moaned. "Oof, oh man, I'm stiff."

Mark nodded in sympathy. "I wish we had some coffee."

Ellen scoffed. "Hmmph, me, too."

Mark opened his palms, "So, about Sabrina?"

"Yeah, that's a problem we gotta deal with now. We need to tell Hawk about this."

"Yeah, the sooner, the better." Mark stood. "I'll go next door and get him. You just sit tight. I'll be right back."

MINUTES LATER MARK returned, with a sleepy-eyed Hawk in tow.

"Morning . . . So, what's up?" Hawk mumbled, and then noticed that Mark's injured arm was free. "No sling? How's the shoulder?"

Mark rotated his elbow in a small circle, wincing slightly. "It's better, more stiff than sore. I think the more I use it, the quicker it'll be back to normal. Come to think of it, it does seem to be healing at a pretty good rate. My wrist is healing quickly, too."

"Let's sit by the fire," Ellen suggested, pulling another chair closer. "We've got a lot to tell you."

Just as they got settled around the hearth, a knock sounded at Ellen's door. Before she could answer, the door swung open and the twin servants filed into the room bearing silver trays with mugs of hot coffee, a full carafe, and crystal cruets of honey and cream.

The twins served the coffee, then stood side by side and spoke, each finishing the other's sentences.

"It was noticed that you had risen . . . "

". . . and gathered in the Lady Ellen's chambers. "

"Should you care to take morning refreshment . . . "

"... here, with the Lady Ellen ... "

"... you might find the view from the balcony ... "

"... stimulating and ..."

"... appropriate for ..."

"... conversation. You may find ... "

"... the coffee more bracing ..."

"... in the clear air."

They bowed in unison, and asked together, "Is there anything further you require?"

Ellen looked to Mark and Hawk; both shook their heads.

Ellen locked eyes with the twins. "No, and thank you."

The twins smiled, turned, and left the room, softly closing the door behind them.

Mark started to speak, but Ellen stopped him with a finger to her lips. Standing, she went to the balcony, opened the doors and, mug in hand, stepped outside into the grey morning.

She stood on a wide stone platform girded by a low balustrade, suspended at least sixty feet above a sheer drop into a murk-filled moat that belched bubbles of noxious gas. Twisted boles of stunted trees sat like squat warts on the opposite bank. Above her, the rough stone wall of the castle soared to crenelated battlements, weatherworn and snaggletoothed, in an obvious state of disrepair. A hunched stone gargoyle sat on a crumbling cornice of the eroding remnants of a former watchtower.

Motioning for Mark and Hawk to join her, she smiled when she saw that Hawk brought the tray with the carafe and cruets. "I think," Ellen said softly, "we were just told that it's safe to talk out here—you follow me?"

"Yeah, some *clear air*," mumbled Hawk, wrinkling his nose, as he placed the tray down on a wide section of the balustrade. "But can we trust them? Mark, did you *get* anything?"

"Nah, not really, but I didn't think to try to probe until they turned to go. It was just a glimpse, but I didn't sense anything ill-intended. I think we're okay."

Ellen and Hawk nodded and shrugged; it would just have to do.

"But, El," Mark cautioned, "what about what you and I already talked about, you know, before I woke Hawk up?"

She hefted her mug and smirked wryly. "You mean besides wishing we had some coffee? Yeah, I suspect we were overheard—which is probably why it was suggested that we have any further conversations out here."

"So," Mark deduced, "we were overheard, and subsequently warned?"

"Yeah, I think so." She glanced back toward the room. "We can only hope the wrong people didn't hear us."

"Why do I feel," asked Hawk as he stretched his arms over his head and yawned, "ahhuuhhh, um, like I've got some catching up to do?"

"Because you do, *Sleeping Beauty*," Ellen teased. "But I don't think here and now is the time and place to get into details. So, just listen and I'll synopsize."

"All right," he grunted, and sipped his coffee.

"Lady Sabrina tried to *seduce* Mark in order to *mark* him—unsuccessfully, of course. We need to get out of here, soon, before the vampires are up and around after sunset."

"Definitely!" Mark exclaimed.

"Now listen," Ellen urged. "I've read a great deal more of the journal and I think I can do a lot more than I've done so far. But like I said, I'm not going into details, not now. Although what I should tell you now is that this castle is warded, I mean protected by some very old magic that prevents certain spells from working. If someone were to try, well, it wouldn't be good."

Mark winced. "Jeez, what next? Wards? Old magic? Vampires wanting to suck my blood or seduce and mark me? I'm sorry; I guess I'm still acclimating to all this. Is this the new normal for us?"

"Seriously, Mark? In spite of what we've seen and been through," Ellen asked, not unkindly, "you still harbor doubts?"

"No, not really." He sighed heavily. "I know it's real, at least here, and now. Oh, don't mind me; I'm adjusting the best I can. This is a real paradigm shift for me. So be it; it is what it is." He opened his palms and shrugged. "So, how do we get out of here?"

"What about one of those transit globe things?" asked Hawk, sipping more of his coffee. "Would that work?"

"No!" Ellen grimaced. "*Especially* not a transit spell! And there's a complication; if we are named by our hostess as *hostages* or *prisoners*, then we have to be granted permission to leave, or else we can't pass the threshold of any outer door."

"That sounds kinda familiar," Mark mused aloud. "In medieval times, to end wars, strife, or a serious dispute between feudal lords, they would exchange *hostages,* noble blood relatives—sons, daughters, nephews, nieces and such, pledged to live in the households of the opposing lords. This was supposed to ensure the *good behavior* of the feudal lords."

"Did it work?" asked Hawk.

"Well, sometimes. Of course, that all depends on how you define success," Mark began, warming to his response. "For example, the practice was far more widespread among diverse cultures than modern scholars initially thought. It was an early precursor to formalized treaties, in fact—"

"All right already!" sputtered Hawk. "I've only had one cup of coffee! Jeez! A simple *yes* or *no* would suffice. I'll bet this is what you did to Sabrina—buried her in rhetoric!"

Mark grinned. "You're right! She'd obviously never dealt with a twenty-first-century litigator. But I really don't want to encounter her again—ever, if I can help it."

"I'm having second thoughts about anyone here actually helping us find Stacy," Ellen admitted.

"I know what you mean," agreed Mark. "There are threats here we didn't anticipate."

"Right! So, we need to depart this castle today," reminded Ellen, "while we're still considered *guests.* I doubt we'll be so well treated after sundown."

Mark shivered involuntarily. "I don't even want to think about it."

She shook her head and sighed. "We need to be away from here."

"About those wards," Mark asked, "why didn't they seem to have any effect on my sensing intentions?"

"Good question, Mark. I think the wards don't really impact you because the *sensing* you can do is basically *passive;* and, I suspect proximity may be a factor. I'd bet that the wards are intended to prevent an *active* attempt at spell casting."

"Okay, I guess that would make sense," Mark allowed. "So, if you were to try to summon a transit globe, then that would be an active attempt, and trigger some negative response?"

"Oh yeah, like I said—big time! We can't chance it. I'm pretty sure the only way we can safely leave here is to walk out—no transiting tricks."

Mark nodded. "Hey, that's fine by me—so long as we're leaving."

Hawk swirled his coffee and drained his mug in a long gulp. “Okay, so departure as soon as possible. I’m game.”

Mark stared into his mug and mumbled to himself. “Me too, the sooner, the better.”

“Getting away from here is only part of the problem,” she reminded them, staring out across the forsaken landscape. “We still have to find Stacy.”

Each wrestling with the issues at hand, they almost didn’t hear the urgent knock on the chamber door.

The twins immediately entered and went directly to the balcony.

“Beg your pardons, m’lady, m’lords . . . ”

“. . . for this intrusion, but . . . ”

“. . . a patrol has arrived, and . . . ”

“. . . they bring a woman . . . ”

“. . . found at the edge of . . . ”

“. . . the Forest of the Damned . . . ”

“. . . who claims to be . . . ”

“ . . . the Lady Stacy. So . . . ”

“. . . would you please come . . . ”

“. . . to the Great Hall?”

CH 25

THEY WASTED NO TIME in getting to the Great Hall, where they found a small crowd of people milling about in a state of excitement. Half a dozen guardsmen in mailed armor stood in a close semicircle around a tall older man garbed in a red robe who was arguing with Gunther, the Lady Sabrina's familiar.

There was no sign of Stacy.

The twins stepped forward and the room grew quiet.

Mark could not help but notice that the other servants, even the guardsmen, deferred to the twins in a subtle way. They clearly enjoyed some level of status in this castle, perhaps due to their proximity to the Lady Leanan. *Hmm, familiars?*

The twins addressed the red-robed man.

"Magus Jalash-el, if you please . . . "

". . . this is the Lady Ellen, Lord Hawk . . . "

". . . and the Counselor. They . . . "

". . . seek the Lady Stacy."

The mage turned from a scowling Gunther—a clear indication that their argument was far from resolved, and bowed to Ellen.

"Ah, m'lady, m'lords, I bid you a good morning. The patrol found a woman on the edge of the Forest of the Damned and brought her here. She rests in a chamber beyond."

"Where?" demanded Mark. "Is she all right? I must see her!"

"Of course, m'lord, but I must caution you," warned the mage. "It appears that she has been bespelled; her memory is clouded. I will take you to her."

Gunther plucked the sleeve of Jalash-el's robe and hissed, "Magus, I warn you! Keep her isolated and confined for—"

"Enough!" spat the mage. "Do not interfere with me—lest you would invite the wrath of my mistress!"

Jalash-el turned from Gunther, and missed the murderous glare directed at his back.

However, Mark and Hawk noticed.

The mage gestured solicitously, and stepped toward a narrow hallway. "M'lady, m'lords, if you would be kind enough to follow me, please?"

At the end of the dimly lit short corridor, the mage's acolyte and a man-at-arms stood vigil before a chamber, its door slightly ajar with morning light suffused around its edge. The acolyte smiled and bowed at the approach of his master; the man-at-arms merely nodded perfunctorily and stepped aside.

As Jalash-el gently pushed open the door to the small chamber, the glare of grey daylight streaming through a large mullioned window was sufficient to cause everyone to momentarily squint.

And there, seated on a divan, was Stacy absently stroking the large gray cat in her lap. She appeared to be staring into nothingness, a confused and displaced expression clouding her face. It seemed to take a moment for her to realize that the door had opened and a number of smiling faces were pushing into the room.

Her countenance cleared of confusion as recognition flooded her wide eyes. She leapt to her feet, gracelessly spilling Smokey to the floor. In an instant she was in Mark's arms, holding him fiercely as he enveloped her in an impassioned embrace.

"I was so scared," he whispered, "that just when I'd found you, I might lose you."

"You didn't," she murmured, squeezing ever tighter, "and you won't."

Oblivious to the others in the room, they kissed.

The mage's eyebrows shot up, and with a twinkle in his eye, he remarked, "I take it that this woman is indeed your missing friend, as she claims to be? Oh, do forgive an old man; I so enjoy stating the obvious."

Ellen just smiled, and Hawk smiled at her. She stooped, unwound Smokey from her ankles, and scooped him up in her arms. He began to purr strongly, a deep and soothing vibration that was audible to those around them.

Everyone started asking questions all at once, but Stacy just held up her hand as she and Mark disentangled.

"Hold on—I'm fine. I just don't remember a whole lot, before these soldiers found me and Smokey near the forest and brought us here. They said that my *friends* were looking for me; I figured it *had* to be you all. Thanks, you guys, for coming for me."

"M'lady, as I explained a few moments ago," admonished Jalash-el, "you appear to be the victim of a *forget spell*, a deliberate effort to cloud your recent memory. If you would answer a few more questions, I may be able to help recover that which is obscured."

Even though Stacy nodded, Mark picked up on her reluctance to cooperate; but, he said nothing as the mage asked a number of questions. He sensed that Jalash-el meant well. However, something else was slightly off balance, *out of sync*.

Then Mark noticed Gunther in the shadow of the doorway, unseen by the mage. Gunther was brooding; but, he seemed to be somewhat in awe of Stacy. Mark did not understand *why;* but it made him uncomfortable. Gunther's intentions were muddled; but some things were clear. He was particularly anxious about that evening's coming sunset, and would do anything to prevent the four companions from leaving.

"So, this man, Salidar, led you from the inn just as the fight started," repeated Jalash-el. "That is the last thing you clearly remember?"

"Yes, sir." Stacy nodded affirmatively, "Uh, that is, until the soldiers found me. I'm sorry I can't be of more help." She leaned into Mark and sighed tiredly. "If that's all, I'd like to go home now."

"No! No one leaves!" shouted Gunther, pushing into the room. "You will remain here until my lady awakens!"

Magus Jalash-el drew himself up to his full height and glared down at Gunther with disdain. "Be silent, you besotted fool! You command nothing here! These people are the guests of the Lady Leanan, and may depart at their leisure. Have you information to the contrary? No? Very well then, keep to your place, *servant*!"

Gunther started to protest, "No, I—"

"Silence!" demanded the mage. He turned to the doorway and called out, "Captain of the Guard! Attend me, please."

Seconds later, a grizzled middle-aged man of medium height and enormous shoulders, whose tunic bore the insignia of a guard captain, appeared at the door.

"Ah, there you are," exclaimed the mage. "Tell me, please, is it your understanding that these people were named *guests* by the Lady Leanan?"

"Indeed so, Magus, as to these three persons." The captain then gestured to Stacy. "However, this lady arrived this morning with the returning patrol; so, I am unaware of her status."

"She is a *wood nymph!* She must be held!" screamed Gunther, smashing his fist into his palm. "I demand it!"

The captain looked askance at Gunther, the familiar visibly quivering with anger. A trace of mild disgust fleetingly slipped across the guard commander's face at this blatant lack of control.

"Indeed? You *demand* it?" The stoic captain repeated. "You have no standing to make such demands, absent a crime accused. What crime has she committed?"

Jalash-el spoke softly, an obvious counterpoint to Gunther's emotional outburst. "She has committed *no* crime or offense. She has more likely been a *victim* of some sort. Even if it were true that she is a *wood nymph,* that is neither crime nor offense. She is free to go, as are Lady Leanan's *guests*. To interfere would breach the rules and customs of hospitality, and no doubt incur the wrath of her ladyship. Am I not correct, Captain?"

"Quite so, Magus, quite so," the captain agreed. "Were someone to interfere with her ladyship's rules, why then, her ladyship's guard would have to step in and take *appropriate* action."

"Gunther," soothed the mage, "may I suggest that you retire to your lady's chambers and await her awakening. Perhaps *she* will find a need for your service."

Gunther bristled at the old man's condescension. However, at the stiffening of the captain's posture and the malice in his grin, Gunther withdrew from the room.

The mage mumbled under his breath "*. . . damned insufferable toady!*"

The captain chuckled. "You know, Magus, there may be not that much we agree on. But when it comes to that *self-important sycophant,* we are comrades-in-arms to be sure."

"Too true, Captain, too true," Jalash-el agreed. "Best beware. Should the Lady Sabrina ever bestow upon him the *Dark Gift,* as he is fond of hinting that she has so promised, then there will be hell to pay."

"Aye, Magus, there is that," the captain acknowledged as he departed the room, his hand dropping to the hilt of his short sword in an unconscious gesture of reassurance.

Ellen stepped forward. "Magus Jalash-el, we deeply appreciate your help, and that of the patrol in finding and returning our friend to us. But it is now imperative that we return to our own realm and our own obligations. I understand that it is not possible to personally thank our hostess at this hour, so may I ask that you convey our deepest gratitude? If she has any questions, or if we may be of further assistance, she is welcome to visit with me. If there are no other matters before us, by your leave, we will be on our way."

Magus Jalash-el, obviously quite pleased with her overt display of courtesy, bowed to Ellen.

"Lady Ellen, it has been my pleasure to be of assistance. I shall, of course, be honored to convey your kind words to the Lady Leanan. You may prepare your departure immediately, if you wish. Will you require an escort? Oh, forgive me! Of course, the Steward would have no need of such. Perhaps some travel provisions from the kitchens?"

"Thank you, but no," she declined, picking up Smokey, "that won't be necessary. We'll just return to our chambers for our things, and be on our way."

"Very well, m'lady," he acknowledged as he stepped to one side, sweeping his arm toward the open door. "I shall leave word at the front gate that your departure is imminent."

AS THEY PROCEEDED TO their rooms, Ellen softly reminded, "Quiet now; no conversation until we're free of the castle."

Stacy accompanied Mark to his room, an arrangement that was obviously just fine with him.

Ellen stuffed her few clothes and the journal in her backpack and slipped the spectacles into their pouch. Pausing, she took one last look around the room; something told her to leave nothing behind, not even a strand of hair.

She turned slowly about and was surprised to find the twins standing there; yet the only door remained closed.

Smokey leapt off the bed and promptly wound himself around their ankles in sinuous figure-eights. Before Ellen could ask a question, the twins pointed to the balcony and stepped outside.

Ellen scooped up Smokey and whispered, "You trust them, too, don't you?"

Smokey just purred contentedly.

Ellen stepped onto the balcony and Smokey slipped from her arms. He walked to the twins, sniffed each, and sat down between them. He looked directly at Ellen, and then began preening his fur, totally at ease.

Ellen accepted Smokey's behavior as his vote of trust. She nodded to the twins, prepared to listen.

"Waste no time . . . "

". . . in putting distance . . . "

". . . between yourselves and . . . "

". . . this castle. Expect to be followed, so . . . "

". . . cast no spell . . . "

" . . . within sight of this castle. Depart this realm . . . "

". . . at your earliest convenience. This . . . "

". . . conversation . . . "

". . . never happened."

Without another word, the twins filed back into the room leaving Ellen and Smokey alone on the balcony.

Ellen did not hear the door to the chamber open or close. When she stepped into the room, it was empty; the twins were gone. She glanced around as she shouldered her backpack. She saw no obvious means, other than the closed door, by which the twins could have left the chamber. That amused her.

Old castles just ought to have mysteries, like secret passageways. Too bad I don't have the time to poke around.

PULLING THE STOUT DOOR open, she found Hawk, Mark and Stacy quietly waiting in the outer hall. Of course, none of them had seen the twins.

Together they made their way down to the Great Hall and out through the reception area. Ellen kept looking for the twins, but saw no trace. A number of servants were scurrying about on various routine tasks, and several guards were at their posts; but no one paid them any undue attention.

As they crossed the open courtyard and came to the gatehouse, the two guards on duty snapped to attention. The portcullis slowly ascended like the teeth of a great predator reluctant to release its prey.

The companions strode across the heavy drawbridge and walked out upon the road unhindered; but they could feel the weight of eyes upon their backs. Ellen urged them to maintain a leisurely pace until they rounded a low hill studded with gnarled trees and thorny bushes. At least there they were no longer in sight of the castle.

Hawk nudged Ellen. "Hold up. We have a tail. Uh, I mean, we're being followed."

"I know. I was told to expect it—don't ask. I don't think we're anywhere close to safe yet. Let's keep moving and pick up the pace. We need to find a secluded spot, a safe spot, so I can try something."

"Yeah? Like what?" Mark asked, glancing over his shoulder, trying to appear casual despite his growing sense of unease.

"Something new—don't ask. I'll explain later. Let's go."

"Well, in the meantime," asked Hawk, matching her pace, "could you do your other thing? See who's on our trail?"

"I already did when we stopped; it's Gunther."

"Damn," groaned Mark, without breaking his stride. "That's *her* boy. This is not good."

"And just who is *her?*" inquired Stacy, with a touch of *pique* in her voice.

Mark asked, "Uh, Ellen, can we talk openly yet?"

Ellen shook her head. "No, not yet. Keep moving. We need more distance from the castle."

"What? Why?" asked Stacy. "Do you think someone can hear us or something?"

Ellen just nodded affirmatively. "Yeah, or something like that. See where the road goes into a wooded area in another mile or so? Let's hold off on any conversation until we get among the trees. Come on, follow me."

SOON ENOUGH, THEY ENTERED the shaded woods; and Ellen felt considerably more comfortable. The road wound through the trees in a serpentine path. The trees here had grown much closer to the edge of the road; their interlocking limbs created a thick leafy roof overhead.

Smokey had taken to trotting a few paces ahead of the group. He turned toward a faint game trail and paused to look over his shoulder at Ellen.

She stopped, holding up a closed fist as she had seen Hawk do to indicate *stop and hold your position*. She cast her perception about and found at least five other people in their vicinity. With a quick gesture she called the group together and whispered, "We have company—five, including Gunther. Mark, can you?"

Mark paused for a moment in concentration, and sighed in frustration. "Damn! They're not yet close enough for me to read clearly; but, there's no doubt that they're hostile."

"Hostile? Now wait a minute," Stacy insisted, wagging a finger at Mark. "How did you do that? I know Ellen can sense energy; so, now you can *read* people?"

Chagrined, Mark shrugged. "Uh, sort of; I'll explain later."

Hawk looked around quickly, scanning the surrounding area. "I don't see anything that would offer a tactical advantage. This is not good; we're too exposed on the road. We need to move into the trees and find a defensible position."

"I can help with that," said Stacy, as she walked to the nearest large tree and laid her hands upon its broad trunk.

The others just looked on in stunned silence as her face took on a serene expression and, after a moment, a mischievous smile. She murmured her thanks to the tree and returned to her friends, scooping Smokey up in her arms.

"There's a small clearing and a narrow stream about two hundred yards down the little path Smokey stopped at—smart cat!" Stacy smiled as she scratched behind his ears. "But, it's a popular ambush site; predators often lie in wait for animals to come and drink. A bear sleeps nearby, having eaten heavily from a deer kill yesterday evening. Other predators, and prey, are staying away—it's a *big* bear."

Mark gaped. "What? How did you—"

Stacy let Smokey slip to the ground and fixed Mark with a wry smirk. "Oh, I'll explain later."

Her concern obvious, Ellen asked, "Stacy, are you all right?"

"Maybe Gunther is right; I *am* a wood nymph. Oh, I'm teasing; I'm fine!"

Hawk tested the wind, and grinned. "Okay, we can make the clearing Stacy told us about work for us. Let's—"

"Work for us?" Ellen blurted. "She said there's a bear—a big bear!"

"Yeah, asleep," Hawk countered. "Let's not wake it. Follow me, quietly."

Hawk went to a bush just inside the game trail and deliberately tore a broad leaf and bent its stem; it was easily seen from the road. He considered his handiwork for a few seconds and silently started down the path; the others followed.

A SHORT TIME LATER, the group sat hunched in the thick brush at the edge of the clearing. Hawk had taken great pains to stay downwind of the clearing, but such a capricious breeze could be unpredictable. The scent of the deer kill was obvious, so staying downwind was relatively easy; but, they didn't know for certain where the bear slept.

Hawk thought they might be safe hunkered down here. After all, they couldn't keep moving around; they'd either stumble across the sleeping bruin or make enough noise to wake him.

Suddenly, Hawk realized that the forest had gone quiet and the breeze had died. He quickly motioned *climbing* to the others and they immediately ascended nearby trees. Hawk found a tree to climb as well, but he stayed on the lower branches to observe the clearing.

TWO MEN, ARMED WITH simple bows and clad in rough homespun cloaks, appeared on the edge of the clearing, about ten yards apart. They signaled to their rear; two more men, similarly attired but armed with spears, entered the clearing from the game path and split up, each following the tree line to the right and left respectively. They kept glancing at the ground as they scanned the underbrush warily. The two bowmen, with arrows notched and ready, watched the spearmen's slow progress as they looked for tracks.

There was a sudden crunching *thud!* One of the archers was flung into the air and out into the clearing. The hapless man lay unmoving in a crumpled heap, his spine twisted at an impossible angle. His eyes darted to and fro, frantically aware, yet completely helpless.

A huge bear charged into the clearing, reared to its full height and roared its angry indignation. It spied the two spearmen, dropped to all fours, and feigned a charge at one. However, the bear spun with lightning quickness and ran down the other spearman who had dropped his weapon and turned to run.

When the bear turned to face the remaining spearman, its gaping jaws dripped with bright blood. It roared a challenge and wagged its massive head side to side, casting crimson spittle in graceless arcs.

The spearman grimly stood his ground, bracing for the bear's imminent attack.

The bear again reared upright, sniffed the air, and suddenly dropped to all fours.

An arrow zipped past, narrowly missing its shoulder.

Furious, the maddened bruin charged the remaining archer, who paled and fumbled in vain for another arrow.

It was over in an instant.

The lone spearman took advantage of the opportune distraction and fled the clearing. He got no further than the tree line when he suddenly stiffened and fell back, a crossbow quarrel sprouting from his chest.

Having seen the fleeing man fall, the bear shambled over to the body. Sniffing the dead man, the massive bruin lost interest and turned back toward the clearing. Reaching the center, it stood up and scented the wind once again.

A slight breeze had picked up and was now coming from the side of the clearing where Ellen, Hawk, Stacy, and Mark were hidden.

Hawk thought that their discovery was inevitable, but the bear suddenly roared in pain and fell over on its side. A crossbow quarrel protruded from the base of its neck, near the shoulder. The great beast convulsed and went rigid. It did not die, but lay paralyzed and panting, its eyes rolling.

Gunther stepped from concealment among the trees near the path. He fit another arrow to his crossbow as he stalked the wounded, and now defenseless, bruin.

But before he could aim the killing shot, Smokey streaked out of the woods and bounded atop the wounded bear's shoulder. Tail twitching and shoulders hunched, Smokey fixed Gunther with a baleful glare, and emitted a low guttural growling hiss.

Taken aback for only an instant, Gunther quickly recovered. He aimed the crossbow at the feisty feline, and sneered, "Tis almost a shame to waste a bolt on you, cat; but, you might be good sport."

"Gunther! Don't you dare shoot my cat!" screamed Ellen as she dropped to the ground and ran forward.

But Stacy was faster, and stepped between Gunther and the bear, shouting, "Yeah! Back off! And if Smokey wants to protect this poor bear, then we'll protect him, too!"

Ellen joined her. They stood together, glaring at the familiar.

Mark gaped in disbelief, but he nonetheless strode forward and placed himself directly in harm's way to protect the women. "Well, Gunther, it seems that the ladies will not permit you to harm either the cat or the bear. So, you may as well lower your crossbow and tell us what you're doing here."

Gunther did not lower his crossbow; his aim wavered between Mark, Ellen and Stacy. His momentary confusion seemed to dissipate; his expression grew harsh.

"You are now my prisoners! You should not have left the castle. You will return with me now, or I will slay you all! Where is Lord Hawk? Answer me!"

"Oh, I'm right here," announced a voice from Gunther's right. "Thanks for asking."

"Stand with the others, where I can see you!" he demanded.

"Gunther, now you will listen to me." Hawk stepped forward so the others could see him, his pistol held in a two-handed stance. "Lower your weapon and place it on the ground."

Gunther spat, "Do as *I* say! I will kill the nymph first! This bolt is tipped with *silver*!"

"No, Gunther, do as *I* say." Hawk's voice was devoid of emotion, eerily calm. "Lower your weapon. Place it on the ground. Do it, now."

Whatever went through Gunther's mind at that moment was enough for him to hesitate.

In that instant, Smokey leapt off the bear to Gunther's right.

Gunther flinched; and Hawk fired simultaneously.

Gunther's flinch spoiled Hawk's aim.

The .40 caliber bullet narrowly missed Gunther's head, impacted the wood of the crossbow, splintering the trigger mechanism, and sheared the bowstring. Bucking from the impact, the stock slammed into the side of Gunther's jaw. He dropped like a sack of rocks, face down, mercifully unconscious.

The shattered crossbow lay on the ground, the silver-tipped quarrel still in the arrow groove. Hawk kicked the crossbow out of reach.

Quickly patting Gunther down, he found three knives, and a vial of some noxious fluid.

When Hawk rolled him over, the true extent of his injuries became apparent. His right eye had been savaged by the sundered bowstring; it lay oddly flattened and distended on his cheek, leaking a thick bloodied fluid.

Ellen gasped, and turned away.

"Ellen," urged Hawk, "the first aid kit, quickly!"

Steeling her nerve, she complied.

WHILE HAWK AND ELLEN administered to Gunther, Mark and Stacy warily watched the bear. Smokey was back on its shoulder, pawing at the protruding crossbow bolt. Stacy didn't think twice; she walked around to the bear's back, crawled up on its shoulders and considered the arrow.

Mark's heart was in his throat.

"Mark, there's something strange here." Stacy pointed. "I'm going to remove this arrow, so stand back."

"Stacy! No!" he shouted. "Don't touch it!"

She ignored him and gripped the shaft of the arrow with both hands. As if a thought had occurred to her, she paused and said, "Listen to me, you great bear. I mean you no harm. I'm going to pull this arrow out because I think it's doing more harm the longer we leave it in there. Now it's going to hurt, so don't move."

With a precise and determined tug the quarrel came free, and Stacy leapt clear. Blood flowed freely from the wound, but then slowed and stopped.

In due time, the bear began to pant and quiver. Mark and Stacy retreated several paces; but Smokey stood his ground, a mere arm's length from the bear.

Right before their eyes, the bear started to shake and a thick mist like silvered steam rose from its body, coalescing into a vaporous cocoon that obscured their view. Within the cloud of moisture a shape was flexing, contracting, and metamorphosing into another form. Muffled sounds of bones realigning, snapping into place, the snick of stretching sinew and tendons as muscles and joints repositioned, barely escaped the opaque mist.

Then it grew very quiet, and an errant breeze began to lightly blow the fading vapor away.

Before them on the ground, where once was a large bear, now lay a very large man, bearded, dirty and disheveled. Mark retrieved a spearman's discarded cloak and cast it over the shivering man's body. As his quaking subsided, Smokey strode up to the man's face and licked his cheek. The big man's eyes fluttered open. With a deep groan, he struggled to sit up, clutching the cloak around him, and felt for the corresponding spot on his upper shoulder near his neck where, as a bear, he had been wounded.

Mark turned to Stacy. "How did you know?"

"I didn't." She offered a wry smile. "But I do trust Smokey."

Hawk and Ellen, who had been tending to Gunther, now joined them, equally stunned.

"Did we really just see that?" Hawk mumbled.

Nodding her head, Ellen breathed, "Uh-huh . . . I think we'd better get used to the unexpected—and just roll with it."

Hawk scoffed. "Hmmph, like we've got a choice."

The man stared up at them and tried to speak; but, he could barely form words, much to his obvious frustration.

Thinking the first bowman dead, Stacy went to the crumpled body and took a bladder bag from his shoulder. She did not notice that the fatally injured archer's eyes followed her every move.

Stacy emptied the bag's stale wine and refilled it with fresh water from the stream. Returning to the sitting bear-man, she offered the water to him.

He drank deeply, draining the bag. Finally, he could manage a few words.

"I . . . th-thank . . . " He gestured with his hand as if to include all the companions. "I am . . . M-Miska . . . Miska, of Ursus Clan . . . Thank you . . . for . . . pr-protecting me."

Ellen introduced everyone, including Smokey, and ironically, Gunther, who was still unconscious.

"I believe we are all safe for the moment. Now, can you tell us *your* story?"

Miska tried haltingly to explain that he was from the Realm of the Were. It was initially difficult to understand his tale, told in staggering starts and confused phrasing. It was uncomfortably clear he had not used his power of speech in some time. However, his diction became more understandable and his delivery more fluid as he continued his efforts to speak.

He had come to this realm three years ago in search of his brother.

Landless sons of a minor noble, he and his brother had trained as mercenaries, hiring out as bodyguards for the most part, but taking the occasional warrior position.

His younger brother, Ivan, had taken a dubious short-term job as a courier's guard, which included travel in the Shadow Realm. He had subsequently disappeared.

Miska had come searching, but found nothing, on two legs or four. He spent more and more time in his bear form, to the point that he had nearly forgotten who he was, and that he could shape-shift. That was an inherent problem for those Were who spent too much time in their animal form.

"But, cat knew me—even as bear," Miska grinned.

Ellen stroked Smokey and agreed. "He is very intelligent, and wise, I think."

"That one smarty-cat!" Miska guffawed at his own pun.

Mark groaned and chuckled along with everyone. "That's pretty good, very *punny*."

Beneath his smile, Hawk had taken on a pensive look. "Can I ask you, Miska, to describe your brother, his physical appearance in his man form, I mean?"

As Miska did so, the companions grew very quiet.

"What? You know of Ivan? Please, must tell," he begged.

"We don't know for certain," Hawk explained, "but your description is close to that of the innkeeper, Boltar. I will share what we know; it may not be much."

Miska nodded. "Please tell. I listen."

Hawk went on to describe all they had seen. "Unfortunately, we do not know more than that; nor do we know what ultimately happened to him."

"This one, this *Gunther*," Miska pointed. "He knows more of this?"

"We don't know," admitted Hawk. "Perhaps he knows something. But it may be that his mistress, the Lady Sabrina, knows more."

Stacy spoke up, "Miska, you must be careful if you go asking questions. These people are dangerous and suspicious. Remember, you've already been shot once—with silver!"

"Not worry, pretty Lady Stacy, Miska spend most time as bear, easier to be sneaky in forest. Spend much time listening."

"What are we going to do about Gunther?" asked Mark.

Miska grinned, rubbed his neck and rumbled, "Miska take good care of him, already hurt Miska once. Miska not bear it again!" His snorting rumble of laughter echoed in the clearing, as everyone else winced at the terrible pun.

"Miska, everybody, listen to me," Ellen demanded. "We must let Gunther go. Let him wake up on his own and make his way back to the castle. He is seriously wounded, and no doubt has lost an eye, but he really knows nothing—not about us, what we've done, or where we're going."

Turning to make eye contact with each of her companions, she continued earnestly. "Think about it! Gunther is unconscious; he never saw Miska in man form. So, Miska is free to continue his search unhindered, and follow up a new lead concerning this innkeeper 'Boltar'.

"Miska, you should certainly find Hilde at the Inn of the Crying Cup and talk to her. I suspect she knew Boltar better than anyone. That may be the best place to start.

"And last but not least, Gunther has broken the rules of the Lady Leanan's House, so he can't even report any of this without implicating himself."

"That's true," observed Mark. "Gunther is certainly not held in any high esteem by Magus Jalash-el or the captain of the guard. But I don't know how Lady Sabrina will react to this situation."

"What about these other men, who helped Gunther find us?" asked Stacy. "They're dead! Won't somebody come looking for them?"

"I had a close look at a couple of them," said Hawk. "I don't think they're anything but thugs, perhaps this realm's equivalent of *highwaymen*. They certainly aren't like any of the men-at-arms we've seen or met so far. Based on how they were armed, I'd guess they were hunters, or more likely poachers—"

"*Poachers?* On Lady Leanan's lands?" Mark blurted. "Not too smart, eh?"

"No," Hawk agreed. "My gut feeling is that they're thieves who prey on travelers on the road through the forest. It's a good bet Gunther hired them on impulse. I don't know if they'll even be missed by anyone at the castle, but I kinda doubt it."

Mark considered Hawk's observations. "That makes sense. So, leave them as they are. If found, they'll appear to be involved in some sort of hunting—oh, excuse me, *poaching* expedition that went horribly wrong. Gunther can't risk trying to prove otherwise, without getting himself in a bind. And Miska can continue his investigation with no one the wiser."

"So, we are agreed," posed Ellen, "Gunther is released, and we go on as planned?"

They considered the situation for a moment until Miska broke the silence.

"Good plan, simple," he grinned. "Miska understand, can keep eye on this Gunther. Go find Hilde, maybe learn more about brother. Besides, if plan no work," the big man winked, "Miska just kill Gunther and eat him."

Ellen just shook her head as the others broke into snorting laughter.

Stacy retrieved the first aid kit, laid out its provisions, and examined Miska's neck and shoulder. She was shocked to find no wound, only a jagged pink scar. Puzzled, she pulled his face towards hers. "Miska, your wound, what happened to it?"

Miska reached up with a huge meaty hand, rubbed the puffy pink flesh of the scar tissue, and grunted. "Humph, arrowhead *silver* . . . hurt, not move. When Lady Stacy take out, Miska heal, only stiff now. Miska heal fast. Miska thirsty again."

Mark helped Miska to his feet and steadied him as they made their way to the stream for more water.

Miska drank deeply and splashed a good amount of water over his head and shoulders. He then clothed himself in homespun salvaged from two of the dead.

They left the bodies where they lay, in attitudes consistent with a bear attack. This would be the scene that Gunther would face upon awakening.

Meanwhile, Hawk took a large rock and repeatedly smashed the crossbow, totally obliterating any recognizable bullet damage. He then went to the area where he'd been standing when he fired the lone shot and spent several moments scanning the ground. Eventually, he found the ejected spent brass cartridge case and pocketed it.

Hawk checked on the unconscious Gunther, and arranged him in a reasonably comfortable position.

Gunther's face was heavily bandaged. More importantly, he would live.

Miska was again focused on finding his brother, or finding out what had happened to him. Promising to be discreet in his inquiries, he would stay in his man form for a while to help clear his mind. He thanked the companions once more and bid them farewell as he ambled off into the forest.

ELLEN STOOD WITH SMOKEY in her arms and had everyone's attention.

"Now that we're alone, I can tell you that I've read much more of Maude's journal. I've learned how to do a lot more, especially regarding transit globes. The good news is that I think I can even get us home from right here."

Hawk grinned and held his palms out. "Hey! That sure works for me; I don't wanna be late for work. Do you need anything? Or do *we* need to do anything?"

Ellen smiled and shook her head. "Nope, I'll take care of it. But before we go, I want to say something. We've been through a lot that most folks would never believe. We've learned some things; and, it seems we may have individually acquired some new skills. I think it might be a good idea to keep all this to ourselves, at least for now—"

"Wait!" interrupted Stacy, hands on her hips. "You're gonna tell your mom, right?"

"Well, of course I'm gonna tell her," Ellen replied with a laugh. "Look, I know we'll talk about all this at length; but let's do it at home, okay? Good! Now, are y'all ready?"

Everyone smiled and nodded.

Ellen closed her eyes and visualized a transit globe. She gathered ambient energies with a skill that was indeed second nature to her. When she opened her eyes, a large globe, the size of a small car, hovered before them.

Ellen wasted no time, and with Smokey in her arms, she passed through the event horizon like slipping into a soap bubble.

Stacy, Mark, and Hawk followed.

They stepped into a grass-covered clearing, encircled by a familiar set of standing stones, near the shore of a small cerulean lake, deep in the old-growth forest of Domaine Delafaire.

Max and Sophie came bounding down from the cabin's front porch to greet them.

It was good to be home.

A UNIVERSE AWAY, IN the Realm of Shadow, a lone set of helpless eyes blinked in bewilderment and shock. A final thought passed through the dying archer's conscious mind.

Ye gods! A terrible mistake—hunting these travelers . . .

(The tale continues in REALMS OF POSSIBILITY, Vol. II of THE STEWARD)

About the Author

M.D. Ironz is the pseudonym of a former government official, based in an undisclosed location in North America, and now serving as a confidential consultant on matters of intelligence, security, and investigations.

www.ingramcontent.com/pod-product-compliance
Lightning Source LLC
Chambersburg PA
CBHW030542310726
48979CB00010B/2001/J
* 9 7 8 1 7 3 3 7 5 9 4 2 7 *